How I Left the Great State of Tennessee and Went On to Better Things

Also by Joe Jackson

A Furnace Afloat: The Wreck of the Hornet and the Harrowing 4,300-mile Voyage of Its Survivors

Leavenworth Train: A Fugitive's Search for Justice in the Vanishing West

Dead Run: The Shocking Story of Dennis Stockton and Life on Death Row in America (co-author William F. Burke, Jr.)

How I Left the Great State of Tennessee and Went On to Better Things

A Novel by Joe Jackson

CARROLL & GRAF PUBLISHERS
NEW YORK

HOW I LEFT THE GREAT STATE OF TENNESSEE
AND WENT ON TO BETTER THINGS

Carroll & Graf Publishers
An Imprint of Avalon Publishing Group Inc.
245 West 17th Street
11th Floor
New York, NY 10011

This book is a work of fiction. Names, characters, places, and incidents
either are products of the author's imagination or are used fictitiously.
Any resemblance to actual events or locales or persons, living or dead, is
entirely coincidental.

First Carroll & Graf edition 2004

Library of Congress Cataloging-in-Publication Data is available.

ISBN: 0-7867-1284-8

Interior design by Jennifer Steffey
Printed in the United States of America
Distributed by Publishers Group West

To Kathy and Nick, as always, and to family, stepfamily, and friends, too numerous to mention, who over the years talked up a storm about life in the Appalachians and East Tennessee.

Have you perceived the breadth of the earth? . . .
Where is the way to the dwelling of light,
And where is the place of darkness?

—Job 38: 18 to 19

Table of Contents

Part I : Foggy Mental Breakdown

How a Mind to Travel Comes Over Dahlia Jean   2
When the Old Man Wakes   34
Never Check the Mirror When You Drive Like
    Hell on Wheels   44
Why Doth the Heathen Rage?   52
Love at Sixteen   63
Why Banks Ain't What They Used to Be   70
What the Serpent Says   79
How Private Mischief Finds the Old Man   104
It's Rainin' All over the World   114
When the Rooster Crows   124

Part II : The South Will Rise Again

Down a Lazy River   150
Justice Is the Old Man's Middle Name   160
Where the Lost Girls Go   169
Night Comes to the Junkyard   180
Sinners Roosting under Satan's Tail   191
The Mansion on the Hill   211
Highway and City   223
How the Elephant Dies   238
Duck 'n' Cover Makes a Mighty Fine Prayer   247
A Prophet's Never Appreciated in His Own Land   259

Part III : The Land of Sunshine

Good Men Are Hard to Find   264
The High-Octane Highway of Bright, White Dreams   275
Everything Speeds to Its Fulfillment   290
Why Bile Rises in the Old Man's Craw   312
Daddy's Tale   313
Fathers Are a Dyin' Breed   322
A Clean, Well-Lighted Place   330
How We Leave the Great State of Tennessee—   339
—and Go on to Better Things   352

Acknowledgments   356
About the Author   357

Part I
Foggy Mental Breakdown

How a Mind to Travel Comes Over Dahlia Jean

MAMA ALWAYS SAID that somebody'd come along and shut my mouth for me someday if I didn't learn to shut it myself. Who that somebody was, was never quite certain, and all day long I'd wonder if the next stranger roaring through Wattles was him. *Who's deliverin' me to the Land of Plenty?* I was desperate to know. Was it the Brylcreemed college boy piloting his daddy's T-Bird down the blacktop? The broken-down farmer hunched behind the wheel of his broken-down Ford? Mama didn't know either, but she'd remind me every morning before school that my comeuppance was comin' soon.

"You, Dahlia Jean," she'd scream as I tried creepin' past her bedroom door. "Bring me a cup of coffee."

I'd bring her a cup of coffee, no cream or sugar, extra strong.

"Too hot! After sixteen years, ain't you learned nothin'? And quit fidgetin'."

I'd try to stand still.

She'd stare through me like a mind reader at a carnival booth till she sighed and said, "I guess you'll have to do." I'd stand a little straighter, never doubtin' that she *could* read my mind. "I swear, child," she'd mumble to herself, reaching for a menthol cigarette, "you make me snap more'n a new pack of cards." Then *scritch!* the match flared and smoke curled 'round her head, always the same . . . always on cue. It was like I woke each morning in the same fairy tale, but try as I might, I never remembered the end. I itched to leave Wattles, she knew I itched, and I knew she knew. She'd been the same way at my age and look how far it got her, she told me, so best give up such daydreams. Her voice rattled 'round my skull so much I assumed it was my conscience, loaded with such nuggets of wisdom as *Trouble wears pants, Don't talk to strangers,* and *Pick up a loaf of white bread at the Piggly Wiggly before you come home.* And that's not countin' the Coker family motto: *Men are no damn good.*

Lord, how I remember that scene day after day after day as I stood there starin' at my scuffed saddle oxfords and my ankle socks droopin' down. Mama'd be propped up in bed yelling, and as I glanced at her thin little legs outlined under the pink chenille bedspread, I'd think, "Another day like the day before." Which was true. Every morning started in this stale-smelling bedroom where Mama wasted away among the pictures of Jesus on the Cross, Christ Healing the Lepers, and The Sinners Roosting Under Satan's Tail. Surely she didn't believe in that stuff, but I do think it made her happy that others could be more miserable than her. It spread through the afternoon to Wattles County High, where I learned exactly nothin', and ended late at Dave's, the diner where I'd worked Mama's old waitress job for the past year. The slot had come open the night the two strangers in an orange Mack truck picked Mama up past closing and dumped her without slowing down the road. She gave a detailed description of those drivers—too detailed, in fact, for family consumption—in the *Wattles Daily Optic.* The Law never found them, though I doubt much effort was made. The town had a good laugh, while Mama left the job and hid away from the world.

I used to have a sweet and pretty mama, but rage can curdle anything, and I feared I'd end like her. "Mama, you ain't as sick as you think," I once begged. "Let's move to a new town and start fresh and new." That was a mistake I never made again. She ripped into me like two cats tied together, her claws exposed. "I ain't *never* runnin' from this town with my tail between my legs!" she snapped, her voice rising an octave. "When I leave Wattles, it'll be in glory, but until a better offer sits at the foot of this bed and extends an invitation, we stay right here." Vines of smoke crept to the ceiling. "Besides, what prospects have we got? What money we got saved? Here at least we got a roof over our head that's all paid up and you got my

waitress job. You think we'd have that much somewhere else?"
Since I couldn't answer, we stayed right where we were.

Not that my days lacked for variety. Take, for instance, the
last day of summer, September 21, 1961. The morning had
already shaped into disaster when Mama asked if I let Arnold
Simpson put his hand up my dress whenever he felt the urge.
"Tell me the truth, you goin' with that boy?" She rubbed the
warm coffee cup against her cheek and watched me.

"No, Mama, I'm not," I answered, knowing all denials were
useless since she'd already made up her mind.

"That's not what his sister Ruth Ann said. Ruth Ann told
her mama you let that boy ramble 'round up there like a
squirrel hoarding nuts before the snow."

"I do not, Mama, what a terrible thing to say!" But she was
only getting started. She scowled like she wanted to leap up
and catch me 'round the throat—which she said she couldn't—
which I truly doubted—which only got her riled. She could get
around just fine, I thought, if maybe a little slowly, but used
her lameness as a yoke to keep me stuck at home. I imagined
her wandering through the house while I was out, picking
up her china knickknacks and setting them back, rememberin' things.

"You let that boy do that to you?" she said. Rather than
argue, I stared at my shoes and noticed one of the oxfords had
a hole wearin' in its toe. I might be poor as dirt, I thought, but
did I have to look it, too?

Daddy'd said the same before he lit out for Florida. "Fortune's just waitin' to be made down there," he laughed the day
before he disappeared. Even as he said it, something in his voice
made me start to cry. We were fishing on the spillway below the
TVA dam and at first I was happy, it bein' a treat to escape Wattles and its yellow mine-choked streams. The spray rolled over
us like a blessing and the fish jumped in the foam. But even so,
we caught nothing and the evening turned deep blue.

"You won't leave me, will you, Daddy?" I finally said.

His rod faltered in midcast. "I'll never leave you, Princess," he said, glancing sideways where I stood beside a granite boulder abandoned by the last Ice Age. He cleared his throat and looked a bit pekkid. "What makes you ask?"

"You and Mama fight so much anymore."

He laughed and asked when I'd added worrywart to my name. All adults had troubles, he said: Ours just happened to be a chronic lack of dough. Trouble was a normal part of life and the best course was to swim with it. He bent forward and looked in my face. "What're these, tears?"

"No, Daddy, only spray."

The next day he was gone. The last I heard, he surfaced on a fishing boat far to the south in a place called Key West. The local mine owner who saw him was on vacation when he spotted Daddy on the dock, arms 'round the shoulders of two Cuban businessmen. All three stood by a big blue shark hanging by its tail, mouth open in a dead and hungry smile. The mine owner said he walked over and asked Daddy what he was doing so far from home, but then he paused in his tellin' and looked up at me.

"Well, what'd he say?" I snapped, annoyed by the delay.

The mine owner nodded down at his plate, empty save for some scattered crumbs of pie. "You cain't expect me to keep talkin' with a half-full belly, can you?" he said. I glanced 'round to check no one was watchin', then slid a second slice of apple pie with melted cheese beneath his nose. He came into the diner every evening at 6:15 to order chicken-fried steak, two cups of coffee, and pie-of-the-day; he sat at the counter with his jiggly cheeks and big baby eyes, smiling like a hungry kewpie doll.

"So what'd he say?" I repeated, tapping my foot to the click of his fork against the china.

He pointed its tines at me. "Your daddy only grinned," he answered, gulpin' down his last bite of pie. "But I wouldn't go away, so he winked at his Cubans and added, 'I'm involved in government work.' Then all three laughed louder'n necessary and called their shark Fidel. I knew then he was makin' light of

5

me, but as I turned to go, I noticed something else. Your daddy'd named his boat *Miss Dahlia Jean*."

After me. That flummoxed me worse'n anything. Long after the mine owner left, I turned his story over in my mind. Some days the image of Daddy fishin' down in Florida was a comfort, but on others I thought I understood Mama's rage. Why wasn't I down there with him? If he took my name, why didn't he take me, too? I vowed I'd hunt him down someday and ask him face-to-face. He'd answer my questions then.

"Answer me!" Mama screamed, hating it when I drifted off, even if only mentally. "You let anything in pants put his hand up your dress, ain't that true? You're no better'n the white trash in the hollers, droppin' their pants for every stranger with an Orange Crush and fancy car." I didn't tell her we was white trash also, but she read my thoughts and threw her coffee cup across the room. She didn't throw it at me, mind you, but aimed at one of her grim pictures nailed to the wall. This day she hit poor Jesus in the face, like he didn't have enough troubles already, hanging there all impaled. The cup bounced and rolled.

"Mama, you know Ruth Ann's been jealous ever since I beat her in the spelling bee."

Yet it never mattered what I said. Mama just squinted at me in the dim light with the dust motes floatin' 'round. "Wipe that smirk off your face, Dahlia Jean Coker," she warned. "You think you're somethin' 'cause you can come and go as you please and I can't touch you? Think again, young lady! You ain't goin' *nowhere!* You're stuck in Wattles, and you'll end up dead or pregnant just like all the other females 'round here. You ain't no princess, and somebody'll come along someday to prove it to you. Somebody'll shut your mouth permanent 'less you listen to them what knows."

Then she pointed at the coffee cup, lying on its side on the stained yellow throw rug. "Pick that up before you go."

I did as she ordered, though it was the last thing in that house I ever did.

That's the way it was that September morning, the day I left the Great State of Tennessee and went on to better things. As always, I was late for school after Mama's good-morning lecture, so I grabbed my books off the wring-washer, slammed the screen door behind me, and sprinted for town. It was such a beautiful day. The leaves were already dropping from the trees, while in the distance I saw the last traces of morning fog 'round the Smokies that took longer to melt as the summer faded away. I hadn't gone ten steps when I heard a motor growl behind me, and without thinking I stuck out my thumb. It was Arnold Simpson and his glued-together truck, the sorry thing barely held together with backyard welds and baling wire. Oh, Lord, I thought, not in front of the house, and sure enough, when I glanced back, there was Mama's face full and red in the window, mouth opened wide. She yelled something I was glad I couldn't hear.

"Get in, you darlin' thing."

Since I was sure to get a tongue-lashing, I might as well deserve it, so I hopped into Arnold's jalopy and he put it in gear. Black smoke poured from the exhaust so bad you'd think it was on fire. "When you gonna buy that head gasket, Arnold?" I asked. "Or did you declare war on fresh air?"

"Never mind that," he answered, his voice crackin' like always when fixin' to ask me for a date. "There's a picture at the drive-in this Friday. Wanta go?" He stared straight ahead, his Adam's apple creeping up . . . up . . . then sticking. I'd learned the hard way that if I said yes, it would plummet to the bottom just before he grabbed my knee and squeezed.

Boys, I sighed. What an exasperating breed. Why was it you never wanted the boys who wanted you, while the ones you really dreamed about always slipped away? Here I'd be getting grief for riding with a pimple-lipped boy who had a lump in his britches *this early in the morning,* and I didn't even like him. Least not *that* way!

"Can't, Arnold," I lied. "We're expecting a rush of truckers at the diner this Friday. You keep that hand to yourself, hear?"

"Ain't never been no rush of truckers through Wattles long as I remember."

"There will be this Friday. What did I say about that hand?"

His voice got whiny and his hand jerked against the seat cover like it was glued there. "It's a good movie, Dahlia. *The Beast with Five Fingers.* Besides, other than Charlie Groanem, who's takin' out my sister, and that pinhead Gurney Jones, you got no one else to see it with."

That was a low blow. Yet even as we pulled behind the gym and I jumped out before he lunged like usual, I knew what he said was true. Most of the older boys had left for the Army on Memorial Day, tempted away by a silver-tongued devil in uniform and promises that here at last was escape from a life of failed crops and black lung. Wattles packed off its patriots with a parade and pork barbecue; while we ate, the mayor told boys like Arney Slover, Abel Mullins, and Luther Burgess to guard them Commies good. Eternal vigilance was the only way to keep our homeland safe. The three stood in a line and scowled like no one better dare try sneakin' past them. The Reds had the bomb, warned the mayor; only a month ago, that dirty Castro whupped a force of patriots at a little place called the Bay of Pigs. What was next? Poison gas? Missiles hidden in the jungle? Some folks bit their lips. Flies buzzed over the steam plates. The pork ribs turned green.

It was depressing when you thought about it, so I tried not to. But that did no good. Everyone was growing up or moving away. How could you forget those who'd left already, not even waiting for graduation or the Army, but simply heading to the "Little Kentuckys" of Chicago and other northern cities where they could draw an honest wage? How could you avoid the ones who stayed: boys who were all hands like Arnold, or born simple, or mauled by a combine like the poor Haley boy on Route 9? It was like the mountains of East Tennessee was one huge prison and we were all thrown in together to see what new strangeness evolved. Only a few escaped while the rest got mixed and mashed together like some drive-in science-fiction nightmare till a mutant popped out and the Army was called in. Maybe everyone had a tiny nightmare in 'em till the times and conditions were right and the monster emerged, growing bigger and bigger like poor Allison Hayes in *Attack of the 50-Foot Woman,* which I'd seen on a double bill with *The Amazing Colossal Man.* "Hey, Dahlia, wanna see *my* amazing man grow colossal?" cried Arney Slover from the next car over, to which I'd walked up and turned his Coke in his lap, transforming his proud monstrosity into the incredible shrinking kind. But he was in uniform now and had to be shown respect. It ain't nice for a girl to make fun of heroes.

School passed like always. Slow. In first period the fire bell rang and we practiced Duck and Cover. "Who's gonna bomb *this* place?" I complained.

"No talking," sniped the teacher. "A warhead could fall on us instead of Oak Ridge." When I pointed out that Oak Ridge was a hundred miles on the other side of Knoxville, I was reminded that anything could happen in such perilous times.

They were perilous all right, if you included death by boredom, and I almost wisht some confused missile *would* scream down on us since it'd at least be a change. But no such luck, and life went on. In Home Ec, the teacher's voice snapped me from my daydreams as my tapioca pudding boiled onto the floor. In Gym, the coach fussed when I climbed the rope to the rafters but was too scared of heights to come down. Some senior boys strolled over from the basketball hoops and said they liked the view. The lunch lady slopped chicken gravy on my skirt in the lunch line. "What's the matter, you ain't heard of soap and water?" she answered when I complained.

In History, we had a surprise. A professor from the Baptist college down in the valley came to lecture on our life and times. He was a bearded fellow, with a nice smile, horn-rimmed glasses and gray Hush Puppies, and until I saw the wedding band I wondered whether he was the one to take me away. I was imagining his wife as one of them prissy sorts investigating food-stamp fraud when he commenced to lecture in a sleep-inducin' drone. He started off how 200 million years ago this place was nothing more'n a vast bog of dying plants, rotting remnants of an inland sea. The plants piled up and turned to peat, then eons later to coal. *Boring*, I thought: we'd learned this already in Physical Sciences. But then a red spark gleamed in his eyes and his own little monster peeked through. We sat on riches, he said, but the riches were cursed and we were cursed with them. His eyes grew creepy and round. Men took coal from the earth and left slag dumps, cripples, and widows. I'd heard this before in church: what was it about this place that sooner or later turned everyone into a preacher? Must be there was just so much to preach against out here.

But he didn't stop there. Hate and violence seamed the earth deeper than the coal itself, he insisted, his voice growing hypnotic as he recited each war and feud: Indian wars, the Civil War, union wars, shootouts between moonshiners and Treasury agents, squabbles between neighbors that turned into deadly feuds. Violence, like coal dust, ran through our veins; ours was a society that had somehow been condemned. The teacher squirmed uncomfortably in her chair, no doubt wondering how to turn off this egghead who thought he was a prophet, while the prophet-professor held his breath and we held ours with him, wondering if we'd been hijacked by some fire-breathin' tent preacher of doom. A hound dog barked. His arms shot up. I jumped in my chair.

"Escape!" the prophet cried. "We live in an age of escape, all around us, right now." He pointed at me and I ducked my head. "Escape from a way of life that's coming to an end. Since 1940, two million people have left these hills and valleys for the hillbilly ghettos of the industrial North. At least one million people left Appalachia from 1950 to 1960, while you were kids. Think about it. Think of all the friends and family you've seen leave and never come back. What would they come back to, anyway? Strip mines and unemployment. No possible future but crime or the dole. Every single one of you will think about leaving, and if you don't actually do it, you'll someday wish you had. What you've lived through has been one of the most significant and unrecognized American exoduses of this century, second only to the flight of the Okies. A tidal wave of broken people. Not since the Great Depression have so many, with so little, gone looking for better things!"

Then he was done. In the stunned silence that followed, a blond cheerleader asked if this would be on the test. Arnold, who sat in front of me, asked about the people who went south instead of north; when he glanced over his shoulder, I knew he meant Daddy. I heard snickers but didn't look around. "There was a migration south, but smaller and mostly made of dreamers and con men," the professor said. When Arnold turned 'round and grinned, I jabbed him in the shoulder with a No. 2 pencil and told him, "I hope you get lead poisoning."

The teacher made me sit outside, but I didn't mind. Being alone was better, allowing me the chance to drift into my favorite dream. It too was of migration, but on the frontier with Jesse James. It always started the same. I'd tramped through the town square on my way to work when I heard the bank alarm. Gunshots popped like distant firecrackers, followed by a gravel clatter up the road. When I turned around, I saw the horseman, his lower face covered by a bandana, his soot black hair and slate gray eyes. "Take me, too!" I shouted, waving my arms. He plucked me off my feet and plopped me behind him in the saddle. We rode west, past Knoxville, Nashville, Memphis, over the Mississippi, through the Ozarks and onto the plains. I wrapped my arms about his waist and held on. As I dozed and dreamed of freedom, the blood sang in my veins.

But then my outlaw stiffened. *Looks like trouble,* he said.

In the far distance waited a tall man. The red sun set behind him. His face was in shadow. He slapped gun leather and strode forward. A guitar strummed a dark chord.

Joe Jackson

The final bell rang.

School ended at 3:30; work started at 5:00. With a disgusted sigh, I picked up my books and headed toward the square. This was always the worst part of the day. At school, at least, I could drop my head on the desk and sleep. At the diner, between homework, side orders, and dirty dishes, I had no time to think at all. But this ninety minutes between school and work, between one life and the other, I'd grown to hate more'n anything.

September 21, 1961 was no exception. It was overcast and gray, a couple of drops falling to remind me I'd probably get drenched tonight when walking home. Someone had run over a guinea hen at the entrance of the square, and somehow I identified. The poor thing lay in the road and twitched, not quite dead. "Damn waste of poultry," a rock farmer spat as I walked past the drugstore. A neighbor on the bench beside him commented, "It's good for business, actually. Cuts down on surplus. Drives up demand."

I stopped before the Kresge's display window, mooning over the pretty organdy blouse with embroidered eyelets in the sleeves that I knew I'd never afford. Next door, the five-and-dime owner had been run out of business by Kresge's and nailed a bedsheet across his window with the words CLOSEOUT SALE—ALL MUST GO. Out front he'd piled his clothes dummies. Plaster arms and legs stuck out every which way. Then came the Army-Navy Surplus, which advertised a Big Bullet Sale. How big could bullets be? I looked across the street at the courthouse clocks, where the bell tower's east face read 4:20 and the west face said a quarter till five. Arnold Simpson drove by in his truck with a girl from the next town over snuggled under his arm. By the grin on his face, you'd think he was on salary. I prayed he'd catch something deadly and turned away.

I caught a ride north toward the diner with a deputy sheriff I knew. As we rolled through a narrow emerald valley, I rolled down my window and watched a line of black cows drift along the contour of a green pasture, their heads all pointed the same way. The air smelled damp and leafy. It was already cooler in the mountains than in the flatlands and up in the coves the trees were already turning their fall colors, like a green carpet sprinkled with gold coins. A white church stood out against the fields of corn; behind it, the lower hills folded like waves. So peaceful, I thought. So beautiful. Who'd ever want to leave a place like this?

When we rounded the curve, it all changed.

We passed a gray tipple built by a rail spur, surrounded by a small mountain of discarded slate and low-grade coal. The place was famous locally. Last year the pile spontaneously combusted, all that piled-up pressure ignitin' the coal. Though the volunteer fire department tried puttin' it out, the blaze was too deep and the pile was too high. The fire smoldered for months, an oily black cloud that drifted up like an evil genie and floated downwind. Sometimes the rain seemed to do what the firemen couldn't and the heap hissed its last, but in a few days the fire would start all over again. As the sulfur fumes peeled paint from houses in its path, housewives watched their wash turn a dirty yellow color called coal camp gray. No bleach made by man could return their sheets to that virgin whiteness that once made them proud. Every time I rode past, my eyes watered, my throat stung. Some nights I could see the red glow from the diner. The fire would never stop. It was on such nights that I knew why Daddy ran.

The deputy yawned and said good girls don't hitchhike, then draped his arm across the seat and drawled, "You're lookin' more like your pretty mama every day." His fingers accidentally curled in my hair. "Some of the best times I ever had was with that woman. How's she doin' these days?"

I jumped from the car as it slowed and watched it speed away. I thought I was gonna have a hissy fit in the parking lot, right under the red and yellow neon DAVE'S. Looking more like Mama every day, he'd said—why, there weren't no resemblance at all! She was blond and blue-eyed while I was all black hair and eyes and smoky skin, inherited from my Cherokee

Daddy. No, what the deputy meant was simply what everyone was thinking: that sooner or later I'd inherit my mama's reputation, the one she'd earned before losin' her legs. I'd overheard men mourning the passing of those long legs, the way she wrapped 'em 'round a feller and drew him in. Good things passed, but there was always hope. Like mother, like daughter, they said.

The cowbell jangled when I opened the door.

Harson Whitley, my boss and the owner, scowled from where he polished the countertop. "It's about time you got here," he snapped. "I don't pay people to waste my time." He turned back to his polishing and pretended I was dead.

Harson was drunk again. I could smell his whisky breath from here. I stomped to the back, threw my books against the metal dish rack, and yelled through the serving window, "I get paid today?"

"You'll get paid when I'm damn good and ready."

"You ain't been ready for the last two weeks! Mama needs money for her painkillers."

Harson's moon face appeared in the serving window. "Your mama's not the only one with pains."

Harson Whitley wasn't so bad, when he was sober. He toddled behind the counter in his white chef's apron and hat, kidding me about any boys who might drop by. On good nights, he flipped a switch on the back of the upright Wurlitzer and played "*The Third Man* Theme" and "Goodnight, Irene" for him and "Moonlight Serenade" for me, at least on the nights when the jukebox worked. Two months earlier Harson had got drunker'n usual and threw his shoe against its glass dome. Most nights now it just played "The Tennessee Waltz" over and over.

But Harson wasn't sober these days, and though I felt sorry for him, that didn't make life easier. Understanding a person just complicates things. Like the night just recently when I'd been studying between customers and he peeked through the window. "What you readin'?" he asked.

" 'Compensation,' " I said.

He stumbled back and polished the table where I studied. "Whossit by?"

"Ralph Waldo Emerson," I added, movin' my book away from his rag.

He goggled at me with that same mad glint I recognized from Arnold, then grabbed for my leg like it was a sale-price drumstick on double coupons. "I'm sure Waldo won't mind if I take some compensation, too," he cried. We wrestled 'round on the table till I grabbed the ladle from the pot of vegetable beef and chased him out the door. Since then he didn't try more foolishness, but then neither was I gettin' paid.

Mama said it might pass, but I wasn't so sure. The drinking started years earlier, she said, when Harson's young wife ran off with his partner, Dave Aikens, back when I was just a little girl. Now his tippling was heavy and constant, like he wanted to drink himself to an early grave. It was the same old story of musical beds, with an old man the loser, Mama said. About a year after leaving Wattles, the two got nabbed in Nashville for trying to blackmail Grand Ole Opry stars with doctored photos. Though the scam was fake enough, the nude poses of Harson's wife were real. The middle-aged judge took one long look at the photos, sighed, and arranged a plea bargain where she testified against Aikens in exchange for her freedom. A couple weeks later, her and the judge disappeared.

Harson'd heard as well. Most nights now, he rambled on to himself about how he was gonna find his dear wife and move to Florida. Or he growled how women were no better'n whores. That didn't make things easy, being the only female 'round. Worst of all was when he sat and eyed me like a hungry cat does a bird. I kept the ladle handy, no matter what Mama said.

Even so, it was sad to think how Dave's was all that Harson had anymore. He slept on a cot in the back after closing and I'd gone home. He kept his few possessions piled in corners and on a shelf: a gold-framed photo of his wife, a Bible coated with coal dust, some tools. He stored his clothes in a locker at the foot of his bed. On slow nights, he shined and polished the place till every smooth surface twinkled. On fast nights, it was amazing how quick everything got done, he knew the place so well.

But there weren't many fast nights these days. You couldn't hide the fact that lately Dave's had gone to seed. Two of the mushroom bar stools at the far end of the counter tipped from wear. Another, closer to the door, had lost its seat entirely, just the metal stem poking from the floor. The windows leaked. The neon letters threatened to fly off in a strong wind.

Things got worse after the Kresge's snack bar opened and drew away the day trade. Sometimes, I went there myself. The inside was clean and air-conditioned; the soda jerk stared at me with cool black eyes while drawing my Coca-Cola and said how someday he'd own this very store. "You work for that old coot on Route 167, don't'cha?" he asked. "Better watch out, we'll bury him just like we did the five-and-dime."

They said in happier days that Harson made the best hamburgers in the tristate area, and folks from as far away as Bristol, Virginia, and Asheville, North Carolina would brave the mountain curves to taste his Double Whammy Burgers with special sauce and chili fries. They said he made the money hand over fist, and his parking lot was always full. I remembered it myself, back when Mama and Daddy were together and brung me in for a treat just for being their girl. "You can't eat a Double Whammy Burger," Harson would kid me, though I remember him being much taller and thinner then. "You're just a mite. An insect. A tiny thing." *Can so, too, Mr. Whitley, you just watch me,* I'd fuss back, then stare overhead at the lights and spin on my stool till I was dizzy. My, how times had changed. Tonight I watched as a bottlefly lay on its back and buzzed among the dry bug bodies piled like ashes in the ceiling light. It whined 'round the edges of the milky glass then lay quiet, weaving its legs in the air.

Where all of Harson's money went, no one seemed to know.
I sure didn't have a clue. Though there were rumors that he'd
squirreled away a small fortune, I'd never seen no evidence.
The mystery of Harson's riches was Wattles's favorite gossip,
eclipsed only by Mama's angry bedroom antics before they
ended on the highway. I knew Harson still made money off the
truckers' trade, but that was dwindling, too. For all his
moaning about Kresge's, I'd once calculated that he at least
broke even. Mama said he lost money in a Florida real estate
swindle, and before that lost more in the Crash, so he kept
nothing in banks. He didn't spend money on the diner, and
he sure as hell hadn't paid me lately. Down what black hole had
his money disappeared?

In fact, the only thing Harson showed the least interest in
was his musty collection of stuffed critters perched on shelves
or hung about the room. A bull moose's head staring down
like Kilroy above the front door. Two ratty ducks breaking
from cover. A pair of weasels fighting, and the biggest gopher
in the world poking its head from a hole. He dusted them off
constantly, making sure their fur was smooth. Sometimes
when I came to work he'd be tending one like an only child.
No wonder he was losing business. How could people eat with
such varmints starin' down?

That's the way it was the night of September 21, 1961,
another grand night on the town. The sky had finally opened
and the rain came down in a gully-washer, Harson was getting
drunker'n Noah from his Clorox bottle of lightnin' under
the counter, and I stared at the moose like some terrible
Angel of Deliverance while scrubbing beans from a cast-iron
pot. It was late already, less than an hour till closing, and it
seemed no one had passed on the highway for ages. With a
final curse at the weatherman, Harson threw his shoe against
the jukebox. There was a click; then, instead of "The Tennessee Waltz," "Bewitched, Bothered and Bewildered" came
out distant and thin.

"I finally fixed it," he clucked, proud as a hen on an egg.

Joe Jackson

The song was halfway over when a car pulled out front and doused its lights. The windows vibrated from its engine a full minute before that cut off, too. I pulled my stool to the window and shifted 'round some pots so I wouldn't get seen. Look strangers over careful before they do the same to you, Mama counseled, even if her words and actions occupied two different worlds.

Right away, I got an eyeful. From my peephole, I could tell this car was more than new, it was *brand new*, a chariot from heaven come to rest in the parking lot of Dave's. Wattles had never seen anything like it, and neither had I, a pink Cadillac convertible with wide whitewalls, white vinyl ragtop and Buck Rogers tail fins. It seemed unnatural somehow, not of this earth, the way it sparkled so in the lights, the neon raindrops bouncing in slow motion off its pink hood. Was this what waited for me in the big world outside Wattles, I wondered: a world where visions of paradise popped outta the ground like mushrooms any time of the night and day? If so, that was the life for me. I didn't know how—at least, not yet—but I vowed to myself that this pink glimpse of eternity would whoosh me outta town.

It was, of course, the Elvismobile—anyone with a brain knew that—but squint and peek as I might, I couldn't see Elvis inside. Instead, I watched as two shadows in the front seat waved their arms and pointed at Harson. Maybe a fleet of Elvismobiles traveled the South, scouting out locations for the King Himself to land. Maybe I was about to be blessed by a Holy Visitation, and my whole sorry life would change. I ran over to the sink real fast to wash my hands of grease, then fluffed my hair a mite, a girl never knowing when she has to make a good impression. When I looked out again, the shadow behind the wheel had stopped gesturing and instead had lit a cigarette as if to dismiss his smaller companion. *The conversation's over, bubba, so there's no need to waste your breath,* he seemed to say. For the length of time it took to smoke half the cigarette, the two faced in opposite directions, apparently miffed at one another. There must be a better way for Elvis to do business, I thought. The driver tossed his ember out the window; then the two shadows stepped from the car.

The diner door flew open and the cowbell said hello. Harson flung wide his arms like his long-lost wife had finally returned. "Gentlemen!" he bellowed drunkenly. "Do ya like coffee in yer cream, or nice hot tea?"

The older of the two, the one who'd sat behind the steering wheel, scowled like he hadn't heard right, which of course he hadn't. "Coffee for me," he said. He glanced at his younger companion; then, as I watched, the whole left side of the old man's face twitched, then twitched again. I blinked, unsure of what I'd seen. Sure enough, his face twitched a third time, like something live and hungry crawled right beneath the skin. Something told me I might be mistaken about Elvis—I mean, surely the King could hire someone who didn't scare the willies outta his fans. I ducked low behind my screen of pots and looked the man over good.

He was for the record books, all right: a face like Boris Karloff's, long and sunken with no fat to it, split up the middle by a thin, peaked nose. Two gray eyes that peered from their bruised sockets like nails hammered into knotted wood. A grin that instantly melted to a smirking, gap-toothed leer. Harson could offer me *four* weeks' pay and I wouldn't go out front with that twitch-faced bogeyman, I told myself, as he sat down at the counter opposite my window. I bet his mother even named him Twitch. *Twitch, honey, get washed for dinner. Twitch, darlin', don't you dare drop that neighbor baby down the well!* Twitch spun once on his stool before answerin' Harson. "Nothin' for my boy," he said.

Now I looked at the boy . . . and as I did, a thrill ran through me as subtle as a coronary. That ain't no boy, I said. That's most definitely *a man!* It was like I had a checklist in front of me. Two or so years older'n me. Cute as a button, if his hair did hang a little ragged 'round his collar. Most of all was his eyes. It wasn't fair giving any feller such eyes! They were dark as his slick, wet hair—dark and sad, and in the bad light he resembled a wandering gypsy, some fugitive prince who'd permanently lost his home. He had a dimpled chin and lazy droop at the corners of his lips like the old man beside him, and I figured they were father and son. But that was just an accident of birth, a bad roll of the genes, and other than that I *knew* there couldn't be no likeness between this haunted dreamer and his father, who stared 'round the room like a happy zombie. The old man made twitchy faces at the bull moose, then asked, "Where'd you get the elk, Pops?"

"Moose!" Harson barked proudly from the coffee urn. He set Twitch's cup and saucer on the counter, took orders and swaggered back to the grill. "Killed him myself," which of course was the biggest lie of this or any century, since he'd bought it at a farm auction, and only then 'cause nobody else wanted the ragged thing. "Shot him right between the eyes," he said.

Well, shoot, I thought, I was Cleopatra if these woods ever held a single moose. Right about then, I saw the gun. I saw it suddenly, and when I did the whole world seemed to move in slow motion, as if mired in tar. My gypsy dug a nickel from his pocket and spun it on the counter; Harson flipped a burger; Twitch swiveled to watch, and as he did, its handle poked from under his slicker. The gun was one of them long-barreled types with a walnut grip, the kind payroll guards toted at the mines. Harson diced some onions as Twitch drew the gun from his waist and laid it on the stool next to his. Harson slapped onions on the griddle. Gypsy spun his nickel. My left knee began to shake. The fly buzzed one last time in the light fixture. I knew that I would scream.

A holdup . . . that's what this was! I could see it elsewhere, but not here. Why would anybody mess with this place? What was I gonna do? More important, what *could* I do? The only phone was out front, the back door was padlocked, and Harson had the key. In my daydreams I'd pictured that if a robber ever stuck us up, I'd barge out screamin' like wild Indians, an iron skillet in my hands, and lay the sucker out cold. Instead, the trembling in my left knee got worse till it spread up both legs and my stool rattled against the floor. *Hush up!* I felt like yellin'. *If this keeps up, they'll hear.* I closed my eyes, held my breath and counted to ten, the same method I used this morning to inch back down the rope in Gym. By eight-and-a-half the shaking stopped, though the scream still hung midway in my craw.

I peeked out the window again. Harson had started on the second burger, slicing tomatoes and humming, happy as a chickie in spring. The old man slid from his stool and leaned against the counter, one hand resting on the stool. "Nice place you got here," he said, grinning. "I bet upkeep's a bitch." Harson, never one to miss a chance to air his troubles, shook his head mournfully. "I tell you, it's little things that eat you up, like equipment and repairs." When he gestured too wild with the egg turner, the burger patty plopped on the floor.

Nothing happened, far as Twitch seemed concerned. "That neon sign out front, I bet that costs a bundle, too. Five letters in bright lights. D-A-V-E-S."

"It ain't cheap, I won't lie," Harson grunted, bending down to scrape up the meat.

"More letters would make it worse, I bet."

"Most likely, so I guess I'm lucky there." Harson chuckled, slopping the burger back on the stove. "I got all the letters I need."

"But say you had more. Say you had A-I-K-E-N-S up there, too."

Me, I had to spell it out, but Harson didn't, the name most likely branded in red welts in his brain. He jerked straight and dropped the plastic spatula on the griddle, where it melted to a yellow glob. He turned 'round and glared at the old man. "What you know of Dave Aikens?" he demanded in the hollowest voice I'd ever heard him use.

"I know enough," he said. Twitch backed one step from the counter. "He's just a friend I pulled from a scrape once. He repaid the favor by tellin' me about you."

Maybe I was missin' something, but Harson seemed to get the point immediately. "Ain't nothin' you need to know about me, mister," he hissed. "You'n your boy get outta here."

"It's wet outside," Twitch answered in a voice that almost sounded gleeful. "Ain't a man got a right to finish his coffee? And what about my burger?"

"You got no rights in here." Harson's hand closed on the mincing knife and he stepped forward. "You heard me, I said get out." Twitch's grin widened. As his hand moved to the stool, I screamed he had a gun.

Right away I wished I'd heeded Mama's warnings about mindin' my tongue. As fast as my words leapt out, Gypsy dove under the counter, Harson dropped the knife, and even the mice froze in the walls. But it was Twitch who took the cake. He grabbed the gun off the stool and leapt away from the counter, clutching the grip in both hands. The barrel swung between my boss and my window. "Come outta there," he cried. "Who are you? Come out where I can see you or I blow this old coot to hell!"

What a pickle. I mean, if I showed myself too sudden, I'd most likely get blown to yesterday; but if I didn't show at all, Harson was history. "You made a mistake," I cried, tryin' to sound reasonable. "We got nothin' here worth stealin'. I bet you want the Kresge's back in town."

"*Show yourself!*" the old man shrieked, eyes wide, spittle flying, a terrible vision if I ever saw one. I grabbed my book of Emerson essays and waved it in the window. "Please, I'm just the hired help with a half-crippled Mama," I pleaded. "She expects me home by twelve."

"It's just a girl, Pop," Gypsy yelled, his black eyes peeking over the counter. "You shoot a girl, you'll end up back in Bushy Mountain forever, and me with you."

At the mention of the state penitentiary, Twitch lowered the pistol a fraction of an inch from Harson's head. "Is that true?" he asked. "It's only a girl back there?"

Harson nodded. Twitch took a deep breath, then let it out.

He stared at my shaking book of essays. "Go get her, Cole," he said to his son, then motioned with the pistol to Harson. "You sit over here."

Scared as I was, it still struck me that Cole was a handsome name. Probably short for Coleman, like the lantern. I felt drawn like a moth and smiled when he edged through the door.

"You can put that book down now," my gypsy said. "You could've got yourself or your drunk boss killed with that stunt, you know that, don't'cha?" He shook his head, disgusted, but even so I noticed how he eyed me up and down.

Well, Dahlia, I thought, you might be many things, but you ain't dumb. I jumped off the stool and ran up to him, just a couple of feet away. "Look," I sniffed, edgin' close, "this place ain't worth two cents and I ain't been paid in two weeks. Whatta you hope to find?"

Cole gaped at me with that dumb, insulted look a catfish gets when he's clubbed on the head. "Pop said this was gonna be a sure bet. Take the money and run."

"But there *ain't* no money," I replied. Why were so many people convinced this diner held Harson's vast fortune . . . that this was the Wattles branch of Fort Knox? My gypsy seemed to have sense, but a weaselly voice inside my head said Twitch wouldn't be so merciful if disappointed, and that thought really opened the dam. Something spun in my chest and my throat grew so tight it was hard to breathe. Between gasps I asked Cole if he had a kerchief, then undid the top buttons of my dress for air. I sat down; my lungs refilled. As they did, I noticed Cole's mournful look centered where I'd just unbuttoned, and when he noticed that I noticed, he flushed deep red. He fumbled in his back pocket for a blue bandanna with white triangles, then handed it to me and turned away.

Now I was really confused. This wasn't the first time I'd caught some feller staring like all I wore was my birthday suit, but it *was* the first time I hoped he liked what he saw. In the middle of a holdup, no less. What would Mama say?

I wiped my eyes, blew my nose and handed back the bandanna.

Joe Jackson

"I didn't tell you to hold a damn church meetin'!" his father cried from out front.

Cole jumped at the voice; as he did, I grabbed his hand in mine. "You won't hurt us, will you?" I pleaded. "You're not like him at all." He gawped at my hand as if he'd never seen the like, then remembered himself and struggled to pull away. But I wouldn't let go. "Please, tell me your name!" I begged. "My daddy always said that to get to know a person, you gotta learn their name. Mine's Dahlia Jean Coker, I'm sixteen and I hate this town! What's yours?"

He flushed a second time, and I realized how shy he was. I tried to hide my smile. It's not every day a girl gets robbed by a shy holdup man. "Name's Cole Younger," he muttered, starin' at the floor. Good-looking, shy, *and* named after an outlaw who rode with Jesse James. Probably a good kisser, too. Why oh why hadn't Cole Younger growed up 'round here?

But such ruminations weren't allowed more time to grow. Cole's fingers closed about my wrist, and he said his father got testy when things didn't move along. From the looks of things, though, everything was proceedin' just as Twitch had planned. He leaned toward Harson, gap-toothed grin painted 'cross his face, and told me to sit in the chair beside him. I did as he said. He spoke briefly on hard times. Life is rough in these mountains, he told us. A man's gotta do whatta man's gotta do. *Oh great,* I thought, *another lecture,* only this time the professor has a gun. Twitch stuck its barrel an inch from Harson's eye, then asked where the money was hid.

I couldn't help feeling sorry for Harson, even considerin' what kind of boss he was. There he sat under the moose's jaw in his apron and little white hat, his upper lip trembling . . . a pitiful sight, if ever there was one. He opened his mouth to speak, but there was no sound. Cole speculated maybe he'd stopped breathing. "Oh, he's breathin' all right," Twitch answered, a nasty edge to his voice, and thumbed back the hammer. With that, Harson found his voice again.

"There ain't no money, 'cept what's in the register," he

babbled. "Dahlia, go get the man the money in the register. Hurry now."

"Keep still!" Twitch snapped, jerkin' the gun my way. Again I did as told. Agreeable me. Twitch turned back to Harson, his face twisting in eleven different directions. "Maybe you're smart, but I'm smarter. Not the money in the register. I want the big money Dave Aikens says you got hid!"

I perked up at that. Big money? Here? No way! Still, it would be just like the miser to stiff his help while he had a fortune stashed nearby. In response, Harson straightened in his chair and got self-righteous. "If Dave Aikens said I got money, he was screwin' you, just like he does everyone."

Even I knew that was a dumb thing to say. Twitch's face puffed several shades of crimson, then he hit Harson across the cheek with the butt end of the gun. "No money . . . ," Harson whined. Twitch twisted his nose between his thumb and finger, and Harson screamed again. Twitch shoved the barrel down to what must've been his tonsils, and said to give it up or he'd quit being nice. "Ngoh muh-ee," Harson answered, eyes rollin' in their sockets.

"Can't you see it's doin' no good?" I screamed, unable to stand the sight no more.

The diner filled with silence as Twitch stared at me as if for the very first time. He blinked in wonder, then the grin stretched back, even wider now. "You know, I think you're right," he said. He curled his fingers in my hair, almost affectionately, then jerked me to my feet and crammed the cannon in *my* ear. "So let's try this instead."

"You didn't say you was gonna hurt no girl," Cole protested, a bit too feebly for my tastes.

"My son," Twitch answered, "it's a mean world, and you must do mean things to get ahead." He smiled and told me not to take this personal, then cocked the pistol and told Harson he'd count to ten and pull the trigger if the old man didn't quit being coy. "Bring out that money or your help gits blowed among the pots and pans."

I pleaded with Harson not to be hardheaded, but his jaw drew tight and his face grew stubborn. He crossed his arms upon his chest. "I'll give your Mama your Christmas bonus early this year," he said.

For once I was speechless, and I think even Twitch was taken aback, for he cleared his throat and gazed at me with what seemed sympathy before explainin' that he'd count to ten and pull the trigger if Harson didn't come through.

He started counting.

Every girl has her special secret. As Twitch counted down the last seconds of my life, I thought of mine. While some girls want riches, others want fame. Some crave independence; others, security. My secret was a little different, and I usually didn't talk about it. But right now seemed perfect.

I'd always wondered how it felt to know you was gonna die.

I mean, for certain, knowing full well the Reaper would arrive on a set day and time, and there was no way to extend the invitation. What if all of life was like those Death Row guys, awaitin' execution in an 8' by 10' cell? The thought had followed me 'round like a stray dog ever since Mama got dumped on the highway and awaited death in her bedroom. It was like an imaginary playmate ever since Daddy ran away. "Good morning, Mr. Death," I'd say in my blackest moments, and Mr. Death would answer, "Are we ready to play?" Everyone knew little Dahlia Jean Coker was *always* ready for games. Mr. Death wasn't scary, not like people think, and his offers of escape from Wattles could be tempting. Perhaps Mama saw His shadow on my face, for soon after her return from the hospital, she sat me down and said, "Dahlia Jean, you'll know your time is comin' when the heavens open up and Jesus stares you down." But she was wrong. The heavens had already opened and all that came forth was rain and thunder—and Twitch sure as hell didn't look like Jesus. The truth was very different. The truth was quiet and cold.

"Four."

I glanced at Cole, frozen behind a chair. He met my eyes a

minute, then grew ashamed and looked away. He walked to the window and looked out, but I could still see his reflection watching me in the glass. I wondered if he'd still be watching when the count reached ten.

"Seven."

And there was Harson. He watched, too. But there was none of that guilt and fear in his eyes like Cole's, just a blank, steady gaze. "You don't have the right, Harson," I hissed. "No one has the right." He didn't answer, just stared back, and I almost lost it, screamin' and spittin' my hate like a varmint with distemper till the finger would tighten on the trigger and the bullet drilled into my brain.

But soon as I pictured that, I realized something else, too. It wasn't hate I really felt, but fear. Not just of that gun, but of Harson, Mama, and all the rest of their kind. I'd feared 'em all along and hadn't really knowed. Maybe it was Daddy's fear as well. This was the land of ghosts, the playground of the dead, and livin' here was like livin' in a graveyard. You hung around the dead too much, you started to get like them. If you put up a fight, you just got buried. You got buried deep enough and you saw the world their way, holding as much interest in life as that moth-eaten horror that hung over the door.

Then it hit me. Dumb old moth-eaten horror. Why else would polish-happy Harson spend so much time pampering the thing?

"Nine."

I cleared my throat, now being a bad time not to get heard. "You might try lookin' for the money in that moose," I spluttered. "And those critters on the shelves. You might want to check them, too."

For the first time that night, I heard each raindrop strike the tin roof. The wall clock tick. The blood drummed against my temples. I held my breath. The counting stopped. I opened my eyes. From Harson's bloodless stare, I knew I'd hit the nail right on its greedy little head.

There was nothing in the two ducks. Twitch kept the gun in place and an eye on Harson while Cole ripped apart the birds. He looked up from the piles of pink stuffing and shrugged. "There's the others," I pleaded, closing my eyes. When Cole shouted, they sprang open again and I saw the hundred-dollar bill taped to the rear end of the gopher he'd just pulled from its hole.

Twitch lowered the pistol and kissed me on my head. My gypsy danced a jig. But Harson stared, not saying a word, a grin with no mirth in it lifting the right side of his face. When I saw that, I realized it'd just be me and him when the others were gone.

I tried to make amends. "I'm sorry, Harson," I begged him. "You was gonna let me die. What was I supposed to do?"

"Nothin'!" The grin spread wider, more murderous. "You were supposed to hold your tongue and do as you were told!" Two tears rolled down the ridge of his face. "That was my ticket outta Wattles. Me and my wife was gonna move to Florida. The good life's waitin' down there."

Oh my God, I thought, staring into his vacant eyes. Cole stuffed the money from the gopher in his pocket, then pulled the fighting weasels from the shelf and pried the two apart. A fat roll of bills dropped on the floor. *Oh my God!*

"Harson, your wife ain't here no more. You was gonna kill me over *nothin'!*"

"She'd come back! When I saved enough, she would!"

"She's gone, goddammit, gone! She couldn't get what she wanted and left to find something better! She's never comin' here again!"

But the old man wasn't listening, and maybe he never had. "You know what it's like to be stuck in a place with no one 'round who matters? No one who'll make things bearable so you don't have to kill yourself with drink?" He glared at me like *I'd* driven her away. "How would *you* know? Why am I talkin' to you? A girl whose father was such a failure he ran off. Whose mother was the biggest whore in town."

"You take that back," I said.

"It's the truth," he spit, all his past besotted hatred for Dave Aikens, his wife, every conspirin' thing that formed the four walls of his prison now boiling up at me. "Everyone in town knows and says it: Like mother, like daughter. It's just a question of who you'll start with, and when. People made bets, you know."

That was more than any girl could take, so I punched him in the nose.

It was a good shot, a left hook Daddy'd taught me in grade school to scare the bullies away. "Boy, what a pop!" Twitch barked in surprise. "Hit him again!" Harson blinked several times in bafflement, gingerly touching the dark trickle runnin' from his right nostril. He stared at the blood on his fingertip, then whispered that after they were gone, it was just him and me.

Boy, was I mistaken when I thought I'd heard the Reaper earlier, 'cause he surely spoke through Harson now. I was stuck, sunk, hopeless, and had merely saved myself for worser things. If Harson didn't kill me, Mama would when I came home fired. No doubt about it, I was doomed.

Unless I left Wattles, that is.

The thought got me all prickly inside. Except to drive to market in Knoxville, Wattles was the length and breadth of my world. It was all I'd ever known. Sure I'd thought of leavin', but when it came down to it, leavin' was plenty scary and I suddenly felt dizzy and small. Yet when I stared in Harson's face, I knew I had no choice no more. Still, were these the strangers I'd always dreamed would whisk me outta Wattles? Was this the Prince Charming who'd drive up in a classy pumpkin and sweep me away? I glanced at Cole, cramming money down his pockets. I gazed outside at the hot pink Caddy with its snow white roof. I peeked at Twitch, grindin' his molars. At Harson, lookin' glassy-eyed.

I gritted my teeth. Maybe things weren't perfect. Beggars couldn't choose.

Joe Jackson

I sidled next to Twitch pretty as Jean Harlow in *The Public Enemy* and smiled. That'd always been my favorite movie: The Biograph never played nothin' but oldies, and I'd seen 'em all. I'd sit in the back during the Saturday matinee and wonder what it was like to be a gun moll, then slump home to stare in the oval mirror with spiderweb cracks at the bottom and hate myself for not being blond like Brigitte Bardot, Marilyn Monroe, or all the really sexy movie queens. Yet blond or not, this was it, the only chance I had. I crooked my hands on my hips like Mae West and nudged Twitch in the side. "I bet you boys could use a hostage. Easy terms. No down payment. What you say?"

You'd think I stuck his finger in a socket, the way he jerked, while Cole took one deep breath, dropped a weasel, and said: "How about it, Pop? Can we keep her, huh?"

Twitch spit against the nearest bar stool. "No women," he growled. "All they're good for is trouble."

"All we ever do is what you want!" Cole answered, surprisin' his father and, I'll admit, me.

"Boy, git some sense," Twitch said, scratching his chin and looking disturbed. "You remember how your mother ran off." He nodded at Harson. "You heard what *his* wife did to him. All women'll give you is empty pockets and a lump on the head."

I see now how that chance remark was the beginning of the end. A comment like that about Harson's sainted wife was the last push my boss needed to go over the edge. He looked about wildly, then commenced this strange, soft wheezing sound. His face grew red, then white, then ashen. "They'll pay," I heard him say. I seemed to be the only one to notice, for at that moment Cole and his father turned their eyes to the biggest prize in the house: the moose head arching above us all.

It's funny when you're desperate how Fate can stack your deal. Twitch, in his happiness, directed me to steady Cole's chair while he jimmied the moose from the wall. When he stepped close to watch, I noticed how his pistol pointed to the floor.

"How's it hung, boy?" Twitch asked, and I tried not to get distracted.

"By screws and these lines," Cole said, pointing to the web of ropes securing the antlers to the ceiling. He dug in his pocket for a folding jackknife, wrapped his arm about the moose's neck, and started cutting.

I didn't think twice. As I pulled the chair out from under Cole's feet, I yelled for my boss to get the nut with the gun. Harson was all over Twitch before I finished yelling. As I stepped back and dropped the chair, Cole tossed away his knife and grabbed the moose with both hands. There was a creak and the sound of tearing plaster. "Ah, God, Pop, help!" he gasped, but Twitch wasn't in the best position neither as he and Harson danced across the floor.

"Take everything I own, will ya? Take my money?! Take my wife?!"

"I didn't take your wife!!" Twitch cried. But, as usual, Harson wasn't listening: instead, he wrapped his hands 'round Twitch's throat and pulled him 'cross the room. Cole and the moose peeled off the wall together and hit the floor with a thud. There came a muffled shot; someone grunted. The dancers slammed against the jukebox. "The Tennessee Waltz" began.

Now seemed the perfect time to leave. My prince knelt at my feet, his pockets lined with gold. He held the pumpkin that'd pay my back wages, plus overtime. The one thing lacking was the coach. Another shot went off, and the light fixture shattered. Glass and dry bug bodies rained down.

"Where's the car keys?" I yelled in Cole's ear.

"Keys?" he moaned. I shook him like a bad puppy. "In ignition," he whined. I grabbed Cole with one hand and the moose with the other, but that was too awkward so I dropped the moose and dragged my gypsy outside. It was raining buckets as I propped him against the car and opened the front; as I shoved him inside, he fell sideways 'cross the seat. I was tempted to hightail it then and there, yet even in the excitement knew we didn't stand a chance without cold hard cash which, of course was still in that moose. But aw, God, I didn't want to go back in there.

A third shot rang from inside. I took a deep breath and flung open the door on a scene straight from a nightmare. Harson and Twitch rolled 'round the floor like lovers, but when I reappeared Twitch broke loose and crawled toward me. "Stop him, Dahlia!" Harson cried, grabbing onto his legs. "He wants to steal my only chance at happiness!"

I saw it then—how Harson had been gut-shot, the blood and some gray slime trailin' from him as he held onto Twitch, who clawed his way toward me. Harson left a track behind him like a garden slug. And then there was Twitch's eyes. They froze me solid in my size 5 saddle shoes. "You ruined everything," that old man hissed, his eyes flaring like lanterns suckin' up all the air in their globes. "I planned hard for this score and waited patiently in prison, then *you* had to come along!"

"Please, please, I didn't want anything to do with it," I whimpered, trying with all my might to break the spell, back away, run out the door. But I couldn't, not with those eyes fixin' me solid. I knew Twitch'd kill me easy as steppin' on a bug, but I was froze in their glare and a throbbing started in my ears. All I could think of was my heart clenchin' and unclenchin' like a fist, and then the gun was in his claws, pointed at me. But I still couldn't move.

"Dahlia!" Harson screamed. Old Twitch smiled. I watched his finger squeeze the trigger; then something cracked past my ear and lodged in the wall beside me, and *that* sure enough broke the spell. I gathered the moose head in my arms and crashed out the door.

"I'll get you, bitch!" Twitch shrieked. "I'm not that easy to shake. Ask my goddamn boy!!"

"Go, Dahlia, go go go!" the voice in my head was screeching, as terrified now as me. I flung open the Caddy's rear door, but the moose wouldn't fit, so I kicked in both antlers and stuffed in the naked head. I ran to the driver's side, soaked to the

skin, tremblin' from more than cold. Somewhere I'd started sobbin', and as I opened the door I caught sight of Twitch and Harson on their feet, yelling behind the window like two fish in a bowl. An emptiness swelled inside me till I wanted to sink to the ground and puke it out. The two twirled into the center of the room and fell across a table. A shot shattered a plate-glass window . . . I started shouting . . . I don't remember the words. If I don't get away now, I told myself, I never would. Twitch's lips worked silent and furious. Harson stared, eyes accusing and wild.

They rolled off the table and onto the floor. A sheet of rain streaked across the glass. I jumped behind the wheel, turned the key, and threw the car in reverse as Arnold had once showed me. I swept into the southbound lane and drove and drove and drove, not feelin' the wheel in my hands. I rolled past the burning slag heap, through the town square, beneath the Confederate Memorial all granite and green. Over the flattened guinea hen now dead in the road. The last light in town was Mama's, where she'd be waiting, alone in her bed, surrounded by her faded pictures, clutchin' the dog-eared Bible in her hands. I started cryin' and weavin' all over the road, a combination that apparently shocked Cole back to consciousness since he started screamin' I'd better let him drive or get us both killed. But I wouldn't hand the wheel over, not for the world. Like Mama and her Bible, it was all I had.

So we headed south, into the mountains, and after a while I settled back in the white seat cushions that smelled so new and tried to block out Mama, Dave's, and Wattles disappearin' in the night. The ground fog thickened at the storm's edge and piled in bunting layers over the highway. I'd never realized how thick it got till you were smack-dab inside.

Cole turned to me and stared. "Do you have any idea what you're doin'?"

His face looked sick in the green dash light when I said no.

When the Old Man Wakes

EVERY DAMN THING that's happened to me, it's been the fault of some woman.

First I got born. That was a start. I always heard I came out kicking and screaming so bad that I killed my poor mama, but I figured it was just her way of escaping my father and me. My daddy saw it otherwise. *Man born of woman is full of trouble*, he shouted as he beat me, to which I always yelled "Amen!" *He comes forth like a flower, and is cut down,* he continued, to which I imagined how fine it would be to cut him down, too.

Next I got laid. I was sixteen, laying in her bed thinking, *No matter what Daddy says, women ain't half-bad,* when her husband stormed into the room. It was a fair fight, but I still got charged with murder in the second degree. When Daddy visited me in jail, he quoted the Ten Commandments: *Thou shall not commit adultery; thou shall not covet thy neighbor's house, nor his wife, nor his ass nor his ox nor anything that is his.* "Fuck that," I answered—I hadn't coveted my neighbor's sagging old house, scrawny old cow, or ragged old donkey. I'd coveted his pretty young wife. It seemed a perfect explanation, but Daddy still cracked me over the head. When I woke in the hospital, the sheriff asked if I preferred charges. But I refused. I'd learnt a valuable lesson that arguments got won by force, not logic. Plus living anywhere, even prison, was safer than near the Old Man.

I served my years and got out, a supposedly wiser and rehabilitated man. But it wasn't long before I got laid again. This girl seemed safe—no husbands or other complications—but when she knocked on the door and told me I was gonna be a father, I remembered the oldest complication of all. Fertility's a bitch, but I tried to take it like a man. "We're part of the same club now, both fathers," I told Daddy, thinking that now he might accept me, but instead he stared at me like a sack of shit ripening on a doorstep and answered, "You'll never be the same as me." Then he popped me on the head again. *It is better to marry than to burn,* he thundered, plus, *I'll kill you if you don't, you hear?*

So we married in his church, the Old Man presiding at the altar. *You take this man, bla bla bla,* he asked, the Bible held flat before him like a serving tray. "I guess," she mumbled. *You take this woman, bla bla bla,* he continued, daring me with one quick look to say otherwise. I shrugged, figuring it was out of my hands. I was a family man for little more than a year: She and me had our rows, but I only hit her with an open palm, better treatment than I'd ever got at home. Still, she didn't see it that way. Soon after our anniversary, she ran off with the Fuller Brush man and left me with the boy.

Daddy was dead by then, so I went and spit on his grave. I'd always said he was meaner'n a snake, but one was actually meaner than him, a fact made evident the day he got worked up at the pulpit, stuck his hand in the wooden box full of canebrake rattlers, and said how-do-you-do to the business end of a female swollen with eggs. His sorrowful congregation gave me that snake to do with what I wanted, but I was so grateful for my deliverance that I let her go in the woods. All along I thought I'd shoot her, so my mercy came to me as a surprise. But as I stared at her in the box, so yellow black and deadly, I had a revelation, and as I watched her slither off a light seemed to fill the woods. *Ain't no pleasure in the world but meanness,* I realized. In my head, my daddy answered: *Man is born to trouble as the sparks fly upward.* Amen, Daddy, I said.

So it was that when I saw the little black-haired girl in the diner, I recognized trouble again. By now I was an agent of trouble, so had an eye for it, too. I could read it in her face, the way she calculated the next step, always looking ahead. And Cole, poor boy, the moment he saw her in that serving window, he lost his senses and sniffed after her like a dog. Given my own history, I couldn't blame him, yet knowing this I should've knocked some sense into him the way my own Daddy'd done for me. For this is the truth: When it comes to

females, every man in my family, and in the human race, must
admit he has shit for brains.

All this I pondered as I swam out of darkness and fiery
sparks danced before my eyes. A knot the size of Lookout
Mountain throbbed atop my head. Why was I always getting hit
in the same damn spot? If this kept up, I'd grow soft in the
head. Nearby, someone wheezed in slow rhythm, while outside
a real storm was blowing, a bona fide frog-stomper. The hail
rattled and chimed on the roof, but somehow I was getting wet
indoors. I reached over and cut the ball of my thumb on glass;
as I jerked away, my knuckles knocked against a gun.

I was confused for just a moment, but then it all came
back. The girl pulling the chair from under Cole's feet. The
old man throwing himself at me. The way she froze when I
tried to shoot her, then ran with my money when I missed.
The sound of the window shot out, which explained the rain
in here. I moaned and rolled over, trying to ignore the pain.
Sure enough, Harson Whitley lay on the floor behind me,
wheezing his life away. His eyelids fluttered weakly, his face
as pasty white as papier-mâché. A patch of red soaked
through the belly of his white apron, spreading as I watched.
I put my hand on his barely beating heart. He opened his
eyes and cried, "Where's my money?" His hand shot up,
trapping mine.

"I-I ain't got it," I stammered, the fine hairs rising on my
arm. "The girl took it, and she took my boy."

Harson Whitley sighed and dropped my hand. "That girl,"
he groaned. "I knew she'd be the death of me. I knew it when
I hired her, but I was too kindhearted and kept her on." He
started to laugh, but this ended in a mewl of pain. "Oh, that
hurts. I don't suppose water would be a good idea, huh?" He
coughed and winced. "That's what they used to say in the
Army. Don't give water to a gut-shot man."

"You're gonna live, old-timer."

"No, I ain't." He coughed again, more hollow than before.
"A guy can tell." He studied me an instant, then cracked a

smile. "She took your car too, didn't she? You sorry son-of-a-bitch, you're nearly as bad off as me."

"How much did she get away with?" I steered the talk away from my failings.

"Just under $100,000," he said.

My mouth dropped open. *One hundred thou!* I'd had a fortune in my hands and lost it, and for the first time in recent memory, I nearly cried. This . . . this was worse than the sum of every woman-born abomination ever visited upon me, and spots danced before my eyes. "*Nobody* knew I had so much," Harson gloated, eyes shining as I dropped back and stared overhead. "Not even your fine friend Dave. I'd heard the rumors about my money, but nobody had a clue. I sold some land to a mine company—not just surface rights but mineral rights, the whole shebang. You know how hard it is to beat a mine-company lawyer at his own game? I was a real wheeler-dealer, pulling that off." His giggles turned into a racking cough. "Look what it's got me. You, too. We're a pair, ain't we, beaten by a slip of a girl."

The coughs got worse, and he clamped me by the wrist again till they finally died away. "God, I hate Dahlia Jean Coker," he sighed. "You never would've figured it out if it hadn't been for her. She's a smart one, watching how things work. I always worried she'd figure out my hiding place, and would've fired her if I didn't need the help so bad." He closed his eyes. "Still, sometimes it was nice . . . sometimes we got along." He breathed slowly, as if falling to sleep; his eyes reopened, outta focus, and his voice was thin. "You can have it all, if you catch her."

"I'll catch her, don't worry. You can lay money on that."

"It looks like I already have."

That was the last he said. His breath rushed out and dust blew from his lips. His fingers dug into my skin, then relaxed. I realized I'd made a bet with a dead man.

I pried off the old man's fingers as the left side of my face started jumping and lightning crackled overhead. I'd gained the tic in prison and usually didn't feel it anymore, but I did now. *One hundred thou!* In one fell swoop, that girl had took everything that mattered—my car, my cash, and my boy. Now I knew how poor Job felt as he sat in his circle of ashes and his wife mocked, *Curse God and die.* He wanted to kill her, then kill her again.

The rain was letting up outside: headlights flashed past, tires swished through the water slicking the road. I pulled myself up painfully and sat on a stool. The old man looked smaller already, the air leaking out like from a balloon. The dead got puny that way, while in your mind they growed bigger and bigger. In my life I'd killed or damaged those who really needed it, but this time I felt bad. Like me, the old coot had been belabored to death by females: Him and me belonged to the same cursed club. If he hadn't grabbed my gun, this wouldn't've happened, but try telling a jury your gun misfired. No, sir, they'd see it as murder committed during robbery, and send me straight to Death Row.

I'd die before that, but the problem was, how to get away? If only I could think straight, but my head pounded in time to the banging in my ears. First things first, I told myself: I had to calm down. I stuck the gun back in my pants where it felt comfortable and grabbed the old man under the arms; I dragged him behind the counter and tucked him into an alcove for pots and pans. He looked so peaceful, like he was home asleep in bed. I swept up glass from the shattered window and mopped up the blood, wiping 'round for prints as I kept a watch on the door. The clock above it read half-past midnight: if I locked up, maybe no one would notice the mess till morning, and by then I'd be miles away. But where were the old man's keys? When I patted his pants, I felt a key ring in his pocket, but I'd wedged him too tight in the shelf and when I tried to pry him out I bumped the same tender spot on my head. "Shit, fire and damnation!" I shouted.

"Who's in there?" an uncertain voice said.

I froze. The voice had come from up front, by the shattered entrance, and it sounded like that of a kid, probably the same age as Cole. Sweet Jesus and Moses, what else could go wrong? Common sense said I couldn't leave no witness, but this was getting excessive, even for me. I'd have to stuff the newcomer one shelf up from Harson Whitley; if this kept up, I'd soon run out of shelves. I pulled the gun out of my waistband, kept it out of sight, and rose slowly.

"You're not Mr. Whitley," the kid said.

I looked him over careful. He was a scrawny sort, not over seventeen, with pimples in the corners of his lips and hair the color of mopwater. The most prominent thing about him was his eyes. They bulged out from his head like a bullfrog, and in my mind he instantly became Frog Boy. But that wasn't important compared to what I saw behind him, for parked in the lot was his Ford pickup, patched with rust and painted puke green. Maybe it was ugly, but it solved the transportation problem. Now I had to grab him before he bolted and spread the alarm.

"What happened in here?" Frog Boy asked.

"Don't get excited," I replied. "The window blew out and scared us half to death. Harson went for help and left me in charge till he returned."

"You're not from Wattles."

My head hurt too much for a gabfest and I fingered the trigger, wondering if another killing wasn't so bad after all. But Frog Boy still had distance on me, and in my wooziness, I was likely to miss. I had to lure him near. *Come closer, little piggy, where I can see you better.* "I'm Harson's brother, here for a visit." I smiled and added, "Come in. He'll be back soon."

"I didn't know Mr. Whitley had a brother."

"We're a big family."

"I have a sister," Frog Boy said, "though she gets me into more trouble with her gossip and lies." He nudged something with his toe, bent down, and picked up a shard of glass, then held it between his fingers like a shiny nickel. "This could hurt somebody." He walked up and placed it on the counter, delivering himself into my hands.

I almost felt guilty, this was so easy. My finger tensed on the trigger as he reached into his back pocket and ran a comb through his unruly hair. "I bet that was something, sitting here, then *smash!* glass flies everywhere," he said, turning his back to me to admire the ruins. I brought the pistol up and breathed in slowly. "Good thing I came by. I knew it was near closin', so I thought I'd see if Dahlia Jean wanted a ride."

Omigod, he knows the girl. Quick as a bunny, I dipped the gun beneath the counter; he heard the sound and turned around. "Y-you know the girl?" I said, a bit too eager. "You know where she lives?"

His chest puffed out a couple inches and he grinned. *"Everybody* knows Dahlia Jean, but I know her best 'cause *I'm* her boyfriend." He glanced over at the serving window. "Is she in or not? I'm surprised she ain't out already. *Dahlia Jean!!"*

Thank you, Jesus, I said to myself—this idjut from Heaven knew where she lived. What if she was still home packing? "What's your name, boy?" I asked, real friendly, shifting my grip on the gun.

"Arnold Simpson. *Dahlia Jean, you ready?"* He cocked his head. "She ain't answerin'. You think maybe she got hurt?"

"Better go look," I said, following close as he glanced through the door. "Hey, she ain't back h—," he managed to blurt before I coldcocked him with the gun.

I searched Frog Boy's pockets and grabbed his keys to the truck, then searched the back room for something to hogtie his feet and hands. A hank of rope tossed beside a toolbox did fine. I hurried out front, locked the door, cut the lights, and surveyed my handiwork. All folks would see now was the light through the serving window, and thinking things were normal, would head elsewhere for a late-night snack. I felt safe again.

I rolled the kid against the wall and poked around. This back room was part kitchen, part bedroom and storage shed. On the shelf above the cot was a Bible and a small framed photo of Whitley's wife: a peroxide blonde with big front

bumpers, just like Dave Aikens had said. When things got dull
in our cell, he'd reminisce how she moaned like a cat when you
stuck it to her, but it's frustrating to hear such talk in the
cooler and said I'd hurt him if he didn't quit. He always com-
plied. I thought about the former partners and the object of
their affection. Look where it had got 'em: one dead, one in
prison, and for what? A woman. *Every man that eats the sour grape,
his teeth shall be set on edge*, said Daddy. When Daddy was right, he
was right—and he was right again.

But I couldn't waste time on memories. I grabbed what I
needed, including a chipped Louisville Slugger no doubt kept
for protection, and told the boy to quit playing dead. We was
leaving soon. His eyes sprang open and he asked, "You gonna
kill me, too?"

"Not unless you make me angry," I fibbed. "I just want
the girl."

"She's not my girlfriend, really. I mean, it's kinda one-
sided. I just pretend she is. To tell the truth, I think she just
tolerates me, and that's on my better days." He studied me a
second. "Why you want her, anyway?"

"Didn't your mama ever warn you not to question
strangers?"

"Yeah, but no stranger's ever knocked me out and tied me
up, neither."

Did all teenagers talk back at such ridiculous times? "Boy,"
I said, "just answer my questions and you won't have to see
what happens when I get mad."

With that, blessed silence returned. My head didn't throb
out loud. I unlocked the back padlock, crept 'round the side
wall, and peeked in the parking lot. The night was dead. I
piled my junk under the Ford's cab seat, hoisted the boy over
my shoulder, and set him next to me. "So where's that girl
live?"

South through town, Frog Boy replied. There was a breeze,
everything smelling fresh of rain. I drove slow and easy,
mindful of the speed limit as I headed through the town

square. Past a red brick courthouse, past a green Confederate Memorial standing guard. The road glistened in the streetlights; pools of water shimmered on the asphalt like the shards of a broken mirror. A lone yellow bulb burned over the door of the police station, moths and gnats swirling 'round it like leaves. An old cop, propped underneath in his cane-backed chair, glanced up as we passed. I kept my face in the shadows and my knuckles went white on the wheel. His eyes flicked back to his lap, his whittling more interesting than us. We rolled past a Piggly Wiggly, closed for the night, its shopping carts lined out front. We passed down block after block of darkened houses, their families tucked safe in bed for the night.

What was it about places like this that I could not stand? What made me want to burn them down? I had dreams like that, where I'd stand at the town limits and laugh as the few survivors running past saw fire dancing in my eyes. The vision always brought shivers more delicious than the cool hands of any woman. I must've shown it, 'cause I caught the kid starin'. I growled at him, "So where's her house?"

"Right there." He pointed with his tied hands to the last house before the mountains. A single light burned in a window.

It was a dark night on a dark street, but even that couldn't hide that this was the kind of house where people barely held on. The white paint peeled in strips from the wood siding. Some tarpaper shingles had blown from the roof and landed in the yard. A dead tree stump was surrounded by plastic yellow daisies, their spinning petals clattering in the breeze. A ripped edge of the screen porch flapped softly. I cut the lights and rolled slowly up the gravel driveway.

There was no sign of a car. No car meant no kids, which meant they'd never stopped or already'd passed on. As Frog Boy watched me think, the clouds broke up and the moon beamed down. The whites of his eyes turned to violet crescents. I asked how many people lived inside.

"Just Dahlia and her mom, and she don't get out much

anymore." The place was probably locked, he added, but he knew where they hid the key. I untied his feet and told him not to be a hero, then prodded him in front of me.

Frog Boy proved good to his word, digging the extra key from a pot of wilted geraniums. The tumblers clicked, the back door squeaked, and we crept in. It was obviously a woman's house, lacy china knickknacks planted here and there like mines. A framed and doe-eyed Jesus stared, reproachful, as we sneaked through the back door. There was the musty smell of a place too long closed up, the mixed scent of moth-balls and dried violets in tiny bowls. It smelled like a funeral home and gave me the creeps. This was how people ended their lives, not lived them.

We stopped and listened but there was no sound, just a lack of it, as though the house listened to us while we listened to it. "Go on," I whispered, poking the boy forward, wanting out of here as fast as I could. He pointed down a short hall: I saw a bathroom, a closed door with a light behind it, and a darkened room at the end. "Dahlia's room is the dark one," he whispered. "Her ma is in the lit one."

I sighed. There was no way out of questioning the mother, since only she would know where her daughter had gone. This was turning into a social event. First this kid, now her.

"You trying to sneak past me, girl? You think I'm deaf?" a sharp voice snapped, the kind of voice that seemed accustomed to being obeyed. "And who's in the house with you? It better not be Arnold Simpson. I saw you hop in his truck this morning! You come in here, *now!*"

I shrugged and pushed the kid through her door. She was propped up in bed; as Frog Boy landed at her feet, she yelped and scrabbled backward. "You're only half-right, lady," I said.

Her chin went up and she stared at me, eyes narrowing to slits. I'll give her this: She didn't glance twice at my gun. "You get out of my house!" she yapped, then kicked at the boy through the covers. "And take *him* with you! You wait till I tell your mother about this, Arnold, barging into a lady's bed-room, bringin' strangers, too!"

"Oww. Ain't my fault, Miz Coker!"

"You're a depraved young man, Arnold Simpson, simply depraved."

I sighed again, with feeling. What had I done to deserve all this? I said my prayers, served my time, was likable enough, tried to keep the body count down. And for what?

Life ain't fair—that's God's truth.

And *nothin's* easy once a woman gets involved.

Never Check the Mirror When You Drive Like Hell on Wheels

WE DROVE THAT night, all night, though it seemed we was standing still. I couldn't leave the nightmare at Dave's fast enough, but the deeper me and Cole shot into the mountains, the more everything looked the same. The road twisted on itself like hog guts, highway signs streaking past in our high beams in a comet-tail of white and green. The black rocks arched up and trees looked lifeless, leaves dull like lead. Behind was only darkness, but the road ahead paled to nothing, broken only by the odd hunched critter frozen in the lights, green eyes blazing as our car bore down.

I *should've* been happy, so what was wrong? Here I was riding off with my outlaw just like I'd always imagined, but I couldn't shake the feeling that if I glanced in the rearview mirror, I'd see the same rain-streaked diner, the same two dancers spinning to their waltz of life and death, Mama's bedroom light twinkling in the rain. What would she think when I didn't come home tonight? Would she call the police? And what would the police find smeared across the diner's floor?

What had I done? I hadn't doubted myself back in the bright lights of the diner, but you think long enough in a car hurtlin' through darkness, and you start doubtin' the day you was born. Maybe I was superstitious, but I didn't dare check the rear mirror. There's an old saying that the Reaper grins over your shoulder when you drive like hell on wheels. I didn't want to see if it was true.

At least Cole kept busy, reaching into his pockets and coming out with stolen bills. "One hunnert, one-twenty, one-seventy, two-seventy." When I glanced over, he was staring dumbfounded at a heap of bills piled in his lap. "You mean all that came from those varmints?"

"Dahlia, there's close to four thousand dollars right here," he said in disbelief. "It's all in hunnerts, fifties, some twenties." He turned around and looked at the bull moose. "No telling how much is in *there!*"

That got my attention, and the Cadillac stopped on its own. "You mean we're rich?" I squeaked, all the air forced from my lungs.

"It looks that way . . . rich and then some," he said. "By God, for once in his life, my old man was right about something. We can start over wherever we want. We can live like kings and queens."

I chewed on this new development as the engine stalled and we sat like lumps in the road. *Rich*—what a funny-soundin' word. Rich was what movie stars lived, Elizabeth Taylor or Princess Grace in her palace by the sea. Rich was a kingdom where dollar signs sprinkled like confetti and happy people filled the photo magazines.

Now I was rich, too, and I was one of them. It took a while to sink in. "I'll be dog," I finally said. But when I said to open the moose and see how rich we *really* was, Cole suggested we get off the road before some semitrailer ran us down. Otherwise, we would be rich and dead. "Good idea," I said, starting the Caddy and pullin' her over. But even then, Cole was not as happy as the rich should be. A worry had come over him. He

demanded we put more road between us and Wattles, while I
wanted to see all that money that'd been starin' me in the face
for so long. I wanted to sniff it and taste it and pile it in a heap
and dive in.

"Trust me, we better get goin'," he argued, staring back. He
seemed pretty insistent, so I shrugged and started the engine.
We headed south again.

But forward motion didn't seem to calm him, either. He
stuck some money in his pocket, then opened the glove compartment and found his old man's wallet, stuck there for safe-
keeping during the robbery. He stuffed it full of bills and sank
back in his seat, but still couldn't keep still. He rolled down the
window . . . rolled it back up. Drummed his fingers on the arm-
rest. Flipped on the radio, got static. Twirled the tuning knob.

"What the hell's the matter?" I blurted.

"Nothin's the matter," he said.

I knew the difference between somethin' and nuthin', and
told him so. But all Cole did was twirl the radio knob. "I just
want to catch the news, okay?"

"The news is boring. We're rich and don't need to be
bored."

He lost his patience then. "You don't get it, do you?
We're rich and that's a goddamn miracle, but my father
knows we're rich, and if he made it out of the diner, he'll be
after us in no time. He planned and schemed for the last few
years for this money. I doubt he'll let it go. "

"It's ours," I said. "We earned it."

"He sees it otherwise."

Now I glanced back in the mirror, trying to forget those
eyes. "I'm sure we shook him," I insisted to myself as much as
to Cole. "We got a good head start."

"Dahlia, how hard you think it'll be to follow a stolen pink
Cadillac through these hills?"

"Stolen?" I screamed, and nearly ran off the road.

So it was I heard the story of Cole, his crazy father, and his
crazy father's crazy dream. Just like a mother and daughter are

at each other's throats, a son never comprehends his father's demons or the ambitions that drive him mad. Every man has a destiny, and Twitch said his was to leave the Great State and live like a king. But as he grew older, that destiny refused to show itself, and instead of rich, he grew mean. At first he tried honest work, tunneling coal from small truck mines with a string of partners, but it soon became clear that the ways to die in that business were varied, familiar, and grim. There was methane gas, the odorless "black damp" that knocked you out and choked you; other gases ate at your nerves, puckering your face in a permanent kiss or making you twitch in the limbs. There was floating coal dust, explosive as gunpowder, that could spark in an instant and send timbers, coal, and body parts belching from a mine. There was roof-fall, the most common death, slate separating from the sandstone above it, a huge slab of rock squashing you flat as a bug. No, it was much easier to rob the mine companies and the small banks that held their payrolls instead. Sometimes Cole's daddy was flush with cash, but that was always a temporary state before Cole's memories filled up with curses and gunfire, with court-ordered stays with kinfolk or foster parents, with his old man tossed in the state pen again.

It was during the last and longest stay in Bushy Mountain that Twitch met Dave Aikens, Cole explained. The two were cellmates, and like a good cellmate, Twitch stood up for Aikens against some guards. For his pains, Daddy got throwed in the Hole; when he came out, Aikens repaid the favor with the only gift he could: the rumors of his former partner's loot. Though Aikens had never found the stash himself, he said, Pop was welcome to it—if it was even there.

Cole's father didn't pay much attention at first, but you mull over a pot of gold long enough, and it eventually takes on a life of its own. The Old Man was in a long time. By the time he got out, all doubt had vanished about Harson's riches; the vague hope had transformed into certainty. There was a million bucks hid among the cans of pork and beans, he told his son; the only trick was making Harson reveal where. After that, it was Easy Street. They were destined for the Promised Land.

Cole stared out the window as I drove, remembering it all. His reflection stared back. "I'd never seen him like that," he said. "He saw it as his last chance, and he was so sold on the stash that I was scared to argue otherwise. The relatives charged with my care took the wisest course—they ran away and hid. A week ago, we checked out your diner, driving by real slow. Nice and out of the way, said Pop—all his experience told him it was a perfect place to rob. The night before last, he got struck by a wild hair. We'd leave the state in style, he announced, and he hot-wired this Cadillac parked in an Asheville dealership as promotion. *Drive Away Like The King,* the sign on it said. As we drove off, I asked if he was crazy. After all, a car like Elvis Fuckin' Presley's was only the most noticeable thing in the state. He slapped me 'cross the face and said cussin' like a sailor was not acceptable behavior for a future gentleman."

There was a pause. "You know the rest. He would've been right after all, except he didn't figure on you." Cole cleared his throat. "Neither did I."

I waited for more. The stolen tires purred beneath us. We breathed in and out, lungs recycling the stolen air. I glanced over. "Don't misunderstand me," he said. "I don't regret bein' here. All my life, in one way or another, I've been under that old man's thumb. All my life I've dreamed of getting free, as if the past eighteen years could just be washed away. No such chance arose until tonight, even if it did come a little fast . . . I mean, gettin' bopped on the head and dragged away half-conscious is not a very manly way to make one's escape, but I can deal with that. The thing that's hard to deal with is my father's vengeance, if and when it comes . . . and I'm inclined to think it will."

Cole's face shone ghostly in the light, his eyes still fixed outside. "It's like my old man never sleeps, but is endlessly awake. He stares into his future like crazy people stare into the sun. He may be blind to everything else, but not to that money. It gives off heat for him . . . he follows that heat the way a poisonous snake finds its next meal. He's after us; I know it. I think of him almost like the Second Coming: nobody knows when or where it's scheduled, but beware its arrival, brother, 'cause things will start jumpin' then."

"You're scared of him."

He laughed. "Always have been, and always will. Considering what he almost did to you in the diner, you should be, too."

It was hard to argue with that. So we drove. The deeper and higher we climbed into the mountains, the more the road curved. The curves lasted forever, doublin' back till we crawled along like a big pink turtle. It was either that or plunge over the edge of the road. The trees climbed the steep hogbacks, their silver trunks disappearing in the fog. Our headlights lit the black sides of barns and crumbling sheds. We passed a lighted truck stop, the semis and their trailers circled in the night like Conestoga wagons 'round a fire. After that the road south was empty, ours and ours alone. A luna moth drifted into the headlights like a pale green leaf and splashed against the windshield. Its innards rolled up the glass in yellow streaks, pushed by the wind.

I twirled the radio to break the silence, but the best I got was some boy preacher with a high, girly voice and new degree from Holy Bible A&M. He insisted that unless I accepted the Son of God in my life, I was surely damned. *Oh shut up,* I thought, twirling the knob again. Sometimes there'd be a snatch of music: Marty Robbins singing "El Paso," Carl Perkins warning about his blue suede shoes, Elvis moaning "Jailhouse Rock." Like I really needed to hear *that* right now.

So I finally asked: "Should we go back and tell what happened?"

"I think it's too late," Cole said.

And so it was. Too many bad things waited for us back there. Questions by cops, my mama's anger, the wrath of his crazy dad. A return to the land of coal and old men. The wind pushed through my window and whistled so eerie; a morning chill climbed beneath my shift and took hold. The musty smell of the moose filled the car. In the distance an owl whoo-whooed, meaning someone was dying. A dog howled even closer, meaning someone was already dead.

There was an ugliness littered through these mountains, and now we drove into the heart of it, revealed by the dawn. We zipped past ghost shacks, barbed-wire fences, rusted Farmall tractors, gray industrial barns. We sped up hills carpeted with fading yellow school buses and abandoned auto hulks, passed forests choked by rhododendron and creeping kudzu, paused for Cole to take a leak outside an abandoned store. Shakes dangled from its roof; the screen door hung ajar. A blister-rusted sign for LUCKY STRIKES and another for 666 COLDS & FEVERS swung by their nails. We passed houses that could barely be called houses, their long front porches sagging in the middle, their props sunk in the clay. A baby with hair like Elvis crawled from one and waved as we sped by. Behind his house were rows of pens for blue- and blood-colored game-cocks, born to kill. Behind this were fields, overgrown with broom sedge, and beyond that the woods. The whole land seemed to wake in the haunted morning, a creaking and rustling of something buried deep and struggling to rise. Over it all seeped the mountain smell of tar, creosote, gasoline, and manure.

Maybe the light played tricks on me, maybe I was tired. But as I drove, I seemed to see the same face staring back at me on every rock farmer walking stiffly by the road. It was Twitch before he pulled the trigger, his eyes like two rubber knobs. Everywhere I went would be these same pale faces, parched like John the Baptist's, returning from the wilderness before he testified.

We crested a long ascent and the road flattened on a plateau. I could see a little town ahead. We rolled through it in the time it took the radio to catch the morning news, the announcer tellin' how police discovered the body of sixty-one-year-old

Harson A. Whitley stuffed behind the counter of his diner in Wattles, Tennessee. He died of gunshot wounds to the stomach, victim of an apparent late-night robbery. No money was taken from the register, but a number of stuffed animals had disappeared. In a related matter, police were searching for his countergirl, sixteen-year-old Dahlia Jean Coker, her mother, forty-five-year-old Burma Coker, and Dahlia's high-school boyfriend Arnold Simpson, all of whom had vanished, too. Although foul play was suspected, police refused to say whether the three missing persons were in league. Meanwhile, in national news—

"Pop got away," Cole said, his words escapin' like steam. I, however, focused on the things that were news to me. *Foul play suspected . . . three missing persons in league.* What'd happened to Mama and Arnold? Even worse, police thought *I* was the killer now?

The ringing in my ears from the diner came back. Tiny spots swam before my eyes and grew big. The town vanished behind us and a turnoff appeared on the right—I jerked the wheel and bounced down a dirt road. Cole yelled for me to stop, but I kept going, barely missing some trees. We bumped down a forest tunnel, branches overlapping above us, the green light like drowning as I went down the last time. There was one final curve—then the road ended in a foggy field.

I flung open the door and flew out, then crouched over and got very, very ill. In a minute, I heard Cole's footsteps. "Don't stare at me," I said, wiping my mouth with my sleeve and thrusting the keys behind me with my other hand. "You drive. You're so smart, take over. I don't care where we go." There was only silence. I jingled the keys. "You want 'em? Here!"

But Cole just tossed 'em on the seat. His fingers touched the nape of my neck and lingered in my hair. His breath flowed down my neck; a trembling passed along my spine. As I rose to meet him, I saw the worry lines etched around his eyes.

He feels it, too, I thought. *He's as scared as me.*

The realization hit us both like Super Glue. Our eyes did all the talking; then our lips pressed together, teeth clacking hard. Our hands ripped at one another's clothes till we lost our footing on the wet grass and tumbled to the ground. So this is how it happens, I thought in that second before temptation won out and clear thinking was a thing of the past—

Maybe love is the drug, but it's fear that makes the world go 'round.

Why Doth the Heathen Rage?

SOMETIMES I SIT and wonder what's behind the meanness that guides me through this world. Was it my sweet and gentle upbringing? My lovely face? A deeper taint my daddy said was reflected in that face, and which he tried to beat away?

I simply do not know. It's truly a great mystery. Is meanness a cloud that floats in and out of events, entering our lungs like poison gas to make us twitch to its tune? Or does it rise within us, like indigestion? Are we born mean, or do we learn it at the hands of our elders? No one seems to know for certain, so I guess I'll have to ask Jesus when I see Him. God help him if He's stumped, too.

Given that, I've become an expert in spotting meanness in others. I thought I knew its every form. I'd seen it in Daddy's flock during their after-sermon gossip, in the dead eyes of lifers and the cruel smiles of guards. I'd seen it in the mirror and someday anticipated seeing it in Cole. Meanness runs through everything: The more you pick it and pluck it, the more everything else unravels, leaving only that black thread. You may not like it, but sooner or later you accept the fact that meanness comes with life, the late-blooming wonder of God's creation, the black hand that rocks the cradle in this troubled world.

Still, I was knocked for a loop that night when I faced the meanness of a woman too early grown old. Beside that, all others paled. I stood in the doorway, mouth open, gun dangling, as the girl's mama sat straight under the covers and stared back at me. Her head cocked to one side as she listened to the kid babble at her feet, but her snake eyes always focused on mine. There were a couple of seconds of which I completely lost track; a pit opened in the bottom of my stomach, a sure sign of either love or terror, and I sure the hell wasn't in the mood for love. Part of me said, *J. T. Younger, you turn around right now and run for all get-out,* but another part conceded I was in the presence of a superior moral force. It was useless to even try.

Given the kid's description, I'd expected an older woman, but now I realized she was old only in heart and mind. Her hair was long and yellow; her green eyes the color of money, with gold laced liberally through the anti-counterfeit threads. I figured her as ten years younger'n me, somewhere in her mid-forties; she'd been a looker once, but somewhere the soft curves had turned hard. Her long legs under the covers looked thin as sticks, and her skin had that pasty look of someone who's been inside too long. Yet there was no weakness in her face, just a rising anger that seemed hotter than any of that atomic stuff leaking from Oak Ridge.

As I watched, she kicked the boy again for spite, telling him she'd heard enough, then turned the full lantern of those eyes on me. "You want my daughter, and why's that?" she wondered. "Dahlia can give a soul the fits, but what did she do to you?"

"I think he killed Mr. Whitley," the boy said. "I-I think I saw his body stuffed under the counter before everything went black. At least I think it was him."

"Arnold, who else would it be?" she said. "The old coot's been a murder waitin' to happen longer than you realize." She studied me close, figuring the lay of the land. "But you, you're a stranger—so why you?" She puzzled it out another couple seconds, then her face lit up like the candy man arrived. "Could it be all those stories were true?"

"What stories?" Frog Boy asked, looking up timidly from the end of her bed.

"Don't be so dense. The stories of Harson's hidden fortune."

"Oh, them."

The world would be a better place if all the nosy people were collected in one pit and a backhoe filled it in. I hadn't made a peep the entire time she talked, but now my face told her everything 'cause she clapped her hands together and kicked the boy with glee. *"That's it!!"* she cried. "But how did Dahlia find it? I was there for years and nothin', but she's there no time and finds it easy as pie." Suddenly her face grew hard. "And the minute she finds it, she runs off, leavin' her mama behind. Would you do that to your mother, Arnold?"

"No, ma'am, she'd hunt me to the ends of the earth."

"As any mother should." She struggled with the covers. "Which is exactly what I'm gonna do. Arnold, fetch that cane in the corner and my suitcase from the closet. We're going with this man."

Frog Boy and I gawped together. "Who said you were invited?" I finally said. She gave me the same look she'd given Arnold, the icy look men have got from women since the beginning of time. The one that draws its authority from the pains of childbirth and says, *You're an ingrate for doubting my wisdom: I brought you into this life, and I can take you out of it, too.*

She was so calm. "Mister, I'm her mother. I can read her mind. I know where she's headed, even if *she* doesn't yet." She smiled sweetly. "Do *you?*"

I felt light-headed, uncertain what to do. She was right, of course—I had no earthly idea where that damn girl had run. To my surprise, the boy pitched in. "Miz Coker, I thought you was crippled," he said, stepping from the closet and dragging her suitcase to the bed. "How you gonna chase Dahlia 'cross the country if you ain't left the house in so long?"

"I can walk if I have to, though it is painful," she admitted, looking sheepish. "I just never told Dahlia Jean."

Warning bells went off in my ears. This was too much for me. With each new stop, the number of witnesses seemed to multiply. The job I'd planned so carefully was spinning outta control. How complicated could one simple holdup be? I leaned against the wooden chifforobe and waved my gun weakly. "Tell you what. Just tell me where your daughter went, and I won't kill either one of you."

"You ain't killin' anyone," she said, grunting slightly as she swung her legs around the side of the bed. The pink nightgown bunched 'round her knees, showing a glimpse of skin. "You kill me, and you'll never know where the money went. You kill Arnold, and I won't tell you. He's irritating, but not enough for murder. It's that simple." She leaned on her cane and ordered us from the room while she changed.

Her hold over me seemed to break when I shut the door. "Is that woman crazy or what?" I said, but Frog Boy just plucked a glass gewgaw from a table and flipped it over, examining the MADE IN CHINA like it was the most amazing thing he'd ever seen. "Don't ask me, I think you're both crazy," he muttered. I picked up a pink Southern belle with a lacy glass parasol; I crushed her to fine powder in my hand.

She emerged, dressed like a cowgirl, a country rhinestone queen. The boy threw her suitcase in the flatbed and we piled in the cab. She took the passenger seat by the window; Frog Boy slouched between her and me. "Which way was Dahlia headed when she left the diner?" she asked. South, I said. She smiled to herself and her green eyes brightened. "Just as I thought," she answered. "South it is."

"How you know she didn't head off on some other tack?" I snapped.

She bet her share of the money that Dahlia was headed for her daddy, she said.

Her share of the money? "Who made you a partner?"

"No need to shout. I deserve a finder's fee."

At which point, the boy pitched in. "If she gets something, I do, too! It's my truck!" I told him he was abducted and didn't have no rights. He answered, "Well, hell, so is she!"

"No, Arnold, there's a difference," she corrected, patting

his arm. "You were knocked out and tied up, so you are literally a captive. Me, I invited myself along."

My headache felt so massive, it threatened to blow the roof off the Ford. I muttered insults about all things female as I backed from her driveway, grinding the gears. "No need to be rude," she said. "You keep that up, you'll strip the gears."

"Who's drivin', lady?"

"Say good-bye to Wattles, Arnold, at least for a little while," she chimed, making a point of ignoring me. She rolled down the window and spat. "As for me, good riddance," then looked back at me and smiled. "The trip'll go faster if we don't squabble so much. Like the Good Book says, 'Whoso keepeth his mouth and temper, keepeth his soul from trouble.'"

"Yeah, and it's easier to dwell in the wilderness than with a contentious woman. It says that, too."

With that, I held my tongue and drove. Maybe I was in the doghouse now, but every dog has his day. I aimed Frog Boy's Ford right where she pointed and dove into the mountains. As the hours passed, I distilled Burma Coker into the essence of every woman who'd ever made my life a living hell. I'd bide my time and salve my pride till the money was mine once more; until that glorious moment, I could at least imagine every means of murder and annihilation possible for my uninvited guest. I was the long, stiff rod of vengeance in the war between the sexes, the speeding twelve-gauge firing squad tearing down the road. I was the dog, all right, but a dog who'd howl all night once he got his bone.

"Could you please quit snickerin' like that?" the woman snapped, interrupting my thoughts.

"She's right, it's creepy," Frog Boy said.

If nothing else, such mental carnage helped to pass the miles. We swooped through the mountains as fast as the heap would let us, clattering at every seam and weld. The road twisted in ascending hairpins; the bluffs towered over us, the trees looking dead in our beams. Soon it was the hour before dawn, the time when all smart predators rose. We came to a crossroads with a highway running east and west; springing from its southeast quadrant was a truck stop with the red sign DIESEL hanging over an all-night diner's glow.

"Keep going south," said Burma Coker.

"Wait a minute, I'm hungry," Frog Boy said.

To tell the truth, food wasn't a bad idea. I liked this kind of stop, the semis growling deep with a kind of hunger, pulled beside each other for the night as if for warmth, with dark canyons in between. After midnight the whores worked these canyons, knocking for business on the doors of sleeper cabs. Now all was quiet, crickets whirring in the stillness beyond the pole lights, a lonely rush of wind as a car passed down the road. I circled the lot in case the Cadillac was parked back in the shadows, though I didn't expect to see it so soon. I suspected by now that Cole had throwed in with the girl; if so, he knew I'd follow and would be running scared.

Inside the diner, I could see a few cross-country drivers drinking coffee in their booths, staring out the plate-glass windows and watching the dawn's scarlet and orange with red eyes. They cradled the warm cup in both hands, maybe rubbing it slowly against their cheek. This was the home of men with no home, nothing but 18-wheelers and the road. Inside were the hard-shelled women who served them, who knew them by face and first name and flirted comfortably while serving ham and eggs. This was a home with no other commitment than a good, fast meal while the jukebox played songs of failed love and lost highways. It was my kind of place, where love was a good tip and a see-ya-later, the way men and women ought to be.

We piled into one of the red Naugahyde booths, the boy and woman sitting on one side, me on the other. The laminated menus showed every kind of breakfast known to man. Each one was dubbed a different rise-'n'-shine name. Regular-scheduled meals was one of the few things I missed about prison, but this was the first real restaurant I'd eaten in since leaving the joint and so it was a luxury. Once I caught the girl

57

and got my money back, I'd eat breakfast, lunch, *and* dinner at a different restaurant every day. I'd eat at places like this, where menus were propped between the napkin holder and the stack of Domino Sugar packets, each tiny white envelope picturing a president's house or the Seven Natural Wonders of the World. A man could eat and get an education at the same time. Frog Boy played with the salt and pepper shakers, shaped like a hen and rooster. He made them peck at each other; then the rooster fell over and groaned.

Burma said to order her a stack of flannel cakes with blueberry syrup as she went to powder her nose. "Don't try nothin' funny, like leavin'," she warned as she got up.

"Yes, dear," I replied.

As she walked off, I noticed that her step seemed a little firmer than before. She wasn't so bad-looking if you forgot that temper, and a couple of truckers confirmed my thoughts by ogling as she passed. "What's with the cripple act?" I asked the boy. He admitted he was surprised by how well she was getting 'round. He told about the episode with the Mack truck drivers, and how before that her wayward husband turned up somewhere in Florida. The two, nearly back-to-back, made her the town laughingstock, so she stayed inside her room and nursed her bitterness, lashing out at Dahlia, the only person at hand.

The woman emerged looking fresher than when she went in, an occurrence that, to me, was always one of the great mysteries of the world. If a man went to drain his lizard, he came out looking no different unless he'd lost his train of thought and sprayed his shirt and jeans. But when a woman returns, it's like the world's been put in order and life is good. "So what's your name?" she asked as she sat, tucking back a wisp of fallen hair.

"Hostages don't need to know that stuff," I said.

"Stop with the kidnap foolishness, all right? If you remember, *I* flagged down this taxi."

I stared out the window, annoyed. "Okay," she continued, "how about your first name, then, seein' how we'll be together awhile."

"At least as far as Florida, right?" I said. Her eyes widened in surprise; then she figured out what happened in her absence and elbowed Frog Boy in the ribs. "Oww, whatcha do that for?" he cried.

"For havin' a big mouth, for one."

"All I said was how Dahlia's father turned up in Florida."

"Did you say *where?*" The boy grumbled that he couldn't remember. "It's a good thing, too, considering it's the only advantage we got, and once he knows *that,* there's no longer a need to keep us alive." Frog Boy quit rubbing the spot she'd poked and looked across the table at me.

"Oh, yeah," he said.

I merely smiled. I had to admit, this woman had both balls and brains, and between her and the prospect of breakfast, I was slipping into a better mood. The waitress came up, the name "Shelly" stitched in red over her right breast, which reminded me of another reason I liked these places: You didn't have to jump through hoops to learn a woman's name. You just read it off her knockers in a fine cursive hand. Even better, you wouldn't catch her asking mine. All she'd ask for was our order, which was pancakes for the woman, scrambled eggs and ham for Frog Boy, and fried eggs, sausage, hash browns, and cheese grits for me. Shelly dropped her pad in her front apron pocket and poked the pen in her hennaed bun: "We're certainly hungry this mornin'," she said. "I don't see many families this early, just truckers and more truckers. I been here since midnight, and I don't think I seen more'n five cars out there in that fog."

This waitress was the talky kind. "We got a long drive ahead of us, so we thought we'd get an early start," I said. Then I had a brainstorm. "Did you see that pink Cadillac? We passed it to the north of here, back around Wattles."

"Pink Cadillac, like Elvis drives?" The waitress was as excited as I'd hoped, and then some. "Oh, I wisht I'd seen that, mister. I surely do. You think it was Elvis?"

"He's still in the Army, ain't he?"

"That's right. You sure it was pink?"

"Pink as a baby's behind."

"I am *so* jealous," she warbled, the red "Shelly" bouncing up and down. "Let me ask around; maybe someone else saw it, too." I told her not to forget our breakfast as she jiggled off. She patted her pocket and said not to fear.

"She thinks we're family? *Yuck!*" Frog Boy croaked once she was gone. Burma Coker stared at me with new eyes. I chuckled and spread my arms across the back of the booth. "I'll catch that car with or without your help," I told her. "So make it easy on everyone, and tell me where they're headed."

"Dream on," Burma replied.

This was turning into a war of wit and wills. The two truckers who'd ogled Burma paid and left; another slammed through the door. Shelly brought our meals. I told the boy to pass the pepper and sprinkled my eggs like dirty snow. He motioned for the butter, which I traded for a jelly cube. I spread my arms, elbows-out, the best way to eat a meal. I'd learned the trick in prison—no one can grab free samples that way. The boy assumed the same position, learned no doubt at home. Prison and family—the best schools ever for learning how to survive.

So we ate. Frog Boy finished first and, as could be expected, reached over with his fork to spear some of the woman's unfinished pancakes. She parried with her knife. "You don't want 'em," he shot back. She told him to try that again, and he'd lose a finger next time.

I put down my utensils and gazed outside, my belly full and rosy, my mind quite clear. The first orange of daylight glowed like a smooth brush stroke over the trees. I wondered if Cole and Little Miss Trouble was watching it, too. Maybe if I drove straight without no further stops, I could still catch 'em. He'd be in her pants by now, knowing my boy. Of course, he'd see as love what older heads like me knew was only a roll in the hay. Still, I trusted in such detours to slow 'em down. Shelly checked our progress, and said the trucker who'd just walked in had seen the Caddy also, though to the south of here. It drove like the devil was following, he said. Shelly tore off the check, slapped it on the table, and said it'd been a pleasure serving us all.

That's when I remembered the difference between the free world and prison. Out here, you had to pay. Unfortunately my wallet, and all my money with it, was in the Cadillac with Cole. I felt my pockets, just in case; looked at the woman, who I *knew* was broke since this vacation wasn't planned in advance; then looked at the boy. I told him to pay the bill.

He goggled in the way I loved so much, and as he did, the doorbell jangled and a sheriff's deputy walked in. The waitress poured a cup of coffee for him and said he was out mighty early. There'd been a diner robbed in Wattles, he answered. "You know, the one owned by the guy whose wife ran off. Poor guy was murdered. See anything strange on the road?"

"Why I gotta pay?" Frog Boy said to me.

Burma Coker, who'd followed my eyes and seen the deputy, didn't look so hungry now. "Hush, Arnold," she whispered. "Not so loud."

But Frog Boy was oblivious to the lawman's presence, and though he lowered his voice a notch, he was still off on a tear. "Everything happens to me," he complained. "Tonight I've had my truck stolen, I been hit on the head and knocked out, I been threatened with a gun. You call me stupid and poke me in the ribs, then won't give me a bite of your pancakes, not even a smidgen. It's like I'm the villain, but I'm not the villain. I ain't even sopped up my egg juice yet. Why I gotta pay?"

" 'Cause I'll kill you if you don't," I said.

Burma shushed him again. "Arnold, honey, look behind you," she whispered. "He ain't kiddin' this time, dear."

But now it was too late: our voices had drawn the deputy's eye. I glanced up and saw him looking over; I felt my face start jumping all to hell. Who needs a lie detector when you got a face like mine? The deputy watched, surprised; he hooked his thumbs beneath his gun belt and strolled up. I shot Burma and Frog Boy a warning glance and dropped my hand beneath the table, letting it rest on the butt of the gun. I wasn't going back to prison, no matter what. Before going back there, I'd shoot up my second diner for the night and everyone in it.

But the deputy was just curious, not suspicious, and his holster flap was still buttoned when he said hello. "Out kind of early, ain't'cha?" he said, eyes searching my face. "Do I know you?"

Only from old wanted posters, I replied silently. "Never had the pleasure," I actually said. "We're from up north, in Virginia. We're out early for a long trip, is all."

"Shelly said you saw a pink Cadillac while you were drivin'." He studied Burma, who smiled sweetly, and Frog Boy, who kept his head down while sopping up yolk with a toast wedge. He turned back to me. "You see it in Wattles?"

"A little north of there," I said.

"See anybody in it?"

"Just shadows—it was too dark to see." That seemed a bit short, so I added, "I heard you mention a holdup. You think they're connected?"

He sighed and looked away. "Probably not. What stickup man would be fool enough to rob a place then drive off in something that said 'Here I am?' "

Now it was Burma's turn. "You think it was Elvis, like the waitress mentioned?"

"Shelly's got Elvis on the brain. Besides, ain't he still in the Army? No, ma'am, it's probably just someone who wants to be like him. Everyone wants to be Elvis nowadays." He scratched the top of his head and looked contrite. "I'm sorry I even bothered you. You have a good trip, hear?"

I sighed from relief as he walked off, then took my hand from the pistol and put it on the table. It shook like a thing with palsy. "That was close," Burma said.

Frog Boy looked up from his plate. "Okay, I'll pay like you want," he whispered, "but if I do, I want better treatment, okay? This was my gas and date money for the week. No more elbows or smart remarks. No more death threats or knocks on the head." He thought a moment and added: "And when we get back, no more phonin' my mama when I ask Dahlia for a date."

She promised and looked at me. "Fair enough, right?"

I shrugged, feeling my headache return. I pinched the skin between my eyes. What had I done to deserve this, I wondered. I worked hard, just like everyone. I paid my debts to society. Didn't I deserve a break, too?

"I want to hear the magic words," Frog Boy demanded, crossing his arms before him.

"Please," said the woman.

She kicked me under the table when I stayed silent. "And thank you," I groaned.

Love at Sixteen

I WOKE IN a green clearing with morning fog rising from the ground. I'd lost my bearings, then remembered, so blinked and lay still. My clothes were bunched around me, the red dirt cold against my back. Sprigs of grass needled my skin. Cole breathed warm into my ear. He gave off heat like an oven, and I nuzzled closer. There ain't nothin' better'n being warm.

Well, I'd gone and done it, just like Mama feared. But the heavens hadn't tumbled down nor the thunder roared. Nothing happened, 'cept what happened, and that was plenty for me. If anything, I felt strange. I remembered the bedtime story Daddy used to read me about the little English girl who kept gettin' into trouble and jumped down a rabbit hole. "Curiouser and curiouser," she wondered, "I'm opening like the largest telescope ever was!" I felt that way, all stretchy, like my feet pushed through the rhododendrons till they popped out on U.S. 3. All kinda funny till a sleepy trucker crashed into my legs.

So this was love—warmth, weird thoughts, and exhaustion,

while your lover snored. It *was* love, wasn't it, the act that flung me into the grown-up world? In *National Geographic* they ran stories on boys in other countries who entered manhood by getting poked with hot sticks or wrestlin' a pig. In Tennessee, the only ritual for a girl was a roll in the hay.

What a strange thing to be sixteen and fall in love. It wasn't like the movies, where soft lights and music told you all was right with the world. More than anything, I felt confused. It was like everything was possible but could fall apart in a wink, like I'd been preparing all my life for this just to get caught unawares. The little niggling voice in my head that I now recognized as Mama's said, *Men never stay, baby,* but it was hard to believe the voice when I rolled over and a smell like wood smoke rose off Cole's hair. I wanted to sink in that smell like in a warm ocean, sinking so deep I'd never have to mind the voice again. Even through my sleepiness I could hear the roar and rush of a semi and knew we was still too close to the highway. The fog wouldn't last forever. "Wake up," I said, nudging Cole in the ribs.

He snorted once and sat up. "Where are we?" he grumbled, then looked about. "Oh, yeah."

"You always snore like that . . . after?"

"Don't know, I'm still kind of new at it. You always yowl?" That was rude and didn't paint me like no delicate flower, so I bundled up my clothes and stamped into the woods. "Where you headed?" he yelled after me. Where it wasn't so public, I said.

In a minute, the trees closed 'round me like a wall. Strangler vine clambered up; white pine and spruce towered overhead like the watchers of Cherokee legend who judge our acts but do not interfere. It was too spooky for me, and when I heard Cole's steps in the leaves, I yelled where I was. He crunched up and his fingers touched my waist; we looked 'round in wonder, the fog swirling between the trunks and light like green smoke, as if the car had never existed and the diner was only a dream.

We were the only people in the world, and that made us a

little scared. We turned together to look at each other—Cole's eyes were dark and terrible; my face felt lit by fire. "Don't stare at me like that," I snapped, embarrassed, and looked away. But even as I said it, the funniest sensations began prickin' at my skin. I lay back on a red gold pile of leaves, pink gaywings pushing from the sod, and Cole lay beside me. I rolled onto my belly and he hesitated, then traced a finger from my shoulder to the base of my spine. "Goose bumps," he said. I wanted him to touch me again like that and arched my shoulders and neck like a swan. He did so, lightly, with the tips of his fingers, then pressed harder till I felt a pulse. His hand ran farther down my back and suddenly between my legs. I yelped in surprise, then started growling deep inside my chest in a way I'd never heard before and without thinking lifted my hips and guided him in. *Is this me?* When I looked over my shoulder, his face had grown soft and questions swam in his eyes like little fishies. I wanted him like I'd never wanted nothing else and started slowly, neither leading nor following, a wheel within a wheel, time outside of time. I closed my eyes and lost track, not in my right mind. It felt somehow like we'd changed places, both of us split like ripe peaches, but suddenly that image was replaced by that of Mama's wide-eyed face floating through the hemlocks. She saw us and screamed, *Animals!*

I turned over and saw Cole instead of her: we were chest to chest, face to face, but all of a sudden we weren't gentle no more. Cole's breathing grew ragged and I gasped and pushed back as frantic as him. *Are you man enough?*, the growly voice demanded. *Who are all these voices in me?* I dug my claws into his hips and he snarled and grabbed my hair. We scooched against a tree, making sounds that didn't seem normal. My legs squeezed him in their vise; I pummeled the small of his back with my heels. "Oww, quit it," he barked, but someone other than the Dahlia Jean I knew had taken control and she wasn't listening. I wanted to drive myself right through him . . . there was white light . . . my body jerked over and over. I fell to the side in the dirt as if struck dead.

Joe Jackson

Jesus, I thought, my mind awhirl. So that's what it's all about, an overwhelming flood that drowns the present, washing away all cares. I finally understood why Mama gave herself to it after her betrayal; I understood why the preachers raged. You were possessed and glad of it—it felt so good, you couldn't help but open up to the possession again.

"What now?" Cole said. He reached out feebly and tried to scrape his clothes together, but finally gave up and dropped his hands by his side. "We can go anywhere, Dahlia. Do anything. We got more money than either of us ever dreamed possible. We got no obligations. It's what everybody prays for. It's the American Dream."

"Do we have to decide this very moment? Cain't we just lay still awhile?"

Which we did. Soon, my thoughts were driftin' through the strangest places, pictures appearin' I hadn't seen in the longest time. I recalled the day Daddy left, how I stood in the screen door and watched the rain. I was eleven then. Behind me Mama raised a bitter racket, clutching his note in her fist, pressing it flat on the table then ballin' it up again. She laughed and cried, one after the other; I'd never seen nothing like it and was flat scared. Half the china knickknacks Daddy'd bought her during their courtship lay thrown against the wall. My heart fluttered when a black sedan pulled in the driveway. Maybe it's Daddy, I thought, and he's changed his mind. But then it backed out, a lost stranger merely turning, seeing how ours was the last driveway in town.

He isn't coming back, I knew then. My thoughts circled like a gamecock in a pit; Mama and I would circle each other forever, seeking weakness, smelling blood. Bad families are like that, never letting go. Maybe good ones, too, but I wouldn't know. All I knew was Daddy had escaped: I hated him for it; I hated Mama for not doing enough to keep him with us; I hated myself for crying, wishing the tears were just rain through the screen.

The rain.

It's blue in the mountains and goes on forever, building to a flood. I wondered if it was part my fault, wondered what I'd done. He'd looked so sad once the mines laid off and each new job fell through. He felt he was a failure and as things grew tighter and tighter, Mama got scared and no longer disagreed. He'd heard of jobs up north, but no one came back from there. Maybe if I'd told him more often I loved him. Maybe we weren't rich, but other things counted, too. Two years later, when the mine owner had seen him down south, I wrote a letter telling him these things. Any day there'd be a letter back, I told myself, with a photo of Daddy beside his boat, smiling that dark smile. Pack and come south, he'd write: I'm a success. Come down to better things.

But that letter never came.

I lay in the woods with Cole and remembered that last day with Daddy, when he told me all hope had fled. It was the lowest I'd seen him since two months earlier, when he'd nearly gotten killed. Jobs had grown so tight that him and some buddies had resorted to robbing abandoned truck mines. Such mines were little more than holes dug straight in the mountain, the slate roof held up by pillars of coal. A robber started at the pillar deepest in the mountain and worked his way out, taking pillars as he went and replacing each with railroad ties. It was nothing but a gamble, 'cause one never knew when the roof would fall.

That day, three went into the mine and two came out. Daddy and a friend were at the drift mouth when the roof dropped in eerie silence and dust and mud rolled out like a wave. They yelled inside for Benny Huff, their partner, but no answer came. When they clawed inside, his arms and legs stuck from the rubble, twitching like a bug's.

Daddy'd seen death before—most miners have. But Benny Huff's last gasp seemed pathetic, and Daddy couldn't shake the image of those twitching limbs. He went to see Huff's folks, who lived on the reservation at Cherokee. Great piles of hubcaps were heaped around their house; Benny's father cleaned and sold them to tourists. They listened quietly as Daddy told what happened, but it was not the first time they'd lost a child to the mines. He'd seen such resignation before; anybody has who lives in these hills, rising from the wet ground like the fog. Benny himself had spoke about it two weeks before his death: how it seemed to hang over the reservation worse than anywhere else, how he'd rather die than go back there. Maybe the entire land was one vast reservation stretching hundreds of miles from West Virginia to the tip of Georgia, where everyone—whites, blacks, Indians—lived in a murk of resignation, a land of seen and unseen cripples. The only way out was by running. Or Benny's way.

So Daddy ran. For about two weeks after his departure, Mama said he'd be back. She'd give him a piece of her mind, she said, and spent the time rehearsin' her words. The next two weeks, she took to their bed, now hers alone. She didn't eat, barely drank, kept the lights turned low. I stood by the front door and watched the road. Sometimes I walked down the road to where the town ended and the blacktop climbed into the mountains from our little valley, but something held me back from taking one step past the ENTERING WATTLES, DRIVE CAREFULLY sign. In a different way from Benny Huff, I, too, felt buried alive.

Another two weeks and Mama emerged from her room. "I ain't dyin' for that man," she whispered, voice raw from crying. "From here on out, I ain't livin' for no one but me." Her reputation, the diner, the orange Mack truck—all followed from that moment and those words.

I lay beside Cole and watched as the light curled high in the fog. I liked it here: the tan-tipped pinecones buried in the dirt, the trailing arbutus with leathery green leaves and white flowers shaped like stars. It was a paradise where I was safe. But soon the sun would burn the fog off and I'd see it more clearly. When that happened, we'd have to put on our clothes and leave.

Suddenly, what I wanted hit me. I'd known since the diner and had even headed in that direction. It just hadn't separated from the fog enough for me to see.

"I want to find my father," I said.

Cole didn't answer right off, staring instead at our paradise like he, too, never wished to leave. "Fathers ain't so great. I got one and look at him."

"True, but this money will bring my parents back together."

"You sure of that?"

"Lack of money was what drove 'em apart." I looked him in the face. "I'm gonna heal my family."

Cole searched my face and smiled, a little sad. "I'm not sure that family's ain't overrated," he answered, then brushed back a strand of my hair. "But all families may not be like mine, so what do I know?" He looked at me and shrugged, then rose to his feet and reached for his clothes. "We might as well give it a shot. We sure as hell can't stay here."

No sooner had he said it than strange laughter filled the woods. It was a high and feminine laugh, bodiless and eerie, as if filling the space between the trees. I sat up and covered myself, the hair rising on my scalp and arms. Next came the swift crunch of leaves underfoot, but getting distant and heading toward the clearing, and we knew we'd been spied upon. "He's getting away!" Cole cried. He skipped and hopped into his pants, then tore off after the sound.

I was just prying on my saddle oxfords when I heard the Caddy engine roar.

I forgot about the bowknots and ran through the woods. As the trees thinned out, I saw Cole atop a rise. "Oh, shit!" he wheezed, out of breath. I sank beside him and looked out where he stared.

The fog had folded back and I could see into the clearing. "You gave me the keys and I tossed 'em on the seat so we wouldn't lose 'em," Cole lamented. "Oh God, I'm sorry!" I glanced around, unbelieving, as a mockingbird scolded from the high treetops. I saw the clumps of mud where our tires had churned the grass, the flat spot where we first clinched and fell.

Only one thing was missing. I didn't see our car.

Why Banks Ain't What They Used to Be

NO DOUBT ABOUT it, I needed someplace to rob. Man is born for robbery, the urge to pillage as ancient as the nerve and blood. When modern life grows cluttered, a feller needs a pick-me-up and thrill. Though greed is good for this country, it's chastised on a smaller scale. I mean, let a man loot corporate coffers or entire nations and folks hail him as a wheeler-dealer, a captain of industry, and a leader of men. But these same people get all upset when a hardworking stickup man enters a store or bank in the hope of moving up, and is that the least bit fair? Let me remind such do-gooders of the advantages of robbery. A good heist entertains everyone, from the armchair Jesse James to the loneliest shut-in. It rebukes the miserly and returns money to circulation. It renews the hope that we still live in the Wild West, the hallowed time of our great land. It gives the bored enforcers of the law a reason to live.

Yeah, buddy, I'd been in the stickup business nearly a quarter-century, so I'm not talkin' through my hat. Holdups provide a public service and are good for society. People think of us as cowboys who barge in shootin', but to me such an entrance is the sure sign of an amateur. A gun is just a prop, violence just one tool in a well-stocked bag of tricks. The best holdup men are actors, able to rob a bank by force of personality.

Right now, this actor needed capital. As I pulled off the road to consider our future, I reviewed these pressing needs.

I had no cash. The gas tank was near EMPTY. I had two extra mouths to feed. It was like being a family man again, a worrisome thought since family was something at which I'd never excelled.

As the breeze sighed, I slumped behind the wheel, stared at the weaving crowns of some mountain laurels, and sympathized. Once a head of household, always a head of household. I surveyed my tender charges, temporary as they might be. While Frog Boy studied a fold-up map with a green dinosaur on the cover and pictures of beaches on back, as if all of life was a big vacation, Burma grabbed her cane and strolled through the long grass outside. His name wasn't really Frog Boy, but Arnold Peavy Simpson, Burma'd told me, adding that I shouldn't refer to him as an amphibian or I'd damage his self-esteem. She was funny, like maybe she was enjoying this, and I watched as she bent one knee, then the other. The joints still popped, but the ole sticks were growing more limber, she proclaimed happily. She plucked a puffball from the grass. As she blew and the white seeds scattered, she spread her arms and smiled.

I considered that image for a while. Ever since breakfast, she'd seemed easier, somehow. Almost transformed. Back at the truck stop, she patted my hand to calm me as Frog Bo . . . uh, Arnold Simpson paid the bill. "Don't worry, he'll do it," she soothed, and sure enough he did. As we piled in the Ford to continue on our children's trail, she watched the sun rise in the east with real pleasure. "Look't that," she said. "I haven't seen a sunrise in way too long."

She was pretty, when you thought about it: Get her in the sun and add a few pounds to her, and she'd look right healthy again. She had nice teeth, no obvious fillings; she'd brushed out the kinks and her hair shone a fiery gold. A squirrel fussed overhead and I thought of squirrel and dumplin's. It'd been ages since anyone'd cooked that for me.

After a while, she tossed the cane aside, then kicked it for good measure. She walked up, put her hand on the side mirror and smiled into the car. "Okay, professor, so what you figured out?" I said we needed to rob someplace. She didn't blink at all.

Arnold's head, on the other hand, popped up from the map and his Adam's apple rose to his collar. "Do what?" he said.

"The closest town is here," I continued, tapping the map at a dot called Muscovy. "I been through there plenty of times. Used to be the biggest deep-shaft mine in the state till it closed like all the rest and strip miners moved in. Right in the middle of town sits the cutest little bank you ever saw."

"But that's illegal," Frog Boy whined.

"Arnold, honey," Burma chided, "it's what he *does.*"

To tell the truth, I'd been prepared for many things—but not agreement. It stumped me a little while. I'd been ready to explain how the gas gauge floated on empty and how we had no money, how general stores were risky to hit since you never knew what was in the register or if the owner kept a twelve-gauge Mossberg handy. I was ready to show how banks had ready cash and didn't fight back, since they were insured. All this, and more, I was prepared to explain, but now I felt deflated, for all the woman said was, "Makes sense to me."

What was up her sleeve? "I'm beginning to think you like this, Miz Coker," Arnold spluttered, to which Burma replied she was just being a realist. We couldn't sit in these woods forever, she said.

"But Miz Coker, he killed Mr. Whitley! Have you forgotten that? Have you forgot how he's after Dahlia? He's not gonna give her *flowers* when he sees her again."

"I know that, Arnold," she crackled, irritated at being lectured to. "I know he's not an upstanding citizen. But did it occur to you that by not crying out for help back there at the truck stop, we're guilty, too? We had our chance to turn in a murderer and we didn't. That makes us accessories to murder, and that means at least two years in jail."

I looked at Arnold and he looked at me, both of us stunned. Why didn't I think of that? She was right, by God, and it hadn't even dawned on me. Arnold bit his lip and turned pasty again. "Is that true?" he peeped. "Two years?"

" 'Fraid so, honey," Burma said.

Arnold excused himself and stumbled to the laurels where, from the sounds of things, he commenced to lose his breakfast. "Sensitive boy," Burma observed.

I studied her carefully, like one might do a lioness who suddenly strolled up to play. Fact is, the boy was right: Robbing banks was not a Sunday picnic. A million things could go wrong, and often did. I remembered the time I robbed a small bank in Oak Ridge. Everything was going fine till a yellow school bus pulled up with the high-school finance club. I shut 'em in the vault, saying this was how deposits was made. Then there was the Knoxville branch that seemed safe enough till my partner's second cousin stood in line behind us; the resurrection of this long-lost relative rattled him so bad he took it as a message and ran out the door. I never saw him again.

Banks just brought trouble, all that loose change making folks do truly foolish things. I'd heard stories of my famous ancestor, the one who rode with Jesse James. As long as the Jameses and the Youngers stuck to trains, they made a right smart partnership and lived high on the hog; but the day they robbed a bank in Northfield, Minnesota, was the day him and his boys got plugged. And that was the good old days. Now cameras, silent alarms, round-the-clock security, and other obstacles sprang up in banks like weeds. Some experimented with exploding bags of purple dye. Try passing money when you looked like a grape; it couldn't be done. Whatever happened to good sportsmanship? The whole damn country was going to hell.

I looked at Burma Coker with new respect, but also new wariness. "What's your game?" I said. "The boy's right. I'm *not* a model citizen. I *do* have a grudge against your daughter. What's up your sleeve?"

She didn't answer right off, so I studied her while she studied me. All that holier-than-thou shit when I burst into her room and later—and now she talked like Bonnie Parker egging on her boyfriend, Clyde Barrow. It didn't make sense, and things that don't make sense rarely put me in a trusting mood. She shaded her eyes, got a strange look on her face, and watched as Arnold emerged from the trees. He wiped his mouth. "Boy's got no gumption," she said.

"That doesn't answer my ques—"

"I'm tired of people with no gumption," she continued. "I didn't have no gumption after my husband left. I'm tired of that in me. I shoulda done what Dahlia's doin', goin' to confront the bastard and ask him why. Instead I hid behind sex, then played the cripple, ruinin' her life as well as mine." She smiled, a little wildly, those white teeth like fire. "I know you don't have the best intentions for my daughter, but right now you're the fastest and most dependable route to her. Hostage or accessory don't matter to me one bit—I just want to catch her before she does something stupid. If it means robbing a bank, it's all the same to me."

I looked at her, unsettled. Something told me *she* wasn't the one in danger here.

By now it was midmorning, and all signs indicated it would be a beautiful day. The sun glowed a friendly egg-yolk yellow; the sky pulsed a robin's egg blue. It was the kind of day when it was a pleasure to break the law. My plan was simple. Burma'd go in the bank first and ask to write out a draft on an out-of-town bank; while she waited, she'd check for cameras and guards. My face was known in such places: if there were cameras, I'd be back in prison in no time flat. If there weren't none, I'd take over.

We rounded a curve and a sign welcomed us to historic Muscovy; the road ran through the town center, a place so small that a shot fired full choke from a .30-.06 would strike every store. Uphill, a line of pine-shingled company houses were nudged against a slate bluff; many seemed deserted, their windows like dead eyes. Everything—the road, stores, and houses—was pitched at an angle, canted downhill. A sheriff's office marked the town limits nearest to us; the blinds were shut and the law seemed closed for the day. Across the street, a barber's pole spun endless spirals. The white-frocked owner sat in the window biting into an apple, the bite repeated forever in the facing mirrors behind and before his chair.

A dark-skinned toddler with full lips like Elvis waddled from a drugstore and sat backward on his diaper as we rolled into town. An old man with one empty sleeve sat on a bench before the one-room Greyhound station at the far end of town. He turned his head as we parked beside the curb. His eyes had the dull sheen of the blind.

Burma and me slid from the cab, and Arnold slid behind the wheel. "Don't drive off, Arnold," she warned him, "or I'll tell the world and your mama how you left me in the clutches of this madman."

"I see why Dahlia's the way she is," Frog Boy said mournfully, and I felt a little sorry for him. He stared at the blind man and shuddered. "Don't stay long. I don't like this town."

The saving grace of small-town banks is how slow they are to modernize. Muscovy's seemed no different when I peeked inside. There were two tellers' booths, only one occupied at the moment, a vault in the back and a loan officer's desk near the door. Two men stood in line, their backs to us. A cowbell jangled when Burma walked in.

This was the hard part for me. Waiting made me edgy and I felt like a watch spring wound too tight; I peeked inside and the line hadn't moved. Burma shifted from foot to foot. Arnold shifted in the driver's seat, fingers tapping the wheel.

I felt exposed outside the door like this, so decided to scout around. I ducked down a service alley lined by a row of garbage cans. A ginger tomcat winked from one. *How many ladies you serenade last night?*, I wondered. A train whistled down the mountain, far away.

I peeked inside again and the line *still* hadn't moved. I studied Burma's legs, so nice and long, outlined under the cotton skirt, but this was too distracting and I decided to look for a back way in. I walked to where the alley opened on a narrow lane, this bordered by a chest-high wall. Past this, an open field of heal-all and Johnson's grass sloped down to some body shops; brown locusts screeched in the weeds. Across a dirt road from the shops was what looked like a county vehicle compound surrounded by hurricane fencing. Inside I could see a backhoe, two rusted cars, and a third gutted by fire. Way over by the gate I thought I saw a spot of shining color. I moved along the wall till I reached a better angle, and the bright spot turned into pink Cadillac fins.

It took a moment for that to sink in. Pink. Cadillac. Fins. *Good God Almighty,* it hit me. Here we were about to rob the town's only bank, the one thing certain to make us unpopular, and those damn kids were already here!!

I took a step to the left, stopped, took a step to the right, took a deep breath, and got my bearings. I ran for the bank, then forced myself to slow; we couldn't afford attention. True, I'd seen the car, but where was Cole and the girl? Maybe the sheriff had stopped 'em in the night, and he'd run the Caddy as stolen. Maybe he'd throwed 'em both in jail. No tellin' where the money was. We had to ditch the bank heist quick and come up with a better plan.

But when I stepped from the alley, the two men who'd been in line in front of Burma hurried out and peeked back inside.

"What was that all about?" the first one asked.

"Beats me," the other said, "but they sure don't like each other."

They crossed the road and the first scooped up the Elvis baby, saying, "So that's where you got off to." I opened the door and the cowbell jangled. I paused a second and looked around.

The only people inside were me, Burma, and the two bank workers. The manager was bald and pink; he scowled from his desk as if sizing me up as one more hillbilly with his hand out, so I palmed back my hair and nodded real subservient to further that impression. The teller was a prim, silver-haired matron, the kind of woman always put in charge of other people's dough. She wore a dark blue dress pinned at the throat with a cameo brooch, her lips bloodless as she stared from her teller's cage. On the other side of the cage and in her line of sight stood Burma, her hands on hips. Her voice quivered. "*What* did you say?"

"I said we don't give wire drafts to *anyone* walking off the street," the teller replied.

Best nip this in the bud. "It's okay, honey," I said, tapping Burma on the back. "I found the money. We can go."

"She said I'm not *good* enough for their business."

"I said no such thing," the teller insisted, setting her chin. "All I said was you needed some ID. After what happened a half hour ago with that pink Cadillac, you can't be too careful, can you, Mr. Buscomb?" The bank manager scowled, looking properly stern.

My radar went up. Cadillac, huh? I had to learn more. But Burma had been insulted somehow, and little sparks of ozone crackled from her hair. "My money's as good as anyone's," she snapped.

"Then withdraw it from your own bank," the teller replied.

I pulled at Burma's arm, but she'd planted her feet. "What do you mean by that?" she asked. My heart pounded out a warning tune.

I could see what came next from a mile away. It was one of those moments when you want to stop disaster, but you can't move. Don't say it, I thought, for God's sake, don't say it. It'll be the end of the world. But nobody—'specially women—ever listens to me. "Do I really have to spell it out?" sneered the teller. "We've seen your kind before." Burma didn't hesitate. She wheeled and told me to shoot the old bag.

I stared back, dumbfounded. *"Shoot her!"* she demanded. By the way her eyes glowed in their sockets, we were long past the stage of reason.

But I still tried. "I'm sure we can work this out," I began, but quicker'n a snake she seized the pistol from under my coat and raised it overhead.

Joe Jackson

"Robbery!" the bank manager screamed, his smooth pate turning cherry red. Burma said to shut up before she shot him as dead as she meant to shoot the old witch, a pretty straight-forward statement of intent, if you ask me. But that old teller had gumption—I'll give her that—and she didn't even blink as she edged close to the front of her booth where I knew the silent alarm was hid.

"Lady," I whispered, "move away from that counter or you'll most likely get shot." I nodded at Burma, who pointed my gun from manager to teller, teller to manager, like she was a spectator at a Ping-Pong game. "I don't have to add she's not real happy with you." The teller scowled like I'd been talking in church, but got the message and moved away reluctantly.

Everything got quiet real fast, so I locked the door and tried to stay calm. The realization of what she'd started finally hit her: When I turned back, the blood had drained from Burma's face and she stared bug-eyed at the gun trembling in her hands. I pried it gently from her fingers. "You got a shorter fuse than I thought," I said.

The teller's attitude reminded her of how too many people treated her in Wattles, she muttered. "I guess I went a little nuts," she moaned.

I needed a new line of work or I'd go nuts, too. I realized my success rate for robberies over the past two days was headed for a world-class low. I told her I'd seen the Cadillac. We couldn't afford a lot of commotion since the kids were some-where in town.

"I really screwed up," she said, but apologies would have to wait. Right now we had to get out of there. I told the boss to fill a bank bag from the tellers' drawers, and no dye packs or other tricks or I might get angry. He was most helpful. Unfor-tunately, country banks don't keep much cash out front, and he scooped only $250 in the bag. The vault looked tempting, but had all the signs of a time lock. I asked how much longer till it opened. "Another thirty-seven minutes," he said.

What a day, what a day. I saw a door in back and asked where it led. It was a supply closet, said the boss, and I motioned with the gun. The Ice Teller was slower than necessary, so I poked her in the ribs with the gun. Burma grabbed the money and headed to the front while I told the teller and her boss to squeeze beneath the lowest shelf. They reminded me of kissing cousins.

"Better come up front," said Burma.

"Don't rush me," I said. People should enjoy their work, even when it's forced on them. I pinched the Ice Queen's cheek and gave her a kiss, then locked the closet. Burma's voice got more insistent. "Better hurry!" she screamed.

That got my attention. I rushed up front and looked where she pointed out the window. In the street, a county sheriff was struggling with his holster. Beside him stood a wild-eyed woman who stared into my face.

And beside them both stood the dark-haired cause of my misery, hanging tight to the arm of my son.

What the Serpent Says

COLE AND ME stared unbelieving at the clearing that was no longer filled with our money or car. The mockingbird kept scoldin' overhead, a sound too much like mornings at home. I chucked a rock. The bird fussed as it flapped away.

"Now what?" I said.

Cole fell backward in the dirt; he covered his eyes and groaned. I was tempted to do the same. Givin' up had its own appeal. Life in the woods would be simpler, the only worries diggin' for roots and grubs. But I was pestered by questions. Who made that spooky laughter? How could a stolen car get restolen in the middle of nowhere?

So I looked for clues. 'Round the car, or at least its last resting place, I found shoe prints different from mine and

Cole's. They was pointy and narrow like a petite lady's, and appeared from a gap on the other side of the clearing where the dirt road continued down the mountain. From the car, they then led up a woody knoll that overlooked the spot where Cole and I had lain. We'd been spied upon, all right. Even teenage romance wasn't sacred anymore. Our Peeping Tom had got an eyeful, then jumped in the car and drove away.

It made me plenty mad. For Cole's part, he counted a coupla hundred he'd stuffed in his pockets, but the rest of the money was in the Caddy. He recalled seeing a bus station in the town before this cutoff, and figured we could still afford tickets to Key West. "But what about the car and money?" I preached. "We gotta go and find it." Cole said he doubted the Cadillac, money, or thief were anywhere close, and suggested we take the hint before his old man arrived looking for us and his car.

It liked to drove me crazy, the unfairness of it all. That money had been the answer to my woes. I'd hoped to arrive at Daddy's doorstep, pockets lined with silver. What would happen now when two ragamuffins knocked on his door? It wasn't just the thief who laughed at me, but God. I was mad enough to spit and imagined shaking my fist at heaven and screaming, "Strike me dead, you Old Cranky Bastard!" But that was pressing my luck, so I kept such opinions to myself.

We trooped back to the highway, dirt poor again. We'd driven further in the woods than I'd thought, and the sweat tickled my back as the morning grew warm. Such early humidity promised rain. We picked up the pace and came on a trail of sawdust and fluff disappearin' among the trees like bread crumbs. It looked damned suspicious, so we followed the trail through the woods to a narrow, sunlit glen. The moose head sat atop a lichen-spotted pile of rocks: gnats swarmed 'round its face; one glass eye dangled from its socket, while the other stared at me. The back of its skull was peeled open and emptied; fluff was stamped and flattened 'round the rock like someone danced a jig. When I pushed the moose with my finger, it flopped sideways, that one eye now pointed at the sky. Not a dollar remained.

"If this ain't shit!" Cole growled, but I was thinking of other things. This clearing had been ripped open by tree fall: The ground was spotted with bird's-foot violets and blue phlox; a breeze lifted the branches, smelling faintly of rain. A turkey buzzard rode the breeze; birds were in the sky and squirrels in the trees. In fact, we seemed the only things glued to the ground. I remembered a Cherokee legend Daddy'd told me: how all life dwelt in the sky till the crowding grew so great that God sent a water beetle to find dry land. When there wasn't any, the beetle dove to the bottom and brought up mud. God sent the Great Buzzard to dry out the mud, but the bird grew exhausted and his wingtips brushed the mountains, forming ridges and coves.

The whole place was filled with stories like that, Daddy said. Old storytellers called this area the *Amoyee,* a rain-drenched, ghost-filled land. The worst ghost was the Cannibal Woman, who preyed on tribal enemies till none were left, then she ate her friends. What if it was *her* laughter we heard? But that was silly . . . no Cannibal Woman really existed, did she? Our footsteps echoed behind us as we crunched our way back to the dirt road through the leaves. I asked Cole if he'd heard the legend also, but he didn't feel like talking . . . like some friendly conversation to fill the silence would kill anyone right now? So I talked for both of us, how mothers threatened rambunctious kiddies with tales of the Cannibal Woman, how she came out at night searching for bad boys and girls. Her laughter creaked like rusty hinges; her shadow passed like a bat's beneath the moon. Another stick cracked behind me and I started running, passing Cole in a flash, antsy to leave this forest with its spooks and eerie laughter and half-eaten moose heads.

He stared like I was crazy when he caught up, so I tossed my hair in his face and led the way. In another fifteen minutes we were on the blacktop again. I saw nailed high on a tree a sign I hadn't seen earlier: GET RIGHT WITH GOD, and under that, KEEP OUT. A group called the Church of True Signs took credit. I asked Cole if he'd ever heard of such people, and he said there were more nuts in these coves than all the acorns on the trees. He led the way back to Muscovy, no curiosity at all, his eyes glued to the road 'less his old man appeared and we had to duck back in the trees and run. We rounded a curve on an abandoned church with busted-out windows and a high cupola missing its bell. The church was surrounded on three sides by a green graveyard, its soil rich with calcium from all the dead souls within. Maybe we should rest, I said, tuckered out, but Cole answered, "We cain't rest, not with my old man comin' closer. I can feel him." He didn't look back. "We can rest when we're dead."

Jesus Christ, I thought, even Arnold Simpson could carry on a conversation, though it was rarely worth listenin' to. Maybe it was me, so I checked for B.O. Maybe I was a little gamy, but not *that* bad. I said good-bye to the peaceful church, wondering if perhaps we wouldn't find something inside worth keeping, but plodded after Cole, not wanting to be left alone.

In another minute we rounded a second bend. A sign pocked by weekend hunters welcomed us to Muscovy, and the trees thinned at a crossroads. Clouds had started to gather, a spot of rain in the pastel sky. The road across the highway angled down the mountain and outta sight; I heard a faint pounding from that direction, like giants buttin' heads. Across the street lay Muscovy's town center: There was a small grocery with the Greyhound sign, and past that a bank and a barber's pole. A Peach Nehi and MoonPie sure would taste good while waitin' for the bus. I took a step forward, but Cole stopped me. "Don't you see it?" he said.

"See what?" I sniffed, still irritated by the way he'd treated me. "I see a banana MoonPie and cold drink callin' me over, that's what I see."

"Look there." He pointed about a hundred or more yards

down the incline where a thin man with chestnut hair and a sheriff's uniform snapped a padlock on what seemed to be a vehicle compound. Beside him, a petite woman in polka dots and what looked like handcuffs kicked him in the shin. "I see a lady who's not real happy with the Law," I answered.

"Not her," he corrected. "Look a few feet over from her, just inside the fence."

Then I saw our car. The pink stood out like neon. "Cole, that's, that's—" I gasped, but he pulled me in the woods as the sheriff placed his hand on the woman's back and nudged her up the road. "Take these handcuffs off me, Bobby Plenty!" she screamed as they walked closer. "That car ain't stolen. It's a gift."

"Oh, yeah? From who?" asked the sheriff.

"It's a gift from God!" But the sheriff was unconvinced and led her down a back alley and through a rear entrance marked COUNTY JAIL.

We waited till it was evident no one would come back out, then hurried down the road to the Cadillac. Signs on the gate identified everything inside as county property. NO TRES-PASSING, it warned, and BEWARE OF DOG. There was no loosening the padlock. I began to climb the fence, but Cole grabbed a fistful of my dress and pointed to a black dog rising from the shadow of a rusted car. It hit the gate with both feet, snarlin' and snappin' like it hadn't ate in years.

The racket brought a potbellied man in blue coveralls from a nearby body shop; "Dwight" was sewn over his shirt pocket, and a socket wrench dangled from one hand. "Don't mind Edgar," he said, "you're safe long as that fence is between you and him." He told the dog to clam up, then studied us and asked, "How can I help you kids?"

Cole said, "That Cadillac for sale?"

Dwight snorted in surprise. "Don't I wish," he said. He turned his head and a stream of tobacco juice sailed six feet over the fence and near Edgar's feet. Spitting like that is a fine art, requirin' years of practice, and is used to mark territory, like a male dog doin' his business. "It's a beauty, ain't it? Sheriff Plenty just brought it in. Turned out stole from an Asheville dealership coupla nights before."

"How'd it turn up here?" Cole said.

"Turns out Sallie Goodnight was emptyin' out her and her husband's bank account when the sheriff ran the plates," Dwight explained.

Sallie Goodnight, I thought. So that's who stole our car. That, and laughed so spooky in the woods. "Who's this Sallie Goodnight?" I said.

"A jailbird now," Dwight grinned. "Lives way back in the woods with her Holy Roller husband, Earl." He looked up from under his grease-slicked eyebrows and added, "Why you wanta know?"

"She nearly run us down," I fibbed.

Mama always said a lie was the first step to perdition, but, to me, a small and well-timed lie could be a beautiful thing. A good lie at the right moment is one of the few defenses a girl like me has. It forms in an instant, like art, and shapes the world into something bright and clean. Unlike real life, a lie can be controlled, and knowing that, I began to lie like sin. When Dwight said he couldn't recall seein' us in these parts, I smiled shy and pretty, and scuffed my saddle oxford in the dirt. "You ain't," I said. "We ran away." Inspiration hit me and I added, "We're in love." Dwight asked if we were elopin', so I ran with the ball. "We're the age of consent—he's eighteen, I'm sixteen," I said, actin' defensive.

"Shack up without a legal wedding and you'll rot in hell, they say."

"My thoughts exactly, mister, but who can do the honors here?" Even as I said it, I knew full well that in little towns like this the sheriff often doubled as the Justice of the Peace. Dwight's eyes twinkled and he glanced uphill at the jail. "Bobby Plenty acts as Justice, and he's up there now, bookin' Sallie." He looked us over one last time. "But don't say I told you so." He returned to his body shop whistlin' the wedding song.

There was a gap of silence before Cole cleared his throat. "Are we gettin' married?"

"No, fool," I said. "If we want our money back, we need to talk to that woman. To do that, we need to get inside the jail."

"Then what?"

"I'll figure it out when I get there."

* * *

One problem with lyin' is that the clock is never your friend. It took all of three minutes to reach the back door of the sheriff's office, not much time to form a brilliant plan. All I knew was that inside sat the thief who'd stole our car and money, who'd watched Cole and me when she had no business, and who'd laughed like an evil spirit and was enough to scare two years of growth outta me. I had to get in there; I had a few things to say.

I knocked on the door, and as it cracked open, a roar came from inside. The sheriff peeked out, looking like a disaster victim on the six o'clock news. His face was scratched, his shirt pulled out, he favored his right leg. "Roast in Hell, Bobby Plenty!" a high voice screamed behind him. He winced and snapped, "What you want?" in no mood for strangers.

"You got my Aunt Sallie in there."

Sheriff Plenty shook his head like I'd boxed his ears. Cole got that green look again. But honestly, what could I do? It was the first thing that popped in my head. When the sheriff regained some sense, his eyebrows squirmed like woolly-boogers. "She's your *what*? I just locked her up. How'd you know she was here?"

"Word gets 'round."

He glared like he didn't believe a word I uttered, but then again, he probably couldn't believe anything else that happened this day. But I knew this—talk is a steamroller that flattens all bumps in the road. Talk saved me in the diner, and now, by talkin' fast enough, maybe I could get through that door. "Sheriff," I said, bending my head in sorrow, "Aunt Sallie's kind of—" then twirled my finger at my forehead. "Religion does that to people, you know."

"Tell me about it," he grunted, glancing back in the room. The man looked six feet taller'n than me, and he still blocked the door. "I've lived in Muscovy all my life and I don't think I've seen you once," he added suspiciously.

"We're on Earl's side of the family," I explained. That needed some embroidery, so I started layin' it on thick and heavy, talkin' a million miles an hour. We was visitin' Sallie and Earl when they had a big row and she took off threatenin' to empty their bank account, I told him. I felt a responsibility to patch things up, bein' family and all. "We mean to bail her out," I said.

He blinked again, surprised, but had reached that point where surprise rolled off his back like water off a duck. "Why didn't Earl report it himself?"

That was a hard one. "Uncle Earl's pretty pissed," I said.

"Drunk?" he asked.

No, I explained, just mad.

"Did you know the car was stolen?"

I'd been ready for that, and my eyes registered true-blue confusion. "No way!" I said. "I wondered why they had a pink Cadillac, but Earl said he, uh, got it as a gift from a convert in Asheville." I wrung my hands together—that sounded far-fetched, even to me.

He stared longer'n ever, but finally blew out his breath in frustration and stepped away from the door. "This is the craziest thing I ever seen or heard," he groused, "but so's the whole goddamn day." He led us through a middle door and into a one-room jail. "These youngsters say you're their aunt and they're here to bail you out. That true?"

It got mighty quiet in that room. Sallie Goodnight occupied the inner half of a double cell, closest to the wall; she rose from the bunk and studied me with narrowed eyes. We faced each other through the bars. In some strange way, she was how I'd imagined the Cannibal Woman, only younger and prettier. She even looked a bit like me, just taller, more graceful, with straighter hair, and feet that didn't stick out like washtubs. She was ten years older and once was beautiful, but time had made her stern as well as striking. Her hair flowed in heavy tresses to her waist, the dark auburn streaked with lines of early gray. She stood tall for a mountain woman and the polka-dot dress showed her figure well. Her long fingers curled around the bars, the skin of her hands so white I could see the blue veins. She stood still as deep water, lips parted to expose white teeth, eyes steady with interest and anger. A wildness lurked beneath the surface, and if we got her out, there'd be no lettin' down our guard. But now she figured out her options, and finally told the sheriff, "My niece is a saint. I don't deserve such goodness from her."

Sheriff Plenty studied us both, just like an explorer might a new tribe of Amazons. "Okay," he said, "I'll let you out, but I want to get to the bottom of this. I won't charge you for theft, not yet, but the Cadillac stays in my possession, and you're still charged with assaulting an officer . . . twice. Once to my face, once to my knee."

"I'm sorry I lost my temper, Bobby," she said, contrite as could be. I recognized a sister in the liar's art, not that such recognition made me feel very safe with her.

"Save it for court," the sheriff said. "Bond's $250 and at ten percent, that makes $25 bail." I looked at Cole, who sputtered his unhappiness, but reached into his pocket and paid the man anyway. The sheriff stepped into his front office to fill out paperwork; no sooner had he left than Sallie stepped close to the bars and hissed, "I know what you want, but you ain't gonna get it from me."

I told her to keep her voice down. She smirked and pulled her face even closer. "You two were cute sleepin' nekkid in the woods."

Someone with a mean streak this wide deserved a good throttlin'. "Tell us where you hid our money, pervert," I said.

Joe Jackson

Her smile widened, exposing canines. *She's outta your league,* that voice in my head said to me. *You've done something stupid,* though I wasn't sure what. But this became more evident when she whispered, "Brave words for a fugitive."

No one moved in that small, drafty room: we breathed the stone silence of all jails everywhere. Cole sank on a bench and cursed women and brilliant ideas. Out front, Sheriff Plenty banged drawers and cabinets in search of something called a Form 26-20 and a working ink pen. "You don't know what're you talkin' about," I replied.

"Don't play innocent with me. That's all the radio talked about this morning, the diner holdup to the north, the way a girl fitting your description disappeared with a moose head. It makes no sense, unless you add young lovers and a fortune, then an old man's murder makes perfect sense to me."

"Be there in a minute!" Sheriff Plenty yelled through the door.

I felt truly peckish, and my squeaks that she was mistaken did not fool this old gal. "Maybe so," she gloated, "but how would others see it? How would Sheriff Plenty, especially if I gave him proof?" Her eyes narrowed to slivers. "He'd be a hero, that's what!" Her smile turned dead serious. "Get me out and I won't tell. Otherwise—" but the last was cut off as the sheriff walked through the door, handed her a sheaf of papers, and showed where to sign. She scritched her name impatiently and wanted out. "Not so fast," he told her. "We're goin' to the bank to see what you told 'em, then goin' to see Earl so I can ask him about that car."

Her haughty look vanished, replaced by something resembling fear. Everybody in here seemed to have a secret, not just Cole and me. "That's not necessary, is it, Bobby?" she purred. "Earl and me just had a spat, like my niece said. But you've showed me the error of my ways." The sheriff smiled indulgently. "Married folks *oughta* live in peace, but that still don't explain a hot Cadillac," he explained.

Sheriff Plenty locked all doors behind him and led the way

outside. Across the street, a barber leaned back in his chair, stogie tilted to the ceiling, head haloed in haze. He glanced at the sheriff and waved. As we crossed the street, I looked both ways. North toward Wattles, rain clouds gathered. South toward the clearing, a one-armed ancient rose from a bench and lurched toward a pale green pickup. Inside the truck, someone scootched low. That someone looked familiar, but it took my brain a moment to ask, *What's Arnold Simpson doing here?*

It was not a question I contemplated for long. We were standing opposite a tiny bank, and inside there seemed some commotion. The glare off the front window was blinding, and at first all I could make out were shadows. Then a cloud crossed the sun, and I saw a man way in back talking to a closet. Closer still, a woman holding a bank bag to her chest started pointing at me. I watched as her mouth opened and shut. The man in back came forward. He held a gun.

"It's a holdup," barked the sheriff, fumbling for his holster.

"Oh, no, it's Pop!" Cole shouted, ready to faint.

"That's my mama!" I yelped, grabbing Cole by the arm.

Granted, I was confused. This couldn't be right—Mama had her faults, but robbin' banks wasn't one of them. I rubbed my eyes and looked again. It was her all right, standing on her own two legs, which took a moment to hit me, too. When it did, a rushing filled my ears. *Her own two legs?* I'd suspected as much, but here was proof that I'd been betrayed. She'd used me all along: *Get my dinner, pick up that coffee cup, take care of me, goddammit,* while she'd been perfectly capable of doing those things herself. I'd been Mama's little puppet, stupid Dahlia dancin' on a string. I took a step forward, ready to burst through the door and let her know what's what, when the realization hit me that I was being shot at again.

Tok. A tiny circle appeared in the window and a spurt of dust erupted near my feet. *Tok,* the glass cratered again and the sheriff spun and fell. He dragged his own gun clear of its holster and as he pirouetted, the blue black revolver flew free of his hand. It landed at Sallie's feet, just one more gift from Heaven on this fine, miraculous day. She bent down to retrieve it, like firearms from God was the most natural thing in the world. "Who's that guy shootin' at us?" she asked. I looked through the glass again and saw Twitch level his gun at me.

"I ain't got it no more!" I screamed, pointing at Sallie. "She's got the money, that crazy woman there!" Not that it did any good. Until the day I died, which could be any moment, that old man would blame me for everything bad in his world. As I opened my mouth to protest, I noticed several details: Twitch's gun aimed at my liver; Mama's glance at the pistol; the way her arm lashed out, throwing off his aim. The glass pocked again and Cole clutched his arm. Sallie Goodnight squeezed two shots into the bank and Mama and Twitch hit the floor. She yelled to run for the puke green truck. When she threw open the door, Arnold cowered inside.

Now let me say something. More than anything else over the last twenty-four hours, the sight of Arnold scootched low in his truck convinced me I'd entered a world as strange as the one on that TV show, *The Twilight Zone*. Not that I could afford a TV or had ever actually seen it, but the show was on for two years already, and I certainly heard about it from kids in school. It was that mix of normal and not-so-normal that threw one's world outta kilter, and I was certainly experiencin' a good measure of both right now. One day ago, Arnold had picked me up outside my home in this same heap. Since then I'd been shot at, witnessed a murder, fallen in love, made love, and gotten spied on while doin' so. I'd celebrated that I was rich, mourned that I was poor, and got shot at a second time. Now Arnold was waitin' for me again. My life was a loop, day in, day out, startin' in this truck, forever greeted by Arnold: "Get in, you darlin' thing!" Any minute now, Rod Serling would pop up in the flatbed. "Consider, for a moment, the case of Dahlia Jean Coker," he'd say. "The place is here, the time is now, and the journey into the shadows that we're about to watch could be our own."

So Arnold and I stared at each other and yelped, "What're

you doin' here?" It seemed a natural thing to say. Sallie seemed a mite surprised also that we knew each other, but had the presence of mind to add that this was not the time to socialize. Instead, she pointed the sheriff's gun at Arnold and told him to get this heap in gear. Amazingly enough, Arnold didn't argue back, as he tended to do. He accepted the fact that his lot in life was to be hijacked by every armed stranger in Tennessee who needed a ride. He even seemed relieved to see me, and I felt grateful and choked up inside. It's good to see old friends, even if they ain't old friends. As the truck clattered south from town, we updated each other on all that'd happened since yesterday. We both learned something new: Arnold was upset to learn the cops suspected him and me of murder, while I was peeved how Mama had volunteered to chase me down. Worse, she seemed to anticipate my every thought, and had already figured out that I was headed south to Daddy. That especially was bad news.

Meanwhile, blood ran from Cole's gunshot wound. It leaked all over Sallie, who cried her favorite polka-dot dress was bein' ruined. She needed a rag to stop the blood and rooted under the high seat for one. She came up with a base-ball bat, a hank of rope, and Harson's Bible, but no bandage. "Goddamm it!" she shouted, and in a fit of pique threw the Bible out the window. It flapped off like some poor bird smashed by our windshield. As we rounded the curve, she ordered Arnold to pull in behind the forgotten church—the truck doors popped open like a pressure cooker, and she warned Arnold not to run. It didn't matter—he seemed resigned to his fate by now. She handed me the rope, grabbed the bat for herself, and motioned us inside.

We climbed the steps to the deserted steeple: a door opened up top and a screech owl winged away. We were at treetop level, surrounded by green. An old-time floral carpetbag lay by the door, clothes piled beside it. She opened the clasp and Harson's money was stuffed inside. "Pretty, huh?" she grinned. I felt sick, rememberin' how we'd passed this place on our way to Muscovy and if we'd stopped, *like I wanted*, we'd've found our money again. I glared at Cole, who looked sheepish through his pain.

"I left it here before going into town," Sallie explained, right proud. "Even in school Bobby Plenty was nosy, but I never considered the nosiness of that damn old lady bank teller. Nothing would've happened if I hadn't gone after the bank account—that teller kept arguing how she needed both signatures to close the account, did Earl know what I was doin', it was highly irregular, maybe we oughta call. And while she's wastin' time at that, Sheriff Nosy walks past and gets interested in the car."

Serves you right, I thought, though I knew better by now than crack wise 'round someone with a gun. Arnold, of course, spoke without thinking. "Greed's what done you in," he said.

"That's what you think, is it?" she answered, voice chilly.

"Everybody's greedy on this trip, 'cept me."

"It must be nice to be a saint," she said.

Well, I'd always thought *I* scored low on the Arnold Simpson Tolerance Test, but I saw in an instant that her score fell way below mine. She ordered me to bind Arnold's hands with the rope; when he objected, she told me to tie his feet, too. I said there wasn't enough rope for both, which stumped her till she glanced down at her blood-soaked dress, so she pulled it over her head and handed it to me. "Tear this into strips," she said. As she stood there braless, her filmy briefs proclaimin' the wrong day of the week, Arnold's eyes bugged from his head.

I whispered as I tied the knots that now was *not* the time to get all horny, but no one ever listens to Dahlia, and sex was Arnold's downfall. Sallie walked close till a nipple was at nose level and asked Arnold if he was getting an eyeful. "Yes, ma'am," he said.

"Honey," she snapped, "I'm not big on *any* men lately, and you're one of the worst." She pulled a daisy-print shift from the pile, slipped it over her shoulders, and tossed me the bat. "Hit him with this," she said.

Arnold and me stared back, unsure what we'd heard. "Knock him out," she explained. "There's no room in the truck for four, so someone's got to go. Either you knock him out or I shoot him, and either way he's off our hands."

"But it's my truck," Arnold complained.

"And we thank you for it, though you should take better care of your things," Sallie answered.

"That ain't fair! Nobody's treated me right this whole damn trip. I ain't done nothin' wrong."

"Fairness got nothin' to do with it, honey. Like you said, this is all about greed."

Ah, yes, I thought, greed. It was greed that made this country great. Greed that greased the wheels of industry. In days to come, greed would creep across the world like kudzu, coverin' everything. Right now, however, Arnold didn't really care. He struggled with the ropes and stared at me with hound-dog eyes. "Don't do it, Dahlia!" he begged. "We been friends forever. You crack me with that bat, and my blood'll be on your hands."

Granted, *friends forever* did stretch the truth a bit, but I still couldn't poleax someone I'd known so long. "Look," I said, dropping the bat, "I'll admit Arnold gets on your nerves, and I've dreamed of brainin' him myself, but it's cruel to hurt someone that way."

"This is pathetic," Sallie said, so without further ado, hefted the bat and swung it like a major leaguer—save for the fact that the gun was still in her hands. That tiny difference probably saved poor Arnold from brain damage, for her aim was thrown off and he got whacked in the ribs instead. He whirled sideways and cracked his head against the wall; his eyes rolled in their sockets and he dropped like a worm to the floor. "Maybe that knocked some sense into him," she commented, dropping the bat and wiping her hands. "He's lucky I don't finish the job, the foul mood I'm in." She told me to gag and truss Arnold with discarded clothes from her suitcase; she tied a loose balloon of fabric 'round his head and face so no one would hear his cries once he woke. "I want time to disappear," she said. "We don't need him announcing our whereabouts." When we were done, poor Arnold looked like a polka-dot mummy.

Next I turned to Cole. The bullet had dug a furrow in his arm, the muscle red and jumpy, but luckily missing the bone. I tied a rag to slow the bleeding, but Cole was in a world of pain. "A big, strong boy like that can take a little boo-boo," Sallie smirked. "Leave him be!" I snapped, gun or no. "You'd be in jail if not for him and me."

Her eyes were like dark mercury, liquid and enraged. "You didn't act outta charity either, dear." Her voice grew almost sad. "We got one more stop, then it's a big world waitin' that I've wanted too long to see." She hefted the bag of money and left everything else by poor, unconscious Arnold. "Hurry, now. We ain't got lots of time."

———— •• ————

So off we sped again, turnin' down the same dirt road, jouncin' through the same mud and grass to the far end of the clearing. It opened to a logging road, more narrow than the original cut, and soon after the clearing began switchin' back and forth down the mountainside. I drove, Cole bounced limply in the middle, Sallie sat by the door, the carpetbag of cash cradled in her lap. Cole's forehead felt hot as he drifted in and out. I mentioned how surprised we was when the car was taken. Sallie was more talkative, relieved to be under way.

"You were shocked?" she laughed. "Imagine me. It ain't every day you find a pink Cadillac in the woods." She'd already hiked miles up the mountain when she spotted it and was still in a panic, hardly taking time to throw clothes in her bag. She wouldn't say what had happened, but whatever it was threw her into a tizzy. But all was forgotten when she looked inside the moose head.

"How much was in it?" I said. She studied me, suspicious how I could have all that money yet still be ignorant of the amount. I told her what happened in the diner and why our flight was so sudden. "No wonder his dad is upset," she laughed. "I would be, too."

I asked again how much she found. "Maybe I shouldn't say, seein' how you lost it," she warned. "Finder's keepers, you know." At first she'd felt guilty, seeing how we looked so cute in the woods, all naked and trusting; but the world is a hard place, and a girl's got a right to survive. And once she counted the amount . . . well, she saw everything in a brand-new light, she said.

"So what was the total?" I pressed. "Thirty or forty thousand?"

"Make it a hundred."

A hundred thousand dollars?" My foot slid off the gas. She couldn't believe it either, she said, head nodding like a bobbly toy. "Isn't it great? I mean, it's what I always asked for. God really is rewarding me for living with a crazy man. He sure does work in mysterious ways."

My head settled against the wheel. So the rumors were true, after all. "Excuse me while I catch my breath," I wheezed. No wonder Mama trailed me down to Florida. No wonder Cole's dad hated me so. And if he ever learned we'd lost it . . . oh boy!

"I was light-headed, too," Sallie said. "I danced around, clutching handfuls of the stuff, then felt faint and had to sit down. Things like this don't happen in real life." But I wasn't really listening to what she said. I could've used that cash to bring Mama and Daddy back together. Me and Cole could've headed west, over the Mississippi, into the vastness beyond. Now all I could do was ask what she had planned.

She giggled like a little girl. "Fact is, now that I can leave this place, I don't know where to go. I do want to visit Atlanta; I know that. There's a big Rich's department store downtown with all the things Jackie Kennedy wears. Black Halston gowns with little spaghetti straps, mulberry silk wraps, those funny pillbox hats." Her eyes swam.

"What happened between you and your husband?" I asked, the nausea passing.

"Don't be so nosy," she crabbed, angered by the interruption of her dreams. "Too many people sticking their nose in my business today." She told me to start up the truck, we'd talked enough, so I grabbed the wheel and continued down the mountainside. Soon the faint roar I'd heard in Muscovy seemed to grow closer. Raindrops fell briefly, like crocodile tears. "Watch that boulder!" she snapped, then relaxed when I eased 'round it and rolled on.

But Sallie could keep no more quiet than I could, and soon started talking again. "The way I see it, things happen for a reason," she said. "Roads cross and recross—down here it all looks random, but seen up high I bet there's some pattern to it all. Look't you and your boyfriend, brought together by the diner. Look how you brought its riches straight to me."

But even so, she mused, she wouldn't've found the money if she hadn't escaped her husband this morning, boltin' up the mountain crazed with fear. It wasn't always that way. "Once I was happy," she said. "Earl was a good man—one of the most famous tent revivalists in these mountains, so handsome in his seersucker suit, and even if he was old enough to be my daddy, I didn't particularly care. I'd never seen the likes of a man so *inspired* before I met Earl. I'd sit on the bench and watch people I'd known my whole life dance to his tune and think, *If this is power, I want some of that for my own.*"

Her voice grew veiled and thoughtful, her mind a hundred miles away. "But power, I learned, has its own life, and right away I wondered where it came from. Did it live in the hypnotic rise and fall of Earl's voice? The way he'd swing back the hinged lid of the snake box and seem to play with Death, but still emerge unscathed? I came to think that Power and Death were kissin' cousins, and Earl's dominion over death was proof of the better things waiting that all humanity craved. At least, that's how it seemed when the money plate was passed around. The serpent Earl held up was the very symbol of life and death, its body a beautiful scabbard, its touch more than sufficient to kill. I'd watch the long body coil around Earl's arm, and it was like I could feel its silky slither, too. I watched the red tongue taste the air and imagined that fleshy fork on *my* skin."

She drew in her breath sharply at the thought, then released it in a sigh. "You know how you see someone and say, 'I want him worse'n anything'? That's how I felt about Earl. One night after the last true believer left the tent, I made my move." Sallie described it like a love scene from a movie. The sun had set and she walked to the back of the tent where she knew he kept his "room." It was hot beneath the canvas, all close and musty, and her dress was sticking to her skin, she said. She lifted back the flap and before anything else, she saw his silver JESUS belt buckle glint back in the shadows as he moved. She cleared her throat and he looked up, fixing her in his blue eyes as the canvas settled back. Since tent preachers worked wide territories, they were always on the move and, she hoped, lonely. "I've seen you in the crowd," Earl said.

I began to feel a little hot myself as I drove the pickup down that twisty road and Sallie's voice weaved its own hypnotic spell. Was this what it took to seduce an older man? "At first I was terrified," she said, "but not for long. I watched his long fingers form a steeple before his lips, and I thought how feminine they looked, almost like a girl's. I watched his eyes linger on my legs and breasts, and suddenly realized I had a power of my own. *Men are so easy,* I thought, even the holiest, and the image of Salome dancing before her father Herod popped into my head. That's all seduction is, I realized—a gradual shedding of secrets. I was the snake Earl couldn't conquer, weaving in the rusty light, shedding my second skin."

According to Sallie, their betrothal was quick, her pregnancy false, and the "miscarriage" convenient while Earl was on the road. "I don't think he was fooled," she said. "To my surprise, he also wasn't mad. If anything, he seemed amused that the old con artist could get slickered by the oldest con of all. I also don't fool myself that I wasn't his first bump on God's moral highway, and the bumps didn't stop with the wedding vows." She smiled to herself. "Still, neither of us minded. It wasn't a big deal. We were both ambitious in what I now see is the peculiar way of the mountains, wanting more than these mountains can ever give us but still reluctant to break free. We saw through each other like glass, and recognized what we saw."

By now, Sallie's voice had adopted that breathless singsong loved by the evangelists and which she must've heard Earl use a thousand times. I followed her directions down the mountain as the narrow road forked and forked again. The trees merged into green shadows; upthrusts of marble gneiss rose from the mold. We'd entered a different level on the mountain, a world of milky quartz, fairy rings, destroying angels with flat caps like shields. We rounded a dogleg and that roar I'd heard all morning was even more pronounced, transformed to a metal chorus of strange whines and purrs.

"Earl had plans," continued Sallie, "but part of Earl's plan was a mystery, even to me." A note of bitterness entered her voice—a note of wistfulness, too. As she explained it, Earl had bought an abandoned logging camp down the mountain by the river, a "woodpecker" camp as such outfits once were called. In the 1940s, the Army needed wood for walnut gun stocks; after that, a postwar boom in mine props and "acid wood" for paper kept small sawmills going another ten years. By then all the woodpecker outfits were getting bought up or driven out of business by giant firms like Union Camp or Champion Paper, and by the time Earl bought the camp, it had long grown over with weeds and seed pine.

"He didn't seem to mind its state," Sallie recalled. "I couldn't stand the place, at least not at first, but Earl saw something else besides the endless fix-it of the two-story office house, something greater than the half-moon Quonset hut with its rusted logging equipment and the long, low sawmill. There was even a small graveyard of lumberjacks in the clearing, killed when trees fell without warning or logs broke their yoke and crashed down the trail. It seemed spooky to me, but he ignored that, too. Earl saw in his mind something unique—a kind of monastery for revivalists, a getaway where the rich urban faithful could return to nature, paying hefty sums to learn the evangelist trade. 'Think of it, Sallie,' he tried to tell me. 'Classes on snake handling without getting bit. Faith healing with guaranteed results. Speaking in tongues. There are people out there who will lap that up. It'll be the nation's first retreat dedicated entirely to holiness, a sanctified fortress out in the middle of nowhere."

I put on the brake as a black bear emerged from the shadows, gave us a quizzical look, and lumbered away. "He was right about one thing, though," Sallie admitted. "It was like no place I'd ever seen." The way she described it, the forest surrounded three sides of the camp, while closing the circle on the downhill slope flowed a tributary of the French Broad River, one of the main sources of the Tennessee. As the forest around us opened to an overlook, Sallie said I could stop the car and see for myself, if I desired.

I did as suggested and got out for a look-see. Some sights are so green and otherworldly, a girl tends to get weak in the knees. The tiny camp way down by the river looked like the last unspoiled place on Earth, but the river had swelled with rain over the last few days and now was creeping uphill. "It has a certain charm, don't it?" sighed Sallie. "Part of me still likes the place, even after what happened the last day or two."

Part of that charm was its isolation, but according to Sallie that was its downfall, too. Those who got drawn here by Earl's praises of mountain beauty got driven away by its solitude. "The place is too lonely," said Sallie, "so lonely it plays with your head. Visitors told me they could hear themselves think, and they didn't like what they were hearing. Word soon got 'round and nobody came. It was only then that Earl told me he'd sunk his life savings in the place, and now we were ruined."

Joe Jackson

A big gray squirrel barked from a limb above us, but Sallie was lost in her memories. "One thing about Earl Goodnight, he's always an optimist," Sallie said. "This was just a minor setback sent to test us, he declared. He hit the revival circuit again with new vigor and I went with him, watching the faithful with new eyes. What did Earl see in them to make him think he could build a utopia? They would inherit the earth, he railed from the pulpit, but it soon became evident to me how badly he'd misjudged. Everywhere we went were more ghost-towns-in-the-making, more victims of the great migration, no young couples with children but just the middle-aged and elderly who were left behind. Those who came to Earl's tent revivals seemed to sip a common bitterness: they suspected they were obsolete, bypassed by the rest of the nation's prosperity. They were the hicks in people's jokes, the new nigger of the social order, dumb hillbillies like Li'l Abner and Moonbeam McSwine. They prayed for a way to deal with such changes, and Earl's gift was to sanctify their rage. But all the rage in the world can't stop poverty, and Earl's followers were too poor to lift themselves—much less us—from ruin."

Sallie stared down the mountain at the logging camp a long, long time. Earl quit and she quit with him, Sallie muttered, holing up in their failed paradise, miles from the nearest neighbor, an orphan named J. Wesley Biggers. "I thought the isolation would kill me at first, but then I discovered a knack for survival, and all of a sudden *I* was in charge. I plastered the walls and calked the casements of the frame house; negotiated rights-of-way for power and phone lines running up the mountain through our property—for a neat monthly sum, mind you; read about a strange demand for wild ginseng, the weed we called 'sang' 'round here. The country was goin' health-crazy and the war in Korea had ruined a lot of Asian ginseng lands. Shoot, the dried root was sellin' for $60 a pound and up, and damn if it didn't grow in our backyard. It was easy to find the bright gold leaves in the forest, and I learned to make cuttings from older roots and transplant the young stems for the future. 'Look't this, Earl,' I told him, 'you were right. We're sittin' on a gold mine!' But Earl didn't care."

His failed dreams embittered him, she said. "He tried to start a new sect called the Church of True Signs. The Apocalypse was comin', he promised, and you could duck 'n' cover till you were blue in the face and that still wouldn't save you from the Bomb. Only isolated enclaves like ours would survive, he said. But no one was impressed. Who wanted to wait for the end way the hell out here? You'd be better off dead."

"But even that's not what finally drove Earl crazy," Sallie ended. "I blame *that* on the opening of the strip mine." She walked me 'round a big set of boulders perched at the edge of the overlook and pointed uphill.

I saw now the source of the metal shriek I'd heard all morning, a graded pit far upslope where, she said, the deserted Muscovy pit mine had once been. "That damn thing is the pet snake of progress," Sallie spit, "creeping on its belly down the mountain toward our home. And for that we can thank the TVA."

I'd heard folks rant about the Tennessee Valley Authority before, Daddy among them, but never understood why till now. Here was the flip side of progress, set like a scar on the mountain. The Authority promised cheap electricity to factories in the flatlands, but the only way to keep that promise was to build ever-bigger generators burning hundreds of tons of coal each week and millions of tons each year. Sallie'd seen the plants herself while ridin' the circuit with Earl; they were hunched on the riverbanks by the TVA's million-dollar dams, gigantic black boxes bristling with chimneys and ablaze with an inner fire. Cheap coal was necessary to feed the beast and keep them going, so the Authority bought mountain tracts where coal deposits lay too close to the surface for traditional extraction. Tracts like the one beneath Muscovy, she declared.

Sallie hugged herself, as if she'd grown cold. "This is Earl's real apocalypse, honey," she whispered. "Not the Biblical one he'd expected. Not bombs from above, but one that's homegrown."

Joe Jackson

I clung to the boulders and stared up and down the mountain, from the cantilevered town up top to the doll-like camp by the river. A crater had formed below Muscovy, a moonscape where once there was forest, replaced by loose earth, tree trunks, massive slabs of blue slate, and abandoned loaders. A gray glacier of "gob" advanced down the slope, blotting out trees in its way. As I watched, a huge D-9 bulldozer sheared off a wave of topsoil and dumped it over the edge of the crater, exposing the coal beneath like black blood. The bulldozer slammed against an oak; the tree held firm a few seconds, then started to lean. Its roots rose from the soil like claws until the strain was too much; the roots snapped and the tree spun into others on the slope beneath it, lopping off trunks with a crack like a rifle volley.

In the center of the crater was that roaring beast I'd heard all day. The mine itself was no more than a series of sunken "benches," the ends of each bench backed up against the seam. It looked for all the world to me like spreading ripples when a stone hits a pond. A giant power shovel squatted dead center, its arms rising up in an arch of pulleys, cables, and gears. I watched as the shovel swallowed tons of coal in a gulp, then pivoted on its axis and spilled its guts into trucks gathered like hatchlings 'round its treads. "Day by day, these benches sink deeper," said Sallie. "Some days the explosions sound like bootsteps marching close to our camp. Someday Muscovy will be undercut, and when that happens, it, too, will join the gray glacier that creeps down the mountain to our home."

I couldn't move or talk. I was fascinated and paralyzed, never having seen such destruction in all my born days. God created the mountain and now man, not to be outdone, was tearing it down. As I watched, black birds wheeled above the scar, a great flock of starlings that circled and dropped, only to rise with each new roar.

"The mine was the last straw for Earl," Sallie explained sadly. "When it came, he gave up and never left camp again. 'Earl,' I said, 'we gotta get out of here. Someday a hard rain will come and wash that river of rock down on us.' But Earl wouldn't listen. He'd watch the glacier creep closer—it was a sign of his failure, a power greater than any one man. He seemed to take comfort in its gradual approach, like he wouldn't have to struggle no more. It was a serpent and most beautiful at night, he told me—that's when the moon shone off the rock above and river below us, and he knew it was God's plan that these two streams should join. 'That's crazy, Earl, and I won't listen,' I said. Then this morning he said he'd found a better solution than sittin' and waitin' for the end."

Sallie's voice sounded funny; when I looked up, her face was ghostly pale. I realized that maybe she *was* a spirit of this place, but not the Cannibal Woman incarnate like I'd first believed. No, Sallie'd been cannibalized herself. She was what happened if you stayed.

"I should've seen it comin'," she said. "Earl still had his snakes, collectin' ever more as his isolation deepened, keepin' 'em in glass cages in a small room on the second floor. He'd go into the woods each early morning with his burlap sack and hooked stick, unearthing copperheads and timber rattlers in their dens. They balled together to mate, a writhing mass of snakes with no head or tail, beginning or end. 'Like evil,' he'd tell me. 'Like man.' He'd bring 'em to that room of cages stacked four shelves high. It was a frightening place with its dim-lit heat lamps and one hundred snakes nosing at their glass walls. I wouldn't go in there, not alone. The largest were fat and grayish yellow, dark chevrons marching down their backs, unblinking eyes like slits as they watched a body open the door. Earl fed them rats and mice, waiting as he dropped them into the pit, watching as they froze in place with fear. The snakes never seemed interested till the moment they struck, and I always wondered what it was like to die like that, headfirst down a serpent's belly, still conscious as you dissolved in stomach acids."

And so it was that early this morning, long before daylight— while Cole and me drove through the mountains and radio preachers cried doom on the world—so it was that Earl awoke to tell Sallie he'd had a most wonderful dream. He'd seen himself completely wrapped in snakes, arms outstretched and curling, red tongues appearing and disappearing like the darts in martyrs. "You're wrapped up the same, Sallie," he said. A rattlesnake's was the most painful of bites, but there came a point where the pain became a sea of clarity that one rode in waves. "You float atop these waves," Earl promised, "until you rise to Heaven. Do this with me, Sallie," he insisted. "Float with me into the light."

It got real quiet as we stood there, her silence punctuated by the shrieks of the strip mine. "What happened next?" I asked.

"Why, Earl was talkin' double suicide," Sallie said, staring at the river. "I couldn't have that. Even in paradise, it's kill or be killed."

She paused and stared at me without blinking. "Now I gotta hide the evidence before Sheriff Plenty shows up and gets all nosy again. I've got a husband to bury, honey. You and me have got work to do."

How Private Mischief Finds
the Old Man

I LED BURMA Coker from the Muscovy bank, too disgusted for words. Disgust was too mild a term. I was so mad at myself, I couldn't see straight. I had the ache that wouldn't stop. In less than twelve hours, I'd gone from zero to three women determined to make me miserable, the latest some wild-eyed stranger who'd fired at me outta meanness or boredom, maybe both. And then she stole my wheels. Even worse, I'd shot my boy. How would I explain *that* when I caught up to him? *Sorry, son, slip of the finger, aim's not what it used to be.* True, it seemed I only winged him, but if he'd ever had doubts about running, they were long gone now.

The most immediate problem was bein' stuck in a town that had every reason to see me dead. Me and Burma had robbed the local bank, and I'd plugged the local lawman. I ran into the street just as Arnold's jalopy vanished 'round a bend in the road. I put my foot on the wounded sheriff to stop his squirming. "Who was she?" I barked. "The one who shot at me!"

"Turn yourself in and we'll talk about it," he moaned.

Why was everyone so dead set on telling me my business? I warned the sheriff not to make me mad, then put my gun to his head. It was like Harson Whitley all over again, like every fuckin' day of my life would be the same as the next, which made me even less charitable than in Wattles. "Where's she headed?" I demanded. "You got to the count of ten."

"You kill me, you'll regret it," he replied.

I felt my face begin to twitch; my anger rose toward that level where'd I lose all control. "I only kill them who deserve it, Sheriff. You deserve it? You're convincin' me you do."

He gazed nervously at my face; then, without further thought, spilled the woman's name and directions where she lived. She might go back, he said, since she'd been acting skittish and might have something to hide. I thanked him for his change of heart, then considered killin' him anyway. In the old days I would, him bein' a witness and all, but Burma walked up and I couldn't do it in front of her. I aimed a gob of spit at the lawman's forehead and walked away.

Burma caught up and said we'd better make tracks—a barber had run out in the street yelling for help, while some blind geezer yelled back he'd call the state police if he could only find a phone. "We can't go yet," I said. "I got something to do." My perfect pink Cadillac was locked inside the fence and, with all the hubbub, I'd never find the keys. That car was the symbol of all I'd dreamed about—and now she was out of reach. She'd spoke to me when I first glimpsed her in the Asheville lot, a curbside siren promising endless roads to luxury. Now she was the symbol of my failure. If I couldn't have her, no one else could, either.

I stopped outside the vehicle compound and shoved cartridges from my pocket into the pistol chamber. *Bang!* I shot her in the windshield, and glass webbed. *Bling!* in the radiator, and steam hissed from the hole. *Whoof!* in a tire. *Clink!* in the hood ornament, and the winged figure flew like a silver dove. Sobs caught in my throat. A bullet pierced the pink hood, tender as a baby's cheek. A black dog rushed from among the rusting hulks, so I shot the fuckin' dog.

A man ran from a body shop with "Dwight" stitched above his right nipple, screaming about that dog. I pointed the gun at him and pulled the trigger, but the chamber was empty by now. "Hold still, I don't want to leave you out," I promised, digging in my pocket for more cartridges. Dwight turned quick for a fat man and ran away.

Burma grabbed my arm when I started to follow. "You've done enough," she said. "I think we better go."

"No way I've done enough," I screamed. "I've lost my son and money, and now my car, forever. I hate this place. I hate every goddamn little town like this in the goddamn state of goddamn Tennessee!"

"My, my, what a mouth," she said, but gently, prying my fingers from the gun. "Why don't you give me that before you do something we'll both regret." She stroked the back of my neck with her thin fingers. "There, there," she cooed, "it'll be all right. You've just had a bad couple of days."

"I've had a bad life, that's what I've had," I sniffed, and then the levee broke. She put her arm around my waist and led me into the woods.

<hr />

What I had was a mental breakdown, I later heard it called: a normal enough thing for a man in my shoes. Even with the knowledge, I still felt ashamed. Me, John Thomas Younger, great-great grandson of one of the greatest outlaws of the West, blubberin' like a baby. What would my pals in prison say? I stumbled beside Burma, drained of life, dog tired. She tried to be of comfort, but was a complete failure at navigating. Soon we got lost in the forest, bumping like pinballs from tree to tree.

These woods were like nothing I'd ever been in—trees so high you couldn't see their tops, green shadows between the trunks as deep as the sea. The only direction we could tell was downhill, so we took that toward a pounding like my heartbeat, *boom boom boom.* "I've heard that sound before, in Wattles," Burma told me, and soon we came out on the lip of a huge strip mine dug in the earth, the *booms* the pounding of a giant power shovel as its toothy bucket slammed into a coal wall. Storm clouds built in the west, and I could see the sun glint off a mahogany river far below. In the mine some doll-like workers pointed at us and we dove back in the forest, only slightly less lost than previous, working our way back uphill.

As we climbed, I thought of recent history. I'd really shot my boy. I'd always said family life was like a series of little murders, and now I'd lived up to my words. "I wouldn't've shot Cole if you hadn't grabbed me," I said to Burma. "You'd of shot my daughter otherwise," she replied. "Besides, you just winged him. Kids heal fast." We crunched through the leaves and emerged on the highway. A rising wind brought the smell of rain with it. The sky was slate blue.

In the distance, the red flash of a police bubble-top sped our way. We ducked back into the trees, and a black highway patrol cruiser rolled past, the driver shining a spotlight into the forest, uncertain if he'd seen something in the gloom. We hugged the ground behind a green-spotted oak till he was gone.

"They're lookin' for us, all right," I said.

"They ain't gonna find us, not if I can help it," Burma replied. She looked up and added, "Right now, I'm more worried 'bout that rain."

Joe Jackson

We plodded south and soon a dark shape rose up—four walls and a steeple among high weeds. The door hung on a hinge and all the windows were shattered, but the roof seemed intact, and that was the important thing.

We ran inside just in time. Cloud-to-cloud lightning lit the interior in brief flashes; the wind moaned through the broken panes. The pews were pushed to one side like a listing ship; the cross hung at an angle; beer cans were piled in one corner. Red velvet curtains behind the altar had been ripped down, revealing a door. We grabbed an armful of the curtains and made a musty nest among the jumbled pews. I still trembled and Burma held me close, her breath smelling like nutmeg.

"Why you being so nice?" I finally said. "I shot at your daughter, remember? Shot at her twice, but someone's always ruinin' my aim."

"That oughta tell you somethin'," she commented. "Maybe you ain't really meant to shoot her."

A few heavy drops drummed on the tin roof overhead. Blue lightning deepened the lines of her face. I watched in horror as my hand reached up on its own to brush back her hair. I caught the traitor thing before it did much else and scratched my nose instead.

Still, she smiled at the gesture and I looked toward the ruined altar. "I don't understand women," I said. "Men wear themselves like patched and dirty coats, open for inspection, while women are like silky stuff hid next to the skin."

"How so?" she said.

"I mean, you spoil my aim, but you're stayin' on and leadin' me to her, too. You want that money bad as me. I half-suspect you don't know *what* you want. My father said as much, how women want the world, and if they get it still ain't happy."

"Ask a bunch of women, they'll say the same of men."

"That don't answer the question."

She moved close and beneath the velvet my Billy Bob awoke.

He'd been in hibernation a long time. She smiled like private mischief and moved against me again. *This ain't smart,* I thought: *This is the mother of the girl I wanta blow away!* That's no grounds for future happiness, not unless the rules of love had changed.

"I don't know the answer," she sighed, suddenly a philosopher as the rain drummed down. "All that stuff about a mother's love kicking in once she has a baby never seemed to work for me. If anything, I felt trapped. Still, you ought'n a-tried to shoot her. There's such a thing as moderation. Or ain't you heard?"

"That never worked for me."

"No, I guess not." Her laughter sounded like chimes. "It's strange. I told Dahlia someone would come along to give her her comeuppance, then you pop up full-grown, like something outta my head."

The lightning flashed closer. She stiffened and I counted her heartbeats against my chest. It still made no sense, I told her. "Don't take no genius," she replied. "I stayed too long in the house and must've read a million of Dahlia's movie magazines, all sayin' the same. Desire's the heart of existence, but anticipation's the best we get." She hummed in her chest as my old soldier rose to attention against her. "What's this?" she teased.

"It's . . . nothin'."

"Oh, there's somethin' there, all right." Her eyes shined through the gloom. "You ain't perfect, but at least you're determined. That's more'n I can say for lots of other men I've known."

The fireworks started then. She unzipped my fly and her smile curled inward as she scooted on top of me. "Way I see it, it's time to live again," she said. "When we robbed that bank, I was scared to death, but it was also like I'd come back from the dead." She grabbed my hand and placed it on her ass; she wore no pants beneath her dress, and my ears began to ring. "If Dahlia takes that money to her daddy, he'll talk her out of every cent and sail off into the sunset." She hiked up her skirt and guided me inside. "I don't plan to let that happen." She placed her hands on both sides of my head and started rocking. "We need each other, whether you know it or not."

"I don't . . . I don't think . . ."

"Don't think so much," she growled, her body moving like the pistons of a V-8 engine. "Just enjoy the ride."

The storm had settled in upon us when I finally woke, one of those long rains washing through the valleys that break in a wave of thunder then stays for the long siege. Rain blew through the windows and puddled on the floor. Something knocked up in the steeple, then knocked again.

Burma was still atop me, weight on her elbows, watching my face. She'd unbuttoned her dress during the excitement, and we lay skin to skin. Her heart beat like a bird's. I ran my hand down her back, feeling the soft hairs at the base of her spine.

"Did I wear you out?" she said.

It'd been a long time since I'd been like this with a woman, I admitted, then realized she might reckon such admission as affection. "Not that I believe in love," I said.

"I'm no teenager, honey. Did I ask if you did?"

"I just want to get it straight. This ain't love. It's fuckin'."

"The last of the true romantics," she snorted, but stayed where she was. "Since you don't believe in love, what *do* you believe in?"

That didn't take much thought. "Money," I said.

"Just money?"

"Well, what it can bring. What it can buy."

She traced her finger down my stomach. "You believe in an afterlife? In God?"

I stared at her in surprise. "Why you askin'?"

"I don't know, a church like this, it makes me think, is all."

The question made me uncomfortable. To tell the truth, no one had ever asked me that, not even my old man. They'd only *told* me what to believe. I stalled a bit. "Do you?"

She shook her head. "No God would make a world like this."

"My God would," I said, surprising her, but really surprising me. Suddenly, for the first time in my life, I knew *exactly* what I believed. "This world is filled with ghosts and walking dead made in His image," I told her. "He watches for entertainment as they feed upon each other. That ritual of the bread and wine is all mixed up. It's *us* who are the meal."

"Sounds like a terrible place," she said, and shuddered, dropping on my chest for warmth.

"It's the only place I've ever known."

"You think it's only like that in the mountains?"

I laughed. "I think it's like that everywhere. There's no gettin' away."

———◆———

I must've dozed again, but this time I dreamed. Thing is, I hardly ever dream, my sleep like a hole I drop through every night and emerge from in the morning. This time, I was riding on the back of a fast black horse and in the distance spotted bony figures, some so weak they barely crawled. The sun was a setting crimson ball, flat at the top and bottom, sinking into the plain. I rode over the bony men: they crumpled beneath the hooves like the flash paper bookies use. A smell rose like rotting fish. "Take us with you," they cried.

I woke and lay still, counting the beats of my heart as if at any minute they'd end. It was still dark outside, and something was wrong. A frosty moon showed through the clouds. The wind had risen, rushing 'round the church in a low and searching moan. Burma held me so tight it hurt. "Did you hear that?" she said.

"It's the wind."

"Not that," she said. *"That!"* I heard it now. The knocking in the steeple had grown stronger and more steady than before. *Thump... thump... thump.* Probably a shingle torn loose or a limb hitting the roof of the steeple, I tried to reassure her.

"Don't sound like no shingle or limb to me."

To tell the truth, it didn't to me, neither. Shingles don't move in circles across a room. Limbs don't crash against walls and groan. "Go see what it is," she said.

"You're crazy."

"Take your gun." She shoved it in my hands.

That was better'n nothing, so I pulled on my clothes and shoes, Burma the same. No one wants to stand before a ghost, or worse, in their altogether. I walked to the back of the altar, held the gun in front of me, and opened the door.

It was like a sound box in here, and the crashes were amplified. *Boom... boom... boom,* loud and solemn as a funeral drum. "Go on," Burma hissed, poking me with her finger. "I'm right behind you." We felt our way up the stairs.

There had to be a good explanation for this, but right then not a single one made sense to me. Burma felt it, too: her face was gray white as an oyster, drained of blood. She hung on my arm, eyes big as saucers and white at the rims. A door was closed at the top of the stairs and behind it the pounding was louder. I couldn't think. The whole thing was maddening. I was too old to be scared of the bogeyman, but I was quiverin' like a kid what knew a monster waited right beneath his bed. *Show some grit,* I told myself, then bounded 'cross the landing, threw open the door, and barged in.

That was the dumbest thing I could do. A figure stepped out of a shadow-filled corner and turned my way. Maybe it was the suddenness of its appearance, maybe its overall weirdness, but a panic took hold of me then like I'd never knowed before. The thing bent down as if struggling with something 'round its feet, then straightened and hopped toward me while waving its arms. Its legs seemed glued together, the upper trunk swaying in the moonlight like one of those tiny plants in stagnant water that wave a host of arms to sting and paralyze its prey. It was white as a sheet but with black blobs on it; it took two short hops and stood between me and the door. Burma froze on the landing, fist to her mouth. I held out the gun but my shaking got worse, and I dropped it to the floor.

"*Iffs smee!*" the woolly-booger said.

The sound of that voice gives me the willies even now. It was garbled, like something was stuffed in its mouth, but even so it sounded familiar—and in a flash I knew who it was. It was Frog Boy, transformed. That crazy woman at the bank had killed him, and now his spirit had returned for *me*. Most spirits come back lookin' like themselves, or at least close enough, but not Arnold. He'd come back as a man-eating plant, and boy, was he mad!

"*Iffs smee,*" the ghost moaned again.

In my defense, I gotta say I tried to stay calm. Ghosts ain't necessarily bad: they're just *different,* that's all. It probably hurts their feelin's—or whatever goes for feelin's in ghosts—that we carry on so much whenever they appear. Still, I couldn't help myself. My eyes bugged out, my mind went blank, and the only command my legs recognized was, *Get the hell outta here.* Yet, the idea of rushing past that thing and letting it touch me brought cold sweat to my skin. I'd rather jump from this bell tower than let that happen; I crept to the side of the belfry, but saw how that was suicide. I groaned, feeling dizzy, and clutched the rail.

Arnold's ghost had lost me for a moment and stood silent, stooping then straightening, clutching the air. My dizzy groan changed everything. It hopped in my direction, coming fully in the moonlight for the first time. There was a blank where it shoulda had a face—no eyes, no nose, just a bubble of pulsing white where a mouth should have been. I knew in that moment that all my sins had come to get me. "*Hoop mee,*" it begged.

I found my voice again. "Don't hurt me, Arnold. I can't help you. I'm sorry, but you're dead."

"*No'm not, I'mlivvf,*" it replied. Then it leaped—or maybe

tripped—clutching for balance with those awful arms. It grabbed my shirt, and as it did I shrieked in fright and struck out with my hands. *"Doanleeffmee, iffs smee, Awnoo!"* it wailed, the voice filling the belfry. I was screaming with it, and Burma, too. I tore loose and bolted past Burma, who was fast at my heels.

We rushed down the stairs, through the church, out the door. We ran through the graveyard where the rain splashed and fell. *"Peas, peas, doanleeffmee!"* it cried from the high tower.

But we wailed like banshees as the moon lit our cold, blue path through the trees.

It's Rainin' All over the World

I WASN'T DIGGIN' a grave for *nobody's* husband, and I said as much as we rolled to a stop before Sallie's home. Hers was a two-story frame house, pleasant enough in the twilight, with flaking white paint, kelly green trim, and some missin' shingles. Give it a touch-up and take out the corpse, and you're talkin' all-American. "You'll do what I say, missy," said the homeowner, patience wearin' thin. She waved the gun to make her point. I was growin' mighty tired of people and their firearms: give a *dog* a gun in this damn country, and the hound'd think he was superior.

But just as soon as Sallie threw open the front door, it was evident all wasn't picture perfect inside. As I steered Cole to the parlor and tucked him in a Scotch plaid love seat, she grabbed a pair of hooked sticks from the closet and ordered me to follow. She bounded up the stairs, then paused at a door near the head of the landing to take a listen. Was that a feeble scratchin' from inside? She twisted the knob, and a blue black abomination tumbled at her feet. "Sallieeee," it moaned, "I knew you'd come back."

"Aww, shoot!" she yelped. "Why aren't you dead?"

I stared at the weird room from which Earl Goodnight had emerged. Snake cages lined its walls, the serpents nosing the glass; in the very back, two cages had fallen from their shelves and shattered on the floor. Earl's shirt was ripped open at the collar, and underneath I saw that his right arm and shoulder had swelled tight with blood. Worse, the side of his neck had turned to black jelly. "What did you *do* to him?" I gasped.

"Snakebite, whatta you think?" she replied.

I stepped back, scared to get a similar dose. In the space between the busted cages, two rattlers climbed each other, the upper two-thirds of their bodies raised impossibly high. "Combat dance," Sallie said. The two were so absorbed in their fight that they paid us no mind. She waited till gravity made 'em topple, then pinned each head with a hook and told me to set an empty cage nearby. As I reached for one, Earl grabbed my feet, mistaking me for his wife. All ankles probably looked the same from his angle, but just the same I screamed.

"You came back . . . I knew you loved me!" he moaned as I kicked free.

"Earl, stop it, you're gonna get us killed!" Sallie said. I set down the cage and dragged Earl from the room as ordered, grateful to get out of there. He flopped sideways as I set him up, his eyes rolling in his head. He'd certainly seen better days. His hair was coal black and flecked with silver; his tanned face was creased with smile lines. He was every girl's vision of the perfect daddy, tall and lean with large knobby hands able to fix anything—except, of course, the venom that puffed him up like a balloon.

Just then a crash came from the snake room and Sallie scrambled out, slamming the door behind her. A moment later, something big and angry hit the wood. "They ain't happy," she said, breathing heavily. "We're not openin' *that* door again." She slid down the wall beside me and Earl, and I asked what was the deal with his wounds. Rattlesnake venom was nothin' more than highly evolved spit, she answered, which meant digestion started the minute it entered the blood. Earl was being turned into meat-flavored soup. "Eeew!" I cried, glad I hadn't eaten in a while.

But how was he still alive? She didn't know, she admitted. Anyone else would've kicked the bucket long ago. A single bite can kill a normal 200-pound adult in an hour without help, but maybe Earl'd been bit so much over the years that he'd built up resistance and it took him longer to die. No matter what he'd done, his fate was cruel. Beads of sweat dotted his forehead and he mumbled nonsense sounds. I asked how she could let him suffer, and she said turnabout was fair play. "After all, he tried to do the same to me."

Snakebite had been Earl's chosen door to paradise, she reminded me. This morning, as he'd dragged her in that room, she realized he saw her as an extension: When it was his time to meet his Maker, it was also hers. Couldn't leave loose ends laying 'round. She screamed he was crazy, but he didn't hear a thing. They'd stick their hands in a cage together, he gloried as he lifted the lid. In a fit of panic, she threw herself against him; he smashed against the glass and the rattler lunged, striking him under the jaw. That cage pitched against its neighbor, and both crashed to the floor. Sallie ran from the room and locked the door from outside; Earl was still screaming as she packed her bag. Only when she slid behind the wheel of his truck did she realize the keys were in his pocket. She began her predawn hike up the mountain rather than stay another instant in that hell.

When she quit talkin', she pulled back his eyelids and listened to his labored breathing. "He's nearly dead already. It won't be long."

We carried Earl between us down the stairs, leaving him on a couch across from Cole, beneath a painting of a mountain stream. The room felt more like a shrine than a parlor, honoring someone's vision of family values. A Slim Whitman record was propped against the phonograph; next to it, Tennessee

Ernie Ford sang America's favorite hymns. The room was paneled in knotty pine; stuffed calico cats were propped on the
chairs. They watched me with their bright fabric eyes. A framed
photo of Earl and Sallie at Niagara Falls smiled from the mantel.
She saw me staring at it. "Love's a trap," she said.

"Just 'cause you and Earl failed don't mean everyone will."

She disappeared into a bathroom, then came out with
alcohol and bandages. She knelt beside my gypsy and dabbed
gently with a cotton swab at the torn skin of his wound. "I
think the failure's in us at birth," Sallie said. "We love each
new man with a kind of madness . . . maybe the *idea* of love is
what snares us, not the man." Cole hissed in pain as the
alcohol stung his wound; Sallie placed a cold rag over his
brow. "Ever notice how love songs are the most romantic part
of romance, and how it's a particular song you later associate
with each new love? Maybe that's why Elvis is so big. My mama
once said she was the same with Frank Sinatra; the newspapers
called girls like her 'The Bobby Sox Brigade.' History repeats
itself, and no one seems to notice but singers. They learn the
secret why all the girls scream. Maybe that's why men have ruled
the world so long at our expense. They've learned the way to
get inside our dreams."

"You sound like my mother," I said.

Sallie looked in my face and laughed. "You're as guilty as
anyone," she said. "The way you tell it, all you dreamed about
was gettin' carried off by an outlaw. Now the outlaw's come,
but he keeps gettin' shot or knocked out, so you carry *him*."
Cole's head drooped sideways in fever. A thread of saliva tied
his lip to the upholstery.

Sallie sighed and said we couldn't waste more time. She told
me to empty Earl's clothes from their bedroom and burn 'em
outside. "That way it'll look like he moved out instead of
gettin' buried somewhere nearby."

The bedroom was also a shrine to domestic bliss . . . maybe
even more than the front room. Two framed wishing wells hung
above their pillows. Quilts and a comforter with a bear-paw

pattern covered every inch of their bed. Their framed marriage certificate hung by the door. In the closet was a set of luggage just like the carpetbag that held all our money. I grabbed Earl's clothes off the hangers, dumped 'em in a laundry basket, got distracted, and walked over to the bedroom window. Storm clouds were piling in the north and west; I tested the casement and it lifted easy. I could be gone before she knew it, but that would leave Cole behind. So far, Sallie hadn't proved real merciful to men.

I carried the clothes outside and past a fenced-off area with dirt mounds and tilted headstones: the loggers' graveplot she'd mentioned earlier. The names on the stones were eaten away by weather, and it was obvious no one had visited 'em in a while. I entered the equipment hut where Sallie said I'd find the firepit; I piled some logs and sticks into a small pyre, grabbed a can of gas and some matches, and *Fwoof!* the flames leaped high. I fed Earl's clothes to the fire.

Job done, I watched a bubble of resin grow and break at one end of a burning log. There was a sizzling-bacon sound, then a knot of black ants spilled from the hole. Poor things, they'd built their nest inside. Some fell into the coals, spitting like grease when they hit. Others climbed to the top, but they were surrounded by the blaze. A flame licked out, followed by a snap and a hiss, leaving a smudge where an ant had been. More flames darted out like serpent tongues. Finally, only three ants were left. They writhed together, their legs curling up, one by one.

I'd been gone thirty minutes, and the sky was deep blue. To the south, stars twinkled through a rent in the clouds; to the north, lightning leaped and played. The sky looked strange, the clouds pilin' up to resemble a huge hornets' nest. There'd be no leaving here tonight, even if Earl had already given up the ghost and we buried him lickety-split. Once that storm broke, the one road in and out of camp would turn to mud.

We'd best batten down the hatches for the wild night ahead. But when I approached the house, I heard arguing. I opened the door. Cole was still asleep, his face half in darkness, half in the pumpkin-colored glow of the fireplace. The carpetbag with the cash was at the foot of the love seat where he lay. Sallie bent before the fire and fed in another stick; Earl stared at his wife, eyes glistening like beetles. "Jezebel!" he groaned.

I walked into the room. "That girl I mentioned is back," Sallie taunted. "She burned all your clothes, Earl, including your seersucker suit. How can you save people's souls without your seersucker suit?" Earl thrashed his arms like a new breed of octopus. That wore him out. His head fell sideways and he snored like Cole.

"He's one tough son-of-a-bitch, I'll give him that," Sallie said. "Anyone else would've been dead by now." I told her of the comin' storm and she seemed resigned to spending the night. If there was no gettin' out, at least no one would be comin' either, she said. She said to get some rest in their bedroom while she kept watch over Earl and doctored Cole. Plus stayed with the money, though that was left unsaid.

I fell on her bed, the mattress poofing around me like a taffeta cloud. I felt tireder than I realized. My muscles softened under the warm quilts, and I ran my fingers along their nap. There was a warm and dizzy feeling, like I sank in honey, then Cole crawled in beside me, I don't know how. Our clothes had vanished and the soles of my feet were up against his shins. *Mmmm,* I said. A sweet smell poured from me and I pressed back. There was a crack outside, and I woke to the real world.

Whoa, mama, my dreams were turnin' into a regular porno show. I looked out beneath the covers, wondering if anyone had seen or heard. There was just the rain drumming against the window, the blue lightning flashing off and on. I cuddled deep beneath the covers and drifted away again. Soon I was walking south, a lightness in my chest, silver spots dancing in the air. The distant sky was lit up red. I walked till the plain dropped into an abyss, where a red yellow light burned at the bottom. I saw movement near the light, an endless line of dots that crawled up the cliff toward me. As they marched closer, I could finally make them out: shiny metal ants with tiny clacking jaws. Their feelers jerked with excitement when they spotted me. They poured over the lip and I pushed them back, but they slipped between my fingers, biting my arms and hands, chewing into the skin.

I snapped awake again, and goggled 'round, confused. An iron gray light streamed through the window: I'd slept through the night, yet the cloud cover was thick and I couldn't tell the time of day. Heavy drops of rain rolled down the glass, collecting others in their path and pooling at the bottom. It must've rained all night: By now the road in and out would be nothin' but a soft slick of mud.

Outside, I heard shouts and screams. "Don't try it, Earl!" Sallie raved. I rushed from the room and saw her glowering at the bottom of the stairs. Earl was sprawled near the top, panting as he hauled himself up another step. It seemed impossible he could still be alive. His hair stuck flat to his head as though painted with a brush; his eyes were dark pits of smoldering coals. The side of his neck and face wobbled like grape jelly. He held the gun.

"Put it down, Earl," Sallie coaxed, trying to sound calm. Her foot was on the lowest step. "You're half-dead anyway. Why make it hard on everyone?"

"I should've shot you while you slept," he groaned.

She took a step up. "I mean it, quit playin' around."

"What happened to us?" he cried, his voice raspy.

"Nothing happened till you tried to kill me!"

He tried to raise the gun in one hand but was too weak, so balanced it in two. "I offered you salvation and you rejected it."

"Bein' bitten by snakes is some kind of *favor?*"

"There are snakes *everywhere*," he said. "What does it matter their form? Snakes rule the world, Sallie, devourin' the earth as we speak. After that, they'll devour themselves. That mine above us is just another serpent, snakin' down the hill. That's what you'll get if you stay among the living, Sallie. Bit and buried. Better to come with me than stay among the damned."

Sallie climbed another two steps. "Give it up, Earl," she said. "The faithful departed long ago. I'm not a believer no more." A tear ran down Earl's cheek and he stared at the gun as if willing it to move. When that didn't work, he aimed it at Sallie. He wrapped two fingers about the trigger and tried his best to squeeze.

Sallie leaped across the remaining space with a curse, face white with rage. She pried the gun from his hand, then grabbed his shirt and dragged him down the stairs. "Come with me," she hissed to me. "We're ending this right now."

I trailed them out the door. The rain came down like gully-whumpers, everything blanketed by sheets of water, the clouds overhead laced tight as steel wool. The camp was one big river of mud flowing downhill. Sallie ordered me to grab the shovel from Arnold's truck; mud channeled 'round Earl's body as she drug him along. Water sluiced down my hair and into my eyes. The ground squelched beneath my feet. It'd rained so hard, the river was nearly up to the sawmill. I saw tree trunks and stumps rolling in its current; big chunks of earth split from the bank and plunged in. This was flood weather, the kind that takes out anything downstream. But what scared me most was the thought that if this camp was sliding toward the river, what about that glacier of rock and mine waste above?

I yelled as much to Sallie as we reached the forlorn grave-yard. She yelled back that she'd seen worse, so quit bein' a baby and dig.

"Do *what?*" I cried.

"Dig! *Dig!* I'm tired of waiting anymore!"

I dropped the shovel. "You mean bury him alive?"

"Exactly. Pick that thing back up."

"Pick it up yourself!" I shouted above the rain.

She started screamin', as crazy by now as the man she meant to plant in the ground like a bulb. "You'll dig his grave or I'll bury the two of you together," she shrieked, pointing the gun at me.

"I won't do it," I shouted back, trying to look dignified in the rain.

"Goddamn it to hell," she roared, "I've had it with everyone telling me what they will and will not do!" She fired off a shot and mud splashed on my shins. "Now *dig*, you little idiot, before I really get mad!"

I dug like a sexton, all my shreds of dignity turned to pudding in the rain. Clay sucked at the shovel; water filled the place of mud. I'd gone down a foot before remembering the buried lumberjacks: I swallowed hard and tried not to think of such things. I hit something hard and a lump stuck in my throat. Another bite with the shovel and a hand flopped onto my foot, tiny white bones peeking through its skin.

I was outta there, screamin' bloody murder as I leaped from the grave. Sallie stared at the hand and even she grew pale. "Okay," she conceded, "dig over there instead."

I leaned into the shovel, skin crawling as if covered with grubs. I went down fast, the soaked clay easy to dig, though half of it was on me. I got down four feet when once again the shovel scraped on something and the yellow dome of a skull popped from the mud like a jack-in-the-box. "I can't do this!" I bawled.

Even Sallie was cowed. "How many loggers did they bury out here?" she said. "Dig to the side, over by the railing, and we'll plant Earl there."

I dug awhile, then looked around and asked, "Where *is* Earl?"

He was gone, all right, crawled off as we unearthed the dear departed, but he wasn't hard to find. His snail's trail led downhill. I had to admire the man's persistence, if not his speed. Here he was, half-digested and delirious from rattler venom, and *still* he fought on. We found him crumpled in a heap against the back wall of the equipment shed, more a pile of rags than a man. "Can't we just leave him?" I pleaded, but for Sallie his attempted escape was the last straw. She grabbed his feet and dragged him back, raging as if the venom had soaked through Earl's skin into her own. She stopped beside the grave and laid her gun on its lip; she flipped her husband into the hole. Water was already halfway to the top, and mud flowed in upon him from every side. Sallie thrust the shovel at me and said to finish up. "I cain't, it's murder," I panted. I flung the spade away.

Her eyes flamed holy homicide—from her look, I figured I was one dead Dahlia Jean. It seemed I rubbed everyone the wrong way. But even as I thought it, it dawned on us both that Sallie didn't have the gun. She looked around wildly—it'd disappeared from where she'd laid it by the grave. That part of the lip had collapsed on Earl. A dark gleam of metal peeked out beside his shoulder, then was covered by mud. She shrieked with all the pent-up hatred of the past two days, grabbed the shovel, and swung it at me. I barely jumped back, feeling the blade slice above my head. She looked from me to the grave, uncertain who to finish first, but Earl was scrambling to get out, and she hated him worst of all. She punched the blade into the shrinking mound of mud and rock, and tossed it down on Earl. He screeched in panic and his arms shot up, reaching for a hold. She dumped another spadeful in his face; his screams turned to gurgles. She laughed as she tossed in dirt, a high, piercing laugh like wind in the treetops; maybe that's why she didn't see his hand reach out till it clamped 'round her ankle. Her laughter stopped and her mouth formed an O of surprise. Earl pulled. The wall caved in beneath her. She fell into the hole with Earl.

There was an explosion of shrieks and splashes that I'll remember till the day I die. The sounds were like the beasts or worse, a concentration of animal sounds. Sallie screamed for help; Earl got on top somehow and pinned her down. His head came over the edge, a grinning skull more terrible than the one I'd discovered. Her hand came up and pulled him down.

The mud caved in. There were a few feeble splashes. Then no more.

I crawled to what remained of the lip and peered over, half-sure I'd get dragged down, too. But there was nothing to fear.

Earl lay unmoving, facedown, body over Sallie's. She stared over his shoulder, eyes dulling quickly, mouth opened in a scream filled with mud.

I fell back and trembled—for how long, I have no idea. The sky cracked like whips and the rain rushed down. When I looked back, the two were nearly buried, just her arm sticking up, so I struggled to my feet and added a few more scoops till I realized how stupid that was. It would all wash into the river soon. I threw aside the shovel and limped back to the house, covered in grime. All I could think was that I had to get clean. I had to get that grave off'n me. I went to the bathroom, but there was no more running water . . . maybe the pipes had washed out—I didn't know. I peeled off my clothes, walked out back and let the rain wash me off, then wrapped myself in a comforter from Earl and Sallie's bed.

I went out front and Cole's eyes were open, the color returned to his cheeks. He peered about, confused by his surroundings, asking what he'd missed. My teeth chattered like a windup skull's as I sank beside him on the love seat. "I'll tell you later," I said.

When we woke it was night and the rain hadn't stopped, but we sprung awake from a voice outside. *Come and join us,* it said, the voice of the tempter. *Let's end this running.*

Cole and I stared at each other, knowing that voice far too well.

When the Rooster Crows

WE RAN FROM the church with the ghost of Frog Boy screamin' bloody murder till we couldn't run no more. Without a doubt, this was the worst patch of luck I'd had in my entire fifty-six years. I'd lost my car and money . . . shot my son, a junkyard dog, a sheriff, and Harson Whitley . . . somehow got messed up with three crazy females . . . and now *ghosts* were after me. In my panic, I'd bolted from the church without the pistol or even the slim pickin's from the Muscovy bank. My skin was nicked by brambles and my clothes shredded by briars. It occurred to me that maybe we'd never get off this mountain. Maybe we'd die up here—cold, wet, and lost—and nobody'd know what happened till some hunter stumbled on our bones years from now.

In the past I woulda said, *Things can't get no worse,* but I'd said that already and they *had* gotten worse. See if I said that again!

"Where are we?" Burma finally said.

I considered our surroundings. We'd stopped in a stand of hemlocks, their green boughs laced high overhead. The cover kept out the rain, but allowed in a silver, scriptural glow. The pine needles at my feet were wove into a soft brown carpet. There was a brief rustle, and I saw an owl glide between the trunks.

"I have no idea where we are," I said. "But it's dry and warm, and no crazy women are takin' potshots at me or ghosts screamin' for my head. Until it's daylight and I can see my way a little better, it's fine with me."

That's where we stayed. In a minute, exhaustion finally caught up, and I fell down a hole into a place of dreams. It looked like here. I pushed through the weave of hemlock and found the girl just as I'd left her, in her simple dress and saddle oxfords, 'cept now she was dead. She'd gotten lost like me. Her hands were palm up, head sunk on her chest, eyes picked clean by birds. The skin of her face was dried and stretched tight, but her hair was long and thick as always, which was how I recognized her. "Where's my money?" I asked, but she wasn't sayin', and a few black ants crawled from the corner of her mouth for answer. She deserved this if anyone did, but I felt a little sad and wasn't sure why. Maybe 'cause I hadn't had a hand in her end. I touched her gray skin and it felt like dry leather. I pushed harder and my finger poked through. She fell over, and when I grabbed for her leg, it cracked off at the knee.

I started laughing then, something in me cracking, too. I threw away her leg and grabbed her hair. I swung the skull in a long arc against a hemlock; it disintegrated in a puff of teeth and dust. What a pleasant thing. *This* is what the chase came down to, nothing supernatural at all. I *whooped* and heard the echo of my voice, then danced a two-step on her saddle shoes.

A hand came down the rabbit hole and shook me awake. "You were dreamin'," Burma said. "Actually, you were movin' your feet and laughin'. You always carry on that way?"

"I feel rested now," is all I said.

It wasn't long before we sensed the glimmers of the iron gray dawn and heard a cock crow through the trees. A second answered him, and we headed their way. We came to a clearing planted with young fruit trees; two dozen tepees made of fence palings and roofing felt were spaced between them, each little hut about ten feet from its neighbor. A water bowl, feed cup, and metal stake was set in the entrance of each, and tethered to each stake was a bantam rooster.

The birds were everywhere, perched on roofs, pecking grass, straining at their neighbors. An old barn with a cinder-block addition stood beyond the tepees, while past that was a farmhouse with white paint peeling from its sides.

"What is all this?" Burma asked.

I looked at her, rememberin' how she was a town girl and wouldn't know this world. "Fighting chickens," I said. "Game-cocks. Not a bad bunch, either, from what I see."

"They're raised to fight each other? That's awful!"

Just like a woman, I mused. "There's a lot crueler things in life than cockfighting."

"Yeah, but getting born to die while others watch . . . it don't seem right."

"It happens to us all," I said. "It's just a matter of how and when. Would you rather be a hen shut in a yard and forced to lay for a year, and then a farmer eats you? A fryer who lives six weeks before he gets the same? Or would you rather be a gamecock that gets two years of life minimum, before you go in the pit—and if you survive *that,* get kept for breeding and your owner loves you like a prize hound?"

"How is it you know so much?"

"I've dabbled," I said.

We were well among the tepees now, and the roosters weren't the least bit afraid. One crowed as we passed, which got the others going; some preened and strutted, while others cocked their heads and looked us in the eye. These were good birds, full of grit and fight, not a scrawny one among 'em—blue, gray, black, and scarlet, with fire red eyes and bright lemon beaks and legs. This was the end of molting season, when birds normally looked sickly, as old feathers dropped and green feathers took their place, but these birds were already in fighting trim. Several pure strains were scattered among the huts—Roundheads, Whitehackles, and Arkansas Travelers—while the results of their cross-breeding were staked closer to the barn. This breeder preferred hybrids with small heads and big breasts, built like walking footballs. Whoever he was, he didn't deal in flash—just birds that took and dealt out punishment, an honorable goal.

I was still admiring the handiwork when a young guy same age as Cole stepped from the barn carrying a shotgun. He was short and wiry; his blue eyes took our measure; his red hair stood up like a comb. He sized us up, the shotgun cradled comfortably, finger on the trigger guard. "What can I do for you?" he said.

"We're lost," Burma blurted. "We was in the woods all night."

He considered us calmly. "How I know you ain't spies for Edmond Klingge?"

"Who's that?" Burma answered, but I knew the name. Anyone who knew anything about gamecocks did. A gambler and millionaire, Edmond G. W. Klingge was one of that Texas bunch that came to dominate the sport over the last few years. Most started as racehorse men with entries in the Kentucky Derby or at Hot Springs, but they diversified, flying anywhere a good hack

Joe Jackson

was promised, their roosters in padded coops and well-paid handlers by their sides. Klingge had won world championships in Orlando three times running; his birds fought in Central America and the Philippines, where it was said they heeled with short, deadly knives. He bragged he'd fly to Hell for a good pitting; it fired his blood to think he was part of man's oldest sport, now banned in almost every state, a trend he considered antihistorical, he once said. There were dark rumors about him, too—hints of cash payments to the Klan and other "citizens' " groups fighting civil rights. But Edmond Klingge kept such business secret, and the rumors were never proved. "Don't take offense," I said, "but why would a man like Klingge come here?"

"To fight Pumpkinhead."

That was all he said, but it was enough. Maybe I'd been out of the sport awhile, but I still knew the breed. Cockfighters were an inbred bunch, plugged into the latest killer or newest bloodline. Young as he was, this boy had bred a money bird. Word spreads fast, and made it to the Texas men. For them, such a fight meant something different. For the boy, a winning hack with a Texas millionaire meant a fast ticket out of Tennessee and on to better things.

"What's your name, boy?" I asked him.

"J. Wesley Biggers."

"Should I know it?"

"Not yet, mister, but maybe someday."

I grinned, taking a shine to this boy. "When's the hack?" I asked. This afternoon, he said, however long it took Klingge to fly into Knoxville and hire a limo.

So there were a few hours left before the fans showed up, and I saw a way out of our fix, cruel as it might be. I told young Mr. Biggers that although we weren't spies for Edmond Klingge, he'd probably wish we were. "We're the two who robbed the bank and shot the sheriff," I said, and the boy's pale face told me all I needed to know. "Your publicity-shy Mr. Klingge hears that two fugitives showed up, he'll fly back to Texas before he even touches down."

"W-whatta you want?" he stammered. "I ain't got money— just these chickens."

All I want, I said, was fresh clothes, a gun, and a ride to the home of a woman named Sallie Goodnight. It sounded reasonable to me, but the boy grew even paler. "Mister, I know the way, but gittin' there takes time. Klingge'll show up long before we could get there and back."

I thought about it and looked at his birds. Call me charitable, but I said after the fight would do. Besides, I'd like to see the famous Mr. Klingge up close, too. The boy smiled, the color returning to his face. He didn't care if we was outlaws— all he cared about was pitting his bird against a millionaire's.

He led us to the house, so relieved that he couldn't stop jabbering. A state trooper had dropped by last night with our description, he said—the two of us were wanted all over East Tennessee. The trooper swore he'd like to get a piece of us hisself. That's the way of the Law, protecting no one so much as its own.

The boy's home was obviously the lair of a chicken man. On the wall hung a painting of a red-and-black Asil, the jungle chicken thought to be the granddaddy of all bantam roosters. Spread on the table were copies of Wortham's Rules, conditioning manuals, and back issues of *Grit and Steel*. Scattered by these were spools of waxed nylon string, old gaffs, and a whetstone. By the sink the boy had stacked bottles of granulated liver, dextrose tablets and vitamin K to coagulate the blood; there was soda, sulfur, and carbolic acid to wipe out lice, Worm-X, Terramycin, and other modern wonders for pip, gapes, canker, bumblefoot, and scaly leg. The biggest jar contained turpentine, the chicken man's cure-all: a feather dipped in turpentine and swabbed on a sick bird's throat would cure most anything. If not, it was probably time to take the bird out back and dig a hole. "You live alone, Wesley?" Burma asked as he handed us clothes from an overstuffed cabinet. He said he preferred J. Wesley, if she didn't mind. "Comes from my father," he said.

"Where are your parents?"

"Ma was always sickly and caught somethin' from breathin' in the chickenshit. Pop felt guilty when she passed and . . . well . . . committed suicide. These are his clothes."

"Who looks after you?"

"I look after myself, ma'am."

Damn, but the boy was an orphan. Burma glanced from the boy to me and shot me a look like I'd gone and kicked a puppy. To tell the truth, I did feel a bit ashamed. Lordin' it over a motherless child is a low-down thing to do. Here was a boy so starved for company that he was kind to a coupla crooks, and the only thing he asked in return was that his precious fight not be disturbed. Out here, alone in the mountains, he'd turned himself into a kind of chicken prodigy, yet even at the moment when all those years of lonely work turned on a few deadly seconds in a killing pit, he was suggestin' to Burma that she put on his father's clothes and tuck her hair up under his hat so she wouldn't be recognized. Word was out about a man and woman, but no one would notice two more gamecock fans. After he gave us a bite to eat, I asked to see this famous bird of his. His face got bright and he led me to the barn.

It was a place of wonder, and I knew then and there the boy was a natural. Why couldn't my own son be gifted this way? J. Wesley led me 'round the place, explainin' how his daddy turned the barn into a pit and taught him the basics of cross-breeding. It was his daddy who installed wooden bleachers along one side and a circle of waist-high fence palings in the center: the floor of the circle was sawdust and hard red clay. The boy had drawn fresh lines in chalk: a long one in the middle and, three feet away, two shorter lines where the birds faced off. A single bulb dangled overhead by a cord; a card table by the entrance was where J. Wesley collected the $3 entry fee. This was his legacy, he said proudly—the barn and the birds. He'd build on it till he was the most famous birdman in the mountains, and make his daddy proud.

It got me all choked up, such devotion to a dead man's

dream. I didn't even *want* to think about Cole and what he'd done to mine. "What's this?" I asked before he saw me all teary-eyed. I pointed to a machine in the corner where a rubber sheet was stretched tight with a level underneath to make it jerk up and down. "My own invention," he said. "You drop a bird on it and he uses his legs and wings all at once, kinda like a bouncin' treadmill." Next to that was a conditioning cage, floor covered with fine-ground oyster shells for lime and ground charcoal for digestion. Pumpkinhead stood inside, glaring at us with shining yellow eyes. He fluffed his feathers as we drew near. The bird was orange as a ripe pumpkin, his tail stickin' out straight like a pheasant's. J. Wesley reached in the cage and picked him up gently. I noticed right off how the bird's legs and feet hung straight down. Birds whose legs hang out of line with the rest of the body are called dry-heeled, which means they can't hit straight, but this one's hung straight as a ruler and he probably flew high when released. He was of medium height, not too tall or short, with a heavy breast and a long-enough reach to reel in the other bird. His head was small and comb trimmed back to prevent another bird's latchin' on. Birds like this got under people's skin, least 'round here. They were fighters, often doomed to an early grave, but if they fought hard and were smart and lucky, sometimes they beat the odds. If not, at least they went out game.

"He looks ready, all right," I said. J. Wesley blew gently on the rooster's head and the bird made a velvety clucking. I dropped a grain of corn I'd been fooling with and the bird's eyes followed it all the way down. Alert, too. He was three-quarters Roundhead, and I nodded to myself in recognition, Roundheads bein' one of the smartest breeds. I asked what he'd fed this rooster last, and the boy said beefsteak for protein and apples to clean his pipes. Considerin' the pickings in his kitchen, I figured this bird's diet was better than the boy's.

I asked the bird's age. "Nearly three," J. Wesley said. Like I figured, nearly midcareer, but when I asked how many fights, he said ten and I whistled in surprise. Most owners fought their birds twice a season, and a bad-cut bird could heal for six months or more. Was he tryin' to kill his prize rooster, I wondered aloud. He just grinned even wider and said as often as not Pumpkinhead got on top first and gaffed the other bird under both wings. Next to a gaff to the brain, which was dumb luck, a stab under the wings was lethal. He'd bred a champ, all right, but the fly in the ointment was that he'd gone sweet on his bird. Owners who did that made mistakes. I watched J. Wesley stroke the bird and wondered what the afternoon would see.

The first spectators arrived before noon. They were locals and J. Wesley greeted them at the barn door. The biggest had his bill cap pulled back and a brown paper bag in his hand. "No gate today, Buddy, but you'll have to leave the bottle outside," J. Wesley said. The bigger man's smile was lazy and loose, but his eyes held a mean glitter as he asked what was a chicken fight without stimulant, huh? J. Wesley shook his head like he was used to this and stepped casually inside the bigger man's reach. "Now, Buddy," he said, "this is an important fight. You wander out back and finish that bottle while comparin' my roosters to your'n, but no drinking in here."

One of the big man's friends patted his shoulder. "J. Wesley's right. Let's take it outside."

I was impressed. The boy could keep his head. Others drifted in, about twenty men all told. They sat in the bleachers, made side bets, talked among themselves. The place had the easy, informal feel of like-minded men who'd known each other all their lives. Burma stayed out of sight in the house—*uninterested in murder*, she'd sniped outside J. Wesley's hearing—which made me the only stranger there. But J. Wesley introduced me as a family friend and the locals nodded politely. We talked bantam roosters. If they had any suspicions, they didn't let on.

The sprinkle outside heightened to a deluge, then slowed to a drizzle again. 'Round 1:00 P.M., a white limo with smoked glass rolled to a quiet stop outside the door. All heads swiveled—none of the locals had ever seen such a thing. A man in doe-colored livery hopped from behind the wheel and opened the passenger door. A hand plump as a baby's appeared on top, gold ring on the pinkie. A pair of rhino-skin cowboy boots appeared next, and Edmond Klingge stood up. He rubbed his manicured hands together. "Well, it took some doing but we made it," he said.

Edmond G. W. Klingge liked everyone to know he'd arrived in more ways than one. He wore a wide-brimmed white hat with a gold medallion on the crown, the metal embossed with the head of a crowing rooster. He wore gold rings on his index fingers and pinkies, a brushed suede jacket, brushed denim pants, tooled leather belt with a shiny gold buckle, and mirrored sunglasses with gold rims. He snapped these off, revealing ice blue eyes. They swept the property, passing quickly over the farmhouse till settling on the yard filled with gamecocks. A lean man with parted black hair stepped from the other side of the car, carrying a steel traveling coop. "Damn ugly day for a fight," Klingge announced. "Where's this famous Pumpkinhead?"

J. Wesley stepped forward, hand extended. Klingge, a six footer, looked down and scowled. "Why, you're just a kid! Where's your daddy?"

"I'm eighteen, Mr. Klingge," the boy said calmly. "If I'm old enough to get drafted, I'm old enough to fight chickens, I guess."

"Don't talk to me of fighting, I was in the Big One, boy!" he roared. The Texan seemed a little young for that to me, but money does strange things to a man's sense of worth, includin' his memory. He turned to the man with the cage and snapped, "Nobody told me I was pitting against a baby." This dark-haired fellow shrugged like he was used to such behavior and said they didn't normally ask an opponent's age. During all this, the driver opened the trunk and pulled out a brushed leather case. He carried it flat, like a silver serving tray. "This better be worth it," Klingge groused, slamming the door. "I got important business waiting in Newport, matters of national import, you hear?" He breezed past J. Wesley, whose hand was still extended; the black-haired man, who I figured as his handler, walked up and shook it instead. "Pay him no attention," he muttered. "I've heard good things about you and your bird."

Up to that point, I really hadn't cared who won this hack, but now I did. Maybe the kid was too green to know better, but I'd seen this kind of act before. It was a common prison trick; all big talk and bluster to scare your opponent and stay the cock of the walk, at least in your cell block or pod. Edmond Klingge was living up to his reputation, all right: a little rooster with a big ego. As the boy followed the driver and handler, and I followed them, Klingge strode around the barn. He touched his hat to a pair of breeders he'd apparently met before; they nodded back, unsmiling. "This place sure isn't Theresa Square Gardens," he crowed at the boy. "Ever hear of Theresa Square Gardens? It's a marble palace in the Philippines devoted entirely to gamecocks. Reclining seats, air conditioning, the pit itself behind glass. That's the way to do it. Then there's this. I guess it takes all kinds."

The boy shrank inside himself. His father's legacy obviously couldn't compare.

"But even that's nothing compared to Latin America," Klingge went on. "Those bastards are *crazy* for blood down there. The more blood the better, and the bigger the bet, the bigger a man's *cojones*. You know what *cojones* are, don't you, boy? Yours even dropped yet, huh? Once in Guatemala I dropped $47,000 on one single fight. That's more than the entire GNP of some of those goddamned little countries. That's big *cojones*, I'll have you know. I had to grin and bear it, too, though I cussed a blue streak when I got home."

Forty-seven thousand was more than this boy would see in his life. Me too, unless I got my money back. "Quit it," I said. We were standing in front of Pumpkinhead's cage when I said it and Klingge wheeled 'round to look me in the eye. "And who are you?" he asked, intrigued.

"Someone who's been 'round long enough to know a line of bull," I said.

Klingge smiled slowly. "Well, well, a ringer," he muttered, and looked me up and down. "Not a very pretty one, though." He turned back to Pumpkinhead, and the little rooster ruffled his feathers. "And this is the famous rooster. Strictly for the barbecue, you ask me. You want a game chicken, take a peek at Widow Maker there."

We turned 'round. The handler entered the pit and opened the traveling coop—out strutted a red-and-gold rooster with a ruffle 'round its neck like fox fur. This looked a faster chicken than Pumpkinhead, leaner in breast, longer in leg. Maybe a little older, which meant more experience with the gaff. Widow Maker strutted 'round the pit like he owned it, then returned to the handler when he held out his hands.

"How much you want to bet?" Edmond Klingge crooned.

The boy had expected this. "I got a thousand saved," he said.

Klingge hooted with laughter. "A thousand? That's chicken feed. You think I came out here for pure beauty? Let's make life interesting and up it to five."

The boy blanched like an almond. "I ain't got that much," he said.

"You have those chickens out back."

"That would wipe me out."

"Why play the game if you aren't willing to bet everything?"

"In that case," I corrected, "five thousand means nothin' to you."

Klingge studied me again, more interested than before. He smiled. "You're right, old man, whatever or whoever you are. I came all this way, I ought to make it interesting. Every man has his price. Name yours, boy."

J. Wesley thought hard a moment, then spoke. "You hire me as assistant to your handler and take me all those places you bragged about. Give me the chance to make it big."

The smirk on Klingge's lips now turned pure mean. "High stakes, then," he said. "At least for you. You might find that, either way, I win." He crooked his finger at the driver, who unlatched the leather case. Inside were small squares of chamois with holes cut in the center, a spool of waxed string, and two sets of murderous-looking spurs.

"Short slashers," he explained. "The Guatemalan kind. Just an inch and a quarter long but a hand-forged steel that's sharp as a razor and has a point like a stiletto. You know what that is, boy, a stiletto? It's the long knives royalty used to assassinate their friends."

J. Wesley plucked the slashers from the case, his face growing hard. He knew he couldn't back out since he'd just set the terms; I couldn't help but think of wagers with the devil. He needed help if anyone did, and I remembered an old trick of my own. I told the boy I'd retrieve his gaff pads and string and hurried to the house, where I grabbed an orange from the icebox. Burma asked what was up; I told her and she mused I'd taken a shine to the boy. I didn't like unfair fights, was all. She smiled, unconvinced, and I hurried back to the barn.

By now the locals' bets were startin' to fly. Most wagerin' at cockfights is done by finger—one finger for one or ten dollars, depending on the stakes, five fingers for five or fifty, clenched and opened fists for multiples. The bets were getting into the hundreds, most in favor of Klingge. J. Wesley sat on his side of the pit like an island, pretending he didn't notice. I stepped before him, my back to the crowd, and told him to pay attention, then dug a hole in the orange with a pocketknife and held the fruit to Pumpkinhead. The bird smelled the juice; when he started to peck, I grabbed his bill, pushed it down to the bottom of the orange, then pulled it back out. The boy looked at me uncertainly.

"Old trick," I said. "Your bird's been without water all day, and now he gits a slight taste of that juice—but no more. It drives him nuts—makes him so mad, he's ready to kill anything."

The boy smiled, regaining confidence. He asked if I'd help with the gaffs, and I coached him like a ringside manager: "Don't get worried, you know your stuff, you just ain't been 'round Klingge's nasty kinda game." It was like I was young again. J. Wesley held out Pumpkinhead's leg and I cleaned his spur stump with alcohol, then fitted the chamois pad tight over the stub. I slipped the metal socket of a slasher over the stump, tying it low and outside with the wax string. I took the bird's toe and moved it to see how the muscle moved. Satisfied, I did the same with the other heel.

"You think we got a chance?" he asked.

"I don't know." I glanced back at Klingge. The millionaire had already tied on the slashers and lighted a cigarette; he held the bird with his left hand and blew smoke at Widow Maker's head. It was another old trick: blowing tobacco smoke also riled a bird. Widow Maker shook his comb and clucked angrily as Klingge blew another cloud.

I turned to the boy and said the odds looked even to me. Pumpkinhead had weight, but Klingge's bird had a longer reach and more experience. "We'll just have to see."

Klingge's handler was made referee. I didn't like it, but knew it was a nod to the trouble Klingge'd took to get here. Balking only owned up to fear. The handler seemed honest, but a ref's job was the most important in a cockfight and he'd keep who buttered his bread in the back of his mind. Klingge would handle Widow Maker while J. Wesley handled Pumpkinhead. They walked to the center of the pit so the ref could examine the birds' heels. Some folks took offense at this, but to me the final check was insurance: Once a fight started, a spur couldn't be replaced. It was also a check that you hadn't honed your gaff, a forfeit, not that it mattered much with this Latin steel. The ref stepped back, satisfied. "This is an extra hack," he said, a formality since everyone knew the season didn't officially start till Thanksgiving. "Thirty-minute time limit or a kill, gentlemen?" Klingge and the boy nodded. "Okay, bill your birds."

The two walked to the center of the pit and faced the birds

bill-to-bill. For the first time, Pumpkinhead saw the intruder in his domain. His eyes glowed fire. Klingge and J. Wesley stood at arm's length and thrust the birds together, then did it again. Pumpkinhead caught the taller bird's comb in his beak and twisted till Klingge ripped him loose. The golden bird was furious, squirming so bad Klingge had a hard time keeping hold. A couple of spectators laughed. "Let's get on with it," Klingge snapped, annoyed.

"Get ready, then," his employee said.

The two squatted down and faced the birds on the short lines, holding them by the tails and watching for the signal to let go. "Pit 'em," the referee said. Both birds came out at once, flying straight up and slamming together in midair. Their feet shot out before they hit, each spurring the other in the breast, then they fell in a flurry of feathers. They tried to pull free, but the gaffs were sunk deep, so they rolled on the ground and pecked at one another's head.

"Handle," the referee said.

J. Wesley and Klingge lunged for their birds. They separated them and returned to the lines. Klingge seemed shocked by Pumpkinhead's speed and looked worried. A spot of blood showed on Widow Maker's breast. Pumpkinhead was just mad.

"Pit 'em," the referee called.

I noticed that this time Klingge watched his handler's lips; he let go of Widow Maker a second before the words came out. The bird flew across the pit, gaffs glittering, before the boy let go. One gaff stuck under Pumpkinhead's wing, the other into J. Wesley's hand, right above the thumb. The boy yelped and leapt up, tearing the slasher from his bird's breast as he did. The gaff and Widow Maker dangled from his hand. Klingge stayed silent, merely smiling as he watched J. Wesley pull out the slasher. Blood spurted with it. I called for time.

The referee said we had thirty seconds. J. Wesley whispered he couldn't feel his thumb.

This was bad. The bird was doomed if released again so slow. I told him to let me handle Pumpkinhead, and told the ref of the change. He stopped the clock, glancing to his boss. This was where the paycheck mattered. Klingge looked at me and seemed a little edgy. "I don't know, the same handler usually starts and ends a fight," he said.

"We could cry foul for jumpin' the call," I reminded him. "Seems the two equal out." Some spectators called how that seemed fair.

The ref glanced at the crowd and said it was fine by him, if fine by all. Klingge scowled, but agreed. The referee checked his stopwatch and said fifteen seconds remained.

I looked Pumpkinhead over, standing him on his feet while I blocked his view of the other bird. He seemed steady enough, but listed a little on the side where he'd been hit. I picked him up and saw blood under the orange feathers. The original wound was bad enough, and the boy only made it worse when he tore the blade out sideways.

"Time," the referee said.

I turned around and reminded Klingge that if he jumped the gun again, he'd automatically lose. Klingge raised his eyes at the ref, who said uncomfortably, "That's the rules, Mr. Klingge." The millionaire looked at me, the easy smile gone. "Pit 'em!" the referee cried.

We let go together, but this time Widow Maker's height made the difference and he landed on top when the two collided in midair. His spurs sank into Pumpkinhead's breast; the birds fell and came apart, then launched up again. Their legs cut and slashed so quick you saw nothing but a blur. Pumpkinhead hit the ground first and rocked back on his tail, hooking up. Widow Maker landed on the slashers and got hung. "Handle!" the referee cried.

I ran over and picked up the two birds. It was Klingge's place to pry the steel from his bird, but as I lifted, I twisted just a tiny bit, evening the odds. Klingge took the bird from me, uncertain what he'd seen, but his face still growing scarlet. I just smiled.

Both roosters were matted with blood, and I saw now that

the tear in Pumpkinhead's chest had punctured a lung. A bubble of blood rose and fell from his bill with each breath; I smoothed his feathers and blew on his head to cool him down. J. Wesley appeared beside me, pressing a blood-soaked towel to his hand. He moaned when he saw his bird's condition, knowing he'd as good as killed his champion. I heard a rattle with each breath, which meant the bird had a clot but couldn't sling it. I put his head in my mouth and sucked in, hoping to loosen the clot this way.

"Time!" the referee said. Both birds were weak, so we set them at the centerline. The ref cried to pit 'em, and they rose together, yet Widow Maker again got the height, a blur of steel and feathers as he came down. Pumpkinhead tried to rise up but was weak from his wound; Widow Maker landed on his back, driving in both spurs.

The orange bird twisted free, kicking up and out and snapping Widow Maker's wing. A cheer rose from the spectators, but the movement left him open, and Klingge's bird nearly severed his leg. Pumpkinhead fell sideways; Widow Maker shuffled in, driving home one steel needle, then dragging Pumpkinhead across the floor.

"Handle," the referee cried.

I pulled the gaff out straight and took Pumpkinhead back to our side. The bird could barely hold up his head. "I think he's had it, kid," I said. Moaning softly, J. Wesley took the orange bird in his arms. He smoothed its feathers, wiping away the blood. He parted the feathers near its vent and blew to cool him off. The bird fluttered and straightened its neck. The referee called the time.

I put Pumpkinhead on the line, wondering if animals knew when they were doomed. Or, like people, did they fool themselves to the very end? "Pit your birds," called the ref, and Widow Maker rose a couple inches, beating his wings as hard as he could. That was still more than Pumpkinhead could manage. He pushed off on the ruined leg and flopped over, exposing his neck and side. Widow Maker came down with both gaffs as

Pumpkinhead thrust up with his beak, and one of the gaffs entered his brain. He trembled and fell still. Widow Maker jabbed at his skull and poked out an eye.

"Take him off!" the kid screamed.

No one said a word. Klingge caught Widow Maker and took off its slashers. J. Wesley did the same gently, handing them to Klingge. He turned away, cradling the bird. The men in the bleachers paid their bets and left. One of the men who'd nodded to Klingge patted J. Wesley on the shoulder, then walked out the door.

"What a fight!" Klingge cried. "I doubt my bird'll survive, either, he's cut up so bad." He gazed at J. Wesley, who still hadn't looked up. "Kid, it's a mistake to get sweet on something—don't you know that? Everything that lives is just a piece of meat." It struck me how this was something I would say, which didn't make me feel too good.

Klingge said he'd arrange to collect on his bet. "I won't welsh on you," J. Wesley replied.

"I know you won't, kid." Klingge glanced at the boy one last time, then shrugged and left the barn, followed by his driver and handler. The engine started, then receded into the distance. The boy smoothed the limp feathers, staring at the empty pit. I listened to the rain outside.

———◦———

"We gotta do something for him," Burma told me.

"We ain't a damn charity," I replied.

Still, as I stood on the porch and watched J. Wesley drag a shovel behind the barn to dig a grave for his hopes, I felt touched the same way. No matter how hard you try or how long you struggle, the rich and powerful always seem to win. For everyone else there was false hope, and that, too, disappeared.

So I followed the kid behind the barn. He leaned on his shovel, a hole at his feet, a shoebox in the hole. The rain dripped in a thin line off his cap. His eyes were fixed on the tepees. None of the chickens were out, huddled beneath their pitched roofs, as if in mourning, too.

"I guess you're ready to go," he said. "There's a couple of slickers you can have. I don't need 'em no more."

I asked what he had planned. Thunder rolled in the distance. "I'll pay the man," he said.

"And then?"

He shrugged. "I'll get a job somewhere, I guess. Gotta keep the farm."

So I sighed and done as Burma asked me. What else could I do? I told him *why* we wanted to find Sallie Goodnight. I offered him a couple thousand—maybe more, maybe lots more—if he got us to her. He could recoup his losses and start again.

His smile was tired, but at least he smiled. "You'd do that for me?"

I scraped my toe in the muddy gravel. "Don't get me wrong," I stuttered. "It was the woman's idea."

We crept down the mountain at a slug's pace, rain drumming on the roof of his daddy's black sedan. J. Wesley steered by feel alone, brooding the entire way. As it grew dark, the fat clouds looked impaled on the treetops, they were so low. Our headlights barely pierced the rain. The only real light was blue lightning. I wondered if it would've been wiser to wait for day.

I'd barely finished that thought when J. Wesley pulled his car beside poor Arnold's beat-up truck. "We're here," he said.

I got out my side of the car and looked around. A drearier place I'd never seen. Prison would be an improvement. The old logging camp was little more'n a wreck, while above it a massive slag drift from the strip mine angled its way toward it down the mountainside. The ground had turned to gruel that flowed downslope, while at the bottom the river crept high. We were parked in front of the main house; one light burned inside, in what I guessed was the front room. The door knocker was shaped like the Praying Hands. To the side of the house and down the hill a little was a fenced-off area, like a garden or something. Just inside I could see something weird poking from the ground.

I pulled my slicker tight around me and reached back in the car, grabbing J. Wesley's shotgun from the backseat. I was tempted to barge in then and there and get it over with, but remembered how that Goodnight woman was handy with a pistol. I cupped my hands to my mouth. "Cole, it's your daddy. The river's rising and you'll be flooded if you don't come out. Let's end all this silliness now!"

We listened, but there was nothing but the endless patter of rain. Lightning lit the yard around us and J. Wesley walked over to the fence where the strange shape stuck from the mud. "Maybe they're not home," Burma said.

"Where else could they be?" I yelled through the rain. "Arnold's truck is here, so it's not like they're on a joyride. Your voice carries farther—maybe you should try."

"Dahlia, it's your mama," Burma pitched in. "It's all been a big misunderstanding, honey. We'll talk things out, I promise. Everything'll be fine."

I watched the boy as she was talking. He touched whatever it was that stuck up, then recoiled in horror and scrambled back. After a second's hesitation, he crawled forward and started scoopin' up handfuls of mud.

"Is that woman with you, Dahlia?" Burma continued. "Don't listen to her; she's not your friend. Just throw out that gun and we'll make up. We'll make things like they were!"

"I didn't like things to begin with!" the girl shouted from inside the house. "Go 'way! Leave us alone!"

Burma's eyes glowed like fireworks, but for once she held her tongue. "You don't mean that, baby. That's just Harson's money talkin'. Nobody needs to be greedy. There's plenty to go around!"

"You lied to me about your legs, Mama," the girl yelled

back. "You made me your slave. Why should I listen? If we give up, you'n that booger with you will just enslave us worse. Either that, or kill us dead."

Booger? I'd booger *her* once she was in my hands.

"Mama, I ain't goin' back to Wattles," that damn girl continued. "I ain't basin' my life on no more of your lies!"

"*Lies?*" Burma screamed. "You're callin' me a *liar?*" She was losing it again—her green eyes bugged from her head. "You dare call me that, you little tramp, while I put up for years with you 'n' your daddy and the only thanks I got was desertion? You think you can take that $100,000 and leave your mama to *rot?* I know exactly where you're headed, and if you think I'll let you hand that money over to your no-'count daddy, you don't know me so well!"

The girl yelled back that she'd hand the whole fortune over to Daddy and spit in our face while she done it if we didn't let them be.

"Gimme that gun!" Burma screamed, but I was ready this time. I held her off and made soothing sounds. "You know this ain't helpin'," I cooed.

There was another second of silence, broken this time by Cole. "Pa!" he cried from inside. "Dahlia and me have talked it over and we'll split the money fifty-fifty with you. Fifty thousand's more'n enough for anyone. Dahlia found some luggage in a closet, so we'll divide the money half-and-half between two identical carpetbags. We'll place the bag with your half right outside the door. You and Dahlia's mother take it and do what you want. Just leave us alone!"

I yelled how that made no sense. "Cole," I said, "you're actin' pussy-whipped, but I forgive you anyway."

"No need to be crude," Burma said.

This sure was getting nowhere. The real question, however, was where that Goodnight woman was lurkin'. She was the one I really feared. But then J. Wesley ran up, his eyes and mouth dark circles, and said the woman and her husband were dead, buried together in a shallow grave. I smiled. That changed everything. Only Cole and the dark-haired meddler were inside.

But that raised another question: That Goodnight woman and her hubby sure hadn't buried themselves. Cole probably hadn't done it, either, since I'd shot him. That left the girl.

For the first time, I seriously considered this waitress from hell. Could Harson Whitley be right? Could Dahlia Jean Coker be more than a match for me? Horseshit, I said. Still, a host of "what if's" entered my mind. What if the girl did more than bury those two and helped Wife and Hubby off this mortal coil? What if she was like me . . . a killer . . . just younger and sneakier? She didn't look the part, but women can surprise you. I'd underestimated her once, and look what happened. It was best to be cautious this time.

I asked J. Wesley if there was a back way into the house, and he said there was. I turned to tell Burma, but she was poundin' on the door. "You get out here and talk sense to your mama!" she demanded.

"Talk sense?" the girl cried back. "I'm not the one hitched up with a killer."

What is it with mothers and daughters? Even when they get along, they don't get along. Burma turned and told me to break down the door, but I said I hoped to bring a little reality to the situation. I planned to go through the back, instead.

That was easier said than done. J. Wesley and me sneaked 'round back, but the door was locked, so I busted out a window and the boy crawled through. He flipped the latch and I entered a dark kitchen, dimly lit from the hall. There were pots, pans, a wooden block of knives, not all of its slots filled. No telling how the girl had armed herself. I peeked toward the front. I could see the edge of the front door and could hear Burma yelling through it, but I couldn't see the girl. Where was she? Maybe we'd got lucky and she hadn't heard us over the wind and rain and her screaming mama. Our best chance was surprise.

We charged down the hall and 'round the corner, yelling at

the top of our lungs. But no one was there. There came a sound from above and a pan zipped past, catching J. Wesley in the shoulder and knocking him sideways. He slumped against the wall as the girl laughed overhead. "You think I'm stupid, you old fart? You may fool my mama, but you didn't fool me!"

She stood at the top of the stairs, holding a Dutch oven over her head. I ducked 'round the corner as she pitched it at me. It hit the door with a *blang!*, leavin' a deep dent in the wood. That could've been my skull. She reached by her feet and hoisted a stewpot. J. Wesley shook his head, tryin' to gather his wits, as I drug him outta range. The stewpot flew through the air and crashed out the window. I peeked back 'round the corner and the girl stood watching, bread knife in one hand. Cole was farther back on the landing, shoulder bandaged, moving slow. Both held carpetbags, like they'd said. They'd divided the money, just like they promised, but nobody divided my money without my say! I stepped out and flipped the lock to let Burma in, then turned back and warned Cole that this was his last chance. "I want my money and I want it now!"

"It ain't yours to want," the girl shot back, meeting my gaze. Like mother, like daughter—two peas from the same pod. Dreaming of revenge, I took a step up the stairs.

Now several things happened at once, and each was confusin' as hell. J. Wesley shoved past me and ran up the steps. The girl backed off slowly, wavin' the knife. She stopped when she reached Cole, who knelt by a door and fumbled at the lock. "Gimme that money," J. Wesley demanded. "It's all the future I got!"

The girl sliced the air between them with her knife. "Stay back!" she warned him. "This ain't your fight. I don't want to hurt you, and there's worse things than this knife behind this door."

What a sorry bluff *that* was. I mean, I could come up with better threats with my tongue tied back and only half a brain. I raised the shotgun to my shoulder and lined her in my sights, but Cole and J. Wesley were too close. I yelled for them to stand aside. Even as I said it, a strange, low rumble came from up the mountainside. I'd heard such a sound before and my trigger finger froze. Burma peeked outside and screamed.

It was a flash flood, a big one by the sound of it, bringing along the spoil from the mine. I looked out the door and saw a squirming wall of mud and rocks—the front of the wall plowed through the thin border of trees at the top of the clearing and rolled our way. I slammed the door, grabbed Burma's hand, and headed up the stairs. Too late . . . the mudslide hit us like a ramrod and knocked us to our knees. A tree trunk plowed through the door; then the house lurched back and the wall caved in. We crawled upstairs as the first floor filled with mud, water, stone, and the remains of poor Arnold's truck—I thought for an instant that now his ghost would really be mad. The stairs started to buck and we hung to the rail. The house itself seemed to lift from its footing and roll sideways, kind of like a fun-house barrel 'cept fun houses don't throw boards and glass at you and this wasn't fun. We clawed to the top of the landing and rolled against the back as the house slammed against something that seemed to stop our slide. I heard a groan like metal, then remembered the Quonset hut behind the house; I gave a prayer of thanks, then saw a muddy wave leap up the stairs at us and knew I'd prayed too soon. This landing wasn't high enough . . . we'd have to make it to the roof for any hope to survive. I pointed up to Burma and she nodded; I tried to warn J. Wesley, but he was lungin' for the girl. She tottered back, knife flying from her hand as he grabbed the bag from her arms. "I got it!" he cried, exultant: He'd lost all hope and then regained it, all in the space of a day. Funny how things work. He smiled and stepped toward me.

Then the metal hut gave way.

The house jerked and tumbled, and as it did, the door beside the boy burst wide. Something flew from it that appeared to *wriggle* in midair. J. Wesley screamed as the girl covered her face with her hands. I had a quick image of fangs

. . . of the boy's white throat . . . of glass cages tumbling through space. . . . Then he pitched against the railing and the whole thing broke free. I watched in shock as J. Wesley clutched the money bag to his chest and fell backward in space, then was engulfed by the flood before even havin' time to scream.

Then it was our turn. The house hit the river with a wrench and crumbled like bread dough, walls caving 'round us, roof ripping off and pitching away. I saw the night sky through the rent; the girl grabbed Cole's hand and climbed. "This way!" I cried, but even as I said it, Burma's eyes widened in warning. She tried to pull me back—too late. Something hit me behind the ear and there was white light and water. Then no more.

Maybe it was minutes later, maybe days—I wasn't sure. I came to, amazed that I still lived. The rolling had stopped and the last wall of the house had vanished. We'd crashed against the bank and gotten hung up, Burma said. She pulled me up the bank, then knelt among a pile of boards and cradled me in her lap. I listened to the roar of the water and heartless rush of the rain.

Our kids? I asked, my voice thin and distant.

They made it to the roof and last she saw, were floating downriver, she said.

J. Wesley?

Tears cut channels through the grime on her cheeks. She simply shook her head.

Part II

The South Will Rise Again

Down a Lazy River

WE FLUSHED DOWN the mountain as if from a toilet, Cole and me straddling the roof and holding for dear life as the current whirled and swirled. Mother Nature was in a bitchy mood. Lightning flashed and I saw the other half of the house ram the bank and crumble. I was certain nothing could live through that, and I cried out Mama's name. I lost my hold as I did so and slid toward the water, but Cole reacted in the same instant, hooking me by the elbows. He winced from the pain of his wound, yet held on tight as the current spun us away forever from Sallie Goodnight's dreams.

We sped like Casey Jones, outta control and no choice but hang on. I remembered the childhood game of setting a bug on a leaf and dropping it in a creek; I'd always wondered what it thought as it dipped and floated away. Now I knew—and wisht I'd been kinder to animals. Now I was the bug. Soon the current calmed enough for me to inch back up the roof till I was face-to-face with Cole. He held the bag of money beneath his chest—the only one left, now that its twin with half our money had gone down with that boy. I wondered if our folks had somehow saved themselves and asked Cole what he thought. "I don't know," he said, but his eyes were sad.

We floated that way awhile, the question of our folks hanging between us like a wall. My thoughts were like ball bearings, rolling in crazy ways. I recalled an Indian tale of how the Flood was the last gush of blood of a dying god, then remembered how Daddy said lightning was when angels peeped at themselves in mirrors and thunder the sound of their vanity. Rain of this intensity was not really weather—it was more like a spiritual condition, signs of sin and violence that overflowed a fallen world. In the brief breaks in the rain, I could see that what had once been ridges were now the riverbanks—folks called out above us to see who it was that'd survived. Sinatra's song 'bout nighttime strangers was ruined forever for me now. The silky darkness rolled back a smidgen; the mountain's bulk was lined against the sky. If my geography was correct, we'd drift till we hit the French Broad River, and that'd take us near the town of Newport, though arrival times were a mystery. High on a ridge hung a neon cross, electric blue, and I wondered how many lost souls like us would see it tonight. It was like we lived in some weird Roy Acuff tune.

I asked Cole who he thought the boy that grabbed the money from me might've been. "Just some poor fool Pop talked into doing his dirty work," Cole answered. "I know how that feels."

I could tell he was feeling cranky over gettin' beat up, half-drowned, and shot, so I grabbed him 'neath the shoulders and said to get some sleep, I wouldn't let go. He scootched the money bag toward me and I settled it under my breastbone. It was softer now than when all filled up, almost like down.

I thought again about that boy. All my life I knew I'd see his face as the snakes shot across the landing at him and he screamed and crashed through the railing into the flood. What was it he'd said just a second earlier? He called the cash "the only future I got," then looked so happy when he grabbed it from me, like all his problems were solved. Then the horror came . . . and he was gone without a trace, like he'd never existed at all.

He was too much like me for comfort, and the $50,000 cushion beneath my breast felt a little less cozy than a second earlier. Me and that boy were flesh 'n blood examples of how nothing ever goes as planned. This trip was a good example. From Wattles in the state's northeastest tippy-tip to Georgia was supposed to be two days' driving, yet two days had already passed and we'd barely made a hundred miles. What started as a flight to better things had turned into some weird Tennessee death trip brandin' anyone who hitched a ride.

My thoughts rolled on some more. I recalled a hill behind our house where Mama and me took long walks after Daddy fled. She walked with no purpose and one day we found a cemetery, one of those forgotten plots that was all that remained of a family that once farmed the cove. Many of the gravestones were speckled green and white with lichen and wort, and worn faceless with years. Some were still readable and I saw how many were infants: stillborn or allowed a few minutes of life before they passed on. The next-biggest bunch was little children, dead before five. Epidemics did it, Mama told me: diphtheria, cholera, smallpox wiping out whole families. It was a cruelty greater than death to take the young before the old and upend the natural order. I found a stone better preserved than its neighbors and read the inscription: "Turn ye to the stronghold, ye prisoners of hope." Mama laughed the strangest laugh and said what a hateful country this was.

Then something happened I always carried with me. A shaft of light pierced the leaves above us and crossed her face, and suddenly she told me the way it was in these hills. Tales of mad old men who wandered the forest, of old women who threw themselves off cliffs, of mothers who fed their children to rivers so disease couldn't claim 'em, of fathers who swallowed powders meant for the tobacco worm. Maybe there's a curse on this place, Mama wondered aloud, passing her hand slowly across the coarse stone. Though in punishment for what stain or sin, nobody ever learned. Maybe people did know once, but the memory was wiped from existence long ago. "Life here is like an insane asylum," she said. "We're bein' punished, but we don't know what for. The preachers call it Eve and Adam's fault, but everybody knows that's a crock'a bull. The only way to stay alive is to get away."

"Let's go, Mama," I said. "You're scarin' me." I grabbed her hand and led her away.

She was gone now and me and Cole had escaped, but in the strangest way. We bobbed down the wine-dark river like in the gospel tunes. Dark objects floated 'round us, some faster'n us, some slower: I looked down at Cole, still asleep, and thought how Mama said all love was doomed. I thought of Sallie, how she insisted there was no such thing as love. What if they were both right and love was just an itch in search of a name? An itch in the blood and nerve that grew tormentin' till someone came to scratch it. Someone like Cole. Maybe I was the same for him, soft in the right places, sweet as an overripe plum. But given a change of circumstance, it could be anyone: Begonia June instead of Dahlia Jean, as if names meant nothing anyway, since deep inside was all red meat and twitching nerve. What I'd called romance was merely meat on meat, and who can get excited kissin' steak, even if it is sirloin?

Even worse thoughts got dredged up by the flood. What if love was even less complicated than that, and just a misfire of the nerves? Like that dead frog in Biology class when the current hit and its leg twitched and I barfed on poor Mr. Potter, the teacher. Maybe what upset me most was not the shock of the dead come to life, but the thought that life boiled down to heaves and pulses like any moist machine. This is a good example of stimulus-response, said Mr. Potter, wipin' at his shirt. Ring a bell and a dog salivates. Zap a frog and Dahlia vomits. Scratch an itch and we fall in love.

So we drifted with the flood. Cole dozed . . . maybe I dozed a little, too. I dreamed I was on a raft like old Huck Finn who I'd read about in English, except my journey was longer since I floated down the Tennessee till it met the Ohio, then joined the Mississippi and beyond that the all-consumin' sea. Problem was, Huck was just a fella in a book and I was a sixteen-year-old idjut-waitress who'd seen four different deaths in only two days. A girl can get a wee bit nervous exposed to such upheaval; not that I was ever the most cheerful person, but I wondered if

I'd feel quite so trustin' of life again. I mean, at the moment we drifted kind of peaceful, but just as easy this river might decide to give a sudden hiccup and me and Cole would join the same fatal club as Harson, Sallie, her husband Earl, and the mystery boy. See if something like that would happen in a book . . . just flip the page and *oops, sorry folks, the story's over, better watch TV*. I don't think so, thank you. When you think about it, what did the author of Huck Finn know 'bout the rules of life and death? What do writers ever know?

Came a dawn that held no light, just a lessening of dark to gray. The channel opened wider and I realized the flood was greater than I'd dreamed. I'd thought we'd ride this wall of water till it petered out, but now the torrent swelled in all its fullness and became an endless, rushing wave. I'd learned in school how a bathtub of water weighed three-quarters of a ton, and how an inch of rain falling 1,000 feet and draining one square mile had the energy of three atom bombs. Those boys at Oak Ridge oughtta rethink their careers. The water 'round us filled every low spot, and ruin fanned out on all sides. We passed a floating raft of livestock: bloated cows, their legs stickin' straight as a table's; dead stallions bobbin' up and down. We were safe enough in the main current, but close to shore the debris piled up, grinding everything in a kind of mill. I saw a line of people sitting on a green hillside, watching the water pass; white goats grazed 'round them, like the world of humans was an irritating dream. The spectators stood when they saw us and waved. I waved back, bein' sociable. They hopped up and down. They sure seemed pleased to see us, I thought. Did they think this was a honeymoon cruise? A man put his hand to his mouth, but he was too far off and I cupped my ear. He ran close to the water and made a sweeping gesture, as if warning us to steer clear. How exactly was I supposed to do that? It wasn't like this was a boat and we had a rudder. "What's that fool want?" I asked, nudging Cole awake.

Cole studied him a minute and answered, "I think he's warnin' us things are gonna get nasty."

Sure enough, they did. The river curved and we sailed for a sunken farm, its roofs and silo breaking the surface to form a trap. A mass of debris was already hung in the ruins. A frame house, top story intact, had drifted into it, and on the roof rode an older man and two blond girls my age, dressed in matching flannel nightgowns, identical twins. A father and his daughters, helpless passengers like us in the flood. They were surrounded by other floating ruins that bashed against the sides of their house and threatened to crack it like an egg. They were close to the bank, but not close enough to jump; a huge willow overhung the water near them and two would-be rescuers had climbed its branches to snag the house with long poles. A crowd at the base of the trunk shouted encouragement and commands. The castaways on the roof watched as one rescuer jabbed for purchase but nearly lost his balance; their raft began to pull away and all grew frantic; the father lunged for the pole and grabbed it, but this jerked it from his savior's hands and he pitched headfirst into the flood. The would-be savior would've followed, too, if not grabbed from behind by his partner. The two girls panicked, sinking to their knees, screaming and begging those on the bank to save their father. The people on the hill skittered 'round like bugs sprayed with Raid. Another man separated from the group: he ran ahead and tossed a rope to the girls, but it fell short. A log reared beneath the eave of their roof with a huge grinding sound and pitched it up at an angle. The girls whirled their arms for balance, but no use—they plunged in the water and, like their father, disappeared.

A sickening silence draped about us, but not for long, for now it was our turn. We banged against a barn roof, the painted words SEE ROCK CITY peeking above the waves. The two girls' screaming faces popped from the water beside us for an instant, then disappeared again. Cole yelled in fright and pointed; I glanced up as a shadow eclipsed the sun. Out of the flood reared a hay wagon wrapped in barbed wire: It loomed overhead like some great sea beast breaching the surface and ready to lunge. Trapped in the wire was the twins' father, throat and chest pinned by its loops, just his right arm hangin' free. He was drowned, but his eyes were wide and staring; his arm jerked with each lurch of the wagon as if beckoning me to follow. Here was the stranger Mama always said would come for me, only the stranger was the Angel of Death and I froze in stone fear. The wagon crashed against our roof, levering us up—the Angel's hand brushed mine as if he was the bridegroom and I his bride. *Dahlia, take this ring,* but the idea was too horrible and I screamed, droppin' flat out of reach of his hand. His fingers swiped where I had been a moment earlier: more wreckage slammed against us, shooting me and my raft from the angel's touch like a bullet from a gun.

We sailed into the open water where the torrent calmed and slowed. We floated past the ruins of a small TVA dam—I realized we were in lake country, low farmland that had been flooded years earlier itself to form reservoirs. It was a sign we drew close to civilization; other signs followed soon. Billboards on the hills overhead urged us to buy hand-stitched pew cushions and eat Jimmy Dean Sausage each morning. A bridge had washed out, and below that the road had caved in; we drifted past a long, cool limo that had once been white but now was black with mud. I saw some silhouettes inside like people, but we were too far off to help and they weren't moving, anyhow. We passed an auto graveyard, half the cars submerged, the other half creeping up a steep hill. A tin-and-tarpaper shack sprouted from the top and a man stood in the door staring. I shifted the money bag and waved, but he didn't return the wave. Down farther an emerald knob of grass and clover rose from the water and atop that sat a mansion with tall white columns. A man on the porch ran to the waterside and snapped our picture. I cussed him roundly as the current pushed us on.

After a while I felt almost like a tourist as I watched the country unscroll. Our raft occasionally snagged on something unseen underwater; when that happened, the water sucked and gurgled at us till one end swung 'round the other and we lifted free. The sun was straight overhead when we nudged against a treetop poking from the surface and hung up awhile. It was peaceful sitting there. Cole mumbled himself awake and I asked him how his boo-boo felt; he laughed and said it felt better, though he'd never heard a gunshot wound called a "boo-boo" before. I filled in spaces in his memory from when he was delirious, then stretched myself beside him in the sun. "Was this a mistake?" I finally said.

"Going down this river? I can't say we had much choice."

"No, you know what I mean. The whole ball of wax. Everything."

He looked at me seriously, then smiled. "Funny time to doubt fate," he said. I grabbed his hand and asked if he thought we'd ditched his father. Surely no one could escape the way that house crumbled. But he wasn't convinced. "My old man's survived worse'n that," he said.

"That might mean Mama's still alive as well." But this was too confusin'—a dead Twitch meant freedom, but the death of my mother, while a live Twitch meant exactly the opposite. Which star did I wish on here? "Even if he is alive, he can't find us, can he? Not in all this mess. That would be impossible."

Cole stretched like a cat on the warm tiles. "I would've thought the same, but you saw how he tracked us to Muscovy, then to that logging camp, both in the middle of nowhere."

"But Cole, he can't follow us forever. That ain't human."

Cole shaded his eyes from the bright sun and rubbed gently at his bandage. "I always considered him more like a natural force than strictly human, kind of like this flood." He looked past me to the water and added, "Besides, he'd follow the river, and it goes only one way."

I stretched out beside him, wondering if this chase would ever end or whether I'd keep lookin' over my shoulder till the day I quit running for good. "It's not what I expected," I finally told him.

Cole snorted to himself. "I never know *what* to expect," he replied.

We were quiet then, peaceful even, watching the flood swirl by. After an hour or so, a dark spot appeared upstream of us, then that grew steadily till I could see it was a chestnut that'd been uprooted entirely, floating serenely our way. A girl was caught in its limbs, face and chest exposed above the water, flannel nightgown swirling 'round her waist like a cloud. Something seemed familiar and I stared harder. Sure enough, it was one of the drowned twins from before.

The strangest silence muffled me in its folds. The tree passed like a slow ship, the girl its lone passenger. She'd drift on forever through the waters of the world, a silent messenger that death took the most lovely and innocent without remorse: *Look on me and weep,* she said. One of the tree limbs scraped the edge of our raft as it passed, jarring us loose of our underwater snag. We followed down the river after it, the girl up front like a carved wooden prow.

Soon we hit a branch in the current; the chestnut angled into shallow water while Cole and me continued down the main channel. I looked back. As the tree lodged in a raft of logs and wreckage, the girl's body unwrapped gently from its limbs. She floated against the obstruction, arms held above her. The water frothed around her like chocolate malt, running up her cheek, ballooning gracefully 'round her hands and arms. I watched till we were out of sight, which mercifully didn't take long.

Only God and this river knew where we was headed, and by now I felt too unraveled to care. For a while thereafter I felt nothing but slow fatigue. The river widened farther; the banks transformed from cliffs to gentle slopes; in the distance I saw hills dotted with white—maybe a relief camp with food and shelter—but we were too far off for help of any kind. We passed white farmhouses jutting from the surface; a herd of fawn-colored Jerseys watched from an island that had once been a hill. Near them a man in a blue jacket steered his small boat beside the long roof of a chicken house, all his breeders no doubt drowned. Sunlight danced in his wake. We rocked gently.

"Look at that," Cole said. The far hills had drifted closer and on them I saw a white thread of road on which a dirty beige VW had pulled over, its driver leaning on the door, his eyes glued to our passage. He jumped in the car and took off, speeding to where it seemed we might land. I felt heavy-bodied, like the sun had sapped me of every last ounce of will. Our raft dragged beneath us like a train pulling to a stop after a long night's journey; a cow kneeling on the hillside turned her head to watch. Others hove in sight, chewing slowly—huge, stupid things. The roof pulled to a stop, small waves lapping against the gutters. I got to my feet and swayed for a minute, then stepped in the slime. Cole followed. The bottom sucked gently at our feet, unwilling to give us up, but we pulled free and walked over the hill, ignoring the cows.

Below us was a plain, and to the left the factory town. The flood had crept through it and down the valley, spreading its slow tendrils toward the horizon like some amoeba, magnified a million times. The water and land formed patches of brown and umber stretching to the blue horizon; the sun shone off massive sheets of water, their jagged edges cutting across the land. I could see tiny trails of dust marking the paths of rescuers who frantically rushed down the few remaining roads. Knots of men scrambled about, piling up sandbags at their edges. Cars sped toward each other then dropped outta sight. Ant people raced from place to place, but the water still broke through.

I couldn't take it in, not all at once. It all seemed a game played beneath the mountains, a strange theater staged for cruel gods. I shielded my eyes with my hand and heard a car engine gurgle behind us. A door slammed shut. "Are you two all right?" a voice cried.

I didn't answer. "Who are you?" Cole said.

"I'm a reporter for the Newport paper." He handed a picture

ID to Cole. "That's where you are, Newport . . . nobody who's floated out of these mountains seems to know where they are. I was over at the relief camp when I saw you. You drifted for the longest time, like, uh, the Ancient Mariner, if that means anything." Yes, I'd read it in English class, I said. He gazed at me quizzically and asked, "Where'd you come from, by the way?" 'Round Muscovy, I said.

"What's your name?"

I looked up at a sky as huge and empty as all understanding. His words barely came together in my brain. He wanted Cole's and my names, but what did names matter? We were no one and anyone. We'd risen from the flood and could start anew.

He asked our names again as he fiddled with a camera, a black, bulky box with knobs and shiny attachments whose proper use seemed to elude him. He'd noticed what I had not, that tears of relief, guilt, and sorrow were running down my cheeks. I must be crying, I thought, and with the realization started to quiver like a leaf. I should be dead after all this. Maybe I really was and this was just a dream.

"Great shot!" cried the reporter, pointing his camera at me. "I'll get you to the hospital once I get another! No, don't wipe away those tears! Look natural! For Christ's sake, don't move!"

Justice Is the Old Man's Middle Name

I LOST COUNT of the times that river tugged at our heels that night and tried to claim Burma and me. No tellin' how we survived. The rain kept up its *rat-tat-tat* in the trees above us, while the muddy water boiled like an unwatched pot. After crawlin' free of the crumblin' house, we rested in our vantage point and watched as whole sections of riverbank split off and fell into the water, as stands of trees crashed into the torrent and rafts of oak, ash, and wrecked houses slammed into the river bends. Me and Burma searched for J. Wesley and the money bag he'd grabbed from the girl and clutched to his chest, but both were gone, gone, *gone*. 'Round midnight the last remnants of Sallie Goodnight's house was swallowed up by the torrent; soon after, a yellow Caterpillar 'dozer from the strip mine glided down the hill on a slick of mud and oil. It plunged into the river, taking half the bank, too. I stared up where the camp had been, but nothing remained, swept off the face of the earth like it'd only been imagination.

"We gotta leave!" I yelled to Burma through the rain. "Who knows if that big power shovel or Muscovy itself won't be slidin' down the mountain soon!"

"Go where?" she shouted back.

"Downriver! After our kids!!"

It was the only way. My guess was that Cole and the girl were still kickin', though God knows survival was a gamble for everyone right now. Burma said she'd last seen 'em float off on the shattered roof; if they stayed in the main current, such a raft might hold up quite a ways. I'd heard of such rides before. Survivors floated miles downriver on barn roofs and telegraph poles during the Johnstown disaster; a doctor's son rode a barn door fifteen miles down the New River two years ago. If I knew that girl, she'd hold tight to the remaining bag of money and I wanted it back. Fifty thousand dollars might not be as spectacular as a hundred, but it wasn't nothin' to piss away.

We started walkin' down the river, seein' how our choices were limited. Trooping up the mountain would take forever, not to mention the angry army of cops waitin' at the top, while angling through the woods risked gettin' lost again. Still, it was a deadly business hanging too close to that bank; the river would rise in a heartbeat and try to pluck us off our feet, while other times the ground melted to a muddy soup and we skated downhill. After a while, we climbed away from the water and followed the sound of the flood.

It was a slow and tiring process, and I found it hard to tell our progress in the dark. After an hour I thought I saw a blue light, like a heavenly beacon, but when we steered toward it, it disappeared. Once or twice I thought I heard screams from the dark river below us, no doubt people sweeping past on roofs or logs and crying from the gloom. "Help us, God, please!" a man pleaded, till his voice grew thin with distance. Burma cried to herself. I felt sick inside.

Near dawn the rain slowed and we came to a two-lane road. This followed the path of the river, easing our way. The daylight made evident what doomsayers had warned about for years: Disaster like this was waiting, but no one had paid heed. It was obvious that more coves than just the logging camp's had spilled their innards. This was a disaster that would touch most of East Tennessee. Walnut-colored water filled every low space, churning like dirty laundry, the banks stripped of soil to the bedrock, trees ripped up by their roots and scraped clean of their bark and leaves. The odor of green wood hung everywhere, like I'd stuck my head in a bag of shavings and breathed deeply.

'Round seven o'clock or so, a panel truck puttered down the road behind us and pulled beside us; an old man with a strawberry birthmark on his pate was drivin', and he offered us a ride. He could take us as far as the nearest village, a place downriver called Del Rio, where he'd heard rescue workers had gathered in hope of finding survivors. He lived on a bluff above the river and all night long had heard the cries and wails of those carried in the flood. "It was the most terrible thing I think I heard in all my life," he told us. "They sounded just like ghosts."

"They probably are by now," I said.

The ruin worsened the lower down the mountain road we traveled; though the highest water had subsided from the river, it left behind huge tangles of trees and mud. Arms and legs stuck from these tangles, as if even in death those trapped inside were clawin' to get free. The flood rejoiced in adding shame to slaughter: bodies floatin' in the eddies were stripped naked, their clothes drippin' from the branches above. We rounded a bend in the road and saw below us a young girl laying in the shallows, her arm wrenched backward at an unnatural angle, nearly from its socket. She pointed back up the mountain, as if to warn everyone to run. Onlookers parked on the ridges and gawped. Overhead, a jet etched peaceful lines in a sky now almost free of clouds.

By midmorning we reached Del Rio, or what was left of it. Rubble and the foundations of ten homes and a general store were all that were left, while ribbons of oil from ruptured heating tanks drifted like black lace between the ruins. A lone electrical pole stuck up from the water, a woman's body draped across one crosstree. A flat-bottomed boat puttered toward her, the rescuers too late to do any good. Beyond this, we passed the ruins of a stone bridge, the mounds of rock and logs a testament to where the flood had dammed momentarily, then smashed on through. Wrecked cars and trucks were lodged in this rubble, their roofs crushed in. A huge pile of the wreckage that had settled in a curve downstream was dotted with rescuers wearing surgical masks. The old man stopped his truck and let us out. "This is as far as I go," he told us. "I knew people in this town. I owe it to 'em to do what I can."

Burma and me approached the giant mound of wreckage, sprinkled with rescue workers. They picked through it slowly, stone by stone, some holding bloodhounds to sniff out survivors; the smell hit us as we approached, a sweet black-jelly feast for flies. One rescuer waved us off. "Get back, there might be disease," he cried. "It's not safe here."

"Anyone seen a teenage boy and girl float by on a roof?" I asked.

The man's laugh was sour. "There were plenty of people on plenty of roofs, buddy," he said. "But they were voices in the night. All we're finding now are the dead."

"It's my daughter," Burma added.

The man looked uncomfortable. "I'm sorry, ma'am. You have to go downstream to the relief center in Newport. They're the only ones who'd know."

We continued to walk downriver on the road. Soon we were on a deserted stretch, no cars or people, the rescuers not yet makin' it this far. In the distance I saw a sandbank and piled upon that what looked like a mound of black rags. Two turkey buzzards spread their wings and flapped off, then the black rags straightened and a white face turned. This scarecrow studied us a moment then ran into the trees, leaving behind it a lifeless form. We walked up. It was the body of a woman, one shoe on, one shoe off, ring finger severed where her wedding band had been.

I gazed at the forest, sure we were bein' watched. "What frightened him?" Burma asked.

I pointed to the woman's fingers, then her earlobes which had also been sliced off. "Quickest way to get the jewelry," I said.

Burma's eyes grew wide in horror; she spun 'round as though the ghoul might sneak up, then opened her mouth to speak and couldn't—probably a first for her. I warned her to expect worse: People who lost everything thought of little else but how to survive.

"But that ain't *human!*" cried Burma.

"It's *very* human," I disagreed.

We kept going, picking our way slowly till we came to a place where our road ran too close to the river and had collapsed into the flood. Lodged in the rock and slabs of tarmac, I saw a snapped-off axle and wheel; nearby lay a radiator grill. A few more yards and we saw the car itself, oozing with mud, its roof and hood nearly flattened. Its front end slanted down into the river and water boiled around it; ugly balls of yellow foam paused briefly in their course, then swept on. Its back half was snared in a basket of roots; the whole thing dipped and bobbed in the current. Something sure seemed familiar about this. Both back doors were open and I saw someone's arm hanging out. When I looked closer, I recognized the passenger.

It was Edmond Klingge. His driver, too, hands at ten and two, head pancaked between the roof and wheel. There was no sign of Klingge's handler or Widow Maker, and I figured they'd been sucked downstream. Gone was Klingge's wide-brimmed hat, brushed suede jacket, and mirrored shades; his shirt was pulled out and a jagged point of rib poked through the skin. He still wore the rhino boots, but the right one and the foot inside it stuck out at a right angle. Klingge's water-soaked skin swelled white 'round the rings on his fingers; he was damned lucky not to've lost 'em yet, like the woman upstream. It was only a matter of time till the local ghoul arrived. I nudged him softly and he opened his eyes. "Don't I know you?" he groaned.

Maybe it was the arrogance of his voice, I don't know. But as I remembered J. Wesley, the old meanness covered me again. I dragged Klingge from the car, paying no mind to his whines. I laid him on the bank and checked the trees. I didn't want no audience for what I had planned. All I saw was a crow chased by a pair of mockingbirds. I walked up to Burma, who crossed her hands over her shoulders, like she held herself in. She stared at the water. "You know who it is, don'tcha?" I said.

"That man who ruint J. Wesley." She stared me in the face. "What you gonna do?"

"Get a little payback, I guess."

I expected argument, but she stared at him coldly and said she didn't want to watch, that's all. No moralisms, no holier-than-thou's. I pointed to a copse of trees up the bank and she walked off without a word. I turned back and poked Klingge with my foot. "Stay awake," I said.

"Get me to a hospital," he gasped, teeth chattering from shock. "I got money in my wallet. I can pay."

I rolled him over, thanking him sincerely as I fished the wallet from his jeans. There were four hundreds inside, so I stuck them in my pocket and tossed the wallet in the river. His eyes got big and he seemed to see me clearly for the first time. "You're that man at the cockfight," he said. I smiled and asked how this had happened. After all, he'd left well before the storm.

"My driver got lost," he said, voice squeaky and dry. "By the time we knew where we were, it was so dark we had to creep along. We—we'd gotten over that bridge back there when there was a rumble and the road fell out beneath us, and the next thing I knew the car was rolling in the water. The doors flew open and my handler and Widow Maker washed away. We rammed something huge, or it rammed us, then the driver started screaming until the roof caved in." The words took a lot out of him; a sweat filmed his forehead. "That's all I remember," he said.

"Do you remember the boy?"

"What boy? I need a doctor."

I twisted one of the gold rings from his pinkie and repeated my question. That got his attention. "Why are you doing this?" he pleaded. "I've got lots of money. I can make you rich."

"The boy drowned in the flood while grabbing for a bag of money."

"I had nothing to do with that," he said. I twisted loose another ring; he tried fighting me off, but failed. I held it in the light, whistled when I saw the engraved *24K*, and complimented him on his taste. "You ruined that boy, Edmond," I continued. "You don't mind if I call you Edmond, do you? You didn't have to take everything he had."

The sweat crept to his upper lip. "It was a bet. Just a bet. *It was just a game.*"

I shaded my eyes, looking in the trees again for the black-clad ghoul. "You'n' I know that, Edmond, but the boy was a bit young to understand."

"This is crazy. You're crazy. Important people are waiting for me. I'm a powerful man."

I stuck the rings in my pocket. "Important people, huh? Who else besides me, the woman, and some down-and-out chicken men know you're even in Tennessee?" I wrenched the last rings off his fingers when one suddenly caught my attention—a seal ring with a smooth black face and an embossed splash of red. I'd seen the design before and held it up. "Is this what I think it is?"

His face showed relief. "You recognize it," he said.

"The Klan's the important people you talked about?"

"They get things done. I came to make a donation, so they could do more."

I bent down and cradled him in my arms. He was heavier than he looked. "I've seen their work," I said.

"So you'll tell them I'm okay, and you'll take me to a hospital?"

I stepped toward the boiling river. "Not quite," I said.

Comprehension dawns so slowly, but it eventually comes to us all. Now it came to Edmond Klingge. "What're you doing?" he screamed. "You can't do this! I'm a millionaire!"

I chuckled as I stood on the bank and watched the river churn. There's something holy in a flood. Noah must've felt it when he stood upon his ark: I bet he gazed upon its surface and mourned how deep and cruel justice could be. "Nature's amazin', ain't it, Edmond?" I said. "She don't care if we're rich or poor, high or low. We're all equals in her eyes."

"You're crazy! You can't do this! I can't die!!"

"We all die, Edmond. Sad to say, it's our common lot." With that, I opened my arms and dropped him in.

He hit the river with a splash, went under, rose again. His head bobbed like a cork; his mouth filled with yellow foam. His eyes grew wide and sorry, the dark pupils like bull's-eyes. I wondered if it was true that your life passed in those last moments: *Maybe I should ask him,* I thought, but by then the current had carried him off and he went down for good. I stood and watched the river, knowing that what I'd done was good in the eyes of the Lord.

Joe Jackson

I walked back to Burma, who searched my face but didn't say a word. When we turned, the man in black rags stood on the hill under the shade of the trees. "I saw what you done," he shouted. "That was murder. I seen it." This time he didn't run.

I looked him over slowly. I saw now he wasn't really dressed in rags, but in a long black coat and pants that hung tentlike from his thin frame. It looked like he hadn't dirtied a plate in ages, and his lean and hungry look was made worse by the powder white face shining over his getup like a wan moon. His eyes were moist and bulging, probably from a goiter; his lips were full and red, like bladders of blood. I thought of a lamprey and told myself to watch my back or he'd latch on.

"Stop right there," he said when we were a few yards away. His hands stayed in his pockets, one poking forward like he held a gun. He had a high, nasal voice, the kind that would quickly grow tiresome. Everything about the man cried ugly: If you dipped him in the river, you'd skim ugly for a week. "I mean it, mister," he said when I reached into my own pocket, "take that hand out slowly 'less you want to see Jesus soon."

I held out my hand, palm up, and on it were Edmond Klingge's rings. "Who you think you're kiddin'?" I said. "If you had a gun, you'd've throwed it on us already. This is what you want, right?"

He looked insulted, but his eyes never left the gold. "You don't know what I want," he pouted, but I just sneered. Could I call 'em or what?

"I know *exactly* what you want," I answered back, "especially after seein' your handiwork upstream."

His lips quivered like jellied cranberries; he glanced at my face anxiously. "You can't prove that, mister, you were too far away," he said. "Besides, that man you threw in the river had money. I saw you take it from his wallet. I need it more'n you."

"These are hard times, and we need money same as anyone." I closed my fingers over the rings. "I *was* willing to trade for a little information," I added, "but if you're not interested . . ."

He edged forward, eyes glued to my hand. "Flood washed away everything I own," he wheedled. "A man's got a right to survive."

I smiled and uncurled my fingers, one by one. "I agree. That man had done something bad to a friend of ours, so we got justice, is all. Times like this, when everything's out of kilter, there's precious little justice left. Times like this, justice becomes each man's responsibility."

He studied me cautiously. "You sound like one of them preachers who says the end times are comin'."

I smiled like a loving father. "They ain't *comin'*, friend. They're already here."

Where the Lost Girls Go

OUR REPORTER WAS good to his word, pilin' Cole and me into his VW and takin' the high roads back to town. "I'd take you to the relief camp, but they're as swamped as the countryside with people, and at least at County General they'll give you a place to rest and some clean clothes *before* makin' you sign a stack of forms." The little Beetle lurched at every pothole, but the reporter, whose name was Johnny Newsome, drove like a madman, foot to the floor. I doubted I'd seen anyone happier in his job. "Last night was just another boring news day in this podunk little town when *boom!*, all hell broke loose and half the mountain and everybody in it washed into our laps! Half the town is underwater, not like that's anything to cry about, and I've been rushing from place to place all night long. Haven't gotten a minute of sleep, but I don't mind. If this doesn't get me in the *New York Times* or a shot at a Pulitzer, I'll give up journalism and lead a normal life in politics or PR."

We switched through country roads, then hit the state route that curved down the ridge to town. Our progress slowed, the road clogged with every kind of refugee known to man. "It's like a war that everyone's escapin'," Cole observed from his cramped backseat. Johnny Newsome said he'd made the same comparison in one of his stories. "But my editor said, 'This is a flood, Mr. Newsome, an act of God and of nature, not a work by Tolstoy. We don't have fifteen hundred pages at our disposal, so keep it under fifteen column inches, please.'"

Still, Cole and Johnny Newsome were right—it was like an entire people had been attacked and now ran for their lives. We passed livestock vans stuffed with cows and pigs, black Ford F-trucks stacked with poultry cages, two-tone station wagons crammed with the inventory of family life: TVs, record players, pots, juicers, toasters, Singer sewing machines, gold-leaf Bibles, steam irons, 3-D pictures of the Praying Hands. At an intersection, a poultry truck had T-boned one of these family arks, littering the road with plates and silver, the air afloat with chicken feathers. Our reporter swerved to the shoulder, jumped out, fiddled with his camera, and snapped off several shots till both drivers turned their wrath on him. He jumped back in the car and floored it when the poultry driver threw dead chickens our way.

The road widened as we closed on the town. A vast lot of mobile homes awaited sale under flapping plastic flags. A fat girl in a dirty blue uniform passed out ice cream cones from the window of a Frosty Freeze. There were Hillbilly Car Sales, Hillbilly Auto Parts, and Hillbilly Fireworks—so many "Hillbilly" businesses that I prayed the flood would do us a favor and wash 'em away. The road in the opposite direction was a crawling corn snake of cars. "Where's everybody goin'?" Cole asked.

"To the disaster camp for help," said our driver, "or just getting out of town—it doesn't matter where."

We soon saw why. Half of Newport was underwater, a thick sheet of red muddy river covering downtown. This was the Pigeon River, which branched off the French Broad just a few miles north; according to Johnny Newsome, every river in this region had swelled three or more times normal overnight and driven half the country from their homes. We pulled to the side of the road and got out so our reporter could play photographer again. The water moved in slow motion, piling debris against the storefronts and pushing stranded cars on their sides. An otherworldly braying drifted up—the horns of abandoned autos whose electrical systems had shorted. The main street ran along the railroad, and this ran along the river: The water'd slipped its banks and invaded the streets, and was now nearly up to the second stories of the brick buildings, turning them to islands. Lampposts and roofs of large trucks and buses poked above the surface; a huge ketchup plant dominated the approach below us, and oily smoke rose from its center where a gas main had ruptured. No one could get close enough to fight it, and the fire burned out of control.

The ketchup plant wasn't the only island in town. The jail was the closest building to the river, and inmates had herded onto the flat roof. I saw no uniforms among them: The guards had either been overpowered or had run away. Not that the inmates were free, for the river imprisoned 'em worse'n any bars. One man jumped as a tree trunk floated past; his buddies cheered as he hit the water and climbed upon it, but the triumph was short-lived. Just as he waved to his friends, something pulled him under. The others watched and waited, but he never rose again.

The hills rose 'round the flooded city like a giant bowl. At its edges, water swirled 'round tilted power lines and sewage gushed from manholes. But many of the buildings higher up were still untouched, and that's where we were headed, Johnny Newsome said. County General was wisely built on higher ground. He fired reporter questions at me as we threaded back streets, and only after the third or fourth did I realize I'd better be a careful little girl. *Who? What? When? Where?* None of these could do me any good. *How?* would link me to Harson's death and call in the cops. *Why?* was something I still didn't understand.

"Is all this goin' in the paper?" I finally asked.

"Of course it is, I'm a reporter, whatta you think?" he laughed. "You think I go around saving castaways from the kindness of my heart? I'm not a bad person, but I've got a job to do."

I pled amnesia to his questions, while in the back I heard a relieved sigh from Cole. But we still weren't outta the woods. County General's emergency room was like an ant's nest just been stepped in: Everywhere was rush rush rush, phones ringing, white ambulances and black hearses, injured calling for help, gurneys parked in the hallways bearing pale forgotten forms. The place smelled of ammonia and ether and gleamed of sea green linoleum. An ambulance screamed up and medics wheeled through the doors a man with an unbelievable lake of blood seeping from his belly. I felt sick and faint; my field of vision narrowed to a crevice; every sound echoed in my ears. I told Cole I had to sit: he put his good arm 'round me as the reporter rushed to the nurse's window and pointed at me.

I focused on the strangest things. The plaster walls were green and rusty yellow; the ceiling was tan. My chair was a glossy green, imitation leather that felt cool on my skin; it had chrome tubing for the arms and legs. *So pretty*, I thought. *So modern. Lucky me.* A woman fidgeted in the chair beside me and read from *Modern Screen*. "Does Liz Love Dick?" the cover asked. "Does Dick Love Liz?" A blond nurse in white dress and white stockings, which made her calves look fat, clopped up briskly and knelt beside me. "What's the matter, hon?" she said.

"I don't know . . . I don't feel so good."

She lifted my eyelids and felt my pulse, her fingertips smooth and cool. There was a rolling wheelchair . . . a small bed curtained off . . . a young doctor with bags under his eyes. "No visible trauma," he said to the nurse, as if I wasn't present. "Probably shock."

"Sedative?"

"Yeah, juice her up and throw her in the women's ward. A little sleep will do her good."

———•———

The rest of that day and the night that followed, I floated in a sea of sleep and drugs. I was tucked between cold sheets in a long room with other flood victims 'round me. I was under a window and light streamed in so warm. An IV bag hung on a metal post beside me; I lifted my arm and a clear tube of liquid dribbled into a vein. Three types of people appeared and disappeared. Doctors and nurses rushed up, poked and prodded me, rushed away. Patients shuffled by in soft slippers, their beltless white gowns gaping open behind. Bewildered family groups searched for those who'd vanished entirely, and these lingered longest. They bent close, brushing back my hair. "That's not her," they'd say before moving to another bed.

Once I was conscious long enough to ask a young nurse what they'd done with my boyfriend. She checked my chart and answered, "Oh, yeah, you're the girl who floated down the river." Cole was in the men's ward the next wing over. "He's just fine," she said.

That's all I remembered till next morning, when I woke feelin' human again. A sparrow chirped outside the window. A breakfast cart squeaked by. A woman shuffled out of sight through an open door at the end of the room. I moved my arm and the IV tube was gone, replaced by a bandage. The white clock on the wall read 9:05.

In the bed to my left, a girl munched a Baby Ruth bar and watched my every move. "You slept forever," her small voice said. She looked like a little elf: blond hair in pigtails, front tooth missing, a Paris green nightgown her parents must've brought in. Her right arm was set in a plaster cast, her eyes and neck were bruised, other exposed parts looked banged up pretty bad. "What happened to you?" I said. Floodwaters picked her off her feet and slammed her into a chain-link fence during the evacuation, she replied. According to her daddy, it was lucky she hit it, 'cause otherwise she woulda kept goin' and drowned. I asked how old she was. Ten, she answered, and added, "Want some candy?"

That seemed an excellent idea. Four days had passed since the robbery at Harson's, and I hadn't had a decent meal in all that time. The mere thought of food made my belly clench inside. The candy was piled on the table between us, left by well-wishers; the goodness of candy washed through my soul. So much chocolate, so little time. Chocolate with nuts, raisins, or toffee; chocolate cups filled with peanut butter; chocolate bars white as a polar bear. I'd read that chocolate bars first appeared at baseball games in 1911. If so, how did folks manage before? Say what you want, a country that produced Tootsie Rolls and Hershey's Kisses couldn't be all bad. I grabbed a grape Tootsie Pop and settled back in chocolate bliss, sucking the hard candy shell.

"I know who you are," she said.

I nearly swallowed that pop—sucker, stick, and all. "How could you?" I asked when I stopped gaggin'. "I never set foot in town before today."

"The paper, silly," she exclaimed. "You're a star." She reached with her free arm to the bedside table, grabbed a morning paper and tossed it over to me. "The nice blond nurse brought it before you woke so I could see all the pictures of the flood." Four large photos were spaced across the front: an aerial shot of miles of flooded farmland; the ketchup factory burning in the night; the dusty relief camp Johnny Newsome had spoken about; and the close-up of me, hair and face slick with mud. Cole watched from one corner, cows from the other.

Nothin' like tellin' the whole world our whereabouts, I thought. This could be bad.

But the little girl wasn't done. "I know something else, too," she whispered proudly. "It's a secret, but I won't tell."

I didn't like the sound of that, either. "A secret?"

"Look on the back page."

I did as she said. My photo stared at me again, this time from a smaller box, and at first I was confused. But not for long. It was my high-school photo with a coupla lines how I'd gone missing and might know something of a murder, with a phone line to call.

"No one else knows," she grinned, toes wiggling in excitement beneath her covers. "Nobody else put the two together, or at least they haven't said anything, and you know they would! You're too muddy in the first picture to be so pretty in the second, which is probably why nobody's seen it but me. But I know, 'cause I been studyin' you all night long. The little photo on the back actually's been runnin' for the last two days, and I saw it on the very first day it ran. 'She's too pretty to kill somebody,' I said to Mama, and Mama said we never know what's in the hearts of others, even our best friends. Beauty's only skin deep, which is what she says whenever I ask why people do bad things. I get so tired of hearing that. Adults are hard to understand."

She smiled pretty as a picture and added, "I also remember your name. It's Dahlia Jean Coker; it says so right there." I thought my heart had failed. "You were asleep when the nurse came and I asked about you. . . . She said you passed out before they got information, and I thought I would bust with the secret, but I still didn't tell. I remember your name because it's so pretty, all except the Coker part, but everything else sounds like flowers in spring. I like flowers, don't you? My name is Wanda Louise Coover, which is also pretty, but not as pretty as yours."

She looked at me and sighed. "You're on the run, ain't you? That's why I didn't tell. The nurse said your boyfriend is a dreamboat, and I bet the two of you are on the run together. That's *so* romantic—I wish something like that would happen to me." She stared at the TV bolted overhead and watched as Tom and Jerry battled it out for the umpteenth time. The mouse got whacked with a croquet mallet. The cat got folded into a squeeze-box shape and made accordion sounds. "Did you really kill that man in Wattles for his money?" she finally said.

I coughed up the Tootsie Roll so hard it shot across the room.

"My daddy knows the perfect thing for choking," she said. "He's a policeman, and policemen know first aid. He puts his arms under your ribs and squeezes and food pops out like a cannonball. You don't want to stand close, though, 'cause it'll ruin your dress if it hits, and you never know what's stuck in there." She looked at the clock and smiled. "It's almost visiting time, and my mom 'n' dad'll be comin' soon. Daddy'll take care of you then."

I bet he would, especially when his darling Wanda let slip who I was. No two ways about it, I had to get outta here. But when I slid from bed, my clothes were missing. Only my saddle shoes remained. Worse, the money bag was gone. "If you're lookin' for your clothes, they were such a mess the nurses burned 'em and planned to give you donated things," Wanda said. She added sadly, "You're not leavin', are you?"

"No, no, not at all. I'm just feelin' restless and want a bit of air."

"Come back soon," she giggled. "I got more questions about bein' an outlaw in love."

I pinched my gown behind me and set off down the hall in search of Cole. The corridor was so alive with comin's and goin's that nobody really noticed me; when some emergency broke out down at the other end, I ducked toward a stairwell. Near it was a door marked LAUNDRY. Inside I found some smocks and scrubs, which quickly replaced my embarrassing gown. I peeked out the door and, when no one was looking, darted out and down the stairs.

So where was my gypsy in this maze of injury? We had to skedaddle quick, faster'n any cartoon mouse on TV. Once my picture hit the state papers, the Wattles sheriff would surely see it; maybe he'd already seen it and even now phoned his pals in Newport to round me up and send me home. If he was slow about it, Wanda Louise Coover would tell the world right soon.

But my luck was right for once, and no one paid me no

notice in these hospital clothes. I wandered down white halls, past a cafeteria, past a glass room full of squalling babies, through a waiting room jammed full of beds. Still no Cole. I turned a corner and clattered down another flight of stairs. At the bottom I found a set of double doors marked MORGUE.

Oh, Lord. I'd had my fill of dead people, but they were wall to wall and having a convention down here. Everywhere I looked were bodies wrapped in sheets or zipped in black plastic bags. It was like the dead outnumbered the living, a state of affairs usually much better hid. The hospital must've run low on formaldehyde or whatever they used for preservin' bodies, since at the other end of the hall crushed ice covered some of the black bags. But the biggest problem seemed identifying the dead. A list of the missing was taped near the entrance, while a new list from the relief center apparently arrived every six hours. Names had no meaning; instead, what one wore and his physical features was the fastest ticket from the morgue. I studied the lists like I might find a secret, dreading I'd find Mama while praying I'd find Cole's old man:

No. 9:   Unknown female. Age 12-15, silver ring on thumb and tiny silver bracelet on right wrist.

No. 12:   Unknown male. Age 50-55, evidence of snakebite.

No. 30:   Unknown male. Age 5, sandy hair, red shirt, jeans and one black sock, five pennies in pocket, one arrowhead.

No. 45:   Unknown female. Age 25-29, long black hair, underwear with "Sunday" embroidered in pink, dress with yellow daisies. Found near body of Unknown Male, No. 12.

I stood reading a long time; it was the saddest thing I'd ever seen. Here was nearly a century of life and experience, wiped out in less than a day. "Can I help you?" a voice asked behind me, and when I came down from the ceiling, a pudgy coroner in white coat and white whiskers gave a big belly laugh. "It takes people a while to get used to this place, even employees," he said. "They send you from the relief camp? You got an ID for me?"

I was about to say I was lost when it struck me I might already be missed upstairs, so best not give myself away. Just before I'd jumped, I'd noticed a description that stuck in my mind: "No. 66: Unknown male. Age 35-37, brown hair and beard, Phi Beta Kappa fob in right pocket, wedding band, no inscription, gray Hush Puppies." The shoes sounded familiar. "I may have something on Number 66," I told him, adding that I'd ended here by mistake while looking for the men's ward.

"Everybody gets lost and ends down here," he shrugged. He graced me with directions, then led me to a white-lit room where the best-preserved bodies, "and not just pieces," rested on stainless-steel slabs. Whole bodies were sent here and to the relief camp for identification, while chunks spit out by the flood's meat grinder were stored in those bags in the hall. It was cold in here, the air conditioner churning in the ceiling, icy air pouring from large vents overhead. He pushed through a second set of doors into an anteroom. "Number 66 is one of the few in better shape. He seems quite popular. You're his second visitor today."

We stopped at a table where a college-aged boy stood quietly, staring at the still and waxy form. The boy had unruly hair and cocoa brown eyes; he'd pulled back the sheet and I recognized the corpse: the professor from the Baptist college who'd lectured in my History class on the day of the robbery. It seemed years, not just a few days, ago. He'd stood in front of the blackboard like some doom-sayin' prophet and roared how violence ran through our veins like coal dust and our society was somehow condemned. "Escape!" he'd cried as we jumped in our seats—and now he'd escaped this life for good. His face was greenish red from decomposition; huge bruises splotched his chest where his ribs were crushed; a great purple gash stretched from under his arm and down to his hip, the wound that probably killed him, the coroner said. He usually performed an autopsy to be one hundred percent certain, but with the number of bodies, there simply was no time. Identification and disposal, or interment, was all that mattered now. I looked in the professor's face. He seemed composed and serene, even in death, like he dreamt of perfect lectures where every student learned something and all the class made As.

When I glanced up, the college boy was studyin' me. "You're not a student at the college, are you?" No, I said, the professor had lectured at our high school a couple of days ago.

Joe College grew excited. "He talked about that class," he said. "That was the one with the girl who disappeared in a robbery that same night. He said she seemed to have a violent streak—she jabbed a boy with a pencil during his lecture."

I was tired of total strangers sayin' the most unnervin' things about me. "What you doin' this far south?" I asked, steerin' his thoughts elsewhere and prayin' he didn't ask the same.

Joe College's real name was Michael Venus, and he was the second driver in a two-car caravan of students and faculty signed up to join a Freedom Ride down in Chattanooga. Their caravan had made it to the valley when last night's flood swept through Newport and surrounding counties. There was no warning, he said. His car was behind the professor's, stuck behind a semi when an entire section of highway ahead of them disappeared in water—and the cars and trucks on it, too. The professor, another faculty member, and two students were in the first car; so far, only the professor's body was found. Two other students were with Michael, but they were too upset to continue and had already gone back home.

I gazed at Michael Venus and felt sorry for him. "What about you?"

"I just called the college, and they said they'd call his wife." He shrugged his shoulders and dipped his head, trying not to cry. "They were my friends in that car. I-I don't know, I thought I'd go on to Chattanooga and finish what we started.

At least I can tell the organizers what happened. There's nothing more for me to do here."

A phone rang in the next room, and the jolly coroner picked it up. "No, I don't think so, but I'll see." He poked his head through the door and asked, "Your name's not Dahlia Jean Coker, is it? If it is, some people would like to see you in the lobby."

No, my name was Sarah Lee Flowers, I said. The door swung shut. "No Dahlia Jean down here," the coroner said to the phone.

I kept a straight face, feelin' like dirt for what I was gonna do. "You wouldn't mind another couple passengers, wouldja? We're headed south to Chattanooga also—the sooner the better."

"Yeah, I'd appreciate the company," my poor, unsuspecting, and innocent Joe College said.

Night Comes to the Junkyard

HARVEY NOBLE WAS observant. Scavengers have to be. He claimed he was in "resale," but he couldn't hide his true self from someone like me. Scavengers pay their passage by noticing the unnoticed, sniffing out the hidden want, finding value in forgotten and abandoned things. They have a built-in radar for riches and a lust for the pretty bauble, a combination that betrays them. Harvey's weakness leapt up full-blown as I held Edmond Klingge's jewelry in my palm. *Just a taste,* I beckoned. *Make a deal with J. T. Younger. It's not like you're sellin' your soul.*

True to his roots, Harvey obliged. "All twenty-four karat," I tempted. "We need is information, that's all." His hand crept from the pocket where he'd said he kept a gun, revealing nothing more threatening than long, knobby fingers. "They'd bring a good price in a pawnshop," I said. It was like holding a bone to a dog. As one finger touched a ring, Harvey sighed with pleasure. I grabbed his collar, slapped his face, and let go.

That startled everyone, Burma included. But this was a delicate moment if I hoped to control the man. "That was for threatening us," I said. As he cringed before me, I picked him up, brushed him off, and held out a ring. A hand lashed out and the ring vanished into the loose black clothes. I said he'd get another if he helped us. His eyes burned with resentment, but he asked what I had in mind.

Had he seen or heard of someone like our kids? Not surprisingly, he had.

"Were they safe?" Burma butted in. She'd stood back during the preliminaries, but pushed forward now. My ragman gave her the once-over, then explained how he was standing in his door watching the river when a girl and boy floated by on a roof as easy as you please. The boy was asleep, but the girl perched real protective atop some sort of bag. Her caution made him wonder if something valuable was inside; with any luck, they'd beach and he could find out what it was. She watched him as he watched her: He didn't like that, since some folks were too observant for their own damn good. The girl shifted her weight on the bag and waved for help, like he'd help those who couldn't help themselves. Who'd she think she was—a celebrity? He prayed to God the roof would snag and knock 'em out or kill them, he so wanted to peek inside that bag. But God never listened to the prayers of Harvey Noble, and as he watched, the roof hugged the current and floated out of sight like so many of the junkman's dreams.

"So what's in the bag?" he asked.

"None of your business," I said.

He looked hurt at that, and launched into how all junkmen have a dream. Take these junk cars, he said, pointing to the gutted Fords and Chevys fighting for space on the knob that was his home. By now we'd crawled up an auto graveyard not far downriver from where I'd passed sentence on Edmond Klingge. Once this hill of wrecks had been extensive, but now the river crept up three sides and portions of cars stuck from the water like prehistoric varmints strugglin' onto land. I saw the outlines of others completely submerged. Down underwater lay a 1934

Joe Jackson

Airflow De Soto and a 1952 Willys two-door Aero, mourned Harvey, once destined for a rich Atlanta fool willing to pay top dollar for "classic" cars. Now all they were good for was a place for snapping turtles to call home.

Because of that misfortune, Harvey felt *particularly* sorry for himself, a circumstance that led to his robbin' corpses. It was a brief madness that, he promised on the Bible, would never happen again. "It's not like I hurt no one, so there's no need to turn me in." The nervous chatter added to my headache as he led us up his hill. At the very top sprouted Harvey's tin-and-tarpaper shack where everything was for sale. Hubcaps hung from the trees and were stacked by the sides of his shack; a dirt road in the back was lined with stacks of tires. In a nook in the road stood a metal shop, and inside rested a jet black '53 Mercury with fender skirts and twin aerials. I whistled appreciatively: Harvey Noble was proving full of unexpected skills. The car glowed from multiple coats of hand-rubbed paint with a blackness that shimmered from inside. This was even better than the Cadillac. The Caddy spoke of glamour, but this was pure meanness. Amid the junk, we'd found a work of art. We'd also found our wheels.

That wasn't all. I heard scratching 'round back and found a clutch of chickens peckin' at the dust. A bunch of night crawlers had wiggled to the surface from the rains. For the hens, it was a feast day, and for us, too. I tucked a biddy under my arm and asked Burma if she could fry it up. "I ain't gonna pluck or gut it," she said, "but do those honors and I'll fry up two or three."

"Don't worry," I said, then reached down and twisted off the chicken's head. It struggled in my arms till I dropped it, then ran a couple of steps and fell over dead. Blood pumped from its neck. "That's what Harvey's for."

Night came to the junkyard. Dogs howled in the hills. I picked my teeth with a wishbone and gazed at the dark sky. The stars winked back; the moon shimmered off the slow-rolling flood. I felt a pleasing rumble in my belly. Burma was hardheaded, but she could cook up a storm.

It all tended to make me reflective. What if I gave up the chase? Let the kids go on with their lives, like Burma said. What would it hurt? Hole up in a place like this where she 'n' me could rob banks for the rest of our lives. I'd never really been happy before, but sittin' here, studyin' the river, maybe I was happy now.

Still, to give up the chase after all I'd been through was an assault to my pride. In important ways, it seemed irresponsible. To do so condemned Cole to a life tied to a pushy woman. To give up meant the girl got the last $50,000, which meant she'd won the game—just like Harson Whitley said she would. I could still see his face in the diner, still hear him hiss, "She's tougher'n you think," right before he died. Maybe I was happy, but no one liked a quitter. I looked to the river for answers. Dark shapes floated by with secrets that they wouldn't tell.

We started early the next morning. We crawled into the Mercury and Harvey took over, the hood a black jewel before us, reflecting the sun into hundreds of white diamonds. He suggested we begin with the relief camp, since they kept lists on the living and the dead. He whistled as he drove, but a shadow crossed his face and he asked, "You really believe what you said about the end times, or were you just stringing me along?"

"I believe it," I said, knowing my man. It wasn't enough for him to fear me—he had to be in awe of me as well. "The TV preachers say the signs are right. We got enough atom bombs to blow up the world twenty times over. The symbols all line up, Harvey. I have no doubt we're in the final days."

"Where'd you figure this out?"

"In prison."

"Why were you in prison?"

"For dispensing justice."

"Whose justice?"

"Mine."

He considered this awhile, chewing his lip like a piece of prime rib. "I tend to believe you," he finally said. "It's hard to explain why, everything's so turned 'round. I fought in Korea, freezin' my ass off while Reds swarmed around us, and for what? Come home and coloreds got a new mess of laws, Jews got their own country, a Catholic's in the White House, but what's in it for the common man? I'm not the only one who wonders. Some pretty powerful folks do, too. Maybe things'll equal out, but before then, things'll get ugly."

"My thoughts exactly, Harvey old boy," I said.

We hit the relief camp by midmorning, a shining canvas city pitched on a hill. The tents were spaced in equal rows and, from a distance, resembled rows of winter cabbage planted in a long field. At the top stood the brain center, a brick-and-glass junior high, the county's second-biggest school. The biggest was now underwater, Harvey said. The river lapped at one side of the camp, the shore littered with the floating wrecks of houses and SEE ROCK CITY barns. Although the flood no longer raged, its waters still inched up the shore.

We parked outside the camp and walked up the road; we came to a sign listing the camp's Do's and Don'ts. *Do* boil your water. *Don't* bring guns. *Do* line up for vaccinations and report all spontaneous abortions. *Don't* dig through the pockets of corpses or loot businesses, or risk getting shot. Burma reminded Harvey that that meant him. Army trucks roared past, their flatbeds heaped with bottled water, blankets, bedrolls. One truck stopped at a tent marked with a red cross; soldiers rushed out and unloaded wooden crosses with black numbers stenciled in the center. Inside, white-clad figures rushed toward a bed. People watched as we passed, eyes out of focus, a zombie gaze. We reached the top and I looked back. A yellow dust hung over it all.

It reminded me of the day my daddy preached on poor ole

Job. Man's life was war—that was Job's message—and this was the aftermath, a last stand where the waters rose. Maybe all of history was like this, the bodies stacking up, all disasters and holocausts ultimately the same. Where man didn't finish laying waste, Nature obliged. Maybe it was a victory to merely stay alive. I watched the dust pulse up like a sorrowful breath, a yellow beacon that sent out our shame. I had the curious feeling that I was weightless and being drawn into the air. I was an atom in a great cloud of atoms, bumping 'round randomly . . . a cipher in a huge namelessness, forced to make choices beyond my control.

"You okay?" Burma asked, grabbing my arm. I must've fallen, though I wasn't aware. I got up, rubbing the dust from my hands, as people paused and stared. We couldn't stop like this, warned Harvey. Someone official would put us to work or poke us with a hypo.

We hurried to the school gym, now an improvised morgue. Big metal fans whirled in the exits but they couldn't erase the smell. The dead lay in straight rows on the basketball court, all covered by sheets, white humps reflected in the polished wood. A portion of center court lay empty, dividing the bodies into separate teams. The New Dead and Old, waiting for the whistle so another game could begin.

A young man in a white jacket sat at a table before the entrance, papers stacked in front of him. His portable radio was turned low to an Elvis tune. I asked if he was doorkeeper for the dead, and he gave me a strange look, like maybe he hadn't heard me right, then asked the name and/or description of the one and/or ones we were searching for. He flipped slowly through his papers, eyes scanning each form. Though no bodies matched Cole's description, he jerked his thumb over his shoulder and said a girl the same age as Burma's daughter lay under a sheet, left side. He glanced at a soldier standing post and told him to lead us there. We walked past bent figures searching among the shrouds; in here, the quick were outnumbered by the dead. The soldier walked outside the lines of the court and stopped before a sheet, then drew it back. "It's not Dahlia," Burma gasped in relief, then started crying. "This girl's so pretty," she said.

"Yes, ma'am, she is," the soldier agreed. I looked at him closely for the first time and noticed his beard was barely fuzz. He said the girl had been found in a mass of wreckage below one of the breached dams. She was tall and slender, in a long dress with lace up to her throat. She wore flat slippers like a dancer, unusual because most bodies arrived missing one or both shoes. Her face showed no disfigurement or swelling, like other victims, and I looked at a band of freckles across her nose. She'd probably hated them. Her hair was still encased in mud and fell in heavy masses to her waist. Other searchers walked up, and I expected someone to say she merely looked asleep, but no one did.

"No one's claimed her?" asked a man with a bandage on his cheek.

"No, sir, they haven't," the soldier replied.

"You won't bury her before they do, will you?" said a woman with the man.

"We'll have to, ma'am, if they don't come today."

"Seems cruel to leave her hair like that. She has such beautiful hair."

"Yes, ma'am, she does," the soldier said. Almost gently, he spread the sheet back over her face and walked away.

The next stop was the survivors' list, kept in the band room. A line stretched out the door. Two lines, actually, all mixed and confused. Survivors were required to stop and register soon as they arrived for help, but this was also the second stop for family and friends of the missing, after the gym-floor morgue. It was like standing in a ticket line: pushing and shoving, foul looks and tempers. I saw now why the camp prohibited guns. The Red Cross lady in charge of our line seemed no happier than the rest. She was in her thirties, slim, blond hair permed stiff, makeup cracked by too many forced smiles. I noticed Harvey eyeing her delicate gold earrings and gave him a warning glance. No Dahlia Jean Coker or Cole Younger registered, said the Red Cross lady, running a finger down her lists. "Next," she cried.

"Wait a minute," I said. "There's got to be more. I didn't stand in line this long for that."

She raised her eyes for a National Guardsman, but he'd drifted away. Her eyes narrowed. "Their names aren't on the list. There's nothing we can do."

"Think a little. Did you get a boy and girl together, sixteen to eighteen, who rode in on a roof?"

She started to protest, but an older lady sitting beside her looked up. "We did have someone like that," she said.

"I would have remembered," disagreed the country-club princess.

"Well, *we* didn't have them, but look here." She unfolded a daily paper at her elbow and handed it across the table. On the front was a picture of our kids. The girl stared at me, eyes dark and haunted. She sat in a muddy field as a bug-eyed Jersey cow peered over one shoulder; over the other shoulder stood Cole. His hands were clenched, face frozen in a black-and-white scowl. The river stretched behind them, filling the background like a mirror with no end.

I handed the paper to Burma. "At least they're alive," she said.

"You know where they are?" I asked.

"No, I'm sorry, I don't," the older Red Cross lady said. "And since they didn't register here in the camp, we don't even know their names. You might ask at the newspaper, though— maybe you can find out there, if their offices aren't under-water."

We thanked her and left the room. I gave Harvey a gold ring for good work and said he'd get the others if we found our kids. We stepped back into the open air. It was hotter now, the sun burning overhead like white metal. An army helicopter hovered over the football field and lit, its skids gently touching the ground. Some dignitary clambered out, hunched beneath the blades, followed by a pair of suits and Foster Grants, all

met by a uniform with a row of stars. Too many authority figures for my tastes, and I stepped away. Near the Red Cross tent
a church meeting had started under low-slung canvas. People
stood inside singing a hymn that Daddy loved:

> A might-y fo-r-tress I-s our God,
> A bul-wark nev-er fa-il-in-g
> Our help-er H-e a-mi-d the flood
> Of mor-tal ills pre-va-il-in-g.
> For still our an-cient foe,
> Doth seek to work us woe
> His craft and power are great
> And, armed with cru-el hate,
> On earth is not His e-e-e-qual.

Their voices swelled in glory, bringing back memories. Daddy
ready to strap on his armor and conquer the sinful; how his
beatings followed its beat; how the belt descended and he said
it made you want to beat the devil yourself, right, boy? "Right,
Pa," I screamed. What would these worshipers think if I
appeared with a belt of my own and chased them from this
temple?

"Take me away," I said to Burma.

What the flood failed to take, I wanted to tear down.

The flood had crept within a block of the newspaper office when
we showed up; it oozed forward slowly, like a patient slug. The
place was in an uproar. A herd of trucks was parked by the exits,
movers racing in and out to empty the place before the water
came to stay. We walked in unopposed. The newsroom itself was
a shambles, some staffers still at their desks and hunched over

phones or typewriters, others carrying files and papers out the door. They were trying to beat a late-morning deadline, one last paper before they abandoned this place and relocated higher up the ridge. The long room hummed of recessed lighting and clicked of typewriters; sometimes the power flickered, threatening to go any second. A writer ripped his copy from a typewriter carriage and shoved it at a circle of editors; one of these editors eyed it quickly and nodded, and the reporter rushed away. In the center of the circle stood a barrel-chested man with a blond mane; his hands looked like enormous slabs of beef covered with stiff hairs. He kept those hands trapped in his armpits, as if unleashing them would cause damage, and scowled at the madness around him. His head was square, the jaw set at a sharp angle, teeth grinding together when a lieutenant handed over a sheet of copy. I thought of paintings of Custer's Last Stand.

"We're not gonna make it, Mr. McTeague," an editor said.

"We goddamn better," the print commander growled. "I've never missed a goddamn deadline in my goddamn life and no goddamn flood's gonna goddamn beat me now." A huge hand left the safety of its armpit and clawed at a bottle of Tums nearby.

I threaded toward him, Burma and Harvey in tow. On the wall behind McTeague hung a line of framed awards and citations, and above them a glassed square of needlepoint with the inscription: "In the beginning was the Word." A stuffed parrot stood in a corner: someone had pasted a cartoon bubble to its beak that said, "Fuck you!" A lieutenant cried we couldn't enter, but I brushed past and stopped outside the ring of good soldiers. I raised the paper with the girl's photo on front and told the yellow-haired man what the Red Cross lady said. McTeague's eyes got hard and dark. "Can't you see we're trying to make deadline?" he boomed.

"I don't give a damn about your deadline," I said. "Where are these two?"

The circle of editors got quiet. Typewriters stopped clattering.

Joe Jackson

All movement seemed to freeze. It was like I'd entered a temple and blasphemed the local god. McTeague, the resident priest, stared back as if imagining me on a turning spit. "There's nothing more important than a deadline," he said.

Burma broke in. "Maybe it is for you," she said more kindly, "but these are our kids."

He sucked his breath between his teeth, no doubt trying to comprehend such rude beasts at his door. But he was human, too. "I'm sorry, lady," he said. "If they're your kids, that's more important than anything else, but for us, all we can think of is that the flood is still rising." He turned to a lieutenant with a head like a coconut and said, "Wilson, where did young Mr. Newsome say he took that boy and girl who floated down the river?"

"County General, boss," said the coconut-head.

McTeague smiled at Burma. "That's your next stop, lady. And if you see my goddamn reporter when you get there, tell him to quit flitting around the country like a mayfly. I need his ass in here!"

What was it about people in the flood zone, I wondered, as we piled back into Harvey's Mercury. It was like they all wanted to drown you in words. Still, we was getting closer to our prey. Our reunion would come quick; this goddamn journey would finally end. It was almost like a squirrel hunt, tramping through cold woods till the varmint peeked from behind a limb and you shot and missed, then tramped after it some more. It was good exercise, sure, and fun in its own way. But you still hated the squirrel.

Our progress was slow. The flood kept creeping higher; the streets were clogged with those seeking higher ground. The moon shone faint in the sky. As fire raged in the ketchup plant, the distant smell of vinegar and smoke mixed with the constant one of sewage. An army chopper passed. Please God, I thought, give me wings.

God didn't hear. It was near dusk when we reached the hospital, and by then our kids were gone. They'd been there, all right, but had slipped through our fingers again. A floor nurse came down to the lobby and said they'd simply disappeared. Everyone seemed interested in those two, she said. First there was a little girl in pigtails who told her daddy all about her neighbor, then a squad of cops who said they may have something to do with a murder. Then that young reporter, the one who checked them in. "She was in my hands," he moaned, "and I let her go."

The only real clue to her whereabouts was down in the morgue, where the coroner heard something about a Freedom Ride, whatever that was. "I'm afraid that's the best I can tell you," the nurse apologized, smiling wanly at Burma. Everyone was sorry these days.

We slumped back to Harvey's car, feeling low. So close . . . always so close. Yet never close enough . . . and never in time. I definitely felt my years.

"What's a Freedom Ride?" Burma finally asked.

"Beats me," I said. "Where do you even find one? Sounds like a church social to me."

Harvey cleared his throat. "I think I can answer both questions," he said. Yet something about the admission made him uncomfortable, too. "I don't want to get involved in this, so if I do, it's gonna cost more'n a couple of gold rings. Maybe some of what's in that girl's bag."

"What you gettin' at?" I barked.

"I know a man. . . ."

Sinners Roosting under Satan's Tail

EVEN IN HIS grief, Michael Venus wasn't no fool. Findin' Cole was easy enough—he was in the stairwell, and like the jolly coroner said, makin' his way to the morgue. His wound was cleaned and dressed; he was decked like me in hospital scrubs; he clutched the money bag. But leavin' the hospital was another thing. Down a hall, a nurse and state trooper scratched their heads in confusion; flashing police lights were parked outside the main lobby. This attention was no doubt for me. Michael even held his peace as we left by a side door and lit out in his rattletrap Corvair. We stopped at a grocery for lunch meat, at an Army-Navy for a cute rucksack to hold the money, and some surplus clothes to replace the scrubs, then by the side of the road when he couldn't stand the suspense no more. "I don't think your name is, or ever was, Sarah Lee Flowers," he announced. "I think you're that girl from the professor's class, the one everybody's looking for."

I looked at Cole, and him at me. We could knock him on the head and steal his heap—to tell the truth, the longer we kept on runnin', the easier that started to sound. The fact that I felt like that gave me the willies, like I was turnin' into Cole's old man right before my eyes.

That was *not* a line I wanted to cross—not yet, anyway. "Should we tell him?" I asked Cole, who shrugged.

"I'm beat, too," he answered. "Go ahead, tell the man."

So for once I didn't fib. Michael sat silent when I finished, digesting my tale. On the radio, Dr. Joyce Brothers warned how the tight skirts and sweaters of today's teenage girls meant a sexual revolution was in the works; you just wait and see. Rob Petrie would criticize his wife Laura's hairdo in tonight's *Dick Van Dyke Show*. "So you're not really murderers?" Michael finally asked. Absolutely not, I said.

"That's a relief," he mumbled, but it was still confusin'. "If I get this right," he said, *"your* father"—pointing at Cole—"*is* the murderer, and *your* mother"—pointing at me—"hitched a ride, and both are chasing the money," pointing at the rucksack of dough. He looked from Cole, to me, to it. "This is like a midterm test. I just hope I don't have to explain it to anyone."

I asked if he meant to turn us in.

"Why should I?" he said, laughing. "This is like the stuff I read in American Lit. You know, people running to or from something, only this time it's real." He tapped the wheel and settled back in his seat. "Which makes me a plot device. I've never been a plot device. It's kind of liberating." He'd take us to Chattanooga, he said, but we had to pay for gas since we were a bit richer than him.

So we drove. It was hard to believe that for once our luck had shifted and someone would be helpful. Michael asked about Wattles and the robbery; in turn, I asked about this Freedom Ride. He laughed again, more relaxed, and said I must really be from the boondocks to miss the civil-rights nastiness of the last few years.

I hadn't *completely* missed it—you couldn't live in this part of the country and miss it—but on the whole it hadn't touched me. I hadn't known any coloreds in Wattles, simply 'cause there weren't any 'round. Folks said it was 'cause there'd never been slave owners in that part of the country, but the real truth was that black folks had moved away. The place was too mean. Folks near the bottom have few tears for those lower'n them. In Wattles, the greatest meanness in people came out concernin' jobs. A job held by a black man meant one less for a white, and only the absolute nastiest labor went to coloreds. Who had it worse?, Daddy asked me once: the Cherokees sent to reservations, or the niggers kept 'round for dirty work? The answer depends on who does the askin', he said.

The Freedom Rides started in May, Michael said, and many were organized in colleges like Vanderbilt in Nashville. Though segregation in interstate travel was outlawed in 1949, he explained, Southern states still forced blacks to sit in the back and barred them from "whites only" facilities. The strategy of the activists was to defy local law, station by station, forcing the federal government to protect the protesters and enter the fight, something it didn't want to do.

Yet protection became a greater concern than anyone dreamed. The first Freedom Ride was firebombed, a second through Birmingham was mobbed by Klansmen, and a full-scale riot occurred in Montgomery. Those who made it to Mississippi were thrown in jail. It got to where Riders wrote sealed letters to their families in case they never returned. "You volunteered for *that?*" I asked, and he said nothin' ever changed in this country without sacrifice. I answered, "It sounds more like suicide to me."

I mean, why would anyone want to make *hundreds* of yahoos angry? I'd made one mad—just one—and look what *my* life had become! Get a whole passel of yahoos upset, and the world as we knew it would end. Hollywood actors would get voted President. Maybe there'd be a nuclear war. These were crazy times in more ways than one, Michael agreed. "All sorts of people are coming out of the woodwork," he said, "not just yahoos. All are demanding respect and all think their way is the Gospel." With that, he launched into a poem.

Mind you, I like a good poem same as anyone. In second grade, I'd hopped on stage to recite "Humpty Dumpty" and the classic—

I had a little dog
His name was Blue
I pulled his tail
And the buttermilk flew

—which proved I had a way with words. But Michael's poem came outta the blue, and it wasn't like neither of these. First off, it didn't rhyme, and was wrote by some New York beatnik named Ginsberg. I knew all about beatniks—they hung out in coffeehouses, had pointy beards, and said, "Oh, daddy-o," like Maynard G. Krebs on the *Dobie Gillis Show.* Michael Venus called the poem "Howl" and at first I thought it'd be a nice little poem about dogs. But when he shouted out lines about starving and naked hipsters, I knew this wasn't no puppy-dog tale. It was more like the effects of bad whiskey, you know, the kind filtered through car radiators and sold in Mason jars. Michael really loved that poem, but more than the poem he loved the idea that entire worlds of misfits and exiles existed in

America about whom folks like me had never dreamed. Crazies who waved poems and peters at unsuspecting strangers, predators prowling the wastes who ran up the body count like hometown football scores. Homosexuals proud and scared of what they wanted; pregnant girls my age crossin' state lines for backroom abortions; straight-arrow boys like Arney Slover and Luther Burgess who rushed to war full of hope and glory, and returned partially assembled. There were too many outcasts in the America of Michael Venus, and just at the very moment when folks hoped for better things.

That made me think of the picture hanging in Mama's room—*Sinners Roosting under Satan's Tail*. Now I knew why it'd always disturbed me so. The naked sinners in the picture weren't repentant, not at all. Look closely in the painted faces and you saw that they were happy, frozen midstep in a terrifying rapture. A woman with black scabs on her face screamed as Old Nick's tail dropped to crush her, but the scream was of joy, not fear. The damned prayed hard for apocalypse. They danced faster, hoping to hurry the ruin.

Maybe folks were right to not stray far from home. Maybe it was wiser to stay in Wattles, where at least you knew your place and didn't end up feeling lost. There weren't no fatal detours if you hunkered down forever in good ole Tennessee. I'd seen too much in the last day or four to make me think twice about goin' on to better things. What if all America was one vast river of night with all the lost sailors ridin' their flimsy rafts . . . a doomed race of Huck Finns goin' nowhere but crazy . . . a jukebox-screamin', rock-'n'-roll moanin' sideshow of cigarette smoke, one-night religion and sex, a land of false hope and cheap ecstasy? Where a fierce wind drilled the sounds of Elvis into every kid my age, from Times Square to Hollywood, from the hillbilly towns of Ohio to the limp palm trees of Florida. What if all America was like Tennessee?

If so, there were plenty of places to get fooled, but nowhere left in which to get saved.

———•———

We reached an overlook above Chattanooga about twilight, pullin' briefly on a kind of Lover's Leap where some eager couples were already parked to spark and coo. Fabian sang "Turn Me Loose" from a radio in one of the overheated interiors; from another, Dion crooned, "Why Must I Be a Teenager in Love?" Still, most of the couples had pulled back from their liplocks to watch the show spread out before us like a personal drive-in. Chattanooga lay in the valley, its million lights twinkling against an indigo sky. At its western edge, the Tennessee had swelled to 'bout a quarter-mile wide and curved into the darkness like a sword. Behind the starry city, Raccoon Mountain and Missionary Ridge blocked entrance to the Southern lowlands, while the black brow of Lookout Mountain frowned over it all. This was the very place all them SEE ROCK CITY signs ordered us to go, but underneath the postcard beauty I knew a lot of misery had started here. The Trail of Tears began in this cleft in the mountains, the point from which at least 15,000 Cherokees were marched west after gold was discovered in northern Georgia, herded first into concentration camps in the mountains' shadows, then sent on a cold winter trek that left 4,000 dead. Twenty-five years later, bloodshed returned for a second visit when Union forces breached the mountain pass and marched on to burn Atlanta. Those responsible for the Cherokees' grief now saw their own society come to an end.

Now a new war had started, or at least so it seemed. The swollen river had slipped into the warehouse district to unleash fireworks and flames. Every now and then we heard a *whump* and sparks arched silver and ruby. "That's magnesium," said a kid in a black jacket, perched on the hood of his car. The flood had entered a warehouse storing tons of the stuff, igniting this late Fourth of July. "They closed off the area when the blast lifted off the roof," said his girlfriend, cuddled beside him. "Isn't it pretty? It's the best seat in town." We watched, all reverent, as burning barrels of magnesium floated silently away.

"That's where we're headed," Michael Venus told us. "Everyone in the Freedom Ride is supposed to meet at the Greyhound station, and from what I understand it's right next to the warehouse district."

"So we're drivin' into town, despite the flood 'n' fires 'n' who knows what else?" asked Cole, more than a little disbelieving.

"Keep your head down," advised the teenage couple as we said good-bye.

"It hasn't helped yet," Cole groused as we drove away.

* * *

Like Michael said, the Chattanooga Greyhound station sat at the edge of the war zone. This was where we'd part—Michael to his Freedom Ride, me and Cole to the ticket window for Florida— yet when we got inside, all was empty and quiet. Strangely so, even with the festival *whumps* and thin sirens in the background. The place was downright creepy. At one end of the station stood a cafeteria with a single bored waitress, balanced on the other end by a ticket window with one bored clerk. There were rows of seats, some with quarter-fed televisions bolted to the arms. Blue gray lockers lined a wall, while a chipped white door by the ticket window said "Colored Facilities." We peeked inside. No one was there either but a sleepy old man.

"You sure you got the date right?" I asked.

"Something's got to be wrong," Michael said. "They're supposed to be here by now. Maybe they're already on the bus."

We walked through the door for "Departures," where buses rumbled in their docks and diesel fumes filled the air. Each bus was a blue-and-silver box of metal and smoked glass, a sprinting race hound painted on the side. A policeman with a guard dog watched and smoked a cigarette as a young man kissed an older lady and helped her up the steps of an idling "Stratoliner." A cool wind whipped between buses to Miami, Cleveland, Chicago. I pulled my army jacket tight and felt the rucksack underneath; it was not a thing of joy bein' so near the Law with all this dough. Maybe it was smarter to keep the pack in a locker till time to depart, so I walked back in the station, paid my nickel, and pocketed the key. When I returned, Michael was chattin' up the cop about the Freedom Riders, while Cole shifted from foot to foot. The officer separated from the wall and flipped away his cigarette. It sputtered on the sidewalk and died.

I had a bad feeling 'bout this. Something was goin' on, and I studied the lawman more carefully. A pair of corporal's stripes were stitched to his sleeve; his black-and-tan German shepherd made to stand, but the corporal signaled him down. The dog's brown eyes never left Michael Venus; as I edged up, his twin doggy beams focused on me. Where were the Riders, Michael asked. Had something happened? "So you're with those civil-rights people," the corporal finally said, and Michael filled him in. The corporal nodded as if this explained all the mysteries of life. He nodded to me and Cole. "They with you, too?"

I noticed when he said it that he'd glanced past my shoulder, so I followed his eyes. Another man-dog team approached across the parking lot. They stopped behind us, the second shepherd sitting on cue but angled forward as if awaitin' word to leap. "Stay," his handler said.

This was worse than no good—this was a hitch in our giddy-up, a nicely planned trap all ready to spring. I edged toward the door, but the corporal stopped me in my tracks. "You with him, young lady?"

I couldn't say no. I'd followed him out, dressed in fatigues like the ladies' auxiliary of Young Tennesseans for Fidel. If it walks like a duck and squawks like a duck, it must be a duck, at least in the eyes of the Law. Any protests to the contrary would just feed suspicions.

Now Cole walked up, glancin' back and skittish, as a *third* dog team appeared. "This one, too?" the corporal said. Michael Venus asked if this was an Inquisition. "Keep your voice down," the corporal advised. "It gets the dogs excited. You wouldn't want that, trust me."

It was obvious now we were hemmed in on three sides and goin' nowhere. Nowhere, that is, 'cept where the policemen said. I kept my face down so my hair partly covered my profile. As long as they believed me to be a screamin' pinko out to change the world, they might not link me with a diner waitress connected to a murder north of here. Michael asked if we were under arrest. No, said the corporal, but he suggested we come with him, anyway. "We got word there might be trouble for you Freedom Riders, so we're keeping you overnight in protective custody."

"Keep us where?"

In the City Jail, he smiled, just a couple of blocks uphill. A dog walked either side of us, and one behind. The one in back sniffed my cuffs and started whining. "Duke don't like the smell of beatniks," his handler explained. "Where you from, girl, dressed like that? You a Communist or something?"

"That's enough," the corporal snapped. "They're under our *protection*, remember?"

"Duke'll guard this'un real good."

I was almost relieved to get to the jail. It was an old stone shoebox, several stories high and built atop the hill. We were marched to a metal door set with a window. The corporal punched the speaker button on the side. "We got three more guests from the bus station," he said.

There was a buzz and the door clicked. "Bring 'em in," the intercom said.

We walked down a long hall. Every step echoed like a coffin lid crashing down. A second metal door swung open and a jailer pointed to a "receiving room." It sounded so polite, like

I'd go inside and receive a prize. There were more lockers on a wall and a jailer behind a desk. By now, the three of us were outnumbered by curious deputies. All seemed bored with their jobs, so bored, in fact, there seemed little danger of my bein' identified long as I played my role. They patted us down and asked us to empty our pockets. I watched the jailer stuff change and my locker key in a brown envelope and file it away.

We were escorted to the colored part of jail. The stone walls dripped; the air felt sharp with an ancient tang of vomit and pee. Metal clanged on metal; the hall rang with voices and footsteps that throbbed against concrete and stone. Handheld mirrors poked from the bars, watching our approach, and prisoners seemed packed five or ten to a cell. "You come to save us, too?" a big man asked, his head shaved smooth, and his cellmates laughed.

"That's Lucas, a regular," said our escort. "Don't mind him."

We were placed in the next cell over from the big man, at the very end of the hall. Though usually the drunk tank, the cell was reserved tonight for Freedom Riders, the deputy said. It was the biggest on the block, a holding tank with benches and a few stained mattresses pushed against the walls. The windows on one side overlooked the courts and police station, while those in back had a view of the water-front and its fireworks show. A message printed in black gave numbers for rival bondsmen: GET OUT FAST FOR LESS. The deputy clanged the door shut and strolled away, jinglin' his keys.

Judging by their looks, Lucas and our other neighbors weren't getting out soon. I could see cell to cell down the row we'd come, and each was little better'n a narrow closet with bunks on both sides and a toilet at the back wall. The row was faintly lit by the silver glow of a black-and-white TV set suspended from the wall in a wire cage. It was opposite our drunk tank, and right now was playing the evening news. "Like that?" Lucas nodded at the set. "It's new in here. The idea is that we'll stay quiet with somethin' to stare at all day."

I gazed down the colored block at the line of cells. The further the cells were from the TV set, the more the light faded from dirty yellow, to grainy gray, to graveyard black. I watched as the silhouettes of men captured in this light merged and split like weird clay figures. I heard rheumy laughter, excited voices, catcalls; the place stank of smoke, cold metal, piss, and booze. A dark face in a top bunk of the neighbor cell watched my inspection. He smiled, then turned his head and covered his eyes.

I examined my own cell. Ours was the only one in the block with blacks and whites together, though mostly blacks—twenty-five to thirty people standing or crouching in groups, sitting on the benches or stretched out on the floor. In other words, enough for a busload. This was a generation headed some-where: men and women, college age and older; serious and clean-cut; geared up for a life of gray flannel suits, Christmas Club accounts, ranch homes and a two-car garage—just like their white counterparts in the suburbs. They were the best and the brightest of a new black elite, and unaccustomed to jails like this; they studied us as we entered, knowing we were not one of them. I was relieved when Michael Venus walked over to the others to tell them of the death of the professor. Our scrutiny was abandoned in the general shock and tears.

That was fine by me. I sat on the floor and leaned against the wall as I gazed around. It struck me how everyone in the other cells, out there, seemed much poorer than everyone *in here*. The inmates in the neighbor cells wore blue jumpsuits, but more telling was how they were accustomed to this place, like they'd been here many times. One man in the next cell was beaten 'round the face and hands, while the man who'd watched me from the bunk had a running sore on his arm. They seemed to expect the worst and got it, so there was little use to worry about when they'd go free. Jail was a second home—maybe, for some, the only one. I heard no screams of outrage from the other cells, no one standin' at the bars and callin' for his lawyer. These folks couldn't afford lawyers, much less the ten percent bail. This was where they'd be tonight, tomorrow night, and a month later. Might as well get comfortable, bub.

Cole sat beside me and sighed. "What is it about you and jails?" he said. "I come from a family that dislikes such places, even if we cain't avoid 'em. You seek 'em out like you plan to move in."

I didn't grace such meanness with a reply. Was it *my* fault we'd ended here? Was it *my* fault we'd hooked up with Sallie—which swept us down the river—which dumped us in the hospital—which got me introduced to Michael Venus in the City Morgue? Was it *my* fault we hadn't caught the bus south to Florida from Muscovy, like Cole suggested, but chased the money instead?

Hell, yes! It was my fault, and nobody likes bein' confronted with their multiple sins. Where'd he learn to treat a girl? Probably from his dad. I left him in a huff and stomped across the cell. I stopped at the back window and studied the moon. How nice it'd be to sprout feathers and unfurl great wings. I'd float from these troubles, my wings bearin' me up till I was just another dark spot on the moon's bright face. I'd look back at the earth's blue luster and the cities twinklin' like a necklace.

"Hey, you!" a rough voice snapped. "What you doing by them bars?"

I jerked awake. A jailer stood in the hall and waved me over. He was a big pale man, Elvis sideburns droopin' below his earlobes, a round face pitted from acne. He seemed too big for this tight space, yet stepped so lightly he'd caught me by surprise. "You with these nigras and agitators?" he asked.

"They seem all right to me," I said.

He snorted with disdain. "I swear, you don't look much older'n my own daughter. If she was in here with this bunch, I'd whip her ass." He scratched his chin and asked if I was in college, too.

Trick question, I realized. If I said yes, the others would

hear and ask why they'd never seen me in class. If I said no, they'd question what I was doin' here at all. "I work 'round colleges," I finally lied.

"How so?"

I thought fast. "Uh, singin'. I sing."

"Country western? Like Loretta Lynn?"

"Folksongs."

"You mean like Burl Ives? I like that boll-weevil song."

"I work in coffeehouses, like, uh, the beatniks."

"You a beatnik? You don't look like a beatnik."

"See, you're typin' people," I joshed.

"Some of my best friends is stereotypes," he smirked. "So sing me a song."

I stared back, hoping I'd heard wrong. "Say again?"

"I like music. It gets borin' down here, these long shifts. Sing me a protest song."

Another deputy walked up, which was bad enough, but on the TV behind them the evening news switched from flood coverage to a full-screen shot of Arnold Simpson lookin' mussed and confused. Oh, Lord, they'd found him in the church, and though part of me was grateful, another part wondered why he had to be interviewed *now*. "I was kidnapped," he told the reporter, "stole my truck . . . one hundred thousand dollars . . . hit me with a ball bat . . . Dahlia Jean." I could barely hear his voice—just what exactly was he sayin' about me? I looked back at Cole. He'd seen it, too, and his eyes were wide. On the screen flashed a photo of the church where we'd left poor Arnold, of the bank robbed by Mama and Twitch; there was film of the bank teller crying, more film of Sheriff Bobby Plenty in the hospital, a photo of Sallie Goodnight, and of Harson's diner, with the words "Owner Murdered" over it. Last but not least, there was the yearbook photo of me.

Through it all, the deputies kept their backs turned and hadn't seen a thing. But I had. Cole had. Big Lucas in the next cell over had. "S-sure," I said, "I'll sing you a song."

"That's fine," Elvis Sideburns said. He looked at Lucas. "Ain't that right, Lucas? We're gettin' some entertainment." Lucas looked from me, to the TV, and back. "Better do as he says, honey," he said. "The deputy gets testy if he gets bored. It's either this or watch the news."

"Gawd, I hate the news," Elvis Sideburns agreed.

But, Lord, I didn't know any protest songs. I started to sing "Bill Bailey," but both jailers said they'd already heard it a million times. I mixed up "If I Had a Hammer" with "Nine Pound Hammer"; I remembered a few lines from "Jailhouse Rock," but didn't think that was appropriate right now. Finally I recalled the poem Michael Venus had recited. "I wrote one called 'Howl,' " I said, then cleared my throat and hummed a key:

"*Hmmm*, I seen the best minds of our generation, draggin' themselves through naked streets, angelheaded hucksters luggin' dynamite, *hooowl*, breakin' down crying as bullies popped them in the ass, *hoooowl*, howlin' to holy mama, *hoooooowl*, thrown off roofs and travelin' a million miles a second, *hoooooooowl*, landin' with a *plop*. But that's the way it is, so sock it to me, Mama, watch your big butt, Daddy, I'll be on you like a sweat, the South shall *hoooooooooowl* again."

Then I was done. I noticed it'd got real quiet in my cell . . . indeed, in the whole row. Both guards had backed against the far wall, eyes wide. The Freedom Riders stared like someone crazy had been dropped in their cell. Only Big Lucas broke the silence: "Deputy, if she was black, I'd say you'd jailed a crazy nigger. But since she's white, I'd say she's *dis-turbed.*"

That broke the silence, all right, and the jailer's face grew red. "Shut up, Lucas, or you'll be on report," Elvis Sideburns said. He slapped his hands against his pants and him and his buddy stomped away without another word.

"That was quick thinkin'," Lucas whispered through the bars when the door clanged shut, "but I wouldn't make a career outta singin' if I was you."

I went and sat back beneath the window, hugging my knees

to my chin. "Not real smart, Dahlia," Cole commented. "Now everybody's wonderin' who we are." Once again he was right, for as I watched the Freedom Riders, they watched me. They'd pretty much ignored us till my free performance; now they turned in a bunch on Michael Venus and grilled him who I was.

One woman in particular watched me as they talked, a tall, lean black woman with a high forehead and large, luminous eyes. Her eyebrows curled in apostrophes, giving the sense that she was skeptical of everything and not that easy to fool. The others huddled and sent her over to check me out. Her eyebrows raised curiously as I met her gaze; her lip curved up, amused. "Who exactly *are* you?" she said.

"My mama said it ain't polite to pry."

"Your mama never heard you sing. I'll try again. My name is Verna Albright. Yours is?"

"Daisy Mae."

She sighed and settled down beside me on the floor. "I don't think so," she said. "My grandmother was a midwife, my mother was a midwife, I'm a nurse, and someday I hope my daughter makes a doctor. My whole family has brought life into this earth, and in the process you learn to notice a few things. You're not a Freedom Rider, and you're certainly not a singer. You know what I think? I think you're that girl whose photo was just on TV."

I looked her in the eyes, which seemed amused and unfooled. "Who else thinks like you?" I said.

"No one that I can tell. The others are plain mystified by your appearance, and I seemed the only one standing at a good angle to see the screen."

"Who you gonna tell?"

"It all depends on you."

I studied my options and they didn't look good. As reward for trying to be so secret, I was leaving a trail a blind man could follow. "I'm just tryin' to see my daddy," I told her, and quietly laid out everything as it occurred.

She sighed again when I was through. A man who seemed to be the leader, an old bald fellow with gold-rimmed glasses, started over when he saw her reaction, but Verna smiled and waved him off. "That's Dr. Singer, head of the East Tennessee NAACP," she said, then pointed up front where an intense young black man, handsome as a movie star, was surrounded by college students, mostly female. "And that's a friend of Dr. King's, who works for CORE." She straightened her back against the cinder-block wall. "In other words, this little trip is pretty important, and these people would die if they knew who you were."

"So you *are* gonna tell."

She shook her head. "No way, honey," she said. "Do you have any idea what would happen if it got out who you are? The law in these towns we pass through *prays* for a legal reason to lock us up. Harboring a fugitive sounds pretty good to me."

"So you're *not* gonna tell."

"I don't know what I'm going to do. I'd like to beat you with a stick, I do know that. And once we get out of this cell, you're not getting on our bus—that much is clear." She leaned her head back against the wall. "But I've got to say something to the others; they're waiting for some explanation, and things will get testy if I don't give them one." Her breath whistled through her teeth as she considered little white lies: I recognized a kindred spirit, but she wasn't as practiced in that art as me. "How about you say we're a coupla love-struck kids on the run from our parents, and we hitched a ride with Michael Venus," I suggested, tryin' to help out. "It's not that far from the truth, you know."

She looked at me in admiration. "Not bad. You always this quick?"

"Quick's not the word for it," Cole groused, listening quietly till now.

"Don't mind him," I mumbled. "He's just mad we're in jail."

"If you're going to have a spat, keep it down," Verna said.

"Okay, I'll tell them this, but tomorrow, if and when we get out, you head in the opposite direction. Understand?"

"Perfectly," I said.

She trotted back to her group, and I settled back to watch the show. At first her friends seemed shocked that we weren't fellow activists; then they looked at us and laughed. Michael Venus looked embarrassed and relieved, at once, when the others started kidding him—what could he do, say Verna had the story all wrong? Kids in love do dumb things, I heard someone hoot. Just usually not *this* dumb.

———✦———

The jailers woke us at 5:00. A pale light shone through the windows and a single bulb burned in the hall. We had powdered milk and eggs for breakfast, and by 6:30 our jailers escorted us through an underground passage. Three lawyers in gray suits stood at the end of the tunnel. As they spoke to the man from CORE and Dr. Singer, word of their conversation passed down the line. The lawyers had wrangled all night and got the hearing changed to federal court. That was good news, Verna said.

We were led into a courtroom big as a church, walls high and dark-paneled, windows stretching from ceiling to floor. Paintings of past judges glowered from the walls. Up front was a raised dais with a massive desk and chair; I was reminded of an altar, separated from the rest of the court by a wood rail. An aisle led down the middle, dividing two long rows of pews. We were led to one side, and on the other sat the sheriff and police chief, both in dress uniform. Straight-faced marshals formed a wall behind us, and in the very back sat a row of reporters.

As soon as we sat, the clerk shot up and yelled "All rise!" A snowy-headed man charged through a side door. He was small and wrinkled, like all the juice had been sucked from him long ago, and he seemed swallowed up by his black robe. The clerk read the particulars of our case and the judge followed along from a handful of papers. He flipped off his glasses and stared at the two uniforms. "Chief, why were these people arrested?" he finally said.

The police chief stood and pulled at the knot in his tie. "They were put in protective custody, Your Honor," he said.

"Uh-huh," replied the judge. "And Sheriff, if these people were placed in protective custody, why were they kept overnight in the drunk tank?"

The sheriff rose and looked even sicker than his colleague. "Overcrowding, Your Honor. It's the only place we could keep that many people at one time."

"Uh-huh," the judge said again. He went back to his reading. The chief and sheriff stood an embarrassed second longer, then sat down. One of our lawyers rose halfway from his seat, bending at the waist as if beginning a painful and elaborate prayer. "Your Honor—"

"I'm reading your bill of particulars," the judge snapped, glaring from the page. "Is there something more you want to add?"

"Uh, no, Your Honor."

"Then sit down."

There was silence again. We shifted on our behinds. Each page rustled as the judge placed it atop a growing stack. He removed his glasses, sighed, and told the police chief and sheriff to rise.

"Gentlemen," he said, "the way I see it, you violated almost every federal law barring segregation in interstate travel with last night's little stunt. Did you know that? I also think you violated these people's Fifth and Fourteenth Amendment rights, but their attorneys only partially addressed that in their brief, so you're lucky, and it won't be considered today. What you did wasn't very smart, do you know that? I could have you both thrown in jail."

"Your Honor," said the police chief, rising. "It was for their own protection. We had information—"

"Didn't I just tell someone not to interrupt?" The judge turned to his bailiff. "Did I just say that, Mr. Murphy? I am old and my memory might be failing."

"You said it, Your Honor, I heard you," the bailiff said. "You were very civil."

"That's a relief," the judge replied. "Chief, another interruption and I'll find you in contempt." The police chief sagged. The sheriff, who had his hand up, dropped it quickly. The judge smiled his sour smile. "As I said, you two violated every antisegregation statute I can think of, and I would enjoy nothing more than throwing you in the same place you put these people. You might argue ignorance of the law, but that, of course, would be ironic, since we all know how often that works in criminal cases, hmm?" He glanced back at his papers. "I also know you wouldn't have acted except at the direction of a few city fathers, who, I notice, chose not to attend today. Perhaps you should reconsider your friendships," he said, somewhat sadly. "I see in its brief that the state proposes to put the Freedom Riders on separate buses back to their homes in order to 'maintain the peace and security of the sovereign city of Chattanooga, the surrounding counties, and the Great State of Tennessee.' " He paused. "Gentlemen, if these people want to stop at every bus station and use every 'whites-only' bathroom from Nome, Alaska, to Key West, Florida, they have that right, and they have it because it's guaranteed by federal law."

He leaned forward in his chair. "Do you understand the law? I thought you did, since the two of you took an oath to uphold it. Of course, the day of that ceremony was quite nice, and maybe you were dreaming of fishing, so maybe you didn't hear your oath all the way through. Let me remind you, then, that you are charged with upholding the laws of the city, state, *and* the nation, and you will do so whether you agree with them or not." He stared down at them coldly. "I am setting these people free. They may go wherever they want, and if I see you here again on this or related matters, I *will* hold you in contempt and gladly throw you in jail. You and your political masters, also, so please tell them that for me. Is that understood?"

"Yes, sir," both men said.

"Then for you, court is dismissed." The two officials hurried out. When the door swang shut, he turned to us and added, "You all stay here."

The bailiff roared that court was ended and the reporters rushed out to write what they'd seen and heard. The judge addressed a lean marshal standing by the doors. "Sir, I want you to escort these people back to that bus station and see that each and every one gets on that bus without exception. I don't want a single one left behind. Get them out of this town for their own good. Take them back to the jail for their possessions, and if they've stored anything in the station lockers, watch over them until they are seated on their bus. They never leave your sight. Is that clear?"

"Perfectly, Your Honor," the marshal said.

"What about us?" I whispered to Verna.

"I don't think you have much choice," she said. "You can get off later."

The old judge cleared his throat. "You may think you won a victory today, but I would like to disabuse you of that notion," he said. "I see that most of you are young. Quite young," and he seemed to look straight at me. "You think you are engaged in a great cause, almost like a war, and I'm not saying you aren't. But wars are begun by the old and paid for by the young for one reason: The young never believe they'll die. Perhaps some of you are terrified of what lies ahead, but you have no earthly idea of the madness you're entering and that you're calling down upon yourselves. This, here, today, was nothing. It was strained, but civilized. Those men were my friends, and I've probably lost their friendship forever. But what you're heading into now strikes me as a kind of rabies, a self-destructive savagery which few can understand. I don't know what is happening to this nation and I doubt anyone truly does. I used to be proud of my country, but I'm not so sure anymore. You may think that my order today is a cause to celebrate, but I'll tell you I'm doing you no favor by sending you straight into the gun sights of people who hate you more than they've ever hated anything. I wonder what your parents think: They are proud of you, no doubt, but you're still their children, and you're marching willingly into a brutality they've spent most of their lives trying to escape. I am a father myself, and one of the greatest kinds of helplessness you can ever know is watching your children encounter evil and knowing there is little you can do." He paused, and when he spoke again, it was almost to himself. "You may feel you've won a battle, but I feel like I'm sending you to your graves. God help you." He rose and nodded, and we rose with him. "Court dismissed," the clerk said.

The marshals escorted us out. I looked at my fellow travelers, and not a one was smiling. I looked at Cole and he looked sick.

It'll be fine, I tried to tell myself. It'll be just great.

I mean, what could happen on a bus in this day and age?

The Mansion on the Hill

HARVEY NOBLE'S "MAN" owned a bar at the far edge of town. It had no name he knew of, and never did—just a glowing BUD sign in the window of a low and yellow building. A mud-splattered Dodge was parked in the gravel lot. "Let me do the talkin'," Harvey said.

Burma and me followed him in. It was a different world in here, untouched by flood, rising water, or half the town drowned. This was a bar as basic as they made 'em: plain wood floor, unpainted walls, fifteen tables scattered 'round with chairs. The corners faded into shadows; in one corner sat a tiny stage protected from local music critics by chicken wire. The long bar itself stretched along the back: pickled pigs' feet floated in a jar of vinegar at one corner, balanced on the other side by a rack of chips and pork rinds. A TV behind the bar bathed it all in a mercury glow.

Two people sat at the bar, neither glancing up as the screen door slammed. The bartender was bald, a T-shirt stretched tight across his gut as he read the morning paper. Across the bar sat an even bigger man, balanced on a bar stool. He was built like a college halfback going to fat, and wore a green sport coat, cowboy boots, denim jeans, and snap-brim hat. An orange feather was tucked in the hatband, and a white button with an orange "T" pinned to the crown. A long leather wallet was secured to his belt with two brass fasteners and a steel chain, in some parts of the country the badge of a man carrying large sums of cash. His eyes were glued to the set, following the annual football grudge match between Alabama and Tennessee. Alabama was only about 100 touchdowns ahead. Harvey nodded to the bartender. "Tennessee losin' again?"

"Whatta you think?" the barkeep said. "I don't even know why he watches. Everybody knows what's gonna happen. Someday he'll drop dead from blood pressure and I'll be out of a job."

"It's not like you do any work anyway," the green sports coat growled. "What you want, Harvey?" he said over his shoulder without looking back. "Ain't one disaster enough for today?"

"What makes you think I want somethin'?"

"You always want somethin', you little fuck. You have ever since we was kids. It's what makes you lovable."

"Meet my brother, Tiny," Harvey said. For a moment, I was tongue-tied. Two unlikelier brothers never came down the chute; the shock must've killed their mother, just like I done mine. Tiny Noble turned around and smiled. "Don't worry, me and Harvey always have this effect on people. What can I do for you?"

"Harvey said you're familiar with somethin' called a Freedom Ride."

The man's big head swiveled till he stared at Harvey, who got nervous all of a sudden. "I told 'em nothin', Tiny," he said.

"Their kids got hooked up with that nosy reporter always askin' questions. They may've gone to Chattanooga, that's all. I said I knew someone might help."

The brother's green eyes returned to my face with a slow, searching gaze. He smiled and said, "I do believe you're a con."

I shrugged. "Ain't denyin' it," I said.

"Bushy Mountain?"

"For a while."

"I knew a guy there," he said, and reeled off a name. I knew a test when I heard it, so I told him I knew the bastard, but not good. In for grand theft auto, right? Took a car what belonged to a judge. Tiny sighed and said they didn't make 'em much stupider, then motioned to a table. "Take your beers and sit. I'll come over halftime." The bartender drew our beers and Alabama scored another touchdown. The first half ended. The big man told the barkeep to turn it off; he'd had enough grief for one day.

Tiny glided to our table and straddled a chair between Burma and me. It's surprising how light on his feet a moose can be; it's a dangerous trait that traps the unaware. "They say Bear Bryant walks on water," he said morosely. "I wish Tennessee would buy itself a holy man."

"Maybe there ain't enough to go around," Harvey said.

"Harvey, shut up," Tiny replied. "You don't know nuthin' 'bout football and never have, all you know is makin' a buck in unsavory ways." He passed his hand over his face to change the subject. "Tell me about your kids."

I told him some, minus the cash and criminal details. He nodded politely, aware more was left unsaid, then sat back and placed his hands behind his head. "Normally I'd say I couldn't help you, but Harvey's kin, so he must have a good reason for this. There's a meeting tonight on this very subject, and we're short a few hands."

The oily way he said it gave me a bad feeling. This meeting, I asked: Who's it for?

Tiny leaned forward, the chair creaking under his weight. He studied my face awhile. "If we help you, you help us. That's the way these things work, you know."

I asked again who held the meeting. He grinned real wide. "Guy like you, in and out of the joint, you've heard a lot of things, met a lot of people. You're not dumb. I'm sure you've encountered the Invisible Empire in your travels."

I sank against the backrest, heart low as any fan of Tennessee football. I'd heard of the Empire, all right. Everyone had.

Without knowing, I'd got us involved with the Klan.

———•———

You couldn't live in the South without hearing of the Ku Klux Klan. They were part of the landscape, like gravy and biscuits or *Gone With the Wind*. Maybe more in Tennessee, the state where they was born. The hoods, capes, and flaming crosses made 'em seem unreal for whites, but for any black, Jew, or Catholic unlucky enough to cross their path, the Klan was very real. They'd been a power in the 1920s, electing twelve governors nationwide and impeaching another, marching 40,000 strong through Washington, D.C. But those days were gone. Today they seemed so far behind the rest of the country, they must be related to cavemen.

The truth was more complicated, as is the case with most violent things. Sure they were losers, but the world is filled with losers who get dangerous when riled. The anger of such folks is a natural force that rises like a tide. Their membership could surprise you at times. There were the greasers and thugs, as you'd expect, but there were also working stiffs who somehow felt cheated by life; there were politicians and money men who rode that anger like Seabiscuit on Derby Day. There were a goodly number of combat vets who'd never lost their taste for battle and who, like Harvey, somehow felt betrayed.

By some strange magic, they'd formed a new class—a new and violent Okie who never quite escaped the dust bowl in their brains. Until recently, most seemed content in their klaverns, recognizing no higher authority than themselves. A Friday-night cross burning was a good excuse for drinking beer and letting off steam. And so it went, and maybe would've continued through eternity, till civil rights became a common enemy and its successes lit a new fire beneath their tails.

The biggest group was the United Klans of America, the Invisible Empire of which Tiny spoke now. I'd met some in prison: their blood-drop tattoos gave 'em away—same as the ring in my pocket, a trinket I shouldn't flash around. A recruiter approached me once in the prison library, the one place in all of Bushy Mountain where I could be alone. He radiated a confidence out of kilter with his hardscrabble looks and started braggin' how there was 10,000 brothers like him in Georgia, Alabama, the Carolinas, and Tennessee. It was like joining a holy order, he promised—sign up and I'd be the last of the righteous outlaws, the last white hope, the defender of the faith when the end times came. They were comin', brother; just you wait and see. As I sat and listened, I realized that, take away the talk of race, this was just another sermon by my old man. Preachin' was preachin', no matter the subject, and I'd had enough of that for *ten* lifetimes.

But I also knew this of preachers and their congregations: Membership made one part of the elect, and the whole world was instantly explained as a stage play of villains and heroes. So what if they're outnumbered? In the South, lost causes draw juice from a million worn-out batteries.

I hadn't been nice to that recruiter. Instead, I'd brought my face close to his. Who were niggers but the ultimate inmate, I asked, drawing years for crimes we only got months for? If you want a fuckin' enemy, why not the bankers and politicians?

"We hate them, too," he stammered, suddenly all pop-eyed.

But I was wound up now. "You know what I'd do if I was a nigger?" I said. "I'd gun down every white-robed son-of-a-bitch who looked at me cross-eyed, then tell the judge I'd done the world a public service."

The Klansman left real quick and never bothered me after that. Sometimes it helps bein' crazy as hell.

But that was not a luxury I could afford right now. Not when Tiny said him and his white-robed buddies knew every stop that Freedom Ride had planned. There was a meeting tonight at the home of some guy named the Colonel. We was invited if we was truly serious 'bout the future of our kids, he said.

I told him thanks, feeling none too proud.

———◆———

That night we followed Tiny, trailing his green coupe up a knob that overlooked the flood plain. The air seemed cold and thin, but it was plenty steamy in our car. "We have to join the Klan to find our children?" fumed Burma. "Of all the lamebrained notions! Why can't we just go to Chattanooga ourselves?"

" 'Cause we're a day behind and have no idea where to head next if we miss 'em," I tried explainin'.

"So we ask the ticket agent. You don't have to be a genius to figure that one out."

"Two total strangers asking after a busload of civil-rights folks who've gotten every death threat possible? Tell me that won't draw attention."

"So we go to Florida and wait."

"You gonna tell me where in Florida?"

She said she wasn't stupid. I smiled back and said, in that case, we'd do it my way.

Harvey listened as he drove, takin' it in. We didn't act like normal parents—that was sure. I could see his mind at work, making connections that led to the bag of money. He wanted more than two gold rings, but he was also out of sorts. "What's the matter with you?" I said.

"We're going to the Colonel's."

"Somethin' the matter with this colonel?"

"Tiny calls him a genius, but I'm not sure. I'm as much against civil rights as the next man, but when they talk of bombing churches and stuff, well, I don't know."

"Why take part, then?"

He drew a deep breath. "The Colonel's a bigwig 'round here, and in my business, you need the right connections. I do what I must to get by."

Burma leaned forward over the seat. "Our parasite has a conscience?"

Harvey's head shrank between his shoulders. "Everybody's got a right to make a living."

"Tell me more about this colonel," I said.

To start off, nobody called him by name. He'd been "the Colonel" as long as Harvey recalled; the name seemed to come from his soldiering days. He'd been a forward artillery observer in the Pacific, an assignment that drove many folks mad. You crept as close as possible to the enemy and called back coordinates, hoping to God a shell didn't fall short and land on you. He came home a hero and got a job with the ketchup plant, his mission to scout out smaller companies which could be bought and absorbed. He rose in the ranks and grew rich, and now lived on the side of the mountain in a palace of glass and stone. But sometimes he'd train his old Army glasses on the valley and once again be the forward observer, deciding the fates of the tiny figures below. Sometimes he forgot who was friend or foe. They all looked the same up here. More and more, as he got older, he thought of them as hostiles. The world was closing in. He should feel safe on his mountain, but there was no cover. His position was exposed.

We pulled up a long drive at the end of which was parked three refurbished cars from the 1930s: a Ford V-8, an Austin Bantam, and a coffin-nosed Cord. Though Harvey said nothing, I understood a little better the relationships here. Not only was the

Colonel a powerful man, he was an important customer. We knocked and a blond, crew-cut boy built like a weight lifter opened the door. His arms stretched tight the seams of his green satin bowling jacket, to which was stitched a single blood drop. On the back, a hooded knight rode a rearing steed above the words KNIGHTS—KU KLUX KLAN.

"Hey, Hector," Harvey said. "Your dad in?"

"He's waitin' for you, Mr. Noble," the young guy answered. "Your brother, too." He led us through a room paneled in knotty pine and held up by stone pillars. The ceiling rose like a church, ending in a huge glass window overlooking the plain below. The living room was sunk below door level; there was a fireplace, and on the mantel photos of Hector in a letter sweater and of a dark-haired girl in a strapless prom gown. It all said money: the TV in the walnut cabinet, the soft leather couch; the kidney-shaped coffee table. I wasn't watching where I walked and brushed a glass saucer with little French poodles traipsin' 'round the rim. "Careful," Hector said, steadyin' its wobble. "Mom likes this one."

We continued deeper in the fortress, past a kitchen, streamlined and white with Formica counters and glistening steel blades. "Dad likes the kitchen best," mentioned Hector, who seemed used to giving the tour. "He says it feels *clean* in here." We passed a bar with bent beechwood chairs, a pool table with a green felt top, and ended in a dark-paneled library. Against the back wall sat a desk flanked by U.S. and Confederate flags. The Colonel sat between them. He smiled mirthlessly as we walked in.

"This is them, Colonel," said Tiny, a little behind him and to the right.

The Colonel studied us as I studied him. He was thin as a scarecrow forgotten in a field. His parted black hair was pulled to one side like a raven's wing; his eyes were dark and quick, his face split by a hawk's beak nose. He wore a houndstooth sports jacket, black slacks, white shirt, black knit tie. There was a large diamond ring on his knobby little finger. If I'd expected a hot-eyed crazy in robes, I was mistaken. His craziness was the colder kind.

"I hear you've been in prison," he said, voice crackling.

"That's so."

The dry smile curled around his teeth. "We have to be careful who we let in our little get-togethers," he said. "Too many informers these days." He picked up an ivory-handled letter opener and ran it down his thumb. "Still, I'll admit, I've been pleased with those who've come from prison."

"Why is that?"

"Prison is like boot camp, teaching endless patience and how to endure punishment. It schools a man in violence—something *he* uses, not the other way around."

"I think he's got experience in that, Colonel," Tiny said with a formal politeness, a fawning that was nearly musical.

"I am glad," the Colonel said. "We need a few good men." His attention shifted to Burma. "Does the woman need to be here?"

"It's *her* daughter and *his* son what got on the bus," Tiny reminded.

"Ah, yes, the children," the Colonel recalled, brightening. "That's what it's all about, isn't it? I saw their picture in the paper. The girl looks familiar. Is she a 4H queen?" He waved the ivory letter opener. "This is a war in every sense, including the hearts and minds of future generations." His voice got shrill. "War is repugnant to Americans and we shy from it, yet our skill at waging war is the very thing that makes us a world power. War is like work, and we are damn good workers. We worked at war against the French and Indians, against the English, Spanish, Germans, Japanese, Koreans, and even against each other. We'll probably work at war against the Vietnamese and all Communists, and someday maybe against the whole world. If that happens, so be it—we're here to save the world from itself, and if it comes to that, we will prevail. If we scorch the earth, we'll rebuild and replant. The best worlds are those built anew. I hated war when I called shells upon myself, but I loved the work because I was so good. I loved my country because it gave me the chance to succeed. It's like a dream I had last night," he said.

Tiny prompted: "A dream?"

"A wonderful dream. A magnificent but mysterious dream. I dreamt of a bright kitchen, much like my own, but one so bright it hurt to gaze upon it too long," he said. "I loved that kitchen, so white and clean, and that was the main thing—cleanliness—which means everything to me. But even as I watched, the kitchen darkened, spots of mold collecting in the unwashed places, grease stains in the corners, smudges on the floor. I tried to clean them; somehow the stain was my fault. I had not kept it under control. It was my own negligence that allowed the dirt to come inside. I scrubbed and waxed and bleached, but the rot still spread. Soon there was only one small isle of brightness amid the advancing sea of dirt, and I stood in its center. I cried out, but no one heard me."

I thought, This is one crazy motherfucker I'm dealin' with here.

"Honey, is that you?" called a female voice. It came from down the hall. "I can hear you all the way in the bedroom. Are you preaching again?"

The Colonel winced and Tiny shuffled. Hector leaned out the door: "In here, Mom!"

A small, waspish woman burst in, followed by two white poodles like windup toys at her heels. She was dressed in the frenchified way of the fashion magazines. Her black hair was cut short; she wore tight pedal pushers, flat shoes, a wool T-shirt with wide black stripes and a red scarf 'round her throat. The only thing missing was a black beret. Her eyes swept the room and lingered on Burma, who stared back hypnotized. "You must be those people looking for your children," she warbled. "Your daughter is so cute, but her coloring is so different from yours."

"Delores," growled the Colonel, "we have business here."

"It's Desirée, honey, you remember that I changed it?" Her eyes scanned the library and landed on her son's bowling jacket. "I hope you're not planning another silly rally. We're a laughingstock already. And what are *you* doing wearing that? Take it off right now!"

"Aww, Mom. . . ."

"Don't *aww Mom* me!" She wheeled on her husband like a frenchified she-bear. "God knows I give you lots of latitude since you're such a good provider, but if you think any college in the country is going to give a football scholarship to a boy who lights crosses for a hobby—" She sucked in a furious breath. "Hector, go to your room."

Now a new voice joined the fray. "Mommy, Daddy, you down there?" A girl the same age as Burma's damnable daughter and dressed like Jayne Mansfield thrust through the door past the pouting Hector. Her blond hair had dark roots; she wore an argyle sweater under which her front bumpers pushed up and out impossibly. I wondered if I was in the presence of a natural wonder, or one of those Howard Hughes, cantilevered, nose-cone bras. She told her brother he looked stupid in that stupid jacket. "You always look stupid," Hector crabbed.

"Daddy, you're not holding another Klan rally, are you? All the kids make fun of me when you do."

The Colonel stared in horror at his daughter's chest. "For God's sake, Delores," he pleaded. "She looks like she's had a silicone job."

"Desirée," his wife said.

"Oh, Daddy," sulked the daughter, "everyone wears 'em these days. Don't be such a prude. Besides, the kids are going to the movies. I need some money."

"I won't have my daughter parade around like a *stripper!*"

"But you would have your son parade around like a thug?"

"Daddy, I don't want to miss the *movie!*"

"Mom, why can't I go to the rally? Dad said I could go."

As the noise climbed higher, the Colonel's head sank into his hands. He held out his wallet and his wife plucked it from his fingers. She told her daughter to change to something less *enhancing* and held forth the movie money as a bribe. The daughter and the poodles trotted down the hall. She stripped the satin jacket from her son's back and pushed him out the door. She turned to Burma and wrapped her arms around her shoulders. "You poor thing, you need a bath and a makeover much more than you need some silly rally with some old Neanderthals. Men and their foolishness will be our death." She closed the door and herded Burma down the hall.

——————⋆——————

I don't remember much after that. We crept from the house like breakout artists and ended at a midnight rally with gallons of beer. I hadn't eaten in forever, and the longnecks hit me hard. There was a burning cross in a clearing; old boys clutched cold bottles and stared longingly at the flames. I wondered what they saw. They must've spotted somethin', for the more they drank, the more they grew hypnotized. There were cars parked in the shadows, deep in the trees. The Colonel stood tall and lean in his red robe and talked to the crowd. He told how the cross would light our way for the hard work ahead. We refused any longer to be passive tools of outside forces, he cried. We wouldn't kowtow to our enemies, and proceeded to name them all. There were so many, I couldn't keep 'em straight. There was international Jewry, the mongrelization of races, the fluoridation of water, the big blue flag of the U.N. The more I drank, the fuzzier it all got, till I wondered how we'd hold back the Jews, mongrels, and blue One Worlders who threatened to fluoridate us all. There were cheers as he made each point, these growing wilder as more cars arrived with beer. There was something how our own nigras from Newport was lured into the plot and how we had to stop 'em before the nigra flood lapped over the doorsteps and into our own homes. If those civil-rights bastards wanted a fight, they'd get it the minute they tried steppin' off that bus, right?

"You got it, Colonel!" his troops roared from the trees.

The Colonel turned to where me and a couple others stood beneath the burning cross. I watched the cinders fly up, hoping they wouldn't fall back and set me on fire. He placed folded white robes in our arms. Only white, Protestant, one hundred percent Americans could take the Klan oath, and he asked the three of us bein' inducted if we were those very things. "Yep," I said, hoping against hope that he didn't ask anything else before I passed out.

He turned to the crowd. "Tomorrow," he said, "we begin our great crusade."

A great boozy shout rose to the heavens. I ran to the woods to piss.

Like it or not, I was one of them.

Highway and City

THE GRAY ROAD beneath us swept Chattanooga away. We sat in the middle of the bus, Cole at the window and me on the aisle. Our Greyhound rolled south down bits of superhighway tied together by detours and old roads, the beginning of what folks bragged would someday be an ocean of concrete linking coast to coast. Right now, it only seemed like miles of aggravation lined by orange construction cones and the shells of abandoned mom-'n'-pop stores. Their owners had seen the future and retired early, their lives rerouted to a Florida trailer park surrounded by swayin' palms.

Still, something that got me faster to where I was headed didn't seem a bad idea. I said as much to Michael Venus as he visited up and down the aisle with friends, a comment that pushed some button of his. "Don't be so sure of that," he said. "It's not like this highway was built for your driving pleasure; it's all part of Ike's 'National Defense Highway System,' like the

German autobahns Hitler built during World War II." He pointed out the window. "See that overpass we just drove under? Its clearance can't be lower than the height of a tank turret. See how few entrances there are on this road? It's so Farmer Brown can't pull from a field in his tractor and plow into an Army convoy."

Trust a college boy to have an opinion 'bout *everything!* "But how's that a problem?" I said. "Once it's finished, you'll have the freedom to pick up and go wherever you please. It'll change everything."

"Change it for the worse, you mean. All a highway planner sees is how to improve the flow of traffic, even if that means cutting down forests, leveling hills, or wiping out those family businesses we passed a while ago. The road, and nothing but the road, will become our national symbol. The cloverleaf will be the national flower and concrete the new suburban lawn."

"What made you so smart?" I said.

"I took a seminar on Lewis Mumford," he bragged. "It might do you good to read him, too. He said in the next decades the highway will change our way of life as drastically as a passing tornado or an atom bomb."

"Oh, can it, professor," yawned one of Michael's buddies sprawled on the back bench seat. "Can't you see we're trying to sleep? We don't need a lecture right now."

Mumford-Schmumford, I grumbled silently. It's not like *everything's* depressing out here. I spotted redbud trees up in the mountain passes, right past the FOR SALE signs. Redbuds grew as far north as Wattles and their twisted black branches could fool you to think they were dead. Then, long before Easter, the gnarled branches sprouted tiny blooms of lavender; as the clusters multiplied, the trees were filled with purple fire. I turned to show Cole, but he was still sulking from his trip to jail. Like Mama said, it's wise at times to hold your tongue . . . so I let him be. As I stared out the window the border sign for Georgia flashed past. The road went bumpity-bump, and quick as that, I was out of Tennessee.

Funny thing, leavin' Tennessee. I'd waited for this moment my whole life, figurin' I'd whoop when it happened: confetti might rain down, or God would write congratulations in the sky. Instead, I felt quiet and kinda sad. I looked back as the state-shaped welcome sign receded to a dot, my gaze passing over Michael Venus, who'd dropped in the backseat after his sermon and started to yawn. Verna Albright dozed one row up from me. The entire bus was quiet, most Riders asleep after their night in jail. The normal order for a bus was reversed: Blacks up front, whites in back or sprinkled in the middle, but that was the whole point and no one seemed to care. Cole and me thought it odd at first, but the world was changin' and there were lots of things to get used to nowadays. Someone hummed the song, "Cigareets, and whiskey, and wild wild women, they'll drive you crazy, they'll drive you insane," and someone else mumbled in his sleep. I looked back one last time and figured I wouldn't see redbuds this year.

To tell the truth, I could use some winks myself after all the craziness, so I nestled against Cole's shoulder and hoped to drift away. But his muscle stiffened and he flinched. When I looked up, his face was froze in ice as he stared outside. "I'm sorry about last night," I whispered. "That was stupid, actin' like a folksinger when I cain't sing."

"Why do you do those things?"

Good question, I answered. I wished I knew.

"I'm not kiddin'," he muttered, trying to keep this private. "All I want is a normal life, but you and my old man seem dead set against it. You probably don't realize, but you're just as single-minded as him. It's like you're both on some crazy quest, reflections of one another, and you drag everyone you touch deeper and deeper till we all drown. In the diner, you looked like such an angel, I couldn't help but fall for you, then in the woods you was . . . lots different, and that was fine, given the circumstances. But after that, *my God*. We been kidnapped by a crazy woman, threatened or shot more times than I can count, washed from a mountain and down a river, arrested by police dogs and throwed in jail—and all in two or three days. I don't think that's normal, no matter what angle you take it from."

"It's not always like this," I mumbled. "At least we're outta Tennessee."

"You think Georgia or Florida are any different? You made any plans for after we find your daddy?" He stared at me and added, "Who's to say those two ain't waitin' when we arrive?"

"You don't know."

"As long as your mama's along as guide, I got a pretty good idea."

That was a possibility I didn't want to talk about, so to change the subject I told Cole I had to go pee. In the back was a little stand-up closet the bus company called a bathroom, and I sat on the cold seat with my poor knees shakin' from the roar of the tires and the road. Cole was right . . . all was outta control. The world was a crazy place, and I just made it crazier.

It's awful to admit you're a loose cannon, but I was like a howitzer. I didn't mean to be that way. Girls were s'posed to be sweet 'n' pretty 'n' caring 'n' smart, but I was smart-alecky with a mouth that had a mind of its own. How in the world, at the age of sixteen, when all the other girls in Wattles had parties and sleepovers and mooned over *American Bandstand* . . . how in the world, I asked, did I end up here? Normal girls ain't murder suspects, fugitives, disaster victims, or jailbirds; fewer still are all four rolled up in one. Maybe Mama was right and I *was* as bad as she said. All I did was daydream, and everyone knew they were the devil's playpen. All I did that pretty fall morning was take a ride with Arnold Simpson in his truck, yet we drove off a cliff into a world like nothin' I'd imagined.

No doubt about it, that had to change. I stood and hiked my britches with conviction, then punched the button on the commode. Wouldn't it be nice if my troubles flushed away that easy, too? I'd sure enough give it a try. I'd go outside and promise Cole to do better. I'd think before opening my mouth. We'd rethink our route and spend our money wisely. We'd buy a house in the suburbs and have a cute little poodle dog.

The latch was stuck when I pressed, and it took an age of poundin' before someone heard and opened the door from outside.

The bus was a different place when I emerged. No one paid my newest embarrassment the least attention, not even Cole. It took me a moment to understand why. By now it was midmorning and the sun was high overhead. We were on a long straightaway, the road sloping from the foothills like inside a bowl. Michael Venus and some of his buddies had turned in their seats and stared out the rear windshield at the road behind us, where a line of evenly spaced dots was headed our way. "They seem to be moving awfully fast, don't you think?" Michael said. They did travel at a fair clip as they sped up, maybe 20 or 30 miles an hour faster'n our bus, and the spooky thing was how none tried to pass the other but kept perfectly spaced, as if punched from a machine. In a minute, the lead dot grew into a green Dodge coupe, and behind that was a night black Mercury that any red-blooded American boy or girl would go crazy for. Another eight or nine cars were spread out behind them.

A ripple of worry passed from the back of the bus to the front. Several other Riders rose in their seats and stared back silently. "I'm sure it's nothin'," said one woman.

Her neighbor answered, "Let's hope so."

The lead coupe pulled up and slowed to our pace, the other cars fallin' in line. All had Tennessee tags. The man driving the coupe was a solid chunk of fat, the top of his face chopped off by the sun visor, while the man beside him in the front was thin and reedy, the kind who bends but never blows away. When he turned and spoke, the fat man's lips opened in a fleshy laugh.

All of a sudden the coupe pulled out to pass and the other cars lined up behind it like a stunt team at the state fair. The maneuver was so smooth and fast, it unnerved me. The riders in each car stared ahead as they passed, which was odd since just about everyone peeks curiously into bus windows. Then I saw him riding in the Mercury. He was up front, the same hawk-nose splitting his face, the same coffin-nail eyes. He, too, stared ahead.

So Twitch had survived. I searched for Mama with him, but the glare was blinding and I couldn't see. Maybe she'd died in the flood; maybe she hadn't, but he sucked her dry like a spider and tossed away the shell. There was no way on earth he could know we were on this stretch of road—yet he'd managed to find us again. The short hairs sprang up on the back of my neck and I think I giggled hysterically. Maybe Cole was right and there was no way to beat such an unstoppable force. As the Mercury cut in front, a line of chills trickled down my spine.

"You okay?" asked Michael. "You look faint."

"I . . . I gotta go," I said.

I plopped in the seat beside Cole as the last car sped ahead. The Riders watched in silence till once more the procession was a line of dots on the shimmering road. What had been a threat had turned into an oddity. "That's a first," the bus driver said. His name tag said Bob and the Riders called him Smiling Bob, because he never did.

An easy chatter of relief filled the bus, and I bent forward to ask Verna why. Everybody had seen the line of cars and remembered Anniston, which happened during the first Ride four months ago in May, she said. Thirteen Riders started from D.C. anticipating the worst, yet there hadn't been real violence till the Alabama border. They'd pulled up to the station at Anniston, and a mob with clubs and chains blocked the entrance, no police around. The mob tried to board the bus and there was a fight; somehow the Riders pushed them off and the bus pulled away. The mob slashed their tires as they rolled out; they piled in their cars and followed in a caravan like the one that just passed until a few miles out of town the bus's tires blew. The Greyhound ground to a stop and the mob surrounded the bus; windows broke, followed by firebombs.

"Anniston's nowhere close, is it?" I asked.

"No," said Verna, "we're not stopping there."

I was happy for the Riders, but wished their relief extended to Cole and me as well. Who were these people that Twitch'd joined up with? Did he draft an entire army just to chase me down? The man seemed capable of anything. "You saw him, too," I whispered, words tremblin' before me. "I see it in your face. You were right when you said he'd follow." But Cole had panic in his eyes, like he'd swallowed a fishbone and couldn't breathe. He'd seen nuthin', he claimed. The glare was too bad.

Of course I didn't believe it, but anyone with a lick of sense would've known to proceed gingerly. Not me. "You're just as scared as me," I said, my big mouth firing to life again. "But you're scared of something different—I see it now. You're scared you won't stand up to him when it matters most. That's what happened in the diner when he was fixin' to shoot and you stared shamefaced in the glass. That's been your problem all along."

Even as the words slipped out, I realized I was a fool. I'd knifed him in his weakest spot, before a bus full of strangers, an act as cruel as if he'd slugged me with my own bugaboo— that it wasn't Mama who Daddy'd run away from, but me. "Oh, Cole, I didn't mean it," I pleaded, but by then it was too late. His face grew white, his eyes got hot, his jaws clenched like he'd never speak again. A circle of silence spread 'round our seats as others realized this had nothing to do with rights or higher purpose. This was the simple down-'n'-dirty of two people not gettin' along.

"What is it you want?" he finally cried, the hurt in his voice carrying from the front to the back of the bus, maybe as far as the vanished line of cars. "You *beg* me to like you in the diner, *knock* me out and *drive* all night on some crazy quest to find your father, then *jump* me in the woods, three times."

"Twice," I mumbled as a college girl gasped in the next aisle up and I thought I'd die.

"Okay," he continued, "maybe I wasn't counting. A few things distracted me. Like getting shot, or nearly gettin' snakebit or drowned in a hundred-year flood. What did you think I was? Did you think I was Jesse James on a black horse come to make everything better for you? Dahlia, I'm not a fuckin' hero. I'm scared to death of my old man. It's been like that as long as I remember—I hear his voice in my head and see his face in my dreams. I'm nothing but a sacrifice to his wants, like that old fart in the Bible ready to slit the throat of his own boy. All the preachers make that guy into a hero, but I *know* they've never lived in the shoes of the son. I want to say to Pop, 'Go away, I got my own life,' but I always freeze. You say I'm not man enough to face him—you don't think I tell myself that every damn day? I say I'll stand up this time, but the freeze catches me 'round the throat and I can barely breathe. I wisht to God I was stronger, but I'm not and I hate myself and I've always hated myself for it. Is that what you want to hear?" He pounded the seat before him as his voice climbed to a shout. "What do women *want*, Dahlia?! I don't understand it. You're such an expert. You tell me."

Absolute silence filled the bus. Then a college boy up front muttered, "Good question."

The silence turned to disbelief that someone else had spoken, and that opened up a dam. A woman in a maize-colored dress snapped for the college boy to stay out of our tiff, but a middle-aged man seated forward said he'd always wondered the same. A low drone of warning rose from the throats of the women, until one across the aisle from him snapped, "If you don't know by your age, you never will."

It was gettin' personal now, but Cole kept up his complaint, unaware of what he'd brewed. "I'm waitin', Dahlia. You're the one with all the plans."

"Go on, tell him," someone said. I'd lost all sense of direction by this point—whether this urging came from the back of the bus or the front, I simply couldn't tell. Meanwhile, a madness gripped Cole like he was speaking in tongues. He pounded on the seat again, which made Verna Albright jump up and glare back; he said his daddy always claimed women were the cause of *all* men's problems, and he'd resisted that wisdom but after the last few days with me he might reconsider. *What* did women want, he cried, as several college girls tried shoutin' him down.

But he was rolling now and I don't think their voices registered. " 'Beware the confusion of women, lest it becomes your own,' Pop always said. 'What confusion?' I asked, and he'd hit me for bein' dumb. 'Listen to me, boy!' he cried. 'All life is a war for power, especially the war between women and men. The one who wins the fight is the one who pays the most attention.' "

"That's ridiculous!" cried a woman in spectacles.

"Makes sense to me," said a previously silent man.

A riot was brewing, but Cole didn't know it or didn't care. "Maybe we was wrong from the start, Dahlia; I don't know," he went on. "I mean, few people meet the way we did. I'd be happy to settle down, get a decent job, lead a stable life. That seems like paradise to me. But you . . . that's too dull. What's next after Key West? Would we ever settle down?"

"Dump him," cried a woman. "He sounds boring."

"Keep him," cried another. "He means well."

Now the women were arguing among themselves. What was required of a man? Stability or excitement? Fun or family? Maybe it'd be easier to shoot 'em all and start a manless utopia somewhere.

"You wouldn't last two months," a college boy yelled.

I held my head in my hands. These folks were just as mixed up as us, and them better educated. Maybe everyone was that way. I stared out the window for relief and watched the countryside pass in a swirl of autumn red and orange. The mountains slowly flattened and the high forest grew thin. Logging trucks roared past in the opposite lane. We passed through a town with a storefront Elvis and a farm stand boasting "Dill Pickles on a Stick." A woman up front said all men were useless. Smiling Bob stared at her in his mirror and asked if she wanted to drive.

That was enough for Dr. Singer, the leader of the Newport group; he rose in his seat behind the driver and called for quiet, please. "We came here to work together, not tear each other down," he pleaded, but some folks were too worked up to quit and one woman yelled that, preacher or not, he was still a man and, being so, just wanted to take charge. He'd held his temper till that moment, but this was the last straw. He strode down the aisle toward us, hands trembling; he passed Verna Albright, who shook her head in despair. "You said these two were just love-struck kids," the preacher hissed. "From what I've heard, it sounds like more'n that, though *damn* if I can make sense of what's goin' on."

"Don't ask," Verna moaned.

Cole looked at me and his voice was like ice. "Maybe when we get off in Atlanta, we should go our own ways."

The ice stabbed me in the heart. "Oh, Cole," I said, "no."

The reverend's eyes were merciless and the reflected light of the windows danced off his bald head. "I agree with the boy," he said. "I don't know *who* you are or *what* you've done; but when this bus leaves Atlanta, you will not be on it. Clear?" He returned to his seat without waiting for an answer. When Verna turned and looked at me, I melted from anguish. When they came to take me off, all they'd find in my seat was a Dahlia-colored stain.

——◆——

The rest of the way to Atlanta, no one talked. No one glanced at the person by his or her side. We were all inconvenient strangers on the bus. Some things run deeper'n race, and one was the ancient war between women and men.

We rolled through the city that I'd always thought of in Cinderella terms. Atlanta touted itself as the New South personified, a place of motion and rebirth, striving for better things. Motion reveals a lot, but hides a lot, too. We rolled past the railroad terminal, where tracks from all over the South laced into a complicated cat's cradle; past the old Loew's theater where *Gone With the Wind* premiered decades back; past the block-long department store that Sallie Goodnight longed to wander, and her memory made me sad. Past all this to the dock of the bus station where the clock on the wall said 3:00 P.M. and the airbrakes sighed. We stared out the windows, but we didn't leave.

We'd been expected in the worst possible way. A chain of state troopers blocked the entrance; each link in the chain stared at our bus and held a nightstick in his hands. Behind the chain stood a second line of policemen facing a crowd that surged through the station doors. They pressed against the line of troopers, but the lawmen refused to give. The mob seemed a sea of red faces. Some cried for us to leave the bus and face their music. Others screamed for us to stay on the bus and leave the city for good.

"You sure you want me to open the doors?" our driver asked. "That seems like suicide."

He had a point. This wasn't the only group that watched us arrive. A ragged corridor had formed between our bus and the police line blocking the station doors. One side of the gauntlet was made of the press, reporters scribbling on pads, flashing blackbox cameras or balancing bulky TV cameras on their shoulders. The third group stood opposite them, but further back, almost as far as the street, the quietest and in that way scariest of all. A group of Klansmen stood frozen in their hoods and cloaks, more like fangs sprouting from the asphalt than living things.

As I watched, one Klansman did something odd. He was taller than the rest and stood near the center; he reached up and drew off his hood. A man standing beside him turned to protest, but the tall man paid him no mind. He smiled at the bus and I grabbed Cole's hand, forgettin' every triflin' disagreement we'd had that day. "Do you see him?" I gasped.

"I see," he said.

"Why's he doing that?"

"To let us know he's here."

Meanwhile, a decision had been made. Dr. Singer had been arguing with some others, and the forceful old preacher prevailed. He stood up front and said it would start a riot if too many got off the bus. Their movement didn't require a massacre, he said. Still, we'd come to make a statement, and if no one left at all, the racists could say they'd won. Therefore, only one Rider need test the station, and that someone would be him.

Stunned silence filled the Greyhound before a cry arose that nearly drowned the screams outside. He couldn't go, not alone! He'd be killed! Dr. Singer begged for quiet: What better way to make a point, he asked, than one man against a mob? In full view of TV, he smiled, which meant in full view of the nation. Besides, the troopers were there, so he hoped to have protection. He strolled up the aisle as he talked and stopped again by Verna. "Besides, I'll have company," he added, then crooked a finger. "You two are coming with me."

"Them?" cried the bus in one astonished voice.

"Us?" I said. "Out there?" I looked from the cops, to the crowd, to Twitch. "You're crazy."

Now Dr. Singer spoke directly to me, and I realized then why he led these people on this dangerous Ride. His voice and face were gentle and sad at the same time they were stern, like he'd seen a lot in this wild life and knew that people made choices from weakness or fear. Evil, in turn, sprang from these. "Young lady," he said, "we can expect a reception like this at every station from here on out, and at least here there's the press to make the troopers do their job. That's not assured the deeper south we go. You've got to go. Maybe in a few more years you would have belonged here with us, but not yet. Right now, I afraid you don't know where you're headed. Once you're off

234

the bus, turn left toward the reporters. Then neither you nor your boyfriend look back and you run like hell, you hear?"

He was right, ashamed as it made me, and I stood up dazed and toasty from the heat of all the angry stares. I tightened the straps of my rucksack and Cole rose, too, staring out the window at the hoodless man. "Don't even look at him," my gypsy said. "Do as the preacher says and run in the opposite direction." I wondered how I was s'posed to do that if my knees felt like water, but the preacher didn't give me time to think. "Let's do it," Dr. Singer said.

I'd always wondered how it felt walking past a ready firing squad. Now I knew. Funny thing, for all his confidence, Dr. Singer looked like he felt the same. He turned as we stood behind him on the steps and whispered, "You kids, I'm sorry I was rough, but you're not part of this, and I've got to get you out of here." His forehead was shiny and he dabbed at the sweat with a hankie. I suddenly felt sorry for him. Sometimes you got no choice in deciding a path; maybe each faith casts up a martyr, and in that instant of light when the martyr sees the future, he freezes like a jacklighted deer. I realized the little preacher was as lonely as a man or woman could ever stand to be, and I laid my hand on his shoulder from the step-up behind him. "My legs feel like jelly," I said. He smiled the oddest smile and said, "Funny, mine do, too."

The folding doors whispered open. Dr. Singer stepped out, and Cole and me followed. "Kill the nigra!" screamed the crowd, meaning the preacher. "Kill the nigger lovers!!" meaning Cole and me.

An arm shot forward with a microphone attached. "How do you feel?"

"Not so good," I said.

I glanced right and Twitch stared back—only at me and my rucksack of money—no emotion in his eyes, nothing human I could read. I froze and Dr. Singer said we had to keep moving. It's too dangerous to stop . . . it makes us an easy target, he said.

Now was the time to bolt through the press, but two troopers came from nowhere and urged us forward, unknowingly ending our plan. Dr. Singer started to say something, but just as suddenly we were at the end of the gauntlet, facing the double line of troopers and the rabid crowd beyond. A police sergeant glared at the preacher with distaste, then at Cole and me with a more quizzical look, like he'd seen our faces before. Oh yeah, buddy, I wanted to tell him, you saw us all right, in the wanted posters, and you'll remember us tomorrow when we're dead and gone. The idea of a nice, safe jail cell seemed so temptin' now, but the sergeant was a no-nonsense guy. "You'll have to get back on the bus," he said.

"Let 'em through," said a beet-faced man behind his shoulder.

"I'm here to test the court-ordered desegregation of this station's facilities," Dr. Singer answered woodenly, as if he'd rehearsed these lines before. "I'd appreciate it if you'd let me by."

"He wants to visit his *pals,*" Beet Face jeered, and something in the way he said it sounded pure deadly.

"Maybe it's better to go," I said, but Dr. Singer kept his eyes on the trooper.

"Please let me pass," he repeated, a quiver in his voice.

"Listen to him," cried Beet Face. "The little nigger's scared."

The preacher drew himself up, behind the pulpit again, where he belonged. Maybe, at that moment, he saw everything clearly in his life as leading to this point. Maybe Beet Face simply made him mad. "Please, now, I asked nicely," he told the sergeant. "I wouldn't want to report you for obstructing the law."

The sergeant's lips crawled like bugs. "If you insist," he said, and moved aside.

What happened next was like a dance, Dr. Singer stepping forward into the arms of Beet Face, his partner on this card. As I watched, the bigger man's hand dipped beneath the bib of his overalls and came out with a length of pipe. As the pipe descended, Dr. Singer raised his arm defensively. There was a sharp snap and Dr. Singer crumpled to his knees.

Everything seemed to whirl in my mind. The crowd surged forward. "They'll stomp him to death!" Cole shouted; him and me grabbed Singer under the arms to drag him back to safety, but the preacher shrieked in pain. I screamed to the troopers for help; Beet Face giggled in a kind of godly transport and raised his pipe high, the downstroke meant for me. "Run!" said my head; "Stay!" said my feet.

"Goddammit!" yelled Cole, hurling himself at Beet Face and throwing off his aim. I fell back, dragging the preacher with me, as two troopers pulled Cole off our attacker and tossed him back in the pile with Dr. Singer and me. A third trooper, younger than the rest and maybe more merciful, aimed his nightstick across Beet Face's knees. The sergeant closed the line back up and I looked in his face. "You didn't try to stop it!" I cried at him.

Now Verna Albright appeared, kneeling down between me and Cole, untangling the three of us, laying hands on Singer. "It hurts, Verna," the little preacher groaned.

"Ssh, James, I know," she said, feeling his forehead and running her fingers gently down his broken arm. "It's a simple fracture, but he's going into shock. We need a hospital."

"Ain't none," the sergeant said.

"No hospitals in Atlanta?" we all said together.

"None here for you."

I started to stand, but Verna touched my shoulder lightly and warned me to stay down. There was strength in her touch, like she'd entered her element and this was what she'd trained for. "Take him back to the bus," she said to me and Cole.

"Good idea, Nursy," the sergeant sneered.

Verna unfolded slowly to her full height like God Almighty in His wrath. "Don't ever call me Nursy," she spat contemptuously. The sergeant stared back, amazed, his face and neck turning bright rouge. He was being talked down to by a nigger . . . worse, by a nigger woman . . . and worst of all, on national TV. A shudder passed along his face as his lizard brain took hold. He stepped in close and his hands twitched upon his nightstick. She didn't even blink. "Go ahead," she dared him, "let the whole world see."

That got his attention and he looked over at the TV cameras, pointing straight at him. He paused a second and the younger trooper who'd saved me from Beet Face pulled him back gently, saying it would be a mistake, sir. The sergeant seemed near explodin', but he held himself in check. "Get the fuck back on the bus," he snarled.

Cole took the preacher's shoulders while I grabbed his feet: he felt like a bag of sand with loose rocks knockin' 'round inside. A host of hands reached from the door to lift him up and lay him across a seat; Verna boarded last and pulled a first-aid kit from underneath a seat, while someone else tucked a blanket under Dr. Singer's chin. When I turned 'round, the sergeant was standin' in the doorway. "No one else leaves this bus," he ordered. "Get goin'."

"Don't worry," Smiling Bob replied. The doors shushed shut and the engine throbbed to life. Bob backed from the dock without checking his mirrors and ground the gears. I stood on the steps and watched the crowd scream its hate and triumph. The bus paused by the corner, where Twitch stood in his robes.

We stared at each other, the thin glass door between us, for a hundred years. Who needed words? We'd gone beyond them now. His eyes said clearly he'd be waiting—wherever, whenever, he'd be there. I could run forever, but a dance like this never truly ended. He was always there to cut in.

He smiled and nodded once, then turned and walked away.

How the Elephant Dies

LATER I WOULD see that gaze through glass as the precise moment the girl and me understood each other. Our bond went deeper than the chase. Our moves curled about the other's like a snake, a new union needing no words.

Even as I stood there, I could've thrust through the

flimsy door and plucked her out by the throat. I'd be gone from the scene in an instant, and the money would be mine. It was a tempting vision, but wrong, for ours was a passion that should unfold slowly, like a flower. I had a bit of my preacher daddy in me after all. Isn't that the meaning of purpose—a patience that's unwavering and constant? Purpose that, like love or lust, exists only to be fulfilled.

So I turned when I heard the others calling, and came to where they'd formed a circle of prayer. The crowd had thinned and only two troopers remained to keep vigil. Since we weren't breaking laws and the Riders had left, we weren't a threat no more, more like a curiosity.

We numbered forty by now. The Colonel had more clout in the Empire than I'd realized, picking up additional volunteers in Chattanooga, including a spry little chaplain, or "kludd." The Colonel gave the word and the happy kludd said to bow our heads.

"O Lord," the kludd said, "we thank You for bringing us together on this most momentous day. We know life is a battle between good and evil, light and dark, and You are the Great Referee. We realize that in such strife as this, it matters not how you play the game, only that you win. Please let us triumph, O Lord, if necessary in overtime, we don't mind. We're Your team. In Your name we guard the ball. Amen."

"Good prayer," the Colonel said, and wanted to add some thoughts of his own. We witnessed a great victory today, but we could not rest until that bus was stopped for good. He would be greatly ashamed if anyone blamed Tennesseans for passing their problems on to others, and some of the audience *Amened* again. The Greyhound's next stop was Phenix City on the Georgia-Alabama border, where a little surprise was planned. He wanted everyone to continue south and he got 100 percent agreement except for one poor slob whose wife was about to go into labor, maybe already had. There was silence, and the father-to-be left, hanging his head.

"Now I've got to say something that may trouble you," the Colonel continued. "We are all at risk doing what we do. One of you"—and he looked at me—"took off his hood today, and that was not wise. I'll tell you why. Some of you know we expected a visit from a benefactor who'd donated considerable sums to other klaverns and had planned the same for us. He'd flown here yesterday to mix business with pleasure, but never arrived. I can now tell you why. Before we left, I got a call that his limo was found wrecked upriver. His body has disappeared."

"The flood killed him," someone said.

The Colonel answered, "Who knows?" Worried murmurs blossomed from the crowd. I jingled the rings in my pocket from nervousness, then thought it wiser to stop. The Colonel sure knew which button to push, and nothing motivated these boys like a hint of conspiracy.

As we drifted to our cars, Harvey edged by me. "That was Edmond Klingge you killed," he hissed. I could smell the fear.

"You would've done the same," I as much as admitted. "Or did you forget?"

"I would've helped him if I'd knowed who he was. The Colonel will kill us!"

"Why should he know?"

"Those damn rings you gave me are worthless. If I pawn 'em 'round Newport, they'll be traced to me."

"That's not my problem, Harvey."

"Oh yes, it is." The edge in his voice gave me a start, and made me consider him more seriously. Maybe he was an obstacle, rather than a tool; maybe the lethal consequences of such a revelation showed plain on my face, for Harvey's voice grew desperate and desperation carries its own bravery. "I don't plan on tellin' him yet, but that girl's carryin' something more valuable than these rings, I know it, and you wouldn't've joined the Colonel if what she has wasn't important to you. She's carryin' money—lots of it—and I want half of everything."

He grabbed me by the arm for emphasis. "I mean it," he said. "Do like I say or I tell the Colonel what you did to

Edmond Klingge. He'll be all over you and that woman in a minute. Think about it. There's nearly forty people here." He turned and walked to his Mercury.

Our caravan was one car short after the father-to-be left, and two new passengers waited by the car. They were twins, and introduced themselves as Burt and Bart True. "You boys sit in back," Harvey piped, mighty friendly, sensing safety in numbers after his brave but unwise words to me.

Burma squeezed between them, a tight fit as they were hefty size 40s. Their faces were baby-smooth, and for all the world resembled identical overgrown schoolboys. The one distinguishing mark was a red scar on Burt's forehead. Last summer, he said, he'd been trimming branches with a chain saw when the chain bounced up, slashing him bad. The wound healed uneven, puckering his brow. "I don't mind, makes me look like a deep thinker," he said.

"Just makes you look ugly," his twin disagreed.

"You're just jealous," Burt responded; he leaned forward and slapped Harvey on the shoulder. "Crank her up, Harv. Boy, I do love a Mercury. Let's have some fun."

"It's not a race, Burt," said Bart, and Harvey just smiled 'cause he knew the boys well. The chain-saw cut had done more than change Burt's looks, he explained. It changed his personality, too. Before, the two were friendly enough, if shy and retiring, but the missing piece of skull seemed to change both of them. Now they seemed tied together by some weird instantaneous radar. Burt turned wild after his accident, and Bart more maternal, like he did the worryin' for both of them. Strangest of all was how each knew the other's thoughts from miles away. They were so talked about locally that a professor at state college hooked 'em up to some brain-wave machine and was writin' a paper about 'em.

"We're gonna be famous," said Burt.

"Natural wonders," said Bart.

"Miracles of science," both said.

I asked how they hooked up with the Klan.

"Burt signed up during one of his fits," said Bart. "I joined to keep him out of trouble."

"Don't put it all on me," Burt answered. "You said yourself it was exciting."

"Boys, boys," soothed Harvey. "It's a small car and you're gettin' loud."

Both shrugged. Bart turned to Burma and asked, "What do you think of the Colonel?"

"He has a nice speakin' voice," she replied diplomatically.

"He likes to use it, too, all the time talkin' 'bout destiny and whatnot. Puts me at sixes and sevens."

"Don't you say bad things 'bout the Colonel," Burt shot back, leaning across Burma. "He's a great man."

"I think he's a basket case, gettin' present-day confused with those bombs fallin' on him back in the Philippines," offered Bart.

"You're the one's confused," Burt shot back, grabbing for his twin.

"Goddammit!" screamed Burma. "Stop pounding on me! Gimme some room!"

The boys pulled back. Burt sighed, while Bart rolled his eyes. They rode like mirror images, arms propped on opposite armrests, heads propped on opposite hands, watching the land change from foothills to piney woods. The road got sucked beneath us and soon enough we saw the bus. It'd gained a trooper escort, so our caravan dropped down a less-traveled farm route while the bus continued on the superhighway.

"How much longer till we get there?" Burt whined.

"Not much longer," I lied. I stared out the windows at the fields of cotton, black branches sticking up like whips, tattered bolls blowing through the red dust like a Southern brand of tumbleweed. Funny how something like cotton came to represent all things Southern. I'd picked cotton in prison, contracted out by the state, and it's a man-killing job. I'd strap on knee pads and hang the long sack 'round my neck, then stoop and crawl among the cotton rows from dawn to dusk under the broilin' sun. The sacks grew heavier the more you picked, till finally you developed a near-permanent hump and it was hard to straighten your back at the end of the day. Callused as my hands already were from a life of shoveling coal, they still grew raw and bleeding from the razor-sharp cotton bolls.

Beyond the cotton lay a grove of peach trees, their limbs gnarled and untended. Burt glanced at Burma. "You were feisty back there. How's about some careless love?"

"What?" Burma shrieked, not believing what she heard.

"I said you stepped on my starter, baby, and I'm rarin' to go."

She backhanded Burt and leaned over the front seat. "That's it!" she yelled. "Stop the car and let me out here!"

"We can't drop out of line, we'll never catch up," Harvey wheedled, though I knew it wasn't losing his place in line that scared my junkman but being alone with me. I glanced back at Burma as she glared at the twins, daring either one to make the slightest move.

But Burt was right—she looked mighty fine. The more we chased those kids, the more she transformed, filling out amazingly since the night I barged in her room. I remembered the church, how she crawled on top, and my tongue thickened, among other things. Her hair glowed in the red light of the sunset; she looked like Marilyn Monroe and Patsy Cline rolled up together, and I suddenly had a hankering for another roll in the hay. I imagined her moving atop me and crooning "I Fall to Pieces." "Leave her alone, boys," I said.

"She's takin' care of herself," said Burt, dabbing at a trickle of blood from his nose.

Time passed. No one said a word. I thought how, according to the hard-shell Baptists, the earth was created in 4004 B.C., yet in all that time no one created a way for men and women to get along. Love had an ugly face, a dark twin it was always better to keep hid. Harvey flipped on the radio and an announcer recited the events at the Greyhound station. Elsewhere, a hurricane was spinning near Cuba, and peanut futures were down. The Platters sang

"Ebb Tide," and Jerry Lee Lewis banged out "Great Balls of Fire."

"Jerry Lee married his thirteen-year-old cousin—did you know that?" said Burt.

"Everybody knows that," Bart replied.

"What makes a man do that?" Burt wondered. "Jerry Lee had to know he was setting himself up for trouble. A preacher said Jerry Lee was goin' straight to hell, right on TV."

"That preacher was Jerry Lee's cousin," Bart added. "That's harsh comin' from family."

"I have a hard time understanding people," Burt went on. "It's like they're hardest on others for things they want to do themselves. I bet that TV preacher's got his own wanderin' eye. You watch, he'll get in trouble hisself one day. Jerry Lee's more honest, that's all."

I noticed how the conversation dragged Burma down in the dumps. "Why is it people are hardest on their own family?" Burt wondered. "The world sure is a funny place."

It got real gloomy in the car. Burt asked Bart, "You think we'll see a lynching this time?"

"Good God, it's not like we're cavemen."

"We're Klansmen, ain't we?"

"Those days are past. Now we're a political action group," Bart said.

"Seems to me like splittin' hairs. Remember the time Mama saw a lynching?"

"Mama never saw no lynching."

"Did so."

"You're nuts," Bart said. "Mama'd never go for that."

"It wasn't a normal lynchin'," Burt said. "She was a little girl living in the mountains, remember? Circus came to town and one of their hippos killed a man and they hanged it dead."

"Oh, that old tale. You got it wrong. It wasn't a hippo, but an elephant. And it was a little girl got killed."

"Harvey." Burt pounded on the seat. "What was it, hippo or elephant?"

"Elephant," Harvey said, and Burt pouted.

"That's stupid," Burma spoke up. "How could you hang an elephant?"

It happened, though, Harvey insisted, in the early 1900s, when everyone's mamas was still girls. He'd heard about it from his own mama. In those days, circus animals were kept in wagons and this elephant, being a star, had one of her own. Most circus elephants were female since bulls were too mean—as if females ain't meanness personified, I thought, an opinion I kept to myself. This little girl came up to the elephant's wagon and the elephant grabbed her with its trunk and beat her on the ground like swatting a bug. Nobody knew why, 'cept maybe the elephant had a gripe against humanity, but just the same the town wanted justice. Some argued that an elephant was a dumb beast who didn't know no better, but the town took a poll and the majority demanded an eye for an eye. The elephant must pay for her sins, but how? No gun was big enough: some suggested a bear gun, but if that didn't work, she'd break loose and mash everyone. Poison might work, but how much do you feed an elephant? If they got it wrong, she could linger for days. They could blow her up with dynamite, but chances were they'd take half the town, too, and bits of dead elephant would be lathered everywhere.

Hang her, someone finally said. The railroad ran through town and the company had a big ole derrick for righting derailments and lifting heavy sections of track. That'd do the trick, they said. They rolled it out and hitched a logging chain 'round her neck and the chain to the derrick. The whole town turned out, just like a hangin' in the West, and when they winched the elephant up, she naturally got scared and started screaming and shitting. It dragged her up on her hind legs, when something awful came in her eyes. Those watching swore the expression was almost human, like a question replaced her fear. Everyone got real quiet. The chain tightened 'cross the elephant's throat and choked off her screams. The derrick pulled her off her feet and she hung there dead awhile. People seemed to realize they'd seen something inside themselves as bad or worse than the elephant's offense, something so monumentally sad and stupid that they'd hung it up like a giant flag. Take her down, they said. We don't like seeing her no more. One by one folks peeled from the crowd and went home. When the street was empty, the derrick lowered the carcass and the circus people sawed their former star into bite-sized chunks for the lions. The circus left and never returned to that part of Tennessee again.

"What about the children?" Burma asked, awed by the tale.

"They weren't allowed to watch, but could hear the squeals. They had nightmares for years after. My mama did, into old age."

There was silence. Burt cleared his throat. "Hangin' an elephant's stranger'n hangin' a hippo."

"The world's sure a funny place," Bart agreed.

It got even gloomier in the car than before. This was turnin' into one hell of a ride. The sun was setting and the fields grew dark. There were people in the fields who looked like ghosts stumbling among the plowed rows. I dug in the glove compartment, found a pack of cigarettes, and lit up, the first smoke I'd had since the night I'd killed Harson Whitley. A peace as black as coal washed through my veins.

"Those things'll kill you," said Bart.

"I'll show you what'll kill you faster," Burt replied cheerfully. He reached under his robes and placed a .22 revolver on his lap. "It's Daddy's, recognize it?" He stroked it with his fingers, then picked it up and pointed it at the dim ghosts in the fields. "Bang bang, you're dead."

"Good God Almighty, you were carrying that the whole time in Atlanta?" Burma yipped.

"You coulda got us arrested!" his brother barked.

"I just brought it for protection," Burt said, cringing like a dog.

"Protection from *what?*" Burma cried. "A bunch of people who won't even raise a hand to protect themselves? The way you all described it, from an ole black preacher who walked like a lamb to the slaughter?"

"All those commies and perverts the Colonel talks about," Burt wailed. "You know they're somewheres on that bus." I threw my cigarette out the window, reached back, and told Burt to hand it over. Harvey Noble glanced sideways and got nervous. "Wai-wait a minute," he said.

"Give it to me," I repeated in my sternest voice, the voice of Angry Fathers Everywhere, the voice guaranteed never to fail. "You'll get us all in trouble. I'll give it back when we go home."

Burt looked sheepish. When his twin said to hand it over, he did as he was told.

"Nice gun, don'tcha think, Harvey?" I asked, smiling as I pointed it at him. "A fellow could solve a lot of problems with this little beauty." My junkman got whiter than cotton. I reached beneath my robes, stuck it in my waistband, and didn't feel gloomy no more.

That's what's so good about this country. Whenever you got problems, God has mercy on you and drops a gun in your lap.

Hell, it's better'n Bufferin for solvin' life's aches and pains.

Duck 'n' Cover Makes a Mighty Fine Prayer

WE ROARED THROUGH a darkness like space, the red taillights of autos dwindling like tiny rockets as they passed us by. As each vanished, I wondered where it was aimed. According to the Duck and Cover drills back in high school, the point where a rocket hit was called Ground Zero. It looked like there'd be a lot of Ground Zeroes in this messed-up world.

We was on a rocket, too, but headed where? I looked at my fellow rocketeers. Their faces were frozen silver, like old photos, as the lights swept past; very few slept anymore, after Atlanta. One of the college boys in back drug out a map and Michael Venus said our next stop was Phenix City, a tough little town on the Georgia-Alabama line named for a mythical bird what rose from its own ashes. One of the backseat boys grabbed the map and said the "phoenix" the town was named after was misspelled. "Trust a bunch of Southerners to do things their own way," Michael said.

I thought of Duck and Cover again. You knelt butt to the floor, knees to your chin, and hands behind your head till every muscle trembled and the small of your back cried "Kill me, now!" The pain was necessary, said our teacher, 'cause apocalypse was 'round the corner and an ICBM was pointed our way. "Who'd bomb us?" I finally wailed in protest, for which I was awarded a trip to the principal's office. But he was not mean to me that day. He reminded me of the Oak Ridge weapons plant, and how missiles rarely landed where intended. The circle of uncertainty stretched a hundred miles to every side, he told me.

It seemed I lived in a permanent circle of uncertainty nowadays.

I sighed. Duck and Cover had become my generation's contorted prayer. If anything, I was tired and sore, and leaned my head against the cool glass window as the steel Greyhound whistled down the road. I'd switched places with Cole, who didn't relish lookin' out the window no more. Since Twitch's caravan hadn't reappeared since Atlanta, I hoped he'd been delayed.

Our trip south took double the normal time. A few miles from Atlanta, troopers swept up and escorted us to a Negro hospital, where we left poor Dr. Singer under guard. Twenty miles from town our escort vanished, yet there was no sign of Klan pursuit and for the moment we had a breather. I wondered about the black students 'round me and wisht I could dive inside their heads. They were on their own long journey together, and Verna mentioned they were the children of maids, cooks, and Pullman porters, often the first of their family to go to college and gain its promise of better things. All that was suspended—at least temporarily—for something they believed was much bigger than their own futures. Everyone on this bus knew they were part of history, young and old, intentional or accidental, like me. Maybe we was different, maybe not, but deep down we all feared the Twitches of this earth . . . the slight twitch of the nerve connecting the finger to the trigger, the personal Ground Zero. When the time came, we could only hope to stay brave.

It was 9:00 P.M. when we turned off the highway into the glittering lights of town. This was Columbus, Georgia, main gate for the army's Fort Benning. We rolled down a neon boulevard strip lined with dark motels, rent-to-own storefronts, tattoo emporiums, pawnshops, and strip joints, the latter ringed by cars. Cops circled outside their lights, patient and watchful, waitin' to pounce when a driver left the pack and showed weakness by weavin' across the white line. A private in khaki lay on the berm, hands cuffed behind his back, policeman standin' to the side and scribblin' notes in a pad. Cars honked as they passed, but the two were in that separate world of predator and prey. A huge billboard towered over them, a Confederate flag flanked by the Stars and Stripes, a membership summons for something called the Confederate Sons of Glory. Our tires sang as we rolled outta sight, crossin' the bridge over the Chattahoochee River. A sign welcomed us to the Great State of Alabama.

"Just like Tennessee," I said to Cole, and grabbed his hand.

But he pulled loose and answered sadly, "Dahlia, I think here's where we part. I'll take enough money to tide me over. All the rest is yours."

I'd hoped that thought had vanished after we'd stood up to Beet Face in Atlanta, but instead it'd just slept, festerin' with each mile. Such was my power to fool myself. It was crazy to split apart, I told him, but everything was crazy, inside the bus and out, like the walls of reason tumbled everywhere.

I didn't want the money, I pleaded, his words hitting me square in the heart, leavin' me gasping and pale. "You're all I want."

It was too late for that, he said.

I put my face in my hands and started to cry. Nothing dramatic, just quiet tears. Life was dividing us. Life ultimately divided everyone, and no one ever knew why. I was the cause of his unhappiness, he of my confusion . . . we couldn't act different if we tried. The gears didn't mesh; the wheels would not align. I suddenly remembered how he first appeared when stepping in the diner with his old man. All mystery and darkness, black eyes, dark skin. A strange, hunted gypsy, I'd thought, when all along it was a reflection of my dreams. I remembered the thrill I felt as he stared at me as if naked . . . our first kiss . . . the sprigs of grass like cold needles against my skin. Our bus rolled past three soldiers, arms about each other for support, singin' a drunken song. What right did they have to be happy? I hated them for their happiness, hated everyone on this bus for thinkin' they had a future and dreamin' of better things. Everything in my future had turned sour, everyone I'd loved run off. Maybe the right words might save us, but I couldn't find 'em . . . I didn't know 'em anymore, and maybe I never did. I was good at lies, but not at speakin' the truth of things.

Then the strangest thing occurred. My mind opened like a leaf, and I saw the world through Twitch's eyes. What else is there but hatred when we're hurled upon this earth to be a torment to one another and ourselves? Hatred was a searchlight, peering into every soul's recess, revealing all with clarity. Michael Venus and his goofball buddies in the back, the college girls so stunning, Verna so graceful and slim—it was all a sham, a shield against the fear. A curtain pulled further and further back the faster we ran and the longer we lived.

Now I understood. Mama had been right all along. Hate began where love left off—the best defense was to drive everyone away. I reached into the rucksack and grabbed a wad of bills. "Take some, then," I spit, thrusting it at Cole.

"Look at all that money," gasped a college girl, so I turned and thrust some at her.

"He doesn't want it, so you take it," I said. I dropped hundreds in her lap, but she reared back like I'd dropped burning matches instead. I reached into the pack for another handful and held it up. "Who'll take it?!" I cried. "Blood money for free, right here!"

Verna was suddenly right in my face; she clapped her hand to mine. "That's enough," she said. She stuffed the money back in the pack, looking at me oddly when she saw the amount inside. She handed it back, eyes sad. "Phenix City is where you leave us," she said.

I closed my eyes and crossed my hands on the bag. When they opened, I'd be waking from this nightmare in my bed. I'd tell Mama what happened, and for once she'd understand. We'd move from Wattles to some new and better place. She'd become the friend I'd always hoped for. I'd find a boy who loved me. Maybe I could love him.

I opened my eyes.

We rolled into Phenix City at a quarter past nine. The town overlooked the slow and greasy river; there were shouts across the water, rambunctious sounds of life, but downtown Phenix City was squat and red-brick, the bars sullen, the look of the main street mean. We pulled behind a station with only three docks out back and a chalkboard announcing arrivals and departures. The air brakes hissed. The door folded open. All was quiet outside.

This was too damn eerie, I thought, determined not to set a foot outside no matter *what* Verna and the others said. Where was the line of cops, like in Atlanta? Where was the hate-filled crowds? We sat on the bus and waited. A radio blared in the distance, a voice like Elvis. A dog barked. A cat yowled.

"Maybe nothing's the matter," Verna whispered.

"Maybe it's just another sleepy station and the problem is just us," Michael offered.

Maybe, always maybe . . . but you sure as hell couldn't convince me.

As we watched, a short, blond woman strolled from the station and peered from side to side. She was pretty in a sleepy sort of way, maybe in her early forties and wearing a scarlet dress with matching high heels. A scarlet purse hung under her arm. She checked her watch, tapped her foot, stared at the bus as we stared back at her. She seemed confused and frustrated, and after a shrug of decision, clip-clopped to our door.

"Is this the bus from Cape Canaveral?" she asked, smiling up the steps at Smiling Bob.

For his part, our driver looked ready to drool. I heard a drawl in the woman's voice—not the heavy syrup of the country—but the faint drawl of the city, and she seemed intimidated by this place, with good reason. Anyone with half a brain knew a red dress like hers might mean one thing in a highfalutin cocktail party with a buncha lawyers and politicians floatin' by like drunken ghosts. But out here, in the dark streets of Phenix City, it was an advertisement for a more commercial enterprise. She was as out of place as a woman could be. I wondered how many drunken soldiers had asked her price tonight, and found it a wonder the local police hadn't hauled her in. Smiling Bob blinked back to life at the sound of her voice and told her this was the bus from Atlanta, not Cape Canaveral. She frowned like that wasn't the answer she wanted and asked, "So when does the other one get in?"

"Ma'am, the ticket agent can tell you that."

"That's what I'm trying to tell you. There's no one inside."

That couldn't be, Bob's expression said, not in the well-ordered world of schedules and stations. "There's always someone inside."

"Maybe so, but not tonight. Maybe the agent went to the little boy's room for a visit, and I'll tell you, honey, I didn't check there. It's spooky in there, so I came out here."

Smiling Bob shook his head. A chanting crowd and line of stone-faced cops was one thing, but a station without an agent meant the end of the world. He pulled a ring-bound notebook from beside his seat and ran his finger down a page. "Lady, no route like that passes through here."

Now this queen bee was the one to get flummoxed, and she clopped up a step or two. "There must be a mistake," she said. "I'm looking for my husband. Maybe I heard him wrong. His car broke down in Cape Canaveral, and he phoned to say he was coming up by bus. Maybe he meant he'd make a connection in Atlanta, then come down here." She tried peeking over the partition that separated the seats from the steps, but was too short. "How many riders got on in Atlanta?"

"No one, lady," Smiling Bob replied. "Fact is, we barely got out of there alive." She took another step, unconvinced, and Bob made a sweeping gesture. "Be my guest and take a look yourself. No secrets on this bus." He looked back at me and added, "Just the opposite."

She sprang up the remaining steps and her eyes grew wide. "This isn't a regular bus," she said, and Bob explained to her back how this was a protest ride. You had to say this; that lady was quick on the uptake: "Oh, yeah, I heard of them Freedom things," she said, squeezin' down the aisle till she came even to me. "Aren't you a little young to be here?"

I glanced sadly at Cole and shrugged. "It's complicated," I said.

My answer seemed to spark a light inside her, and her eyes narrowed as she studied Cole and me. "Honey, those kind of complications happen to everyone, including, it seems, me. I wish I could do somethin', but right now I've got my own complications."

She squeezed back to the front and thanked our driver for his kindness. Her brisk heels clicked from the bus and through the station door.

There was a breath of silence; then everybody howled. Someone said that woman's husband had a lot of explaining in his future. A neighbor doubted he even had a future once his wife got hold of him. If anything, she broke the tension, and the CORE leader said an attack would've come already if one was planned. Him and a white teammate walked through the station door; they reappeared and motioned us in. Relief swept the bus. We'd been spared, and went in the building.

The station was a gleam of white: white counters, white lights, white tile. It was like being buried in a white tomb deep underground. The few windows were set so high near the ceiling I couldn't see out. This was a place apart from Phenix City, where no taint of a desperate world crept in.

Most of us headed for the bathrooms, and when I came out, Cole stood by the ticket window. Verna talked with some undergraduates by the door to the dock, while Michael Venus and the man from CORE stepped out the front doors. I tightened the straps of my rucksack and straightened my shoulders. I'd give it one more shot. I'd tell Cole how I felt, but wouldn't beg. I'd take what came, and cry alone later. I stepped before him and cleared my throat. "Cole—"

Smiling Bob appeared in the ticket window in a state of panic. "Everybody back on the bus!" he screamed.

Talk about bad timing, and my eyes shot daggers . . . but Smiling Bob hadn't waited 'round. He was racin' from the booth, voice echoin' through the station 'bout finding the ticket agent hiding in the break room, and even as we tried to make sense of that Michael Venus and the CORE official stampeded through the front doors screamin' for us to get outta here! All too late, for the station was an anthill, one mob at their heels and knockin' 'em over, a second plowin' through the back doors and swampin' Verna and the college girls. "The bus is our only chance!" Bob tried to warn us, but a baseball bat cracked the wall near head level and two men dragged him down. Cole and me grabbed hands and turned to run, but there was nowhere to go—every exit was filled with men, women, and children, holding chains, bats, and clubs. "We're in trouble," I said. We looked at each other and maybe I saw forgiveness, but there was no time anymore. The doors were blocked and the crowd was howlin'. It was payback time.

Michael Venus and the young official went down first, swept

back till they pitched over a row of chairs. Verna and the college girls got sucked into the mass foaming through the back, each cut off from her sister, alone. It was like fighting against a stormy sea. Verna shoved without success toward a girl who dropped to the floor: a fat woman flogged her with a gold purse, while a skinny kid with bad skin danced in front and kicked her shins. I turned to help them and someone hit me behind the ear. I dropped like a head of beef in a slaughter pen; between the legs and feet I thought I saw a clutch of journalists push through the back and the mob turn on them instead, forgetting Verna and the college girls. A man ripped a heavy camera from the shoulder of one newsman and used it on him like a club. Two girls dragged Verna out the back, while others followed fast as they could.

It's all a mistake, I tried to shout, but no one could hear. Cole straddled my back, fending off blows with a chair. *He does love me,* I thought, but then another dizzying rush carried him away. He was thrown backward, arms windmilling to stay aright. Then he passed from sight and I was alone. For once in my life, Duck and Cover came in handy. I rolled up like a pill bug for protection as a pair of calf-high work boots stopped before me, the kind with steel toes. Red mud caked the yellow laces. I looked up at a gray face with the prettiest blue eyes. *You don't want to kick me with those steel-toed boots,* I tried to say as he stared back. *I'm too nice a person. I'm just a teenage girl.* But his receiver wasn't workin', or he simply didn't care.

So I covered my head. He kicked me in my kidneys. The rucksack absorbed some of the force, but oh, Lordy, a sharp hot needle coursed to my center and a scream rose from the pain. I didn't deserve this. This couldn't be real. It sure as hell couldn't go on. I grabbed the man's foot as he prepared another punt; he fell over backward, but other boots came up and field-goal practice continued. Waves of heat passed up and down my body; white light shot out from each impact till the whole station seemed to glow. Luckily, my original attacker was takin' shots as bad as me; I dived into his arms like a bad romance and as he screamed, "Get off me, you bitch!" I rolled him over and over, using his body as a shield. I could hear the *whacks* as others hit him; his breath smelled of SpaghettiOs and beer. We rolled through an alley of legs and feet, and all went down like bowling pins.

In that brief moment of reprieve, I caught sight of the strangest thing. A squad of Klansmen marched through the front and stopped in the center, calm as the eye of a storm. At the very heart of the group stood the red-robed man from Atlanta, his arms crossed on his chest; a few Klansmen broke from his side to join the fight, but he remained still. Their entrance was noted by the journalists, who were holding their own: As a front line held off attackers, others behind them filmed. They focused on the man in red. He sensed their attention and his shoulders squared.

In the same moment I spotted Cole, positioned to the group's left, still clearing space with his chair like Davy Crockett swinging Old Betsy at the Alamo. His struggle was watched by a tall Klansman standing by the man in red. The tall man pointed at Cole, but the red robe waved him off. When the tall man stepped toward Cole, the red robe ordered others to stop him. So the tall Klansman pulled a pistol from under his robes.

Everything stopped except the pain. It got very quiet. The tall Klansman pointed his pistol at the red leader and in the silence told him, "Leave the boy go!"

It was Twitch. Oh, God, I knew that voice anywhere, and here I was within hailin' distance with him holdin' a gun again. I tried to hide within the woven arms and legs of my attackers, but Twitch's attention was elsewhere. The old booger waved away Cole's assailants with his pistol and grabbed his son's sleeve. He pulled Cole close as the man in red took a threatening step forward. Twitch pointed the gun and laughed; then, with his free hand, pulled off the red man's hood.

"Get that!" a newsman cried. "He may be someone important!" The camera motors all went wild. The man in red screamed somethin' about exposure and lunged for Twitch, who pulled the trigger smoothly. He stepped aside as the robed man fell.

In an instant that mob changed from attackers to the attacked, a sound rising in the station like pigs in a slaughterhouse as the hammer falls. Twitch realized what he'd unleashed and dragged Cole toward the door, but the crowd was on them quick and spun them sideways. I heard a shot and a scream, then Cole and his murderous daddy vanished in a human wave. Maybe this was my own chance to escape, so I rose from my tangle just as a new crosscurrent sucked me in. I was carried backward, but this time the rush lifted my feet from the floor. Somehow it was the worst thing yet, and I screamed out in panic; I looked over my shoulder and realized I was the tip of a flying wedge headed for the front door. We hit, but the opening was too narrow to pass; as more bodies piled up, I felt like a bag of oats ground in a mill. This is it, I thought—I'm one dead Dahlia Jean—yet in that instant the doors snapped their hinges and we was hurled outside like shotgun pellets and I spun 'round and 'round. My wave crashed through the parking lot, over cars, through the spaces in between. In passing, I saw Smiling Bob leaning against an Edsel, gobs of blood dribbling down his leg; a man grabbed a girl as he passed and ripped her white dress down the front. There were brakes and flashing lights. I grabbed for a lamppost but missed; I hit a solid wall across the road. Sounds crashed 'round me and faded. I rolled over on the rucksack, the clear stars above me, the grass cold on my skin. I smiled at a red neon DINER that seemed to hang upside down between me and the stars.

Hard as it was to believe, I'd survived. How, I had no earthly idea. I pulled myself to a sitting position and saw I'd stopped against the front of a diner 'cross the road from the bus station. Bodies lay in strange angles between here and there. The girl with the ripped dress held a thin shred of fabric 'cross her breasts and sobbed. I moved my body parts till convinced nothin' was broke, though every inch of me was sore.

"You!" someone yelled.

It was a strange, guttural cry, coming from a man I didn't know from Adam. He was crawlin' my way. He was a Klansman, one side of his robe ripped open, hood pulled free. His face was pale and his eyes were bulgin', while his bottom lip was severed like a worm. One leg stuck out at right angles and nearly made me sick to see it, but he dragged it behind him anyway as he clawed through the grass toward me.

"I want that sack," he said.

This was spooky indeed. Everywhere I went, it seemed some stranger wanted my money, but to live through that mob then be addressed by this cadaver was more than anyone could stand. I tried to get my feet beneath me, but the stars whirled and I stayed where I was. "You're the girl in the picture; don't deny it," he said. "You got the stolen money in that backpack. Give it to me. I deserve it. It's mine."

I clawed sideways till the diner's wall and stairs blocked my further progress, yet even so he crawled on. I was trapped, and in another moment he'd squirm all over me like some slimy wiggle-worm. *"Leave me alone!"* I screamed.

"No," he said, as much to himself as to me. "A crazy man is chasing you, and it was me who brought him in. He shot the Colonel, did you see? He shot him in the chest. My life in Newport is over. They'll blame me." He touched my foot with his cold hands and I kicked at his face, but he grabbed my ankle and used it as a lever to pull himself up. "I need that money so's I can get away."

Two high heels appeared beside me and one swung back, landing against the stranger's broken leg. The man howled and rolled off, and I looked up into the face of the red-dress woman from before. She gazed down at me and smiled. "Honey," she said, "this is not your day. Good thing I stopped to eat before huntin' down my no-'count husband." She crouched beside the bug-eyed stranger, pulled a dainty pistol from her purse, and asked, "You want me to use this? I'd be happy to, really, since at the moment I'm not kindly disposed toward men."

The man's eyes bulged in fear; he shook his head and made little whimpering sounds. She patted him on the cheek, rose, and kicked him again. "You have strange friends, sweetie, and really should be more particular," she told me. "In fact, maybe you should come with me."

A weakness washed through me and it was impossible to say no. A little red sports car was parked before the diner; she helped me into its seat and closed the door gently. The place was filling fast with cops; their sirens filled the streets; their spinning lights bathed the buildings in carnival red. *Let it burn so bad the rain can never quench it,* I thought, and started laughing. My savior looked at me and placed her finger on my lips.

"Don't act crazy," she said, glancing back in the glow of her mirror.

"The world is crazy," I shouted back.

"Maybe it is," she answered, "but that doesn't mean you have to be, too."

A Prophet's Never Appreciated in His Own Land

I STROLLED THROUGH the field of carnage, pleased with my handiwork, slightly amazed. With only one shot, I'd accomplished all this. It was a personal best. I'd never known such efficiency.

The fallen lay in heaps: Freedom Riders, Klansmen, reporters, some whose allegiance was unknown. Yet all were injured and I was their teacher. Tonight's lesson, class—pain brings kinship to all.

Some shrank back as I walked close, but such is the lot of prophets, and I paid them no mind. Tiny Noble looked up from where he knelt, cradling the Colonel's head. The old man's robe was redder where the bullet entered—a royal color, as he would've desired. His chest barely moved. "You killed him!" cried Tiny, his hand trembling on the wound.

"Maybe," I answered. "Maybe not. He's survived worse." I stepped past, unconcerned.

Bart True dabbed with his robe at his brother's old head wound, open again. What would this do to their relationship now? I thanked Burt for the gun as I passed; his eyes blazed in anger, but his twin covered his mouth. "Better than a lynching, huh?" I said, and walked on.

I saw my boy, crumpled by a Coke machine, but I wasn't particularly worried since all Youngers have thick skulls. I picked him up and carried him out the door to where Burma waited by the Mercury. Her eyes were wide from all she'd seen. "What were you thinking?" she gasped. "Didn't you know what would happen? The police will be here soon and I can't find Dahlia." She was right . . . I couldn't see the girl neither . . . but something just as important attracted my attention across the street. I handed Cole to her.

Harvey Noble lay on the grass beneath a diner window. He panted in pain, his leg fractured maybe beyond repair. I smiled gently as I walked up, the neon bringing memories of DAVE'S. "You devil!" he screamed. "You've ruined us all."

"You and your friends did it yourself, Harvey. I was just the spark." I smiled pleasantly. "So where's the girl?"

"She's gone," he answered stubbornly. Such a child.

"I know you followed her out, so what happened?" I stepped on his leg for emphasis and the bone shifted beneath my heel. Harvey screeched like a rabbit. "Tell me the truth," I said.

"I had her but some woman came and put her in a red MG and headed east. That's all I know, I swear."

I rolled him over and dug in his pocket, disregarding his screams. More sirens pulled up. I couldn't stay long.

"Thank you, Harvey," I said, jingling the keys to his car. I dug into my pocket and tossed the last two rings on his chest. "Fair exchange," I said. "Take 'em, you earned 'em."

He yelped and brushed them off. "I'm dead already," he

said and started to blubber. Such pitiful weakness in a man. "Just who the hell do you think you are?"

I wondered why people were so blind. "Harvey, I'm the same as you. Just more efficient, is all."

I rose and walked off, ignoring his cries. The station was bathed in rouge and crimson strobes. Police crouched low as they neared the entrance, guns drawn, faces scared. They never even saw us as we started the blue black Mercury, a hole in the night, a shadow without form.

"This is a nightmare," Burma whispered, staring out the back. Her face was a pale rose.

"No nightmare," I answered, gripped by the strangest joy. "I think it's pretty. It's a fine kind of Hell."

Part III

The Land of Sunshine

Good Men Are Hard to Find

MY SAVIOR'S NAME was Laney Frank, but at first I didn't pay her no mind. I was too licked by the double whammy of Phenix City and losing Cole. I was undone. I'd dropped in the hands of another stranger, passed from palm to palm like a bad penny. It'd happened to Mama, and now it happened to me. I didn't wanta think about it. I didn't want to think ever again.

If there was a teensy bright spot in all the darkness, it was that I still had the money and I still rolled south toward Daddy. Both were fine by me, though not quite as important as before. Still, they were all I had. I rode in silence and thought about this while my savior talked to herself and drove. The more she talked, the more she grew convinced she'd been played for a fool. Realization worked into her like a thorn. Take away the fancy dress and she was no different than Mama, just with a gun to strengthen her debate and some wheels to get her there. Her husband was a NASA scientist based in nearby Huntsville, a place where they made first stages for the space rockets and maybe the one town in Dixie where the future counted more than the past, she said. Oscar—her hubby—was due back from Florida, where he'd gone for tests on the Mercury boosters; at the last minute he'd phoned how his T-Bird was in the shop and so was buying a bus ticket home instead. Maybe he'd stop at Fort Benning to see old Army buddies, he told her, so don't worry if he was a little late.

But Laney Frank believed in homecomings, so she put on

her red dress and planned to surprise him when he pulled into the station. The surprise was on her.

Oscar Frank was cattin' 'round. He'd done so before and got caught—to save his marriage, he'd promised never to do it again. She'd wanted to believe him, she told me, wanted it as bad as anything in her life. But in the end, he was just a man. There were too many temptations in the Land of Sunshine, too many space groupies willing to kill time with a rocket scientist if a silver-suited astronaut wasn't at hand. Laney worked herself into a lather at the thought of all the big-boobed, bleached-dyed Marilyns who prowled the astronaut bars. She'd take 'em both out, she promised, then write her "Memoirs of a Scorned Woman" from death row.

What Laney had in firepower and determination, she lacked in basic planning. She didn't have a road map; she'd packed a single overnight bag for the trip to Phenix City; she neglected to fill the tank as we zoomed outta town. Now it was after midnight and we were lost south of the sprawling army base. I watched the needle dip below one-quarter full.

But I was too exhausted to care. I slept and dreamed myself to Kansas. "Auntie Em," I said, "I want to get my boyfriend back." *Child,* growled Em, *people in Hell want ice water, too.*

I came awake to fireworks, wonderin' what in blazes Auntie Em was tryin' to say. In the real world, it was 3:00 A.M. Spots of red and gold flashed above the treetops like the ruby-colored dots and dashes of some cosmic Morse code. "It's tracer bullets," said Laney, "which means we're still at the edge of Fort Benning. The boys must be holding war games."

"Are we safe?"

"Safer than back in Phenix City, which, unfortunately, isn't saying much. Help me find some landmarks so we can get out of here."

On we drove. 'Round a bend we saw a sign for MA'S PIES & TRANSMISSIONS, but the gas pumps were locked for the night and we pulled on through. Not much further, we passed a sign for "NUEVA VISTA, 15 MILES." Laney was happy till we passed the sign again fifteen minutes later. "How'd that happen?" she yelped. "Have we been goin' in circles?" In answer to her question, the engine coughed and died.

We coasted to a stop on the shoulder of a straightaway surrounded by fallow fields. These, in turn, were circled by piney woods. In the moonlight I could see a tall wire fence to our left, separatin' the trees from the fields. Laney studied the landscape, tappin' her wedding ring absently on the steerin' wheel. It was a big ole diamond—two carats at least—and as I stared at that rock, she caught my gaze and grinned. "We're a pair, I'll tell you," she said. "You've lost your fellow, I've had mine too long, and we're both in the woods." She tugged at the ring but her knuckle was swollen. "See? I can't take it off if I try."

On my side of the road leaned a burned-out sharecropper's shack, half-hidden by high weeds. Beside that stood a leafless oak, its branches hung with bottles that glinted coldly and rocked in the breeze. Laney stared at it a second, then asked what it was. "A spirit tree," I said in surprise. It was something Mama'd only told me about and which I'd never figured to actually see, one of those old Southern beliefs that most folks said had disappeared. "The idea is that by trappin' bad spirits in the bottles, you keep bad luck from your door," I said. Laney said maybe the people in the shack could've used more bottles. I laughed and said this place had probably been empty for years.

Laney stretched and said we might as well get comfortable since no one would probably come down this lonely road till morning. She reclined the back of her seat and showed me how to do the same. She reached into the back where she'd thrown a couple of car blankets; she balled one in her lap and handed me t'other. I tucked it 'round my legs and arms against the chill.

"Where exactly are we headed?" I asked finally.

Cocoa Beach, she said. The bedroom for the Cape. "I know his haunts," she yawned. "I'll find the bastard, all right. Don't worry, he's history."

We grew quiet and listened to the night outside. In the distance, on the army side of the fence, I heard a groanin' and clankin' like a herd of huge wring-washers lumberin' our way. "Don't worry, it's just a bunch of tanks," Laney said without glancing over. "They travel in packs for war games."

"How do you know so much?" I mumbled, the warmth of the blanket makin' me cozy.

"You hang around as many military bases as a rocket wife, you learn a thing or two."

"Why they holdin' war games? Any reason in particular?"

"Like the Bay of Pigs, or Berlin, or something? Who can tell anymore? Everybody's nervous these days." She snorted in disgust. "Besides, you know men. They probably got bored and thought it would be fun."

I remembered Luther Burgess, one of the recruits from Wattles who'd been honored in the Memorial Day BBQ, and how he'd said he was getting sent to Fort Benning. I wondered now if he was in that passing metal herd. Luther hadn't known me from squat (at least I didn't think he did), but I'd always had a crush on him. I hoped for his sake there wasn't a dustup in the world somewheres, in some unknown hole-in-the-wall. Luther'd never made a mean comment about Mama or Daddy, least not to my face—one of the few kids in Wattles to be that kind of decent. That counted a lot to me.

Which got me thinkin' of Daddy, and how the mine owner'd seen him act so rough 'n' tough around his Key West Cuban pals. I wondered if he'd got drawed into that botched invasion-of-Cuba thing during the five years he'd been gone. Surely he had sense to steer clear of something so messy, but Mama always said he was a man for blunderin' into trouble. I drew the checkered blanket to my chin and stared past the fence. My tummy rumbled and I asked Laney if she had any food.

"Just some Necco wafers." That'd do, I said.

Laney fished inside her scarlet purse and gave me the gun to hold. It was a small thing, .22-caliber, pearl-handled grip, something Dale Evans would've used in a Roy Rogers matinee. "Don't you think it's strange," I asked, "someone like you carryin' a pistol?"

"You should be glad of it, or that bug-eyed Klansman back in Phenix City wouldn't have been so reasonable in leaving you alone." She handed me a snack and I handed back the gun; she held it up to the moonlight, admiring how it sparkled. "Oscar gave it to me for protection while he was away on business and me alone. That raises an interesting point. Do you shoot a man with the same gun that he gave you as a gift? Doesn't seem fair, does it, but there's a justice to it, too. I bet it'd be a stumper even for Dear Abby." She returned the gun to the purse, and placed that in reach in the footwell.

We nibbled our Neccos in silence and looked at the stars. Such talk of guns and ethics made Laney philosophical. She pointed out Orion, in the west, and above him, the Twins. "I always thought stars were where the angels lived," she said. "That's what my daddy said when I was little, that angels came to earth and perched outside our windows, watching like great, silent doves. Isn't that a lovely idea? They waited around to take us back to Heaven when we died, but could not interfere in our business or risk losing their immortality. So they waited on the ledge like that, invisible, immortal, and alone. Sometimes I wondered what would happen if we somehow got to the stars before we died. Did that make us honorary angels? Would they be able to talk to us then?"

"So you married a rocket scientist to find out?" I wondered, reachin' for a scrumptious wafer. These things were good. Maybe I'd take some of this money and invest in Neccos someday.

"I've wondered about that," she admitted. "I wish I'd found the answers for myself, but good girls are encouraged to marry, and it's easy to believe the accepted wisdom. Everybody else is doing it, so there must be truth in numbers." She tapped the wheel again to some tune in her head. "Life is funny that way. Oscar and I have a nice house, two nice cars, a nice son in a nice engineering school—not that different from other NASA couples, mind you—but I think we're waiting for the other shoe to drop, like it's all destined to come to an end. The bill will come due on all the good times, and nothing's saved to pay the creditors. The most exciting thing in Oscar's work is a rocket launch, something which seems to defy the laws of physics, but the most beautiful sight is when that rocket explodes. It's a green-and-white pinwheel shaped like our galaxy. He's been at the Cape preparing for the launch of the first Mercury Atlas, our most powerful rocket yet, with its silver-suited hero sitting at the top as helpless as a poor chimp, but everybody knows the hero isn't the point. The point is the ultimate payload, and that is a warhead. Oscar's missile will put an American into orbit around the earth, but the real goal is destruction. I think the contradictions have undone him, and it's up to me to finish the job."

I shook my head to clear it, completely confused. What did all this have to do with love? It was worse'n a lecture by Mama . . . at least *her* I could understand. "You don't believe me?" Laney said. "Honey, for every good intention, there's it's opposite conse-quence. For every speck of matter, there's a speck of antimatter." She looked at the dark sky and grinned. "There's a great black hole at the center of our galaxy that beats like a human heart and drives everything. Nothing escapes but positrons, the opposite of light and life, which search desperately for their twins. That union is annihilation, total and complete, but still the search continues, bent forever on that exploding moment when they join like lovers. Opposites attract. It's a natural law."

It was all talk to me, and I told her so. "You and every other adult I've met over the last week, all you do is talk, talk, talk, tryin' to find the truth, but the real truth is that nobody knows! That's what confused me in the first place, listenin' to such talk. If I'd listened to myself, I might still be with Cole."

"But would you appreciate him as much?"

"All I appreciate, lady, is that I want to go to sleep and forget we had this conversation." With that, I closed my eyes.

Joe Jackson

Maybe I slept . . . maybe I dreamed. I was in a rocket that had reached its highest point; the engines had cut off, and I glided silently. Maybe I *was* the rocket . . . I couldn't tell. The stars burned above me in endless night, while beneath me the earth glowed blue and green. It was the most beautiful thing I'd ever seen, but I didn't have long to appreciate it, for my rocket began its silent fall. Beneath me, people rose from their bunkers; they'd been in hiding too long. They emerged into a land where they hoped every valley was exalted and each desert made green; where each man and woman was a pilgrim and no longer a refugee. *Look up!* I screamed, but sound doesn't carry in space. *You've come out too early: it's nowhere as safe as you think.* I dropped from the clouds like stone Jesus, come again to fix everything.

I woke in a sweat to Laney's voice. "I think we've got company, dear."

I opened my eyes to white light, then realized it came from behind the high fence, deep within the trees. There seemed a whole host of spotlights, diffusing in the foggy mist, silhouetting the trunks of the tall, thin pines. Beyond the lights and trees I could see something like a black square roll up, then another and another, all built like boxy dinosaurs. "What'd I tell you? Lots of tanks," Laney said. There was a creak like a vault door openin', then an electric shriek and a voice across the fields like God.

"If anyone's in that car, get out," warned the voice in the bullhorn. "Show yourselves."

"Better do as they say, honey," Laney said. "Never argue with boys and their cannons."

We crawled from the car as advised. I put my hands overhead, but Laney said that wasn't necessary—not yet, at least—so I put 'em down. *Approach the fence!* squawked the metal voice, and more spotlights swept the field, lighting our way. They drenched our car and the empty shack in white; they glinted off the spirit tree. The bad spirits trapped inside the bottles sparked to life and flashed back a merry code of their own. We walked to the fence and waited—except for the diesel growl of the tanks, it seemed real quiet in the woods.

In a minute, a young lieutenant and a private with a radio walked from the light and stopped on the other side of the fence. They looked us up and down, like they'd never seen females before. The radio crackled and squawked, demanding why the play-war was put on hold. The lieutenant finally asked, "May I ask what you're doing out here, ma'am?"

"We're not doing anything wrong, are we, soldier?" Laney asked in a chirpy voice. "Our car ran out of gas, and we were waiting for morning for someone to come along."

"It's not safe out here like this, two women, alone."

"I've got a gun—want to see?"

"No ma'am, that's not necessary," the lieutenant said. He turned to the radioman and said something softly; the private repeated his words into the radio, which honked and bitched like no tomorrow. "You know," he continued, "some of my boys wanted to shoot up that deserted shack. We've been in maneuvers all day and haven't fired our ordnance once. What's the use of joining this man's army and driving a big tank if you can't shoot at something, and to tell the truth, I was tempted. But it *is* on the other side of the fence, and though my map says the shack's deserted, I wasn't 100 percent certain. You know what I'm trying to say?"

"That we're lucky you didn't go ahead and give the order to shoot?" Laney guessed.

"Yes, ma'am," he said. "But you sit tight: a couple of MPs should be out soon with gas, then you can be on your way." The two soldiers turned and faded into the light. We stumbled through the field and got back in the car.

Soon enough, a pair of headlights appeared on the road ahead. These became a Jeep with two soldiers up front; it pulled off the road and stopped, and the soldiers walked toward us in the headlights, each wearing an armband stenciled "MP."

The senior of the two, a sergeant, peered in Laney's window

while the one with a single stripe stood on my side. Something about him looked familiar, maybe how the light hit his square chin. "You the two we got a call about?" asked the sergeant.

"We're the ones," Laney said.

The way the two soldiers glanced at each other, it was obvious they wondered if we'd make a stink. Laney saw it, too, and assured 'em all we wanted was some gas and we'd be on our way. That same moment, the light hit the younger soldier from a slightly different angle, and I finally remembered whose chin it was.

"Luther Burgess, is that you?"

The lantern jaw dropped and the gray eyes above it squinted. "Dahlia Jean?"

"You know this female, soldier?" the sergeant barked, scowling through Laney's window to check me out, too.

"Y-yes, sir, I think I do," Luther replied. "She's a girl I went to high school with." The sergeant bent forward and peered closer, while Laney pulled her wallet from her purse and flashed some kind of government ID. The sergeant looked at it, then at her, then me. "At ease, soldier," he told Luther. "I guess everything will be okay."

I opened my door and followed Luther to his Jeep as Laney and the sergeant gabbed. "You look good," I told my old classmate. "The army's treated you well."

He grinned and straightened. "Put on weight, too," I added, to which he flexed a muscle so's I could *ooh* and *ahh*. "Not an ounce of fat, either," he boasted. "Go ahead and feel."

"My, my," I said, pinchin' a bicep, "ain't you somethin'? What's this stripe mean, and 'MP'? Mr. Perfect?"

"Military Police, Private First Class," he said, then glanced at his sergeant and lowered his voice. "Quit foolin' 'round, Dahlia. What's goin' on?"

"Just passin' through, Luther, gettin' threatened by tanks, that sort of thing."

He gave me a dirty look. "You know what I mean. It's all

been on the news, but nobody knows what to believe. First Harson Whitley shows up dead and you missin', then Arnold Simpson's missin', then your mom. First people thought Harson was robbed and you raped, and your body'd be found in some ditch. Then when Arnold vanished, they thought maybe you two robbed the place and ran."

"Me and Arnold? You know better!"

He grinned. "That's what I said. You spent most of high school fightin' him off, so all of a sudden you're gonna commit murder with him? I don't think so. When your mama turned up missin', the cops interviewed everyone in town, my folks included, then Arnold reappeared all trussed up like a mummy in an abandoned church, and the tale he told was the strangest thing of all. Seems some crazy lady told you to brain him with a baseball bat, but you refused, so she did it herself. Seems you missed your chance after all those years."

"Yeah, well, I was feelin' merciful," I said.

Luther repeated Arnold's tale—how an old convict came to rob the diner, how I fooled him and fled with the money and his boy. How the old man was chasing me cross-country, but the cops didn't believe a word. If I was so innocent, they said, I'd turn myself in. Every old classmate they hunted up and interviewed heard the same line, even Luther down here. The police were real nasty about it, like they suspected anyone who said otherwise. "They smell some kind of double cross, though they ain't sure what," Luther said. "Maybe you and the convict were in together at first, but you tricked him and ran. All they know is that anyone who eludes 'em so long has *got* to be guilty."

"That's crazy," I said.

"That's what I told 'em, not that it did any good. They've convicted you in their minds already, 'specially after that sheriff got shot in Muscovy. Then you popped up in Newport on the front page. What's it been now, seven days since Harson's diner? There's been all kinds of sightings of you, Dahlia; it's like a regular tourist industry back home. You're the biggest thing since Davy Crockett, but I'm not sure I understand. I mean, you always had some wild ideas, but you also had a lot of sense. I always felt sorry for all that happened to your family, but the way I saw it, you just tried to make the best of a bad situation."

I was touched. Somebody'd had some faith in me, after all. I touched him on the shoulder. "I didn't plan it this way, Luther, it just happened." I filled him in and asked if he was gonna turn me in, him bein' a military cop and all.

He thought it out slow and deliberate, then shook his head. "Part of me says I should, since it might keep you out of further trouble. But another part says you wouldn't be treated fair. Besides, the army would have to explain, and threatenin' civilians is frowned on these days." He gave me a lazy grin. "Plus, there'd be all the paperwork. So who has to know?"

Without thinking, I hugged him till the sergeant cleared his throat, so I stepped away. Luther blinked uncertainly and asked: "You really think you'll find your dad?"

"You gonna try to talk me out of it, like everyone else?"

He grinned again, and poked me on the shoulder. "Like anyone ever won a fight with Dahlia Jean Coker." I giggled and punched him back. It felt like old times.

"You tell your daddy he made a big mistake when he left you," Luther said, turning serious. That was so sweet that I kissed him on the cheek, and he turned red. The sergeant walked up and pretended not to notice. They grabbed a gas tank from the Jeep and emptied its contents into Laney's tank; I heard the sergeant ask about me, and Luther said, "Just a girl from high school, Sergeant." They started up the Jeep and drove off. Laney and me were once more alone.

By now it was dawn. A bobwhite called in the distance. I shivered against the chill. "I was wrong," Laney said as the sun peeked above the treetops. "Men *are* good for something."

"What's that?" I asked.

"They'll give you gas," she said, and grinned.

The High-Octane Highway of Bright, White Dreams

I KNEW MY boy was smitten when we got a ways from town. It was still dark when I heard him struggle from the deep. "He's comin' out of it," said Burma, so I pulled to the shoulder of the road. I watched his lashes flutter and was reminded of Cole's mother; I'd seen her traits in him a lot, the ghosts of past mistakes that always haunt the blood. I thought of him swinging that chair in the bus station, daring the world to do its worst, and I was proud of him like I'd never been. Maybe love had made a man of him. But that was over now.

Still, it softened me a bit when Cole finally opened his eyes. "Nice chase you gave, better than expected," I said. "But admit it, you always knew your daddy would win." The smile left my face and the small talk was over. "Where's the money?" I asked him.

Cole said he didn't have it, and to my surprise, met my gaze. "I gave it to the girl," he told me.

"You did what?"

"Dahlia had it from the first. It was always hers."

"But one hundred thousand dollars—"

"Only fifty now. That boy took the other half when he went under, remember? Who was he, anyway—a flunky like me?"

"Nothing like you," I said.

I knew that was a mistake the instant I said it, and silence filled the Mercury. Burma leaned against her door, scanning our faces. Cole's left eye was swollen and would likely turn into a shiner; there were scratches on his face and dried blood. I'd often looked worse at the hands of my own father—what the hell, the boy would live.

"The time for games is over," I said to Cole. "Where was you two headed?"

My boy seemed genuinely surprised. "You don't know?" he blurted. Burma stared hard enough to drill a hole in his skull. Her message was plain obvious. *Don't tell!*

"Somewhere in Florida to find her father, I think," I replied.

Now Cole frowned all puzzled at Burma, trying to figure what the hell was going on. "She hasn't told you, has she, Pop?" he finally said, and started laughing. "Dahlia was right—you can't read my mind." I reminded Cole not to mock his father, but my quiet threat, usually enough to shut him up, failed to make much headway. And that made me uneasy. "No doubt you knew our general direction, *she'd* fill you in on that," Cole added, glancing back at Burma, "but if we'd abandoned that route completely and headed somewhere else, you'd've lost us for good. You had me so brainwashed, I figured you'd find me, wherever I was."

"Don't laugh at your father," I said. I thought I was bein' exceptionally lenient, considerin' the circumstances. "Tell me exactly where she's headed so this foolishness can end."

"No," Cole said.

I shook my head to clear it, since surely I'd misheard. *No?* He'd never said *no* to me before.

"You heard me right," Cole said. "You don't know and I ain't tellin'. The only one to know's her mama, and she ain't said yet, either—and you're obviously unable to drag it out of her. She's as tough as you are, Pop, maybe tougher—just like her daughter. And Dahlia's tough as nails."

"That girl ain't so tough!" I snorted.

"No, you're wrong," Cole said. "I've never seen anyone like her. I'm only realizin' it now. It's too late, of course, but I'll say it anyway. You can always kill her, Pop, but you still won't get the money. I never thought I'd see it, but you've lost. All this was for nothin'. This pot of gold turned out like your other schemes."

He was taunting me! That fact took a minute to register, 'cause it'd never happened before. He'd never dared. At his age, I'd never dared with my old man. Nor him with his daddy, and so on back to the very first Younger, when all the world was new and everyone was scared shitless of the original Old Man. Back when it was decreed that no son could equal his father, that every man would be his papa's pale shadow. As the Good Book says, thou mustn't taunt the Lord.

So I hit Cole. Punishment, just and swift, helps a youngster grow. That's how a dog learns best; the same holds true for sons. I backhanded him across the unmarked eye so he'd have a matching set. His head snapped back but his eyes never left my face. That stare scared the Mighty Jesus outta me.

So I hit at him again. He'd slid against the back door, back where it was harder to reach him and do as much damage, and I started to scream. "You think you're better'n me, don'tcha?" I said. I poked out my chin and dared him to strike me, but his eyes only narrowed.

"No, Pop," he spit back, "I'm nothing like you."

My hand stopped its punishment of its own accord. I dropped it to my side. He was right. He'd never hit me back, no matter how many blows rained down. Fight back, I like to begged him, just this once—but he'd never do it. That damn girl I chased would pop me a good one if given half a chance, but not Cole. He'd never be mean enough. He'd never be like me.

"For God's sake, stop it!" Burma screamed, but by then I was done. "You got what you wanted," she said. "At least you got your boy back! You won!"

"I don't win till I have it all!" I replied.

With that, I jerked up the latch and kicked open the door . . . stumbled outside as my anger boiled up . . . lurched through the ragged field of cotton, to the woods. To the woods, where all sounds carried—the mad cries of fathers, the carrion call of crows. I fell to my knees and started to groan. I'd done this as much for Cole as for me—the robbery, the killing, the chase—but in the end every father's effort is mocked by his son. Come hell or high water, I realized, Cole would stick by that black-headed girl. Dahlia Jean Coker had gone and made my son love her, upsetting the balance of all good and natural things.

I knew I couldn't beat that. Who ever won out over teenagers in love? Just as suddenly, with that realization, I knew I was gonna be sick, too. I scooped out a hole in the dirt and drove my face into it; an acid froth rushed from my center, scalding my throat. But the hole in the dirt couldn't hold it. I scooped out another—dug a hole to put the devil in.

Finally I was done. I lay back, weak, arms out from my sides. The stars wheeled above me. I remembered the first time I fell in love.

It was with Cole's mom. There'd been other women before her, sure, but they were only holes—holes like these in the dirt for leavin' part of myself behind. But with Cole's mother, the feeling took me unawares. I remembered it well. I'd come in from a day at the mine, lathered in coal and sweat, feeling as low as a body could. The dog saw me and knew my temper, so ran under the house and hid. But people ain't as smart as dogs, and Cole's mom continued stirring a pan of sausage and beans. Her hair was stringy from the heat; her short shift hung off her shoulders like a rag. It was ten months after we got hitched and Cole squalled in the back, his cries piercing my head like hot tongs.

"Cain't you hear he's hungry?" I yelled at her.

"He's always hungry," she replied.

"I'm hungry, too, so where the hell's *my* dinner?"

She turned and her cold gaze traveled from the top of my dirty head to the soles of my filthy shoes. "You can kiss my ass," she said.

I took a swing, but she'd expected it and ducked to the side. She hefted the pan but I'd expected *that,* and beans splattered on the wall. We squared off, feinting right and left, eyes locked, moves attuned. We each took swings but none landed, and after a while something changed. As I sighed, her shoulders slumped. "Won't it never get better?" she said.

"I don't know baby, I wisht I knew," I answered.

Then we clenched in a different way.

I guess I loved her then. Maybe I had before, but this was

the first time I knew it for sure. When we fell apart, she lay on her side, facing away. Her chestnut hair fell in a dark spill on the pillow; her tanned back looked strong in the light through a crack in the curtain. I counted the knobs of her spine. She breathed deep and moist like a swimmer goin' down. That's what love is like, I thought. Like drownin'. You open your mouth and let the green water in.

Three months later, Cole's mother was gone.

Soon the fit passed from me and I walked back to the car. "We all been through a lot," I told Burma and Cole. "We're tired and we ain't actin' like ourselves. All we need is sleep, then we can talk reasonable again." Twenty miles further a neon sign of an Indian in a feathered headdress stared across the night:

The Happy Warrior Motor Court
Cabins, Kitchenettes
Day, Week, Month
TV, AC, AAA

I ripped some sheets and tied Cole's hands and feet, so he wouldn't think of leaving. I laid him on the couch and covered him with a blanket, to dream of a love that was, and that would never be again.

———— •◆• ————

I woke in the middle of night to an empty spot beside me in bed. Muffled voices came from the room outside, through the closed bedroom door. A light shone underneath. I crept close to listen: like most of these places, the walls were made of paper. The first to speak was Cole. "He send you in?"

"He's sound asleep, though not for long if you don't keep your voice down," Burma replied.

"Come to gloat?"

"Don't be foolish."

"You're here to untie me?"

"That's even more foolish. Your father'd kill me. Do I look like a suicide?"

"Then why *are* you here?" Cole said. Good boy, I thought: Never trust a woman. And I, too, wondered what that woman was up to now.

Burma sounded hesitant when she spoke again. A little confused. "I'm not sure why I'm here. Maybe I want to get a look at the boy my daughter fell for so hard."

"I'm no boy, lady, and your daughter's certainly no *girl*. Not no more."

It took me a moment to figure what he was getting at. I felt strange when I did. A bit older, too. But Burma merely laughed. "Oh, I'd figured *that* already," she said.

"You did?"

She laughed again, sad and even sweet. "It's fairly obvious, the way you and her stuck by each other. Even Romeo and Juliet weren't babes in the woods."

"Dahlia said you'd hit the roof if you thought we'd done it."

She laughed. "Once I would have, certainly, but not now. My little girl is smart, but she don't know everything. Besides, things happen to the best of us. Look't me and your pa."

"You and my pa?!"

"Not so loud. You want him to hear?!"

But I'd heard, all right, and I was bouncin' off the walls. Why'd she have to go and tell him *that?* That woman's mouth was bigger than the entire Mississippi. Why not go stand on a roof and announce it to the world?

"You and Pop?" he said again, softer. "But that's impossible."

"He may be old, honey, but he's got all the right equipment," she said. Oh, Lord, I thought, next comes a detailed inventory. Cole seemed just as flustered. "Any man likes sex," she added, "given the proper circumstances and the fact he's not dead."

"No, I mean . . . he doesn't like *anybody* . . . you saw how he hates me."

Her bantering stopped. "He doesn't hate you."

"I've never been good enough for him. You saw how he talked about that boy who drowned. It's always been that way."

"You ever think it's himself he hates? Not you?"

It got real quiet in our little cabin then. What did she mean, I hated myself? I liked myself just fine. It was the rest of the world that was the problem.

But Cole didn't buy it. "That's crazy," he said.

"Oh, yeah? Drivin' away your only child's a good way to prove your worthlessness. I got lots of experience in that department, so I oughta know."

I wisht I could see Cole's face, but was right grateful I couldn't see my own. Meanwhile, Burma's tongue wagged on. "It made me proud the way you and Dahlia hung on to each other even when everything seemed against you. That showed more spirit than I gave her credit for." Outside in the parking lot a horn blared twice, then died. Her voice was angry when she resumed. "But going to find her daddy's a dumb mistake. Don't look so surprised—I knew her intentions from the start, that's all she ever used to talk about, how if a fortune dropped in our laps she'd walk right on his fishing boat and ask him to his face why he ran. I know Dahlia better than I know myself, and everything I know as a mother tells me she's headed there. Now that she's lost you, she probably thinks she's got nothing else. But the minute she arrives in Key West, that man'll suck her dry."

My breath caught in my throat—I nearly choked out loud. Did I just hear what I thought I heard? I listened for some confirmation, but Cole turned suspicious again. "He did send you in here, didn't he? He's trying to find out where she's goin'."

"You stupid, stupid boy. I'm trying to save my daughter. Don't be dumb as her."

I hurried back to bed. They talked a little longer. Then the light flicked off and Burma crept back in the room. She slipped beneath the covers, spooning herself agin me. After a while, her breathing got regular and her body grew warm. Outside, the dark night barely lightened. The first bird sang. I eased from bed, eased into my shirt and pants, eased out the cabin door.

Key West, huh?

I'd heard of the place, a big spot for fishing, the last in a chain of islands strung together by bridges. As far south in this goddamned country as you could drive. During the Great Depression, a hurricane had nearly blew it and the nearby islands into the sea. According to the radio, another big one was brewing out beyond Cuba, and folks worried it might grow as nasty as the earlier storm. How you could live without solid land around you, I wondered, always eyed as a tasty treat by sharks and crocodiles? Yet all sorts of people did, fishermen and treasure hunters, government spies and spooks, artists and other bums, even that famous writer guy who'd blowed off his head with a shotgun a couple of months ago. Chances are, I'd never blend in good enough to escape notice, but with only one way in and one way out, what did it matter? That girl would never get away from me. Not now.

All this I considered while standing alone in the parking lot, all the other motel guests still asleep in their triple-A beds. I figured the Mercury had already been reported, but I sure hated to dump that smooth-runnin', black-souled car. Maybe the old shell game would buy us some time. I switched the Mercury's plates with those of a Chevy a couple of cabins down, then switched those with the plates of an Edsel parked near the shadow of the woods. Switching plates was as easy as switching women. Everybody did it, and there was always another at hand.

I wondered if I'd be switching Burma the same way soon.

I couldn't think about that now. I burst through the cabin door, rubbed my hands together, and said, "Wakey-wakey, children. The bird is on the wing, the dew is on the bud." I shivered with the chase. It was time to hit the road.

———————

We cruised the Merc across the Florida border before lunch, and stopped at a welcome center with a big orange ball balanced overhead. A sign announced "The Great State of Florida Welcomes You." Inside was air conditioned, even this late in the year. One whole wall was lined with ads for alligator wrestling! Trained parrots on bikes! Girls dressed like mermaids and swishing their tails! Strange state, I thought. And people made fun of Tennessee.

A girl with an orange pillbox hat and green skirt held a Dixie cup filled with orange juice under my nose. I swallowed it all, smacked my lips, and called for more. "I'm sorry, sir, only one per guest," she said, and pointed to a sign. I walked to the sign, took it off the hook, and tore it up. I held the cup back out. "Don't stop till I say." It was like drinkin' gold.

"What're you so happy about?" Burma asked as we sat outside under the palms. Such trees didn't grow natural so far north and looked sad and scraggly, but folks here seemed convinced life wasn't worth living without a palm tree 'round. You had to respect a place so determined to be a paradise, no matter what the obstacles. I could play that game, too. There was a traveler's advisory posted about the hurricane, how it was growin' stronger and now was named Isolde. It seemed a whole lot of worry 'bout nothin' to me. Up above, the sky was still blue and the sun as yellow as a daffodil. I hummed a little ditty. Nothin' would get me down.

We got back in the car; I settled in and drove. There's something spiritual about driving a good car. It's the American church on wheels. You skim across the earth's smoothed surface, the power of the V-8 engine traveling up the pedal and into your soul. The road was the nation's bloodstream, and Florida the most perfect expression of that truth ever devised by man.

I mean to tell ya, in Florida it seemed like roads were everywhere. They led in every direction, and if they ended in swamp and palmetto, who gave a damn? It was the ride that mattered, that and the road itself, and before long, we linked with a four-lane turnpike that seemed to form this great state's spine. The lanes north were packed with cars fleeing Hurricane Isolde, but for every one of them leavin', there seemed another headed south like us, and I realized we were all replacements here. I looked at the faces in the car windows and saw a constant hope for better things. That promise was everywhere. Sun, sand, surf, sex, this place had it all, and if that wasn't enough, the billboards promised more. There were green hills of golf, where grass grew ready-clipped and weed-free. There were kidney-shaped pools where the old dived in and came out fresh, shapely, and young. We all thirsted for the promise, this southbound herd in my lane. Every year they scrimped for this week or two off work, dreaming of this road.

But what if they got to its end, I wondered, and the promise wasn't there, or wasn't what they'd dreamed? I knew a lot about such promises. I could tell them a thing or two. Maybe the sand gets in your suit and chafes. The surf is piss-warm, filled with slimy, stinging things. The sex is never as good as promised; the sunburn returns years later as skin cancer; and in all likelihood, that cancer has spread throughout the blood. This wasn't how it was s'posed to be. Something must be wrong. Look at the billboards—the people in them were laughin', but not us. They'd reached the promised land, but got off on the wrong exit. They needed another map. Maybe they'd get it right next year.

And at the end of the high-octane highway lay Miami Beach, the brightest, whitest dream.

We reached there by supper and I veered east, hoping to see the ocean after all these years. I hit a street called Collins Avenue, and the three of us fell quiet, our differences forgot for now.

Deep in the land of sunshine, we'd entered a frosted world. Everything was white, a fairyland of white more spotless than the Colonel's sanitary dream. On a flat strip of sand dividing sea and swamp, someone had created a world contrary to sense, a pearl white heaven paved upon the jungle where white-furred matrons walked tiny white dogs and snowy stretch limos floated lazily toward a blinding sun. The white hotels rose above them— hotels crowded together so tight you couldn't see the ocean— hotels resembling gigantic household ruins. That day, I saw leviathan iceboxes, sugar cubes, can openers, all sunk into the earth or tilted on their side. We rolled past hotels with names like Eden Roc and Fontainebleau, sprung from the earth like white fuzzy dice, like twenty-story Westinghouse freezers awaitin' their monster housewives. They existed in their own special space, a space completely opposite anything the Great State of Tennessee could ever know or be. A world so divorced from the black coal pits of my life that I wondered if I'd lost my mother fuckin' mind.

It made me nervous—that's what it did. It made me wonder if the world had passed me by. Everywhere was water, and so as well as goin' blind from all the white, I felt seasick, too. Water rocked the boats in endless marinas, gushed from fountains, bubbled over colored lights in silver pools. It glinted off a thousand mirrored surfaces till the buildings themselves were columns of water that tied the sky to this splashing, spurting, insane dream of an insane tropics where nothing was steady and everything floated away.

I was gettin' hypnotized. I had to get away. "You're drivin' like a maniac," Burma said.

Collins Avenue ended in a park and more water, but a causeway veered toward the mainland and the city of Miami. I took a quick right past cruise ships and island strongholds in a shimmering bay. I left the redoubts of the rich and entered a part of Miami called Liberty City. But what the hell, I didn't see no liberty here. Ruin and tumble was crammed along the street; the faces on the street burned black with hate for all things white across the bay. What would it be like to service the flake white mansions, the silver white hotels, day after day, then come home here? I'd seen want before in Tennessee, but at least you didn't stare at the source of that enslavement hour after hour, day after day. The hate burned deeper as you waxed the sleek cars, shined the crisp loafers, buffed the smooth nails. The faces stared as I drove past, lost as hell. I knew such hatred, too, I wanted to tell 'em, but I represented with my very pigment all the things they didn't have. So I rolled up the windows, locked the doors, and prayed to God to get us out of here.

"Oh, God, this place!" said Burma. "How can such things be?"

How, indeed? I wisht, in that instant, that I'd never left Tennessee. This was America boiled down to its essence, the richest and poorest side by side yet never touching, tucked away in the nation's southern pocket, out of sight and out of mind. Maybe it would fall through a hole in that pocket and disappear. I doubted those Freedom Riders would ever make it this far; I doubted anything could ever set this place free. More likely, Miami would become a nation within a nation, a kind of mutant America like in the movies—a land of gold and blood, fire and doom, surrounded by water, miles of water, fathoms of the stuff. The fires would break out, but there'd never be enough water to put out these flames.

I, for one, didn't want to hang around. Not me. I stepped on the pedal and in an instant passed from Liberty City to another part of Miami called Little Havana, as if entire worlds lived side by side in this goddamn city but glanced off each other at crazy eight-ball angles—as if once you entered the city limits, you'd never get out. "Where the fuck are we?" I cried in despair. Cole pointed to a sign that said SW Eighth Street, and Burma added, "Ain't that where all those Cuban exiles live?"

So it was. We were starving by now, so I pulled over; it was like parking in a carnival. Latin music pulsed from store-fronts, renovated theaters showed anti-Castro movies, women like sweet, ripe fruit walked past in high-heeled shoes. I smelled fried bananas in the air. I saw El Cuño cigarettes stacked behind glass with trapped flies buzzing; pyramids of gourds and strange tubers stacked in produce markets; iced coconuts served with a straw. There were seashell shrines built to the Virgin Mary and love potions sold in botánicas. Radios tuned to Spanish-language stations played the Cuban national anthem and voices spit out their hatred for Castro. These people called themselves los exilios. The exiled.

Maybe the exile was only temporary, they seemed to hope. Maybe Miami was just a strange vacation before they all went home. But no one seemed to agree on the terms. Stenciled on the stucco walls or plastered up in mildewy posters were the names of the exile groups: Alpha 66, Acción Cubana, FLNC, Pragmatistas, MIRR, El Cóndor, Zero—each at odds with the other, each convinced their rivals were all commies, traitors, or fools. It was like being dropped in a swarm of angry bees, ready to sting themselves to death if a common acceptable enemy wasn't quickly found.

We came to a corner booth selling sweet brown coffee and black beans and sausage; I sank onto a stool and tried to make sense of things. It seemed that under all this hubbub lay sorrow, sorrow at their exile, but even more than that, sorrow for the Bay of Pigs. Signs of mourning for lost sons and husbands hung all over: a black armband worn by our shopkeeper; a framed photo of a young man the same age as Cole. He wore a black beret sewn with a patch, "Brigade 2506." The owner, his father, had written the boy's name beneath the portrait. Under that, Muerte: 17 abril 1961, and under that a red rose.

And something else. I saw the word verdad scrawled everywhere. The masthead of a folded newspaper. Painted on a wall. "Truth," and nothing more. I picked up a paper at my elbow and the pages were filled with letters, some Spanish, some English, about the blood of los mártires, martyrs because of "the betrayal," "the abandonment," that moment when President Kennedy withheld air cover, they said. After Castro, JFK seemed the most hated man down here. It was a chorus of fury

made worse by dependence on their betrayers, and the knowledge that there was nowhere else to go.

But wasn't it like that everywhere? Just in different forms?
The black rage of Liberty City, the Colonel's rage that he
passed on to his Klansmen, my father's rage that he passed
down to me. This was the age of betrayal. The fury built forever. We all despaired of some vision, always out of reach. We
counted the promises broken, and watched our dreams drop
and scatter like beads torn off a string.

And so we went mad. There were too many struggles, all
merging into one. The struggle assumed a holy light, got
bathed in the blood of martyrs, was pointed like a spear at those
who lost faith. Everything was struggle. That was the one *verdad*.

By now it was getting dark and we drove west down SW
Eighth toward the setting sun. Maybe there were motels there.
We drove past gun shops and firing ranges, U-Rent shops,
burglar-alarm installers, strip joints, and package stores. We
drove where pink and baby blue tract homes gave way to sewer
plants, and the glint of water revealed the end of the road.
Beyond that stretched the Everglades, and here at its edge were
fleabag motels. Neon flickered and I spotted another Happy
Warrior Motor Court.

It was a sign. I got a double, with an extra bed for the boy.
"You're not gonna tie me up like last night?" he asked as I
stepped outside.

"Naw," I said, oddly depressed. "Where you gonna go?"

I walked through the parking lot to a tiny brown beach
overlooking a sea of grass. It looked like you could walk across
that grass, but I'd heard you'd sink in an instant and never be
seen again. I wondered how many bodies had been dumped
right here, then found the next day. A sign stuck from the
water's edge: DANGER! PROCEED NO FURTHER! I looked
at the grass and half-submerged logs and wondered why.
Maybe quicksand. I peered at the horizon and the sky looked
on fire. The light was like amber, deepening to tangerine and
blood. Some wispy clouds seemed to burn underneath, while

above that a thin band of plum deepened to blue black and the night's first stars.

Why, so close to my goal, did I feel so glum? Cattails grew at the water's edge and slimy clumps of eggs were glued to their stalks. I'd never seen anything like it and stepped close for a better view. A splash came behind me and I backpedaled quick, remembering the sign. I looked 'round but didn't see nothin' . . . nothin' but a half-sunk log with two knobs on top. It sank from sight as I stared.

It took me a beat to realize this wasn't no log. It was a gator, longer than I was tall. He'd been eyeing me all along. I started to laugh even as my heart pounded. No matter what your precautions, the unseen finally gets you. That was the real *verdad.*

The fire in the sky went out. A kingfisher rattled. I went back inside.

After that, it didn't take long. We left Miami early the next morning, past flashing police lights, down the Coastal Highway, away from the boomtown. We rode past trailer lots, tattoo parlors, body shops, construction yards, and reptile sales. People feared the hurricane and store owners nailed plywood across their windows. I looked at the sky—maybe the air felt heavy and wet, but there was still no sign of a storm. These people were just plain paranoid. Or maybe paranoia was part of life down here.

We drove on and on, past Homestead, the last town before the Keys, past miles and miles of water, through islands with names like Largo, Islamorada, Boca Chica, Marathon. All the cars seemed headed in the other direction and I thought good riddance. There'd just be fewer witnesses for what I had to do.

"When did you figure it out?" Burma finally asked, the only time she mentioned the subject. I told her how I

listened in to their conversation t'other night. Burma glared
out the window.

"Shit," Cole said.

And then we were there. Key West, Conchtown, the Isle of
Bones. Past a white Sears shopping center, into the old part of
town. A tarnished metal sign beneath a ficus tree announced the
end of U.S. 1. "The End of the Rainbow," the sign said. This
was such a little town, not much bigger than Wattles, really. I
knew Burma's ex was a fisherman, so looked for signs pointing
to a marina and soon saw them everywhere. CAPT. BILLY'S
SWORDFISH CRUISE, said one. Bragged another: CAPT.
SHAGGY, CHARTER CAPTAIN OF THE STARS.

It didn't take long to arrive. The charter boats and shrimp
boats were all tied willy-nilly, gulls wheeling above them for
scraps, pelicans squattin' on posts and clackin' their bills.
"What's the name of his boat?" I asked.

"Figure it out yourself, you're so smart," Burma said.

It didn't take much figurin'. We parked the Merc and walked
on back, and there, big as life, its paint newly splattered with
blood and fish guts, was where we'd been headed since all the
craziness began.

"Jesus, I can't believe it!" Burma echoed my thoughts exactly.
Painted in black on the stern of a boat was the sign that said our
search was over. I took a deep breath and climbed aboard the
cruiser its captain had named MISS DAHLIA JEAN.

Everything Speeds to Its Fulfillment

WOULD SHE OR wouldn't she? Kill him, that is. With her
pearl-handled gun, in her blood red clutch bag, kept on the
floor of her tiny red car. I wondered this all the way to Florida.
The entire way, she argued with herself. East across the state
till we hit the Coastal Highway; south beside the ocean

through Jacksonville and St. Augustine. The Florida cities had a dusty, overused look, like the sun and salt had leached 'em dry. The ocean went on forever, and the radio said a storm was brewing out there.

"He's good as dead. I swear to God I'll kill him," Laney muttered as she drove.

What was this thing called love? I thought I'd known a week ago in Harson's diner, but now I hadn't a clue. I'd never been more alive than in the forest with my gypsy, but look what love and loss did to people's minds! It drove Mama to bed, then pulled her out—though whether that was love or money, I wasn't sure. It turned Sallie Goodnight into a murderess, Laney Frank into a scorned woman, and an organized group of idealists into a busload of squabblin' kids. Love and lust was the greatest power on earth, but half that energy was spent on talk and the other half on makin' so much trouble you finally believed that monks and hermits had the right idea. Talk, talk, talk, till you drowned in trouble and it was a miracle to get a breath of air.

Take Laney, for one. "Men!" she cried as she drove. "Who needs 'em? Someday they'll be obsolete. Someday a few will be kept on ice for sperm production, while the rest can be lined against the wall. We'll start with Oscar first," she added, swervin' past a station wagon filled with beach balls and screamin' kids. The expression of the man at the wheel suggested that a firing squad might be a relief. "Road hog!" cried Laney, and laid on the horn.

We cruised past the Cape in late afternoon. Cars were pulled along the road; drivers got out and shaded their eyes. We crested a drawbridge and to the north a spindle of fire rose up, tracing a ribbon of smoke through the sky. A deep rumble shook our windshield. "Is it a space shot?" I cried, excited, but Laney shook her head and said it was just an unmanned Air Force Atlas, probably with a Telstar payload, as if that meant anything to me. We pulled over to watch the launch—it was beautiful, so elegant and slow-motion. Yet even as I watched, the smoke began to loop in a lazy figure eight and before I could ask what was the matter, that Atlas exploded all over the sky. Jade and white fire spread from its center like a flower. Smoke trailed like confetti out to sea.

"Destruct button," Laney said. *"Poof!* several million dollars down the drain." She turned the key and restarted the MG. "They're always blowing up," she sighed. "Those missiles are actually very fragile. Something goes wrong—pitch, gimbal, auto-guidance—and that's the end. The Germans made 'em better, which is why we kidnapped a bunch and brought 'em over after the war. God help us if we ever start shootin' them back and forth at each other. God help the astronauts who sit on top of those things."

Immediately south lay Cocoa Beach, the town where she said all the space people stayed. Cocoa Beach seemed equal parts salt spray, sand burrs, and giant water bugs; a single road traced its entire length, a north-south route along the ocean called A1A. It would be hard for anyone to hide long from a determined searcher, and Laney started in immediately. She drove straight to the fanciest motel, a square doughnut with a tiki bar and pool shaped like a kidney, both in the middle where the hole should be. This was home of Walter Cronkite, astronauts, presidents, and congressmen when they came to watch the rockets; it was the place where Oscar would take his home-wrecker, Laney said.

But his T-Bird was nowhere in sight, and Oscar was not on the grounds. We didn't linger, but continued south to the town line; this nudged against an Air Force base, where the spy planes snooping on Cuba landed at all times of day and night, Laney explained. We played a different kind of spy, stayin' in a fleabag motel where Oscar wouldn't be staying and so accidentally spot us, she said. We showered and slept, then rose for the hunt that evening, our first stop the fancy motel again. We circled the lot but no Oscar; we entered a court of banana palms and bamboo lanterns, and emerged by the pool. A man and woman smooched in the deep end, but no Oscar. We made our way north 'round other motels, but no tattletale

T-Bird; we cruised by the bars and strips joints, dodging fly-boys as they raced down the main drag.

I'd never seen anything like it. These folks lived each moment like their last; the afternoon explosion of the Atlas was merely part of the continuing show. Life wasn't lived like this in Tennessee. "You can get anything you want down here," Laney said as twilight became night, *"so why can't I find my husband?!"* Maybe she'd jumped the gun, I suggested, and he wasn't cheatin' on her after all. Maybe there'd just been a mistake with the buses. Lord knows, I told her, I'd made a mistake gettin' on that Freedom Ride.

Laney glared at me like I was in cahoots with the man. "He's here, I feel it," she hissed. "He's just being cagey." At the northern town limits, we pulled outside a place called The Happy Kitty, home of *Hot Women!* and *Girlzz!* A white T-Bird was parked by the door. "See! I told you!" Laney screamed. A fat man sat by the door on a padded stool and squinted past his cigarette smoke as Laney slammed her door. I followed more meekly. "Can I help you, ma'am?" he said.

"I'm looking for my husband," she replied.

"I'm sure you are," he smiled, as if vengeful wives landed on his doorstep every day. "The cover's three dollars, and you have to leave that purse with me."

"I need my purse, my wallet's in it."

"You can take that out, no problem, but what else is inside? Want me to check?"

She glowered at the doorman, whose teeth were white and smile broad. She reached for her wallet, paid the cover, and handed over the clutch bag. The doorman set it by him on his stool. He looked at me and added, "There's no way you're legal, baby. You stay here, too."

Laney snorted in disgust, but I said staying here was fine by me. I really didn't want to go in there with her. She said she'd only be a minute, then rushed through the door.

The doorman wrapped his hands around one knee, leaned back on his stool, and grinned at me. He wore a green and pink

Hawaiian shirt, shorts, and sandals, the kind of getup you'd never see in the Smokies but seemed some kind of uniform down here. He said I wasn't missing much by not followin' my lady friend. "I'm the owner, so I should know. A strobe light, some loud music, some girls not much older than you wearing a whole lot less. It's a dead-end job."

I sat on the curb, my shoulder about even with his hairy shins, and wondered what Laney would do now. "You don't fit my idea of a strip-joint owner," I said to break the silence.

"You ever known a strip-joint owner?"

"Well, no, not really," I said.

He laughed, showin' them pearly whites again. "So you can't really judge. Actually, I was a philosophy major in college, but philosophy doesn't pay the bills. At least, not these days. You know what Aristotle said."

"Ari Who?"

"Aristotle, a great man, maybe a bit before your time. He said everything in Nature moves toward its own fulfillment. Maybe Nature designed me to own a strip club."

Two cars raced down the street, tires squealing. "Where you from?" he asked.

"Tennessee."

"You're a long way from home."

I told him in a nutshell (minus the criminal bits) how far away I really was. He whistled and asked if I was that girl in the papers; one and the same, I told him, no longer carin' who knew. He studied me awhile and said, "Some of my bouncers inside are off-duty cops . . . they'd love the write-up they'd get for turning you in."

"I'm sure they would," I sighed. "Maybe you should tell 'em. The law could make the wrong choices, instead of me."

He laughed and poked me with his toe. "Why ruin a perfectly elegant proof on the way to its completion? You're approaching some fulfillment, like the old Greek said." He stared at the cars on the street. "Besides, I hope you find that boy again."

That was sweet of him, and I told him so. I looked up at how he sat there, fat and happy on his stool, judging the passing show. If I stared long enough, only his smile seemed to remain. I said I liked his Hawaiian shirt and thought the colors went with his eyes. The waves crashed on the beach and a seagull floated overhead. He asked if I saw today's explosion and I said I was impressed. "Lots of explosions down here," he said.

Screams rang from inside, followed by the sound of breaking glass. The owner rose and stretched like he'd expected this, and opened the door. A tanned bodybuilder emerged with Laney tucked under his arm. "She thought some poor guy was her husband, boss, and flew at him screaming. Should we charge her?" But nothing was hurt except a shattered glass, so the owner shrugged and said to let her go. Laney brushed herself off.

"You satisfied now?" he said.

"So I made a mistake," Laney answered, tucking back a loose sprig of hair.

"I suggest you go back to your motel and cool down." He fished the cover charge from his pocket, separated a one, and handed her the rest. "That's for the broken glass. Don't come back. Your husband's not here." He smiled at me as we left and waved good-bye.

We called it a night and returned to our motel. Laney sat cross-legged on the bed, cleaning her pistol, which seemed to calm her nerves. "You're not really gonna kill him, are you?" I asked. She wouldn't know till she found him, she said.

We were out early the next morning, hoping to catch the fox in his lair. We circled the fancy motel first, and sure enough a white T-Bird was parked out back, as she'd hoped. She checked the license plate and smiled. "No mistakes this time," she said.

We drove around the front to the lobby; the motel clerk was pouring himself a cup of coffee as we walked in. He balanced the cup in his hand and blew gently across the steam, his face alight with that kind of sleepy expectant smile you never thought existed outside coffee commercials. Laney leaned over the counter, snuffing out one of his life's quieter pleasures. "I am Mrs. Oscar Frank," she demanded, "and I want the key to my husband's room."

The clerk set the cup down slowly, so not to spill a drop, flipped through a register, and looked up, confused. "He's already registered with a Mrs. Frank," he said.

"That's what I'm here to correct," Laney replied, slapping down her ID. I'm not sure if the clerk saw the gun in her purse or not, but his eyes got big and he handed her the key. We walked past the deserted tiki bar, past the pool with dead bugs floatin' on the surface and a discarded bikini top draped across the diving board, through another breezeway and to her husband's door. Laney turned the key gently in the lock till it clicked, then pulled her gun from her purse like Joe Friday, and kicked open the door.

A bar of light sliced through the dark room. There were two double beds set side by side, both beneath identical paintings of a green Eden. The bed closest to us was untouched, while the one farthest back was rumpled in every possible way. From under the bedclothes rose the upper halves of two rudely wakened sleepers. The man rubbed his eyes and groaned; the woman screamed once in surprise, then a second time when she saw the gun. She gathered the covers to her chest, and though it may've been a trick of the light, it seemed there was more to cover than was humanly possible.

"Size 44, at least," said Laney, observin' the same. "Oscar, I'm disappointed. You promised to lay off the strippers."

"I can't help it, Laney," he yawned. "Old habits are hard to break. The bigger, the better." He patted the knee of his bed partner. "Don't worry, she won't shoot you," he said. "Just me."

The woman had regained enough composure to answer, "I thought she was in Alabama!"

"My wife is a determined woman," Oscar said.

"Is that a silicone job?" I asked Oscar's bed partner, still amazed.

"Damn straight," said the woman, fishing under the bed for her clothes. "Cost three months' wages, plus tips. Can't even see the scars."

Oscar watched sadly as his bedmate slipped into a pair of panties and pulled on an oversized shirt. He wasn't bad-lookin' for a man in his late forties: Fine gold hair covered his chest; light streaks of silver shone at his temples among the blond. He gazed in regret as she picked up a pair of stacked heels by their straps and scurried from the room.

"Nice," Laney said when she passed. "Your taste improves each time."

Oscar ignored the comment and peered at me through the half-light. A lewd light came to his eyes. "Who's the elf? A little friend?"

"You really are beneath contempt," Laney observed. "She's a very nice girl who doesn't deserve to see what I'm going to do to you." She scooped up the key ring by her husband's wallet and held it out to me. "Wait a minute—what're you doing?" Oscar cried, his first real show of emotion since we arrived.

"Hitting you where it hurts most," Laney answered, and turned to me like her husband wasn't there. "These are the keys to his car. Take the road out front and just head south. It will take you to the Keys."

"You can't give away my car!" Oscar screamed. He wrapped the sheet around his waist and stepped across the mattress, so Laney turned and shot him in the foot, right where the instep meets the ankle. "You're such a bore, Oscar." Her husband stared at the hole in his foot and dropped between the beds.

"You shot me with the gun I gave you!" he yelped.

Laney giggled from a case of nerves. She pressed the keys into my hands and pushed me toward the door. "Hurry. The neighbors will call the cops soon."

"What about you?"

"Oscar and I will take this time to get reacquainted. Right, my darling?"

"Oww, my foot, it hurts, and you're giving away my T-Bird!!"

"See, Oscar's fine. Keep the sea on your left and you won't get lost." She kissed me on the cheek, then pushed her pearl-handled pistol into my hands. "Here, take this, I don't need it anymore. It may come in handy for you." She handed me something from the dresser and asked me to hang it on the doorknob on the way out, then pushed me from the room and latched the door.

I looked at what she gave me: a plastic hanger reading DO NOT DISTURB.

——•——

For the first time since leavin' Wattles, I was alone.

I realized this now as I pointed the T-Bird south and left that motel of misdirected love. All trip long I'd been paired with talkers, it seemed. The whole country liked to talk, each voice demandin' equal time. That was the nice thing about Cole. He was quiet, no need to fill up the silence, happy to let me *be*.

But I only realized it now that he was gone. Down the road I pulled over, folded down the ragtop, and stuffed the money bag in the trunk, then drove some more. It was a pleasure to feel the sun in my face and wind in my hair. I turned on the radio, and there was more talk and beach music. I found a pair of purple shades in the glove compartment and put them on.

People stared or waved as I drove by. Maybe they wondered, Who is that girl in the white T-Bird? Maybe it's her rich daddy's car, and she's out for some fun. Or she's a secret agent on a mission to save the world. It seemed so easy to change your image: a new car, a pair of glasses, whether or not you rode alone. I realized I rarely saw anyone else alone in a car. A partner confirmed your presence, but all alone you floated outside space and time. You could be anyone. Older couples, past retirement, stared in resentment, sure I lived in the fast lane. Young guys, surfboards piled in back, honked on the straightaways and dared me to drag. I was the dream girl-next-door from *Playboy*, out for fun, makin' no demands. Middle-aged couples looked at the car and saw Daddy's daughter rolling dice with the insurance payments. A group of girls smiled as they passed and maybe saw themselves.

The road I drove followed the dunes, while beyond that lay the ocean. The sky looked like lead on the horizon, though overhead it was still sunny and warm. It's that storm, I thought, the one the radio called Hurricane Isolde. Funny how they named 'em after girls—maybe someday they'd name one after me. Right now, Isolde was parked west of Cuba, but it seemed to be pickin' up speed. Maybe it would spin off south, into the Caribbean, or maybe north along the Eastern Seaboard. Maybe it would head for landfall here. Just like a fickle woman, said the radio weatherman, but I wasn't amused. Locally, he warned, a storm like this piled water along the coast, making for bigger waves and a stronger undertow, so be careful out there.

I came to a beach town with a STEAMED SHRIMP sign and some picnic tables, and across the street from that a department store like the Kresge's back home. SUMMER CLOSEOUT SALE, said the sign in its window. ALL 2-PIECE BIKINIS MUST GO. Mama'd have a fit if I bought a bikini, I thought, so I stuffed some money from the trunk into my pockets and went in. "You're definitely a petite," the lonely clerk said. She came from the back with a little off-white number that looked to me like panties and a training bra. "That's so cute on you!" she gushed, and I was sold. I wore it out of the store after buying Coppertone, a cotton shirt, some flip-flops for the stickleburrs, and a kerchief to keep the hair from my eyes. I got in the car and kept goin' south. Maybe this state wasn't half bad after all.

Soon I passed over a high bridge across an inlet with rock jetties on both ends; these jutted out to sea. Fishermen climbed out as far as possible, where the waves broke hard and furious, but they didn't seem to care. The weatherman was right: Inland, you couldn't tell the difference, but Isolde could be felt here. I rolled over the bridge and on the other side saw what looked like stick figures riding on the waves. I pulled over and climbed the dunes. They were surfers, the oldest in his twenties, muscled like lifeguards, hair dripping and long. The sun stained their skin brown while bleaching their hair a pale white blond. They seemed another race entirely, poised where the earth met the sea, sitting atop big six- or seven-foot planks and bobbing up and down as swells passed beneath them to curl and break seconds later on the sand. They searched for something out to sea that I couldn't fathom, and the sight was somehow sad. They sat there, silent and coiled, like exiles staring back home. The land was unfriendly and the sea didn't want them, so they were stuck forever in the space between the two.

Suddenly they spotted something and straightened on their boards. I squinted and saw what looked like a deep trough in the water. They flattened on their boards, kicking and paddling toward shore. Why were they scared, I wondered, then realized they only hurried to catch a wave. Somewhere out there the perfect wave was comin', and maybe this was it. The trough deepened behind them and the swell grew high. The water changed from dirty green to blue with foamy tips; they stood at the very moment the wave curled forward then wrapped 'round itself like a tube. The quickest surfer hunched low on his board and disappeared inside the hollow, poised between one element and t'other, balanced perfectly between two opposing worlds.

If only I could be that way. A breeze swept off the ocean and prickled my skin. I'd come so far from home and seen so much, just like I'd always wanted, yet an emptiness had opened inside me that might never end. Few ever rode that tube and found the silence in it; most of us were lucky just to paddle to shore. Some fell off and got dragged along the gritty bottom, sucked out by the undertow. Most searched and searched forever, and in the end there was just a vision of tiny souls watching for a better moment, bobbing like corks on the sea.

As I watched, one tiny surfer looked up in the dunes and waved, then all the others did. Just friendly flirtin', but I felt alone. If Cole was here, I'd've wrapped my arms around him and in that brief instant known the connection of all things. He would've liked the moment, too. But Cole wasn't here, so I brushed myself off, waved back, and walked to the car.

Soon the beach road ended and I swung inland—and in no time I was lost. The sun hung to my right, so I knew I pointed south, but instead of breakers and bathing suits, I was on a long road surrounded by miles of sawgrass and water. The only other life in sight was stringy cattle with horns built for business, white egrets floatin' 'round like snowflakes, and bugs. An eternity of bugs. Black clouds of mosquitoes that landed if you stopped movin'; green dragonflies that dipped and dove among 'em, some as big as your head. Huge brown and yellow locusts marchin' slowly 'cross the asphalt, not the least bit mindful of the rolling shadow on them or the vibration of its wheels. Black fleshy flies, called blind mosquitoes by the locals, that had no other purpose in life but to make babies, then splatter 'gainst your windshield.

Around noon, I came to a town built on a limestone island called a hammock, the island grown over with bald cypress and palms. I filled the car with gas and wiped away the bugs. There was a general store advertising airboat parts, a post office, and out back a dock that jutted into a brown canal. Standing to the side was a stucco church, the white walls turned yellow, and beside that a two-story building that looked like a school. The strange thing was, I couldn't hear kids. I stopped in the store for some lunch fixin's and a map, then went on.

I was barely five minutes from town when I felt the temperature change. Looking west, I saw a storm bearin' down. The leading edge was purple black and rolled forward like a wave; underneath, rain blurred the landscape and lightning forked in the sky. I stopped the car and tried to pull the ragtop up, but it ballooned in the rising wind. I looked up once more and the storm was even closer, the trees in nearby hammocks whipping like reeds. Up ahead was a tiny hammock, so I drove for it, turnin' down a crushed-shell path that connected to the main road. The wind was on me the minute I pulled under the trees; it whistled through the knife-grass and brought a brief spatter of drops, then warm sheets of rain. The lightning came down, too, a whole sky of white electric cracks like the strobe inside the strip joint owned by the fat philosopher. Other hammocks turned black and the river turned white, like a photo negative; the wind whipped at my cotton shirt and I was drenched, cursing myself for not wearing something more substantial till I realized a bikini was perfect deluge-wear. Palm fronds tore loose from their trunks; flying shells stung my ankles and calves. A bolt struck close and my hair stood on end.

Fast as it hit, the storm was gone. There was silence as Nature herself took stock of the damage, then a rush of smells and sounds. The hammock around me smelled like cypress mulch; frogs and toads announced their presence like warm-up bands. A narrow-mouthed toad hopped into sight and cried *ma-a-anh*. He was answered by every tree frog in the world. *Erp erp erp. Ark ark. Ack ack. Ik ik.* It like to drove me crazy. A kite darted near the water; a mottled duck poked from the reeds across some open water, followed by three clumsy chicks. They swam toward the hammock, but the bank was steep; as they searched for a place to land, a small alligator separated from a tangle of mangroves. I felt like yelling a warning but the mother duck'd had already seen and flapped madly, calling for her young. They put on the gas but the gator was on 'em in a second and overtook the rear. He grabbed the first duckling from behind and threw him in the air. The bird came down squawking, straight into its jaws. *Clack,* the duck was gone, and the gator sped after the other two. "Get out of there!" I cried, looking for something to throw, but in that time it overtook the second chick and swallowed it, too.

Now it started after the third. The mother quacked like all hell had broken loose; I yelled bloody murder as the last chick plowed forward, inches ahead of the jaws. There was a burst of spray, a quack and *clack*, and the little duck hopped up on shore. The gator floated at the edge of the water, just its eyes showing. "Missed him!" I shouted.

"Psst, lady," a voice behind me said.

I nearly jumped in the water on top of the gator. When my heart stopped poundin', the gator and the ducks were gone. In their place stood a girl of ten or eleven, her skin light olive, her black hair the texture of silk. Her large, intelligent eyes watched me carefully.

"Who are you and where'd you come from?" I yelled.

"Mi llama Rebeca Duquesa Hermosa," she said, then pointed deep into the hammock. "I saw the storm coming and got out of the rain."

"No, I mean, *where* did you come from? Surely you don't live out here waitin' to jump from outta the bushes and scare people?"

She took that for a joke and giggled, and I recalled the last little girl I'd encountered, little Wanda Louise Coover in the bed beside me in the Newport hospital, her with her big mouth and daddy, the policeman. Every bad thing befallin' me this last week seemed due to some crazy adult or overcurious kid. "I have lived the past months in the town you just passed," this newest girl said. Her tone was very serious and her way of talkin' strangely formal and grown-up, like she'd been weaned on a dictionary and was afraid to break the rules. She had to be a runaway, and like it or not, I couldn't leave her here. But when I asked about her parents, her dark eyes grew angry. "I did not run away," she snapped. "*They* sent me here. But I am going back. I have an uncle in Key West. His name is Jesus Perdida Hermosa and he has a boat. He is a good fisherman, and a smuggler. I have saved thirty dollars and thirteen cents for passage. You will take me to him, and he will smuggle me back home."

"Who said I was going to Key West?" I said.

"That is why I offer to pay you, to make it worth your while. Key West is 160 miles southwest of Miami. I have looked it up. I am good at details. What is 160 miles to an American girl with a car?"

"You ran from that church school the last town back, right?" I said.

"That is not a school," she snapped, and spit in the white carpet of shells. "It is a concentration camp. I am a political refugee!" She was a victim of *una estafa*, a big swindle, she said. She and other children in the school had been flown from Cuba that January. Others still arrived. Her father and mother ran a small *libreria* in Havana, and sponsored many readings of poetry and *novelas*. Last year the regulars to their shop stopped talking of literature and politics, and spoke instead of something new. They discussed how Castro was closing church schools and had confiscated church property; they feared he planned to send their children to work on Soviet farms. No one knew where the rumor started, but everyone accepted it as fact; she listened as the talk turned into a kind of madness and her parents grew scared. By January there was word that the Church in Miami was letting children fly alone from Cuba to the care of the priests and nuns. There was an official name for the program, but everyone called it Operation Pedro Pan and the children soon called themselves the Lost Boys and Girls. The nuns objected to such jokes. They were not lost, they said. They had been saved, and the separation from their families was only brief. But the brief time stretched on longer, the nuns and priests treated them like they'd never grow up, and their parents never came.

Strange tales circulated among the Lost Boys and Girls. Some children had uncles or cousins who worked at the hundreds of boat shops, gun shops, or travel agencies in South Florida owned by a mysterious group called the Agency. Since these uncles and cousins were young men, they liked to brag. The hundreds of shops . . . the Agency . . . Operation Pedro Pan: all were part of a grand plot to overthrow Castro and go back home to their island, these young men claimed. The uncles told of conspiracies in which they took part, of not-so-secret guerrilla camps and small-boat training in the Everglades; of teams dropped "black" in the Sierra Maestra mountains to harass Castro as he'd harassed Batista; of the long, huge crates these teams reported seeing unloaded from Russian cargo ships and sent by train to secret bases in the jungle. Some great confrontation was building between Russia and America, and Cuba was somehow in the middle of it, the uncles and cousins warned. The fate of the world would be decided in the lands or seas of little Cuba, and in such a world, what did a few children matter? Who cared if they never saw their parents again?

Rebeca would no longer wait for the kindness of others, she said. She would find her uncle and his boat, and he would take her home to Cuba. He would sneak her back into Havana like a spy. She would be with her family again, whether I helped her or not. "You can take me back to the school," she announced, "but I will leave again because no one is there." Everyone had left that morning to escape the hurricane; when hurricanes came, there were great floods in this low grass sea. The priests, nuns, and children had boarded fat yellow buses and headed north; when the children lined up for a head count, Rebeca had edged to the back of the very last line. Two boys started fighting and she slipped behind the bumper of the last bus, then ducked behind the trees; she was never missed in the confusion and probably would not be until the buses unloaded and they counted heads again.

She gloated at her cleverness. "I decided to leave last night when they told us of the evacuation," she said. "I am going back to Havana and you will help me." *Right,* I thought, like I needed more complications right now. Taking her along might be the same as kidnapping, which would be my kinda luck. "What if your uncle's not where you think?" I asked.

"That is impossible. He will be there."

"Maybe I should take you back to the school and hand you to a custodian or somethin'. They'll know who to call."

I reached to grab her, but she jumped back. "I will not allow it," she screamed, voice haughty and high. "I will run into the swamp where there is quicksand. You saw the alligator, but I have seen his brothers and they are ten or fifteen feet long. At night you hear the cry of *las panteras*. I will not survive a week. My blood will be on your hands."

I threw open the car door. "Stop this foolishness and get inside."

"I do not talk foolishness," she replied, backing away. This irritated me no end. I was hungry and my lunch was probably soaked; I lunged for her but she dodged around me and sprinted to the water's edge. The gator had resurfaced and moved his tail with interest; he glided forward. He'd brought along a buddy, one with even bigger eyes.

She saw him, too, and looked back at me. She trembled, but didn't budge. She stuck one foot in the water. It disappeared beneath the brown surface like it was clipped off clean. "I won't go back to the mission," she said. "I miss my mama and papa. I miss their arguments about books. I miss my father helping me with my homework, how he teases that I will never get married because boys are scared of too-smart girls. I miss the sweet potato dumplings and bread my mother makes and how she sings me to sleep when I am ill." The larger gator glided past his younger brother and into the main canal. She saw the movement and her face grew white—if I waited another second, she'd jump into my arms in a panic. I'd take her back, no problem, get this brat straight outta my hair. "I just want to find them," she said. Now she was sobbing, no longer a confident child apin' her elders, but a homesick girl not much younger'n me when Daddy ran away.

The gator glided forward. Just a second longer.

I felt like such a heel.

I touched her fingers lightly and closed my hand on hers. Pulled her from the water. The gator slid beneath the surface. Not even a ripple showed where he'd been.

"I'll take you to your uncle, but after that, don't ask me no more favors," I said. She hugged me 'round the waist and skipped back to the car. She grabbed the bag of groceries from the seat and asked if I had peanut butter.

I sighed and felt a headache knockin'. *Why me?*

I'll say this for Rebeca Duquesa Hermosa: She knew her way around this bleak land. We were inside the northern Everglades and still had a ways to go to the Keys, she explained. We passed a huge lake lined with cypress trees and Spanish moss, then drove through scorched savannas where fire had recently burned for days. They'd seen one of these fires from the school, she said. The crows and gulls rioted among themselves to eat the crispy remains of the huge grasshoppers too dumb to flee. Sometimes the peat smoldered for weeks, poppin' out in fiery pockets long after the main fire died. We sped through a Seminole reservation, the only American Indians never to sign a peace treaty, she said. "Do you know much about Indians?" A bit, I said. Before I could say more she proceeded to tell me how the Seminoles warred to escape the fate of the Cherokees. Did I know much about the Cherokee, she asked. "To me," she said, "all exiles are the same."

We crossed a web of drainage ditches and she pointed out the spot where her favorite priest, Father Richard, hooked a ten-foot catfish that resembled one boy's grandfather, whiskers and all. The boy screamed in fright and the priest let the fish go. Off to the left we could see the lights of Fort Lauderdale and Miami reflected against the low clouds. At Homestead, an air force jet screamed past; there was a final stretch of swamp and gators, then a long bridge and we were on the island chain called the Keys.

Joe Jackson

"What is it like being sixteen?"

"Just like any other age." I kept my eyes on the road, watchin' for these weird plated critters called armadillos. They leapt straight in the air when a car roared up, like their one goal in life was to be a hood ornament. They scared me to death, and all that girl did was jabber.

"You did not have a party, the one they call the Sweet Sixteen?"

"No," I mimicked, "I did not have a party, the one they call the Sweet Sixteen," though I knew plenty of girls who did, Arnold's sister included. Not that I was invited, though.

"That proves what they say."

"And what is that?" An armadillo waddled toward the car and jumped, but I was quick and swerved away.

"That Anglos do not share a passion for important things," she said. "In my country, we have what are called *quincerias*. They are very special and are held when you turn fifteen. You are a woman then. There are cookies, cakes, and presents; when it is over, you dress in your very best dress and go to the most beautiful place in town to have your picture made. You do not grin foolishly like some girls, but must look daring to show the mystery burning inside. Or so I've been told. Your brother or cousin hangs nearby, guarding your honor in case you drive men mad. They say men have no control when looked at in such a way. I have tried it myself on my cousins, but they only laughed, so I still have much to learn. Your mother is there, directing the photographs, since they go to relatives and so cannot be *too* daring." She tapped her finger against the window. "Are you a woman yet?" she said.

Another armadillo waddled from the bush and I swerved sideways. "I told you, I'm only sixteen."

"That is not what I mean. You said you had a boyfriend." Her face grew red. "Did you—how do you say it? English is so difficult. Did you become a woman with him?"

"That's kind of personal, ain't it?" I said, laughing.

She stared outside, flustered. "I do not have a mother to tell me such things."

Boy-oh-boy, I thought—I should've lent her mine. "It's called making love," I said. "Yes, I made love to him."

She picked at one of her nails. "Was it nice?"

"It was nice."

"Did it hurt? I hear that sometimes it hurts."

Yes, but not in the way you think, I wanted to say. But she wouldn't understand. "It hurts a little," I said gently. "But then it passes and it's worth it. Why? You got someone lined up back at the mission?"

She made a spitting sound. "Those boys are *idiotas*," she said. "There is one who steals kisses in the lunch line and pulls my hair, calling it a horse's tail."

"Sounds familiar," I said.

"When I fall in love, my lover will be tall. He will be handsome and brave, with a profile like a hawk. He will be a writer, not of silly flights of *la imaginación* like in this country, but of things he has seen and felt. Only with that kind of man will I become a woman," she said.

"That's a mighty tall order," I said. "You wouldn't settle for someone who's nice, but maybe as mixed up as you?"

"No, I have principles." She cleared her throat, and when I glanced over, she was redder'n before. There was silence. "So, how do you know when you are ready for love?"

I rolled my eyes. How had I inherited a daughter, and all her questions, just when I was about to confront my own dad? It was easier dodgin' armadillos. "Are you askin' how you know when you're ready to fall in love? It just hits you, that's all."

"No, that is not what I mean." She moved her foot back and forth, staring like she'd never seen it do such a thing. "Your body. How do you know?"

That's what I'd figured she'd meant. "You mean your monthlies?"

"*Sí.*"

"Your mother never explained?"

"*No.* I asked about it once, but she said it was not yet time."

That sounded familiar. Maybe mothers were the same all over the world. Here I'd started out this morning with a lesson in breast enlargement; now I was bein' asked the facts of life by someone I barely knew. I rubbed my temples. "Has something happened?" I asked. She'd noticed a spot of blood, she said. That was all? Yes, she explained. I told her what to expect and filled in some gaps on procedure. She listened close, then asked, "What was it like the first time?"

I recalled the day my monthlies began. I'd gotten a monster bellyache and was sure I'd die of appendicitis like Cootie Pressum on Merleysburg Road. Or worse, my whole gut would explode. Then I felt a gush and rushed to the bathroom. Since there'd already been some spots, I knew what it signified. I was so relieved, I forgot to consider Mama's reaction. When I left the bathroom holding my undies, she took one look and dragged me back in. She reached beneath the cabinet for the pink box of Kotex, her face stretched into a grimace that made me sick again. She grabbed the elastic belt and showed how to hook the metal ends together, her fingers so cold I gasped and sucked in my tummy. She explained the birds 'n' bees, like I hadn't already heard *that* song 'n' dance, then asked how it felt to be a woman. I shrugged. "Hah!" she cried. "My thoughts exactly." Then she put the pink box away.

Rebeca Hermosa looked slightly green and said maybe it was better that she found out on her own.

We stopped at a food stand shaped like a seashell and ate some springy things called conch fritters. They weren't half-bad if you covered 'em in ketchup and drowned 'em in lemon juice. I pointed the car southwest and let the wheels do their job. I wondered how many revolutions of the wheel it had taken to get from Wattles to here. The wheels traced a straight line, yet returned to the same point. What a depressing idea!

Our road was a two-laner hopping from island to tiny island, each connected by a bridge. Our lane was empty, but the opposite one, headed to Miami, was full of cars. On the bridges we had a better view of all the water separatin' us from Cuba—the Florida Straits, Rebeca said. Way past the horizon was that storm scarin' everyone, and the sky in that direction was a dark and angry blue. For the first time, the threat seemed real.

"Look at that," Rebeca said, pointing out to sea.

At the edge of the horizon, a thin white rope curved from the sky to the sea. *"La tromba,"* Rebeca said. I couldn't take my eyes away and pulled to the side of the road. A second water-spout formed behind the first, each the spittin' image of the other. They seemed peaceful in their progress, keepin' the same distance, tracin' stately, destructive paths along the rim of the world.

"It is a sign," Rebeca said.

"Of what?"

"I do not know. My mother says there are many signs we do not understand."

I gunned the engine and we pulled back on the road. After a while, we crossed a long bridge and then it was night; crossin' water in darkness was like walkin' a tightrope across a void. There were a series of small bridges and a sign said Key West, and we drove through town to where another sign said Mallory Square. Past that were some docks, where some people still lingered, among them three bums singing on the steps of a church. With them, but separate, a conga drummer beat out a tune. "We are der-e-licts, der-e-licts," the three bums harmonized. "Nice car," the conga drummer said. "Shame to lose it in a hurricane." He shook his head sadly. "Storm wash da music away."

I asked the drummer about the marina and he pointed the way. "You think you can spare some pennies, sistah, so dis poor bandleader and his boys can stay somewhere dry?" I dug into my pocket and dropped an uncounted wad of bills into his drum case. His face lit up. "We all right now, boys," he said.

Then there were the docks and a dirty white boat with

strange chips and holes in the paint and my name painted on the back, just like the vacationing mine owner had said. A dim light glowed in the cabin. I switched off the engine and felt its vibration die beneath me. I sucked in a breath, held it, and let it out. I shoved the key under the seat and closed the door.

The water splashed beneath me as I crossed the warped, uneven boards of the dock. I climbed into the boat and clutched the handle.

"Daddy?" I called, and walked inside.

Why Bile Rises in the Old Man's Craw

I STOOD IN the cabin door as Burma confronted her wayward hubby. As we entered, his eyes grew round. His shock filled this seedy sea-room, this smoke-filled cabin that faintly smelled of rotten fish and unwashed fishermen. Here were the last sips of love that Burma never quite finished; here sat the father her girl had crossed half the South to find. How do you define father, I wondered. Learned, wise, and prudent? None seemed to apply to this guy.

What a disappointment. What a fuckin' shame.

"Burma, where'd the hell you come from?" her husband finally said. She told him where she'd been, then told him exactly where he could go.

I leaned against the frame and thought about the girl. She'd gone through a lot, shown a kind of grit that even gave me pause, and for what? For this? Someone who'd lost himself so completely to become the butt end of a bad joke? God was a prankster, all right. Bile rose in my craw.

"What you gonna do when your daughter shows up?" Burma spit, hands flat on the table.

"Dahlia's comin' here?"

This was painful to watch, so I looked away. But one thing

was clear. The girl hadn't made it here yet—somehow, we'd slipped ahead of her. I noticed strange gouges 'round one window like gunshots had chewed up the wood. A spiderweb crack radiated from the corner of another window and spread through the glass. This boat had been through a war and barely survived. I walked down a flight of steps into a hold belowdecks. I glimpsed some books and blankets, a hammock strung from hooks. This man lived among his wreckage, a regular Harson Whitley of the high seas.

"Dahlia can't see me like this," whined Burma's hubby. "What'll I say?"

I looked out the cracked window to the south, where the storm was gathering strength. The skies were gray and angry, whitecaps rushing forward like fleeing sheep. I thought how we are the teachers of what is true and what is not, advancing into a storm of ignorance, heads bowed. Our children follow blindly, trustin' that we'll know the way. I thought about the girl, speeding toward her fate, and my boy, tied up in the car.

It left a bad taste in my mouth. It was time to get this over with. I returned to the cabin and made the girl's daddy an offer he couldn't refuse.

Daddy's Tale

"So you made it," Daddy said.

It was the last thing I expected. No "Hi, Princess, I missed you." No "What the hell you doin' here?" I hesitated in the doorway. "You've made it this far," he scolded. "Don't stop there."

He sat at a table bolted to the floor. His cigarette glowed red as he drew on it; he tapped the ashes in a white ceramic cup; a gold-foil ashtray set before him was heaped full of butts. A fat roach scuttled into a corner; silverfish hugged the walls. A red light burned on a shortwave radio as it crackled out a weather report. One half of Daddy's face was bathed in the green glow of his instrument panel. The other half was hid in shade.

I stood and stared. I'd imagined a gleaming white cabin cruiser, a fiberglass beauty that slid through the sea. Not a garbage scow. Poor Daddy had been sick to death of disappointment when he left Wattles, but he was Mr. Giggles then compared to now. I'd never seen someone so beat down. His hair hung 'round his collar like ragged strips of cloth; his eyes were dark circles; he'd chewed his cuticles to bloody nubs.

"Oh, Daddy, what happened?" I asked, but instead of answerin', he studied me through the smoke and dim light and I was reminded of a character from one of my gangster matinees.

"Come in, Dahlia, I won't bite," he said, but I wasn't so sure. Was this the man against whom I'd measured all others? The man against whom I'd made Cole compete—whose disappearance left a hole in my life that I'd always tried to fill?

"I guess the mine owner was right about your whereabouts," I said.

"Damn busybody, I should've chucked him in the sea. I would've, too, if not for the Cubans aboard."

"You know *Cubanos?*" Rebeca cried. I'd forgotten her entirely; she peeked around behind me and stepped toward the table. "Perhaps you know my uncle. His name is Jesus Perdida Hermosa. He is a fisherman and a very great man."

Daddy seemed jolted by the name. "Who's this?" he asked. "You still adopting strays?"

"You are very rude," Rebeca said. "*Mi madre y mi padre* live in Havana *y mi tío* will take me back to them. I am not a stray. Uncle Jesus has a boat like this, only nicer. You do not take care of your boat—it needs a new coat of paint and has a very bad smell."

Daddy started laughing, but it had a cruel edge to it that I'd never heard in Tennessee. "I know your uncle, all right," he snorted. "I owe everything I am to him."

"You would not laugh like that if Tío Jesus walked in," Rebeca mocked.

"I guess not," Daddy said. "If that happened, I'd jump off this boat and never look back."

"Because he is strong and you are weak?"

"Because I'm alive and he is dead."

It was like he hit her, and the proud smile vanished from her lips. "You lie!" Rebeca said.

"Why should I lie about the man who promised me a future but never mentioned the terms?"

"Daddy," I interrupted, "she's just a little girl."

"I am nearly a *woman!*" Rebeca screamed. "You lie because you are not half the man of Tío Jesus. You lie because it is all you know how to do."

Daddy shrugged it off. "Think what you want. Makes no difference to me."

"*I'd* like to know the truth," I said softly.

He looked me over hard. "You just feel sorry for this girl."

"It's not Rebeca I feel sorry for. You're different, Daddy. I'm sorry for you."

He winced and mashed his cigarette into the foil tray. "We're all different now. Even you. You're nearly grown up. It looks like I've missed a lot the last few years."

"You could've wrote. I *adored* you, Daddy. I had a right to know how you were."

"I was a failure back in Wattles. I hoped to do better down here." He laughed again, real bitter. "Besides, bein' on your own toughened you."

"I was too young to be tough," I said. "Tough means acceptin' what is. I did the opposite, makin' up stories how you'd come back to Wattles and take me to better things. When that didn't happen, I said you'd died tryin', but nobody believed that tale but me. It was like I dropped down a hole you dug for me. I always wondered what I'd done to make you go."

His face got a pained expression. "You didn't do anything, Princess," he said quietly. "You could never do anything to me."

"Why didn't you write and say it?" It was all coming back: the day he left . . . the hours I stood watching for him by the screen door. "I was just a little girl. You said you'd never leave."

There was silence in that boat as Daddy and Rebeca watched me, both a little scared, like I'd roared in with the hurricane and threatened to blow the house down. After all this running and dodging . . . after watching Mama's diminishment, fearin' it was my own reflection . . . after every day turned into one more rejection or humiliation till finally the only way not to go crazy was lose myself in a goddamn dream of better things. *I hated better things!* They never, ever came true. And now Daddy like this . . . a daddy who couldn't give no answer to my pleas.

But then, no one could. I finally saw the truth and didn't like it. I wished it'd stayed hid. We run because we run. That is all there is. Part of us is missing and we search the wide world over, but still we never find it. We don't even learn its name.

"I *did* write," he finally answered.

"I never got the letter," I said.

He got a guilty look and his eyes darted to the side. "Well, I wrote it, but I never mailed it. I figured your mother'd tear it up or that you'd reached a kind of peace, so I threw it away."

"He lies, just like he lies about my uncle," said Rebeca. I smiled sadly, knowing what she said was true. He lied about the letter, just like he lied he'd never leave me that day beneath the dam. In a sense, his lies wrapped me in their silky threads and he had never left. I had a strange vision: how we scuttled our lives through webs of betrayal. One misstep and the spider arrived.

I sighed, so awfully, awfully tired. "At least tell her what happened to her uncle," I said. "It seems mixed up with how you are now."

Maybe he felt he owed me something . . . at least some explanation, so he spun his tale. How he'd drifted after leaving Wattles, how nothing panned out and he became a bigger failure in his own mind than even back at home. All the time he drifted south till there was no south left, and he got a job as a deckhand for a charter captain called Old Man Zed. According to the locals, Zed had been around since the rum-smugglin' days of Prohibition. "He didn't have no family," said Daddy, "just this boat and his stock of fishing tales." How a swordfish nearly dragged him to Cuba back in '47. How a grouper almost took him to the bottom, a huge lump of fish that stared back with greedy pig eyes till he cut the line.

"Everything's simple with fish," Zed pronounced: "You kill them or they kill you," and Daddy came to agree. One morning Zed didn't turn up at his regular hour and neighbors found him dead in his sleep. The next day, a lawyer showed up with a brown envelope: "Thanks for listening to the fish stories," said a handwritten note. The old man left Daddy the title to the boat and what little money he had.

That said nothing about Tío Jesus, Rebeca complained.

He was gettin' to that, he said. By now it was 1959, and he'd been away from Wattles for three years. For the first time he had something he could call his own, but owning the boat just opened a new set of problems. He was new to the fishing fleet: The vacationers chose captains who'd fished the Keys forever, and when he tried to cut his rates, the move was seen by locals as an unpardonable sin. Just when he thought he'd have to sell out, the Cubans fleeing Castro poured in. Businessmen and the wealthy flew to Miami, but fishermen—who'd always hopped the Straits anyway for legal and illegal reasons—came to the Keys. Jesus Hermosa was among the first, and he took the slip right next to Daddy's.

Rebeca was right, he said. Her uncle *was* an important man. A major player in the anti-Castro circles, though Daddy didn't think much about it then. All he knew was that everybody seemed to like Jesus Hermosa, and he ran a hell of a business taking Miami big shots out for marlin and tarpon. Business was so good that he fed Daddy the overflow. "I know what it means to be an exile," Jesus told him over beers, and Daddy was grateful. Anything his new friend said was fine and dandy by him.

Now Daddy's voice grew spooky, just like the day he told Mama and me about the cave-in and death of his friend. The next year, he said, all of South Florida went mad. The CIA moved in, calling itself the Agency, spending money like it was going out of style. It was the biggest shot of cash down here since Henry Flagler built the railroad to the Keys in the 1930s, and all for a bunch of cloak-'n'-dagger stuff aimed at deposing Castro. For all anybody cared, the spooks could overthrow Captain Kangaroo long as the money continued. "Daddy, nobody believes that spy malarkey," I interrupted.

But Rebeca interrupted *me*. "For once, he speaks the truth," she said.

"Thank you," Daddy answered, surprised. Just the same, he admitted, it was hard to believe. It was like every town from Miami south was gripped by a fever. For all the talk of "secrets," there were no secrets; instead, it was all a big game. The Agency set up a front in the University of Miami and called it Zenith Technological Services, the biggest employer around. Those Zenith guys were everywhere, in training camps back in the mangroves, zipping between the islands in Boston Whalers, running practice missions against a Southern Bell microwave tower. It was like waking up in a spy movie, and one day after a year of such prosperity, Jesus Hermosa sat Daddy down. "My friend, do not look a gift horse in the mouth," Uncle Jesus said. "There is so much money these days, 300 to 400 Zenith caseworkers, each handling four to ten Cuban agents, guys they call 'amots,' each amot paying 10 to 30 assistants to hire boats, safe harbors, or anything their hearts desire." It was the largest pyramid scheme in the history of South Florida, which was saying a lot, and all to retake one tiny island and bring one man down. This wasn't paranoia, said Uncle Jesus. It was good economics.

Jesus Hermosa never said where he fit on the pyramid, but he did make Daddy a deal. There was a big training exercise coming up, and the Agency was a few boats short. All Daddy had to do was carry some guns and soldiers for a mock invasion. War games. "If I kept my mouth shut, I'd be paid well," Daddy repeated. Enough for a new coat of paint on the boat and some fish-finding equipment. Maybe enough for a new boat entirely with twin inboard Evinrudes.

Jesus was a good salesman, and visions of a shiny Chris-Craft danced in Daddy's head. Of course he'd help an old friend, he said. The next night, April 16, 1961, his passengers arrived, seven young Cubans led by a fat fellow named Jorge. They carried a box of weapons between them, M-16s and .30-caliber automatics, and for the first time Daddy got scared. "Jesus, you sure this is just practice?" he asked. But Daddy's benefactor slapped him on the back and told him not to worry. "Would I lie to a fellow fisherman?" he said.

It was, of course, the Bay of Pigs, Daddy said. They left at night, and as they headed south, they were joined by more boats from hidden coves and tiny keys. "Jesus did say it would be a big war game," Daddy tried to tell himself, but 'round daylight they entered Cuban waters and the flagship lowered its Panamanian flag. Up came the Cuban one, instead. At about the same moment, his passengers came up from the hold wearing berets and camouflage uniforms with a patch reading "Brigade 2506." Jorge wore sergeant stripes and made a speech about destiny. The radio crackled to life and ordered all boats to the beach; there were booms from the shore, as if in greeting. Geysers erupted around them. There was a *twang!* and part of the windlass flew past Daddy's head.

That was when he panicked—the moment he realized he'd been tricked and this wasn't a game. "These charter boats are built for punishment, but not for cannon shells," he said. He turned right, to starboard, and the chunky sergeant stepped up with a gun in his hand and said Daddy was going the wrong way.

"There's been some mistake," Daddy shouted.

"No mistake," replied Jorge. "Follow the others." He dug the pistol into Daddy's ribs.

By now Daddy's eyes were like fire in the telling, and Rebeca and me didn't say a word. "It was the invasion the rumors had told of all those months," Daddy recalled, "but it was the sorriest invasion I'd ever seen. Where was the Navy? Where was the air cover? Something was mighty wrong. Even my passengers looked sick, like they'd expected more than a ragtag flotilla of leaking boats, and seeing their worry made me mad as hell. They'd been betrayed, I'd been betrayed . . . it was all somebody's idea of a joke, and I was gonna get killed. I lost it then, whipping the wheel back and forth, determined not to make an easy target, my passengers yelling as they bounced around. One man pitched over the side. 'Go back and get him!' Jorge screamed, and I screamed back: 'You said head for the beach, so make up your fucking mind!' It was like the coal mines all over, the smoke and lies covering up a million ways of death, just to make some rich man richer. Like I'd never gotten out of Tennessee. It made my blood boil. Jesus's cruiser pulled close and I saw him in the forecastle, laughing and enjoying the hell out of it all. 'I think you dropped something back there,' he shouted through a bullhorn, pointing back. It made me mad enough to kill. *He* was the enemy, not the guys shooting from the beach . . . *he* was the one who'd sold me down the river. 'It is a great thing you are doing, whether you mean to or not!' Jesus shouted. Then a shell screamed from shore and his forecastle disappeared."

Rebeca gasped. "He was thrown clear?"

"More like he ceased to exist," Daddy said. "His boat curved off and another shell found it, then there was nothing."

Rebeca's face screwed tight, then she started to cry. I led her to the hold and helped her into the hammock. I covered her with a blanket and she turned away and sobbed.

I came back. "That this was mean, Daddy," I said.

"It's a mean world, Princess."

"You don't need to prove it to a little girl."

He raised his palms as if to say such things were beyond his control. He wouldn't've acted like this in Wattles. It wasn't that he'd turned mean, he just didn't care.

"So how'd you get away?" I said. Daddy's voice grew cold.

After Jesus's boat exploded, the gunners on shore seemed to find their range. Shells flew everywhere. Other boats were hit. His passengers hit the deck, but someone had to steer the boat, and standing there in the face of it did something to him. "I'd been fooled, lied to, mocked on my own boat, and now they expected me to stand like an iron man and take them in to shore. I hated every goddamn thing in this goddamn world. I wouldn't take it no more! I started yelling like crazy, whipping the wheel from side to side, laughing as my passengers thrashed about, trying to grab hold. I was the Indian warrior I'd always imagined, screaming a war cry. Jorge hit the table post and lost hold of his pistol; I picked it up and aimed it at them. 'Get off my boat,' I said. They said I was crazy . . . we were out too deep . . . they would drown. They were terrified, and I didn't care. They'd trained for a beach assault and hadn't learned to swim? What a fine joke. 'So start learning,' I said. Jorge begged me in God's name to show some mercy. 'God has nothing to do with it,' I replied. A minute ago, they hadn't cared if I lived or died, so why should I feel sorry for them? As the last one jumped, Jorge looked me in the face and said, '*Un bicho malo nunca muere.*' Then he went over. I didn't stay around to see if they were picked up, and I never learned what he said."

Rebeca's translation came from the hold: "A bad insect never dies."

There was silence in our cabin. "You cut and ran," I finally said.

"I saved my goddamned skin, though nobody saw it that way. Word got out and I was treated like a leper. The Agency refused to pay the money Jesus had promised I'd get. The Miami bigwigs stopped booking fishing trips with me. The marina plans to cancel my lease. There've been weird break-ins at night when I'm away from the boat. I wish I'd never left Tennessee."

Then he looked at me strange and said there was something else. "Dahlia, I don't know how to tell you this, but your mother arrived earlier today."

Maybe I hadn't heard him right, and I stuttered a bit. "You heard me," he said. "There was some geezer with her, scary as all get out. They said they got your boyfriend and you got their money. They want to make a deal, and they expect you'll do it through me."

Fathers Are a Dyin' Breed

THE SHARP KNOCK to the door came later that night than expected. We'd camped at a motel back in town while waiting for the girl to show up; how we pulled ahead in this race, if only for a half day, was something I never understood. Still, waiting is a bitch, no matter for how long. What if something happened to her after Phenix City? What if she never appeared? I breathed easier when Burma peeked out the curtain and said, "It's him."

I went to check on Cole as Burma let her hubby in. "Where you been?" she asked.

"She just got in a coupla hours ago," he said. "Her and some Cuban girl she picked up along the way. I gave 'em something to eat and set up some hammocks so they could stay overnight on the boat."

"You're always so thoughtful," Burma said sarcastically.

I closed the bedroom door behind me so they could keep the sweet talk to themselves. Once again I'd tied Cole up, but left him on a bed. Discipline don't necessarily rule out comfort; discipline is best served with love. But Cole didn't seem to appreciate such thoughtfulness; he asked if that was Dahlia's father while I propped a pillow behind him so he could watch *It's a Wonderful Life* on TV. "Lemme go," he wheedled. "I just want to be with her, is all."

"We're arranging that," I lied. "Till then, you stay tied. It's for your own good."

"Thanks, Pop. You're always thinkin' of me."

I sat on the bed beside him and patted his leg. "There's two kinds of fathers," I told him, nodding to the front room where the voices of Burma and her hubby droned on. "There's the one out there, and me. The difference is responsibility. That's what fatherhood is all about, and it's a hard lesson to learn. The job is fairly easy at first—you keep the brat in food and diapers, maybe a warm blanket, and most dads can handle this since there's not a lot of room for confusion. But when the kid grows up, it gets harder. You gotta teach him right from wrong. But how to do that, if you're not so sure yourself?" Just like a kid, his attention wandered from me, so I rapped him on the head. "This is what I'm talkin' about," I said. "It's a thankless job. Did I thank my old man? No, not once, so I'm not surprised you running off either. Betrayal's built into the system. The son betrays the father 'cause it's the only way for him to break free."

Cole looked at me odd, and asked when I turned philosopher. Maybe I should lay down and take it easy, too, he said.

But I couldn't keep still. Things seemed to be finally falling in place, though I wasn't sure how. I looked about our room. It was a good room, one of the best in the motel. We'd got it half-rate, since all the other tourists had fled the coming storm. The owner himself was nervous and asked that we pay in advance in case he decided to run, too. In exchange, he gave us the key to the adjoining room so's we could spread out more. I'd never had so much space and felt like a king. Outside, an evacuation was in full effect: Though most of the tourists had left, most of the natives stayed. The coral reefs 'round these islands tended to deflect hurricanes so good there hadn't been a direct hit since the '30s, and locals usually rode 'em out. The only signs of Isolde I'd seen so far was wind flapping through the palms and hurricane parties starting in the Grinnell Street bars.

But all was quiet in here. A painting of a calm ocean hung between the beds. A happy fish smiled on the shower curtain.

Jimmy Stewart told his movie angel that life was wonderful. Cole asked me to turn up the volume and I did.

I closed the bedroom door behind me and went out front again. Burma and her hubby sat at opposite ends of the sofa, knees angled in. The lamps cast their faces in shadow; light played off a glass ashtray, where I'd thrown my change and keys. Some of it spilled over onto the lacquered wood. A painting of a shrimp boat in an orange sunset hung between them on the wall. They seemed like a still life, two people caught before intimacy. I felt like a Peeping Tom.

But the vision didn't last. They looked up when I entered, and I could tell something still linked 'em after all these years. I walked over to the window and peered outside. Burma's husband said the girl had agreed to our deal. "Dahlia said you can have all the cash if you want," he said. "She calls it 'blood money' now, and says it just brought grief from the start. She wants her boyfriend back, that's all."

I smiled at my reflection in the glass. All was goin' according to plan. Yet even as I gloated, the damn hubby spoiled my mood. "But Burma, before Dahlia agrees to anything," he added, "she wants to talk to you."

"Me?" she said, sounding shocked. "Why me?"

"She wouldn't say. There's a little diner near the docks. You probably saw it earlier. She'll meet you there, at eight tomorrow morning." There was a pause. "Don't bring *him.*"

I wheeled 'round and said that wasn't part of the arrangement, but for once the Chief, as I now called him, showed a bit of backbone. "It's a family thing," he said. "You can understand that, can'tcha? After all, you're a family man, too."

Burma was off in her own thought bubble. "I thought she hated me," she wondered aloud.

"She said she doesn't hate anyone," the Chief answered. "Not even me. Not anymore."

"She's up to somethin'," I blurted. "I don't like it, not one little bit."

"Shut up!" Burma snapped. "Nobody asked if you do." I stood rooted in place. What was going on in here? First the Chief and now Burma were standing up to me. This was getting worrisome—an epidemic of stiffening spines. Burma's voice softened a bit and she added, "Keep still for once, okay? This doesn't concern you."

Didn't concern me? I'd come all this way, suffered like a saint, killed or maimed so many strangers I was a shoo-in for the record books, and it *didn't concern me?* "This is a mother-daughter matter," said Burma, "something I wouldn't expect you to understand."

I scooted back to the window, stumped and tongue-tied, 'specially after the heart-to-heart in the other room with my own flesh and blood. I peeked out the window and two drunks stumbled down the dark street, their coats flapping in the wind. The storm seemed to be getting closer—a gust blew up and pushed 'em backward. "To tell the truth, I don't feel good about the whole deal, either," said the Chief. "I'd tell her to forget it if not for your promise that nothing will happen to her."

Burma and the Chief looked at me for confirmation. I smiled back, poker face aglow. J. T. Younger, the original Trustworthy Soul.

"Nothing will happen," she promised, still eyeing me. "The money's all we want, right?"

"Scout's honor," I echoed, nodding my head.

"I'm just screwed here, that's all," the Chief whined. "I didn't tell her this, but I've been getting death threats. What I need is a fresh start, just head up the Gulf and tie up somewhere new like Gulfport or Galveston. A couple thousand's all I need."

"That's always been your way, ain't it? Always movin' on."

"Burma, it's the only way I know. I thought we agreed not to start on that."

"You're right," she relented. "This is about Dahlia, not you 'n' me." She paused, then added, "So who's this Cuban girl she brought along?"

"Some runaway who says she knows an old friend of mine."
He looked at her a moment, then laughed in an intimate kind
of way. "Remember how Dahlia always used to come home
with stray dogs and cats? Now it's people. She wants me to take
the girl back home to Cuba."

Burma snorted. "Did you tell her it's a good way of gettin'
shot?"

"You know her. She's hardheaded."

"Tell me about it," Burma groaned. She eyed him carefully,
as if sensing something new. "You gonna do it?"

"I don't know. It's a war out there. Patrol boats, overflights,
all sorts of crazy people."

She lowered her eyes. "I don't blame you," she said.

He bristled at the disappointment in her voice. "I didn't say
I *wouldn't* do it, just that it's crazy, is all. It's like, if she can't fix
her own family, she wants to fix another."

Burma's voice sounded a tiny bit affectionate. "She didn't
get such crazy ideas from me."

"I think it comes from both sides, Burma."

"I guess it does," she answered wistfully.

They were absorbed in each other, like I wasn't even there.
Like I'd never even existed and the years had never passed.
Burma stared at her hubby for the longest time. "Why didn't
you come back?" she finally asked.

"Because I was ashamed," he said, voice almost too low to
hear. "I was a failure in my own eyes when I left, and even
worse in yours. Then I started to see it in Dahlia, and I
couldn't take it no more. I thought leavin' might make
things better, but instead they just got worse. One part of
me said I should come back and own up to bein' foolish,
while the other part couldn't bear the thought of what you'd
say. You've got a sharp tongue, Burma, and always did.
Then, for one brief moment, I fell into some luck and was
doin' well. I thought with that maybe I could go back and
face your anger, and try to make amends. But too much
time had passed. I really did write a letter—two or three, in

fact—but I just tore 'em up. Nothing ever came out the way I wanted it said."

It was uncomfortable bein' in the same room with this kind of talk, so I drew back the curtains and stared outside. It sure was dark out there. "I fell apart after you left," Burma said behind me. "I guess Dahlia told you that."

"She did," the Chief replied. "She's also pretty pissed how you lied about bein' crippled and all."

"I hid from failure, just like you. I took it out on her, since you weren't there."

"We really ain't that different, huh?"

"No wonder Dahlia's take on love is so screwed up," Burma snorted. "It's true, though, ain't it? She really does love that boy."

"She really does," her husband said. "Maybe we should give her a better chance than what we gave ourselves."

There was something in the sound of that I didn't like, and I wheeled from the window in time to catch a frightened glance from Burma before she, too, looked away. The Chief also seemed to realize he'd overstepped some bounds, so he started some fresh, nervous patter to cover up his words. Currents here were running deep, something I hadn't counted on. I'd have to rethink matters quick or things might get out of hand.

The Chief was tellin' Burma 'bout a dream he'd had. "Remember our honeymoon, how we got in the car and drove till we reached the ocean?"

"Atlantic City," she said. "What a dump it was."

"Remember the guy in the sequin jacket and his elephant? On the boardwalk?"

"The elephant that could count?"

"That's the one. I dreamed I rode it, Burma. It was the craziest thing. I was on its back and its stiff hairs poked through my jeans like wire bristles and its front legs were giant pistons pumping up and down. I was in the lead of a circus parade or something—I didn't look back, so I'm not sure, but I felt like the highest thing around. I looked out to sea and saw you and Dahlia just *drifting* over the waves. You wore that low-cut yellow dress you used to like so much and your hair was shoulder-length, the way it used to be. Dahlia was just a toddler, holding tight to your hand. I watched and was suddenly no longer ashamed. I started waving and cried, 'Look at me, on this elephant!' You heard and laughed, and headed my way. For once in my life, I was proud—not of anything I'd done, but because the two of you were proud of me."

Burma giggled in a way she never had with me. "You're such an idiot," she said, the words slipping out soft, like endearments of love. I wished I'd never heard 'em: Things *had* gone outta control like I'd feared, and from now on would never be the same. "You always had the goofiest dreams," she said.

"We really loved each other, didn't we, Burma?"

She smiled, real sad. "We did at first, that's true."

"You think . . . maybe . . . Dahlia remembers?"

"I don't think she's ever forgotten," Burma replied.

—•—

He left the room and said we'd meet tomorrow to arrange the final handoff of the money and my boy. I watched out the window as he glanced down the dark street toward the hurricane parties, then hunched his shoulders against the wet and headed that way. I grabbed my hat and coat and headed for the door, but Burma jumped from the couch as if to grab me. "Where are you going?" she said.

"Just out for a walk. After all those memories, I need some air."

"I'll go with you," she offered, sounding afraid.

"It's nasty out there. I'm just going down the street for a drink."

"You'll appreciate the company," she said.

I laughed. "Burma, we leave that boy in here alone, and he'll either get away or choke himself trying. Where would we be, then?"

"You're talkin' about your son like somethin' at a swap meet."

"I'm only thinkin' business, that's all."

"Why are you really goin' out?" she pleaded. "Tell me the truth."

I kissed her on the cheek and looked her in the eyes. "Listenin' to you two got me thinkin' 'bout my own life. Can you blame me for feelin' a little blue?"

She softened a bit. "I didn't expect things to happen like that."

I just smiled and answered softly, "Neither did I."

She returned the smile and peered past me at the storm. I could see the young girl in her, and why her husband never fell out of love. Why he carried it in him like a bullet that couldn't be removed. "Don't be long," she purred. "I could use a little comfort."

"I'm your man," I said, and went out the door, leavin' her with Cole.

At first I thought I'd lost the Chief, but then I saw him down the street, walkin' slow, hands in pockets, head down. He'd blend into the shadows of a ficus tree, then reappear. Lights beckoned across the street and he looked up; there was a bar and inside, warmth and voices. He looked both ways across the street; I ducked into the shadow of an alley and froze. He crossed the street and went inside.

I waited a beat and crossed over, too. The bar was hung with tiki lamps, fishing buoys, and photos of that famous writer; tiny paper parasols stuck from the glasses of booze. The Chief walked to the bar and pulled up a stool, his back to the window. The barman frowned as he spoke; the Chief's head bobbed in reply. The barman walked over and drew a beer. There was a long mirror over the bar, and the Chief glanced in it as he drank, but I stayed back in the shadows and was sure he didn't see me. A bunch of rummies sang at a table in one corner, while a black man stood before them and waved his arms. The rest of the bar cheered the performance—everyone but the Chief. He grabbed his beer and sat at a small table, back to the street. A painting of an old battle hung on the wall above him: a castle under siege with archers firing. A high tower crumbled and a soldier plunged headfirst, the scream frozen on his face, arms windmilling in the empty air.

The Chief rose from his table and set his empty glass on the bar. The barman ignored him; no one spoke as he left; no good-byes as he closed the door. Wherever he went, it would always be this way. He'd always be the outcast, always enduring some insult like this scene in the bar. Wherever he landed next, there'd be a betrayal—by him, against him, all one and the same. It was the path of his life. Such paths don't change.

I hung back long enough so he wouldn't see me, then followed the Chief into the gloom. He walked past a church, its blue-and-red stained-glass windows glowing warmly, some organ music piping softly within. He paused a second to listen, then walked to the end of a dock at the end of the square. He stared over the water. Waves slapped against the pilings. This storm would be a nasty one, I thought. The chop would batter anything in its grip, pound it way past recognition, then suck the remains to sea.

His shoulders bunched as I came up, but he didn't turn around. "You took longer than I expected," he murmured.

Maybe I gave him the peace he'd always sought.

Me and Christ have a lot in common that way.

A Clean, Well-Lighted Place

THE WEATHER HAD turned plenty ugly by next morning, and nobody took Isolde for granted now. The weatherman said the hurricane had sucked up enough heat and moisture to turn into a monster, graduating to what he called a Force 5 storm. Her eye was small—just twelve miles across—but what she lacked in size was made up by punch and speed, he said. She'd hit Cuba 'round midnight and flattened scores of towns, then bounced in this direction. The next few hours would tell whether she landed here.

If this was just a preview, I didn't want to stay for the main event. We put on Daddy's slickers and headed for the diner as planned. Raindrops hit the dock with an angry *splat;* the wind had a gamy scent and howled like wild dogs. The waves crashed against the harbor breakwater and barely lost any steam. "Your father better come back or all that will be left of his boat is driftwood," said Rebeca as the boats around us dipped and rose in the swells like horses on a merry-go-round. We ran from the marina, but even with the rain gear were soon dripping like rags. We wrestled shut the diner door and wrung out our hair.

I won't lie, I was worried. Daddy'd gone out the night before to talk with Twitch and Mama, while Rebeca and me waited in the hold. The boat was close and bouncy; it banged against the dock, but rubber tires hanging from the sides absorbed the blows. I crawled into a swaying hammock and the boat rocked me into dreams.

But when I woke, Daddy still wasn't there. Rebeca claimed he'd been paid for arranging the meeting with my mother and ran off. I wasn't so sure.

The diner was a pretty thing. The white counter was lined with sea green stools that didn't wobble. The long mirror over the fountain looked hand-rubbed. Nothing like Harson's dump at all. In a corner, the jukebox sang merrily.

We took a booth by the window as a man wearing a T-shirt and shorts punched in "Yakety Yak," followed by "You Talk Too Much." An angry voice behind the serving window cried, "Not again!" The man returned to his stool, picked up a newspaper, and rustled it deliberately. He was small and fat, with a day's growth of stubble and hair that stuck up from the rain.

"It's my dime," he told his critic. "I plan to enjoy it before the end of the world."

"Don't start again," the voice in the window said.

It was obvious these two knew each other and that this was a long-standin' feud. "It says so right here," proclaimed the chubby diner, stabbing the page with his finger. "Huge storms up and down the East Coast, killer floods in the mountains, and now this hurricane is headed our way. It's the end of the world."

A waitress my age stepped briskly from the back. Her hair was blond and kinky, her skin all gold like it sucked vitamins from the sun. She wore a pale pink lipstick that matched her pale pink uniform. The customer pleaded, "Tammy, can I have a beer?" He made a grab at her, but she swerved in what seemed a practiced move.

"It's too early for that," she said. "Besides, I'm too young to serve alcohol."

"You'd think this place would bend the rules for the end of the world."

She passed a rag over our tabletop, and set our places with plastic mats and silver rolled in paper napkins. It was a nice touch, the kind Harson always called a waste of money. "What's his problem?" I said, indicatin' the doomsayer on the stool.

The waitress looked me up and down, and smiled. "Dennis? He's just nuts. Lots of nuts drift here to stay, probably because it's where the road ends."

"I heard that. I'm not nuts," Dennis said.

"You are too and you know it. But you're *our* nut and we love you, so quiet down and I'll bring you another cup of coffee, okay?"

"With cream . . . I like cream," he said. He mumbled one last time that the world was ending, then faced the counter and calmed down.

Our waitress rolled her eyes. "My boss said to tell you we're closing early because of the storm. But don't worry, you've still got plenty of time to eat."

The Land of Sunshine

"You think it'll really hit here?"

"Who knows?" She almost seemed bored. "I've been through five evacuations, and each time the storm veered off, so no one really takes them seriously." She flipped her hair back over her shoulder. "You two sisters or something? You're both dark, kind of exotic." She waved her pencil tip. "Your hair is so straight, kind of Greenwich Village and artsy. Me, the salt kinks my hair like a Brillo pad."

I told her we weren't sisters. "She's from Cuba and I'm from Tennessee."

"No offense, but we're *overrun* with Cubans, them and all that hush-hush stuff, Jeez, give a girl a break." She popped her gum in disdain. "None of it's *real*, anyway. I don't think they even *tried* to invade Cuba, no matter what they say. I think they went offshore and got drunk, then came back with a pack of lies."

Rebeca's mouth began to open, so I kicked her under the table and it shut again. "But Tennessee," the waitress continued, "that's different. Like, up around the Smokies? I've heard the mountains are really pretty. What I wouldn't give to leave this dump and *go* somewhere, you know?" She showed a perfect set of milk white teeth, some tipped with pink lipstick. "I'd be happy if the hurricane came and blew everything over. You ever feel that way?"

"Tammy, quit yakking and take their orders, will ya?" the voice in the window cried.

"And I want my coffee," Dennis the customer added. "The end of the world's upon us, and I need caffeine."

Tammy the Waitress puffed her cheeks in frustration, then leaned close. "So, Mr. High-and-Mighty in the back says to make every customer feel welcome, and how do you do that except by talking? But if I talk too much, he yells I'm wasting time."

"He is a dictator," Rebeca said. "He should be shot."

"Isn't that a little harsh for a short-order cook?"

"My country has a big dictator. Your country is filled with little ones. It is all the same."

333

"I used to be the dictator of a big newspaper before I went nuts," cried Dennis. "I hired and fired with impunity. I was a happy man! Those were the days."

"What did I tell you?" Rebeca said.

"You're pretty smart for a little kid," replied Tammy, then poised her pencil above her pad. I ordered the special with ham and biscuits, and Rebeca wanted steak and eggs. "That's a pretty big order for such a little shrimp," Tammy said, winking at me.

"I need strength because I am going on a long journey," Rebeca replied.

The wall clock read 8:10. I glanced outside and spotted a familiar figure bent against the wind. I watched her in silence, paying no attention as Rebeca stacked her Dixie sugars into a pyramid. It was the first time I'd really studied Mama since I left home—sure, there was the time outside the Muscovy bank and then a day later at Sallie Goodnight's, but you tend to pay less attention when you're in danger of gettin' killed. As I watched, I saw how fine her legs were workin' as she sprinted through the rain. She picked 'em up and put 'em down, splishy-splash, the same legs she'd told me would never work again. She'd stuck 'em under the covers and made a new pair of legs out of me.

I was so mad from the memory that I could hardly see straight when those same legs carried Mama into the diner and she slid beside Rebeca. "You that Cuban girl I heard tell about?" she asked.

"*Sí*. You are Dahlia's mother?"

"That's me."

Even through my anger, I could see she looked better'n she had in years. Her cheeks were flushed from running; her eyes glowed with that green and yellow light that always fascinated me so. She ran her fingers through her hair and tucked it back from her face, and I saw how she'd painted her nails with clear lacquer. She cared about her looks again. She cocked her head and asked how I was doing. I said living with a killer had done her worlds of good.

The smile left her lips. "Don't start, Dahlia," she said.

I pushed my coffee cup 'cross the table, remembering how she used to toss hers at me. "Wanna throw it, Mama? It was only a week, week-and-a-half ago, I think. I've lost track. Go ahead. You can pick it off the floor now, thank you."

She sucked in her breath sharply, fighting her temper. "Your daddy said you were steamed."

"Where is Daddy, anyhow? I wasn't sure you got the message." Then something bubbled up that I couldn't stop. "Or did he no longer matter once he told you I'd arrived, and you had your killer-boyfriend do him in?"

It was like I had slapped her in the face. She caught her breath and gave me the strangest look—scared, sick and sad, all rolled into one. "He was okay when he left last night," she whispered. Then she shuddered, closing her eyes.

That shudder traveled down some invisible wire to me. I'd tried to be mean, but we were still connected, and I'd uttered something she feared, too. I forgot my anger and grabbed her hand; her fingers closed tight over mine. The waitress came back with our breakfasts and a cup of black coffee for Mama. Beside it she set a creamer shaped like a smiling, spotted cow.

"I can not eat all this," Rebeca said. "It is too much."

"Told you your eyes were bigger than your stomach," our waitress replied.

Mama opened her eyes. She gazed at the steak and eggs like it was the last thing she'd ever see: She wanted to enjoy every moment—the steam, the taste, the smell. "It's okay, I'll eat it," Mama said. But Rebeca was still hungry, and asked what she could have.

I looked up at the waitress and asked if they served ice cream. Maybe that would shut Rebeca up and give me some time with my mama.

"We have vanilla, chocolate, and strawberry," said our waitress.

"Give her what she wants," I sighed. I looked at the chubby prophet sitting alone at the counter and told Rebeca to treat him, too.

"But he is disgusting," she pouted.

"He just needs a friend."

Mama smiled as Rebeca left and said I wasn't half-bad as a mother. I ignored that and hissed, "Daddy's dead, ain't he, Mama? Something's happened to him."

"Something happens to all of us eventually," she replied, then tried to put a good face on things, as mothers will. "Oh, Dahlia, you know your daddy. He probably has a girlfriend and didn't dare to tell us, and spent the night with her." But she was out of practice lyin', and her face mismatched her words. With that, all my fine speeches flew out the window into the wind. All the words I'd rehearsed about love, freedom, and Harson's money got jumbled in my head. All that mattered was the loss. I'd lost Cole by not holdin' tight; I'd lost Daddy the moment after I found him. Everything important in life blew away.

What did it matter, I said. You run and run forever, just to end up where you started. You strive like a slave, and exhaustion and death is your reward. When you think you've figured out what matters, it's nothing more than night and fog. It's all talk, talk, talk, a whirlwind of words. You chase after what you think's important, and before you know it, you're far from home.

But what *was* home? For some it was a place, for others a place in time. For me, it was a Sunday long ago. I was a little girl and it was early morning; I walked into Mama and Daddy's room. They were young, and tall, and seemed to know everything there was to know. Though it was snowing outside, it was warm in their bed. They were awake already . . . they were always awake and vigilant . . . nothing could ever happen to me when they were 'round. They were reading the Sunday paper, Mama in her flannel nightgown with the lace 'round the collar, Daddy in the silly black boxers he'd wear, making us laugh by posin' like a bodybuilder. I burrowed into the covers, down between them both. It smelled of bread and wood, of coal and musk; it smelled mysterious and adult; it smelled like *them*.

I remembered how Daddy folded the funny papers to Prince Valiant and started to read. The Prince was dark like Daddy while Mama was as fair as the Queen. There was danger all about them, but they triumphed in the end. They always stayed together and always stayed in love. In time that love became flesh with the birth of a little princess, and that princess was me.

Mama moved from her side of the table and slid next to me. "Oh Mama," I said, my voice breaking, "what happened? I thought I'd come down here and find Daddy; I'd talk to him and things would be all right again. But everything happened with Harson and Cole's father and the people we encountered and—"

She held my face in her hands and looked me in the eyes. "And it didn't turn out the way you planned?"

"What happened?" I said again.

She laughed softly to herself. "They call it life," she said. She picked up her spoon and swirled it in the black coffee; but the coffee, the diner, the pudgy little man touched by Rebeca Hermosa's shy offer of ice cream, the young waitress who dreamed of escape to better places, the storm raging outside the diner . . . all this, and more, were far, far away. Mama looked so sad. "You haven't figured it out?" she asked. "You need your mother's guidance one last time?" I looked in her eyes and nodded. She flipped back a damp strand of hair. "Not that I've been the greatest mother, Dahlia, but do you really think I planned my life this way? You start out so full of hope, then end up so twisted you wouldn't recognize yourself in a mirror. 'That's not me, it has to be a trick,' you say. But things happen that you can't predict, and you make choices that seem right at the time. Soon enough you learn the choices were dead wrong, that your mistakes are the same mistakes made by everyone. You're part of one huge, bloody mistake and no one knows who started it and everyone blames the other guy. Maybe that's what history is. It's like a current you swim against, and when you finally think you got it right, you look back to see how your own struggles caused other folks to drown. You ain't part of the solution, you're just a bigger part of the problem, so you try to get away. Maybe you hide like me, or run like your daddy and so many others we've known back in Tennessee. Maybe you fight back, like Cole's daddy, but an anger takes over and that anger becomes who you are. Whatever you do doesn't really matter, because any victory is only temporary, and the current will always get you. There's no escape. It grabs you fast and drags you down."

"So what're you sayin', Mama? That I should've stayed in Wattles? That I should've hid when I saw Cole through the servin' window? All I wanted was a chance. Was that so wrong?"

She looked up from her coffee. "You cain't prevail," she said. "At best, you get a draw." Then she searched my face like she used to search it each morning right before school. "Do you really love that boy?" she finally sighed.

"I do," I said. "I didn't have the sense to know it, but I learned."

She picked up the spotted cow and poured a thin line of cream into the cup. "Moo," the creamer said.

Mama smiled. "I don't think I ever taught you this, how to read fortunes in a coffee cup," she said. "My mama taught it to me, and her mother taught it to her. The whole trick is that you create the fortune based on how you pour the cream. The amount you pour's important, as well as the height you pour from and the steadiness of your hand. The idea is to pour it so you break the surface without splattering; you do it right and it hits the bottom and wells up and spreads like a blossom, see? You get overeager and you make a splash, which forms lots of globs and eddies, always a bad sign. The smoother you pour, the smoother the cream swirls out, which means the smoother your fate will be. If the cream swirls in tight patterns and doesn't mix, you've got problems; but if it spreads so evenly that you don't even have to stir it, then you know you've done well."

I looked inside Mama's cup. The cream curved off the bottom and came up in a tight, cloudy spiral that whirled counterclockwise. Mama groaned and said she was a little out of practice, then mixed it all together. She blew across the top and took a sip. "It's funny. I lose you when I finally find you. Your daddy, too." She smacked her lips. "Dahlia, go get that money—"

"Always the money," I said.

"Just listen for once, okay? Get that money and whatever

else you've got with you and head for that church near the square. You know the one. Go inside for shelter. I'm not sure when, but Cole will meet you there."

"What you gonna do?"

"Don't worry about that. When Cole arrives, you two run, you hear? Grab your boyfriend's hand and go. Don't waste a second askin' him what happened; don't even look back. If you feel so bad about the money, put it to good use and get that little girl back home. Do something for her, I don't care. And you and Cole be good to each other. That's your job from now on."

A wave of sadness hit me, like she was saying good-bye, and it made me scared. "But Mama—"

She cut me off. "Don't worry about me, Dahlia, I've always looked after myself." She picked up her steak knife and wiped it on her paper napkin. "I'm able to do so again."

How We Leave the Great State of Tennessee—

I LISTENED TO the wind while awaiting Burma's return. The wait stretched on and on—the wail changed in my brain from the moans of ghosts to cries for revenge. I tried talkin' to Cole but he was sulking, so I went out front and played with the loose change and keys in the ashtray. It made a jingly, happy sound, in contrast to my mood.

Burma's stabbed me in the back, I thought, as she failed to return. She's betrayed me for her daughter. Or the money. Or both. Not that I couldn't find them. The last thing the weatherman said before the power cut off was that escape from the island was impossible. The hurricane had turned and was headed straight for the Keys.

My daddy'd always claimed to hear voices in the wind. You

just have to listen, he said. Moses spoke to the whirlwind, and God spoke back. Now, as I listened, I remembered how once before a storm had spoke to me.

It happened long ago—the night my father died. The storm that night was one of the biggest I'd ever seen. Daddy was dying from the bite of the canebrake rattlesnake he'd grabbed in his holy fit, the swollen snake I'd released soon after in the woods. Outside, the gale bent double the crowns of the surrounding hemlocks, a high voice that circled the house and invited Daddy out to play. I'd straddled the chair by his bed, finding it hard to believe that this snake-poisoned wreck clutchin' the covers in absolute agony was the same man who'd pounded me into his own image for all these years. I remembered the line from Scripture: *Who will pity the charmer bitten by the snake?* Not me, brother, I said to myself. Not me.

My mind drifted as I waited for Daddy to die. He was taking way too long. I thought of Cole's mother and her increasing signs of restlessness—within a month, she'd use the Fuller Brush man as a quick excuse to leave. I thought of Cole, barely a year old, and wondered if I'd raise him the same way my daddy had raised me. All I needed was a bit of luck to free me from this cycle of meanness that plagued the Youngers since the very first one crawled from the slime. "God, give me a lucky break," I whispered. "Anything will do."

"I hear it," Daddy groaned.

"What do you hear, Old Man?" I snapped, dragged from my reverie.

"A voice. I hear a voice in that wind outside."

I sighed and rolled my eyes. Crazy old fart—next he'd claim to see angels dancin' on a pin. Partly from boredom, partly from curiosity, I asked what the voice had said.

He opened his eyes and looked in my face. "Them who shun understanding remain in the house of the dead."

"Meaning me?"

His laugh was like a croak. "Meanin' you."

Old Man, I thought, I've had about enough of you. I had

a bright idea. After all, he was half-dead already. No one would care if the vigil ended now. I was half-dead myself from a life filled with this kind of venom, always disguised as righteousness, like a voice of conscience ringing in my head. But something held me back and I gave him one more chance. "Why, in all my life," I asked, "was there never a kind word for me?"

His laugh was like a bark this time, a whole menagerie in here. "Like life is kind, you idjut? Everything I done was for your own good."

"Well, Daddy, I got a saying for *you*. 'Whoso keepeth his tongue keepeth himself from trouble.' " Then I covered his face with the pillow. The wind sucked up the sounds of his struggles, hiding them from those of his congregation who kept deathwatch outside the door.

Once again, I listened to the wind, only now its name was Isolde. Maybe I heard Daddy's voice again. "You can't call me nothin' I ain't been called already," I mumbled to myself, turning up a battery-powered radio the motel owner had graciously left behind. There was only static. The wind tugged at the roof and thudded against the walls. Cheap piece of shit, I thought, and threw the radio against the floor.

The door flew open and Burma flew in with it, holding onto the latch. She pressed her shoulders against the door and pushed it closed. "Where the hell have you been?" I demanded.

"Just walking," she said. "At least at first I was, but then when I saw a tree torn up by the roots and fall on a house, I decided to find shelter. That church by the square looked solid enough, so I sat in there awhile."

I considered her carefully. She was a windblown mess, torn up and drenched, but there was a strange calm about her, too. A peace I'd never seen in her. "I thought—"

"You thought Dahlia and me had run off with your money?" She nodded to herself, reading my mind again. "I knew you'd fret, so that's why I returned through this gale."

She looked at me strange, her eyes shiny. "After all this, I still don't know your first name."

What a strange thing to say at the moment, and it made me uncomfortable. Why'd she go and ask me that? Whoever knows your name holds power over you, which was why God denied Moses when the little squirt dared to ask the same. Still, these were crazy days, and I answered her question. "John," she repeated. "I could get used to John. John's not bad."

The wind boomed outside and she moved to the couch, just a smidgen unsettled. There was something in her face that unsettled me, too. Something percolating in that complex female mind that I'd never understand and probably didn't want to consider even if I could. "Why don't we just let 'em go?" she pleaded suddenly. "They love each other. Let 'em have the money—we don't need it." Her eyes danced bright. "We could rob another bank. I'd be happy if we did that again."

"I made a bet with a man when this started," I replied. "I can't go back on a bet."

Her eyes held mine in a look that was half sad, half regret; her expression took me by surprise. "Just because you start something wrongheaded don't mean you have to end it wrongheaded," she answered back, her hand flat on the table.

"There's no debatin' this. You knew it would always come down to this. The best thing is to get it over with, okay?"

She shrugged her shoulders and smiled. "You're right. The best thing to do is get it over with." She turned and headed for the bedroom. I asked where she was going; she squirmed her hips and asked if I minded her using the little girl's room. I laughed and she closed the door.

I picked up the broken radio. Burma was right in one respect: I did act without thinking lots of times. Throwing the radio was a stupid thing. The cover had broke off and I pushed in the batteries. I twirled the tuning knob, but that broke off. I grabbed the stem and turned it slowly, but only got crackles and noise.

A sound came from the bedroom that didn't sound like flushing. I glanced at the table near where she'd placed her hand—right by the ashtray. I realized she'd taken the key to the next room.

I leaped over and threw back the door. Cole was gone, the severed ropes lying limp on the bed. Burma blocked the door outside with her body. "Stay back!" she warned.

"What the fuck have you done?!"

"You didn't plan on lettin' 'em go, even when you got the money," she said. "You was gonna kill Dahlia, and possibly even me, just like you did my husband." Her voice got very still. "I told you from the start that I'd always protect my girl."

"Get out of the way," I screamed. "I can still catch him!"

"I mean it, stay back."

I was on her in an instant, brushing her aside, so didn't see the knife till she slipped it in my ribs. It went in deep, hitting something soft, then scraped out nice 'n' slow. I batted her backhanded and saw it; a serrated steak knife poised at waist level, ready for another dig. I took a quick breath and it felt like she'd stabbed me again. I grabbed for my waistband and backpedaled, but tripped over my feet and fell backward through the bathroom door, wedging into the tight space between the tub and the commode.

"You're crazy!" I screamed, my words ringing off the tiles.

"Crazy as a fox," she said. "I'm sorry to say it, but you're too dangerous to allow to keep livin'." She filled the doorway, her knife held overhead.

That was her mistake, since she made a better target—a fact I think she realized when I finally pulled the gun free of my waistband. She gasped just before I pulled the trigger, hitting her square in the chest. But Burt True's little popgun didn't have much stopping power, and she lurched when it hit, then gathered herself and staggered forward.

So I shot her again.

That did the trick. And then there was silence. I waited a second, the gun trembling in my hands. My eyes finally focused and I saw the shower curtain with the happy fish hangin' cold and limp beside my head. I looked out the door and saw one foot, toes pointed up, on the bedroom floor. I waited, but the foot didn't move. I put my hand on the toilet for leverage and pushed up; it felt like the knife was turnin' in my side. I groaned and shifted my weight, pushing from the tub.

I crawled to the door and peeked outside. Burma lay on her back, staring at the ceiling. The bedroom window rattled, blinds clicking like a small bird's bones. Blood oozed from her chest through two black holes.

She'd dropped the knife and, just to be safe, I tossed it even farther away. Her eyes were wide and pleading as I bent down. I placed my hand on her side. Her small body vibrated, and I remembered the movements of that body in entirely different circumstances. Now she seemed to get smaller, her vital stuff soaking into the carpet. Her lips parted slightly. "I was your last chance, John," she said.

"I can't change myself, Burma."

"Oh, I don't know," she sighed. Her head fell back; she closed her eyes. "It's been fun, honey, but I think it's catchin' up to me." She took a couple of breaths, then died.

I stared at her for a while—I don't know how long. The wolves howled outside. I picked her up and her blood was damp, sticking to my shirt, already a mess from my own wound. The pain from her knife thrust seemed to travel to my heart. I pulled back the covers and laid her out, tucking in the sheet so only her white face showed. Her expression seemed so calm—it was true, she'd always been calmer than me. My stab wound throbbed like a bitch and I ripped some sheets and wound them 'round me tight as I could. I felt dizzy . . . scooped out like a melon . . . emptied of all life and soul. I lay down beside her and thought how every damn thing that'd happened to me in this damn life was the fault of some woman. Isolde shrieked in agreement. I covered my eyes with my hands and wisht I was made of stone.

The wind stopped as if cut with an ax and all was deathly still. I must've passed out, and the sudden silence brought me to again. Waking is a kind of realization, and in that moment I knew where the boy had gone.

The church. Burma'd mentioned a church by the square. The same church where I'd given the Chief his final payment, the one that pulsed with warm light from within. A church would mean permanence to Burma, a certainty down uncertain roads.

I got up from the bed. The wound still throbbed, but I could bear it if I held my hand tight against my side. It *had* to be borne. I grabbed my gun and walked out the door, leaving Burma in the bed. Maybe when I retrieved my money and ended this Southern-fried train wreck—maybe then I'd come back and burn the motel down. It'd be a fitting tribute for the closest thing to a real partner I'd ever had.

I gazed around me, amazed. I couldn't see the sun, yet a red light filled the sky. Key West lay in shambles. Across the street, the wind had peeled back the metal roof of a house like the skin of an onion, while closer still, a huge magnolia had toppled into the parking lot, roots sticking up and trunk squashing my poor black Mercury. I hadn't even heard the crash. Two dream cars—the Caddy and the Merc—both gone to squat, the story of my life in a nutshell. Fuck it, I thought—let me get my loot and I'll buy something even better. A Corvette Stingray with a scoop and mag wheels.

Still, it was hard to get a grip on this island's new look. Key West was changed to the point of unreal. Though the sky was calm, a solid wall of clouds filled the horizon, the tallest things I'd ever seen—towering up, up and up like gods who'd finally made their presence known to man. The little town resembled nothing so much as a scattered pack of cards, and I thought of that kid's game, 52-Card Pickup, where playing cards flew everywhere. Buildings of stucco or concrete, like the motel, stayed more or less intact, retaining their basic shape while shedding off a roof or losing all windows, while wood buildings were simply picked up and flung to high heaven, nothing left but the outline of the foundation, or maybe a single wall. Reminders of the lives lived in them were strewn up and down the road.

But the eeriest thing was the sound, since there wasn't none. A vast silence lay over Key West, a silence so heavy it went beyond sadness to something mocking and cruel. Up where the cloud towers watched, I imagined laughter . . . a terrible, mirthless laughter that mocked our flimsy dreams. By what right were we treated like this?, I spit. Life was hard and we tried our damndest. We weren't playthings. It made me mad enough to kill.

I picked my way through the shards and splinters toward the sea. The trees that still stood were stripped of their leaves by the wind; they leaned against each other, drawn by mutual gravity. Exhausted birds drooped in their branches, while the bodies of their dead brothers littered the street like exploded balls of feathers, plucked completely clean. A dead cat floated in a pool of water, ripped free of all nine lives. Dazed survivors poked through the ruins.

I walked on. The church was at the end of the street. Its steeple had canted to the side, but somehow failed to topple. A gravelly voice called out, and I glanced over at a man who was inspecting what was left of his store. The glass window had burst out and the display tourist items had got sucked into eternity. The man wore a sky blue T-shirt with one arm torn off; gray chest hair poked above his collar like from a Brillo pad. A line of blood ran down his cheek. "Don't get far from shelter," he warned me. "See those clouds on the horizon? We're in the eye."

"The storm's not over? But it's calm now."

"The eye of a hurricane is always calm," he said. "The last half's still coming, and it's the worst, they say."

I stared numbly at the tilting steeple. "I gotta get to that church."

"Down by the water is the worst place, buddy. The waves get even bigger. There's a chance of a surge . . . a huge wave."

"I can swim," I said, and moved on.

The waterfront was quiet. No one moved. The metal awning on the front of a public aquarium was ripped half off. Conch shells were strewn about, their points sticking up like tire spikes, rosy mouths opened in screams. A small gray shark flopped weakly on the asphalt and died. A shrimp boat that had broken loose of its mooring bumped against the concrete posts. The broken steeple leaned above me, its shadow cutting like a black knife across the square.

The huge door of the church hung open, broken off its hinges. The stained-glass windows had exploded; a few jagged shards of glass remained in the frames. Organ music came from the interior. I took out my pistol and replaced the two rounds I'd left in Burma. I patted down my hair and walked inside.

I stood in the door and stared down the long, thin aisle. Cole and Burma's daughter stood up front by the altar. That little Cuban girl the Chief had described was up front, too, perched on a rail. I figured I'd have to shoot her, too. The ceiling was high and vaulted, the interior a checkerboard of light and dark. Guttering lamps hung from the ceiling; two had pulled loose from their bolts and crashed into the pews. Recorded music came from the balcony—"A Mighty Fortress," soft and heavenly, just like in the relief camp back in Tennessee. I grimaced when I recognized the tune.

At first they didn't see me and I stared quietly, holding my side as I breathed. Cole was wet from the storm, hair streaming down his face. He'd taken a beating from the storm before arriving here. He stood with his hands on the girl's shoulders, fingers firmly planted, staring straight in her eyes. I wondered what he saw. She stared back, just as firm. I thought of her mama; how she, too, met your stare.

The girl had the rucksack full of money on her back; the red light from the window caught her hair and trailed down her neck and her arms. Maybe it was the light that made me drift away. I was in the field by the laurels before we robbed the Muscovy bank . . . the field where Burma tested her legs. I recalled how she plucked a puffball and blew it, the floaters scattering their seed. She spread her hands and smiled, that smile bursting with the joy of life that she'd wasted away. She twirled like a girl, then brushed the seeds off her hands and walked up close. I fell in love with her then.

Not that love saved anyone. Not her. Not her girl. Not me.

The Cuban girl was swinging her feet in boredom, but then hopped off her perch when she spotted me. "Is that the man you're talking about?" she yelled. Cole and Burma's brat came apart and turned. My gun was already up and pointed; I had the drop on them. I moved further into the church and noted that the red light trailed behind me. The light, the music, the gun. It was perfect, like something from John Wayne.

"I'll turn off the lights!" screamed the little Cuban girl. "He won't see us so well!" She ducked for cover and scurried through a side door as I squeezed off a shot, but she was quick and got away. What the hell, I'd kill her later.

"We got the money, Pop," Cole said. "Just take it and leave us alone." He moved down the aisle between me and the source of my heartache, but I waved him aside. "I can shoot her before you take another step," I warned him. "Move off. That's right. Don't make another sound."

"What happened to Mama?" the girl wanted to know.

"She's grown cold, as we all shall soon. It's a natural state, nothing to be afraid of."

"What're you talkin' about? You're not makin' sense," she said.

"I'm talkin' about the ice and cold. You don't even feel it after a while. The ice gets thicker as it piles up, and if someone tries to melt it, all that's affected is the top layer. But that's been your insulation, but now you really feel the cold. Soon enough, it reaches your core. She's done you no favor by warmin' you up, 'cause ignorance is bliss and you know you'll never be truly warm again."

"You're crazy," she said.

"That's the problem with this younger generation," I snarled. "You try to pass along some hard-earned wisdom, and all they do is criticize." I took a step down the aisle. "I want you to know I did your mother a favor. It's better to stay cold permanently."

"You killed her, just like you killed Daddy. Just like you mean to kill me."

She didn't flinch as she said it, but met me gaze-for-gaze. Gone was the scared rabbit from Wattles, gone the terrified bus rider in Atlanta. She wasn't afraid no more. She wasn't afraid of me. She'd learned the important stuff: when to run and when to stay. It made me proud. Too bad such knowledge came mere seconds before I finished her off; but better late than never, I always say.

I raised the gun up and, like a good pupil, she gathered herself for the exam. "I'm not afraid of you," she hissed. "You made me plead once. I won't do it again."

I lowered the gun and studied her face. I smiled. She reminded me of me.

"Dad," Cole pleaded, "don't do it."

"Stay out of this, boy," I said.

"I don't understand you!" she shouted, words ringing in the sanctuary. "I'm willing to hand over the money, but it doesn't matter to you. It never mattered from the start, I can see that now. It's always been about more than the money, or even about me and Cole. I got in the way of some purpose, messed up some grand vision. I need to pay for that, even if I don't understand!"

I pressed my hand against my wound. "You're too much like your mother. She wanted explanations, too."

"Too many choices!" the Cuban girl yelled from the balcony overhead. "Too many switches! I cannot tell which is for lights, and which is for other things!"

I waved the gun, disgusted. "Toss over the money," I said.

Burma's daughter slipped the rucksack from her back; she leaned forward carefully and pitched it down the aisle. I chuckled in my throat; I walked up and nudged it with my foot. I'd won, all right. The old man was wrong.

But somehow, the winning seemed hollow. I'd had the time of my life during this chase. Now it was over. Now what would I do?

I bent down and touched the sack and at the same moment "A Mighty Fortress" boomed through the speakers, the deep chords vibrating each bone in my body and rattling the church walls. I remembered how the refugees sang it in the relief camp outside Newport, singing their defiance, and the song took me there again. The waters had drowned what mattered to them, yet the singers would not die. I flinched and looked up and the lamps swayed overhead. Each singer was just a drop in a vast cloud of namelessness, but they came together anyway and the song was their voice and the voice was enough. They sang and endured.

"Turn that damn thing down!" I screamed.

The music stopped and the Cuban girl cried, "Sorry, wrong switch." In the fallen silence, I heard the rising wind. The light dimmed through the windows. But that wasn't what got my attention most, for when I looked up, Burma's daughter held a pearl-handled revolver, and it was pointed at me.

"Where'd you get that?" I asked, amazed. I looked at my own, the barrel canted aside.

"You're not the only one who's made friends on this trip," she said. "Drop the gun, take the pack and go forever, *please!*"

The wind howled through the open door and broken windows, a high, mad sound. It marked the eye's departure, announced Isolde's return.

I had two choices. Her way, or mine.

I smiled to myself. What the hell.

I straightened quick and swung the barrel. The first slug hit me hard, followed by the sound. I staggered back, not from pain, but the blow. There really was so little pain. My arm felt heavy and I tried to raise it and she looked into my eyes. I saw no enjoyment in them . . . no appreciation of this horse opera, this slap of flesh against gun leather, metal through flesh or dark, romantic music that took the place of words. "What a waste," I mumbled. She wasn't like me at all.

The second bullet hit almost exactly opposite her mother's stab wound, perfect bookends. I could feel the bullet exit through my back and parts of me scatter in the wind. The force turned me 'round, and the open door beckoned. Something was out there that I had to see. I walked through the door and into the square. The red light had deepened and the wind was a true bitch singing the storm's wordless tune. The rain flew sideways past my face, stinging when it hit; a conch shell chunked against my side. I could care less, for I was part of a miracle now. In the distance I saw twin waterspouts, but that wasn't the miracle—the miracle was even closer still. I saw what looked like a fog bank, huge and dark, rolling in fast from the sea. But that was ridiculous, I thought, 'cause fog never moves that fast, and maybe I was hallucinating. Maybe this was Death, my old companion, and when He finally comes, you see things that are not there. I watched, curious, but still the miracle would not go away. Instead it rolled closer, building higher than the dock, higher than the square. Only then I realized it wasn't fog but water, a rolling wall of water, the wave the man had warned me about, the one to wash me clean forever, headed straight for me.

My knife wound no longer hurt me. My gun hand no longer felt heavy. I screamed out my bitter laughter. I felt young and danced a jig.

I raised the popgun up and now it was a cannon, a fucking howitzer. I squeezed the trigger again and again. I emptied the chamber as the wave reared up but the bullets passed through with no harm. Daddy's voice was in the wave, his evil face within the boiling foam. "One can do nothing against God who is not God himself," he cried out.

I screamed back: "But I'm your son, the Son of Death Hisself!"

The wave roared out its anger.

I laughed and took my medicine, roaring back, *Come on, you bastard! You'll never get rid of Me!*

—and Go on to Better Things

I DON'T REMEMBER much after that. The wind went crazy and the rough water blew. I followed Twitch to the door as he staggered out; as he froze, I looked to where he stared. A black wave had grown as huge as the ocean itself, mounting higher and higher as though it held something against us and meant to wash the world clean. Twitch stood in its monstrous face, shoutin' and firin' as it crashed on the square, and I stood transfixed, not exposed to such sights every day. Cole grabbed me from behind as the wave burst through the door; it threw us back toward the altar and rolled us under the pews. There was a roar like the voice of all floods together and through it all Twitch's grotesque laughter ringin' in my ears.

Soon I couldn't breathe and tried to rise up, but Cole and the pews held me down. Good thing, too, for the next second the backwash tried to suck us out the door. My head banged against the seats and my vision receded down a whirlpool. *If this is drowning,* I thought, *it ain't half-bad.* It almost seemed peaceful as I got smaller and smaller and drifted with the waves. I drifted in silence, the whole world in watery silence . . . all life waiting in silence for some secret that we all dimly felt but would never truly know. I drifted past Mama and Daddy and they were together again and happy; as I watched, the years washed like dirt from their faces and they were that age when I remembered them best, young and hopeful and me between them feeling as safe as I ever would. They'd reached their true expression: the best they'd ever be. There were many like that, drifting in search of a moment's grace yet unaware when they found it, then passing to suffering instead. Suffering flowed through life like water, a moving finger writing on the water, our brief stories a moment's eddy in the greater stream. It flowed down the mountains and through the valleys, all of us borne in that green flood till we hit the sea and slept, dreaming of better things.

"Dahlia!" Cole was shaking me.

"You think she is dead?" Rebeca asked. "She is out so long, I fear she is dead."

"Don't be silly. Look, she's waking." He put his hand on mine.

I opened my eyes. Cole and Rebeca smiled down at me, both soppin' wet and worried. We'd all seen better days. A deep gash crossed Cole's cheek; Rebeca'd lost a tooth and her hair stood on end. I had a nasty scalp wound and they'd already tied a bandage 'round my head. The church was a wreck, the pews and tables washed up in a pile by the altar like a massive close-out sale. Part of the roof had stripped clean off, and Cole said the steeple fell completely when hit by the wave. He didn't mention his daddy, but I could tell from his eyes that Twitch was gone.

It dawned on me that our money lay buried somewhere in this rubble, too. We only had to dig. Twitch had barely touched the rucksack when the music went up and he'd glanced away. He never picked it up before he staggered outside. For a second I was tempted, then remembered how, from the beginning, all it brought was bad luck and woe. Let it be, I said. Let other people find it during the cleanup. This place needs a little help. It'd seem like manna from heaven, or at least from the flood.

So we walked outside.

A cool breeze brushed my face, and we stood on the steps and listened as it whispered from the sea. Some survivors were already out and picking through the ruins. Key West looked like schoolbook photos of Hiroshima, with lots more standing water. It was for this—not the Bomb—that we'd suffered through the Duck and Cover drills.

"Look there," Rebeca said.

I turned to where she pointed at the marina and the sea. The sun had set and the waves lapped against the concrete. Boats were tangled in the swells—ripped loose from their moorings and jammed and smashed together in a giant raft that knocked gently against the piers. We called out, but no one replied. We climbed on the floating tangle of vessels, looking for survivors as we hopped from boat to boat, but this was a ghost fleet and no one was aboard. A catamaran rode low in the water and looked not long to sink; a shrimp boat rode higher in the water but its outriggers had folded together and crushed the wheelhouse. A sailboat lost its rigging. Daddy's boat was bound to be in here somewhere, but search as I might, I still couldn't find it. If it still existed, it was past recognition now.

We picked our way to the very end of that tangle and climbed aboard a cruiser in better shape than the rest since it wasn't battered from all sides. It was deserted, too. Water sloshed in the cabin, but more from overwash and not from any gashes we could find in the hull. The boat looked in better shape than most of the buildings back on land. I suggested we spend the night here.

On the horizon, the last streamers of light were fading and soon it would be dark. I opened the door to the hold and saw the keys dangling on a hook. I turned on the ignition, and the gas gauge rocked to Full. The lights on the instrument panel glowed.

"Look at that, it works!" cried Rebeca. She grabbed me 'round the waist and hugged as hard as she could. "You will take me home to Cuba, now? Or maybe when we are certain the boat will not sink?"

I remembered what Mama said about doin' something good for Rebeca—then remembered that Mama, too, was gone. I looked over at Cole. It was just him and me now—oh, yeah, and this girl. "Dahlia," he cautioned, "you're not thinkin' seriously of doin' what she asks?"

"But you promised," Rebeca countered. *"Someone* promised!"

"This boat ain't even ours," Cole said.

I stood between the two of them and shrugged, saying neither yes or no. I turned the switch all the way and the motor turned over, rich and powerful as a Cadillac engine, voice deep as the waves. Maybe I should paint this boat pink. Maybe we'd find a workin' radio in all this mess and I could tune it to the King. *Which way?* I wondered. *Where do I go?* I didn't have a clue, but for once I wasn't scared.

"Dahlia," Cole asked, "do you even know how to steer a boat?"

At least I knew the answer to that. My gypsy's face looked green in the fish finder when I grinned at him. "I can always learn."

Acknowledgments

Over the years and in several incarnations, this novel has received generous grants and fellowships from the Mary Roberts Rinehart Foundation, the Ohio Arts Council, and the Virginia Arts Commission. I am grateful to everyone.

About the Author

A five-time Pulitzer Prize nominee, Joe Jackson is author of the Edgar Award-nominated *Leavenworth Train: A Fugitive's Search for Justice in the Vanishing West*, and is co-author of *Dead Run: The Shocking Story of Dennis Stockton and Life on Death Row in America*, with an introduction by William Styron, which is in development as a feature film with HBO.

Jackson holds an MFA from the University of Arkansas and was an investigative reporter for the *Virginian Pilot* for twelve years, covering criminal justice and the state's Death Row. He was the writer-in-residence at the James Thurber House in 2001. His current nonfiction book is *A Furnace Afloat: The Wreck of the Hornet and the Harrowing 4,300-mile Voyage of its Survivors*.

His journalism has resulted in the acquittal of a man wrongly convicted of murder, the federal investigation of a jail where 16 prisoners died of medical neglect, the investigation of federal agents for misconduct, and the recantations of two men whose testimony helped send men to Death Row.

He lives in Virginia Beach, Virginia.